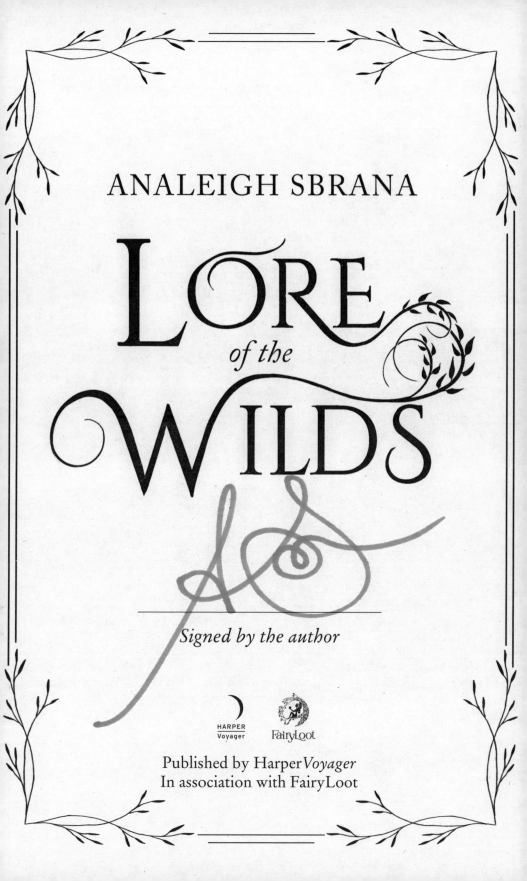

ANALEIGH SBRANA

LORE
of the
WILDS

Signed by the author

HARPER
Voyager   FairyLoot

Published by HarperVoyager
In association with FairyLoot

LORE
of the
WILDS

ANALEIGH SBRANA

MAGPIE

Magpie an imprint of
HarperCollins*Publishers* Ltd
1 London Bridge Street
London SE1 9GF

www.harpercollins.co.uk

HarperCollins*Publishers*
Macken House,
39/40 Mayor Street Upper,
Dublin 1
D01 C9W8
Ireland

First published by HarperCollins*Publishers* Ltd 2024
1

A catalogue record for this book is available from the British Library.

ISBN: 978-0-00-867172-3 (HB)
ISBN: 978-0-00-867173-0 (TPB)
This novel is entirely a work of fiction.
The names, characters and incidents portrayed in it are
the work of the author's imagination. Any resemblance to
actual persons, living or dead, events or localities is
entirely coincidental.

Printed and bound in the UK using 100% Renewable Electricity by CPI Group (UK) Ltd

This book contains FSC™ certified paper and other controlled sources
to ensure responsible forest management.

For more information visit: www.harpercollins.co.uk/green

For those who seek magic within the pages of a book

CHAPTER 1

L ore Alemeyu collected stories like the raven that lived
above the apothecary hoarded shiny pebbles.

But her favorite was the one Mama told about a foolish god whose tricks led to the ruination of humanity. When
Lore was little, Mama would use animated gestures, different
voices, and accents that became more outrageous with every telling. Lore would fall into giggle fits on her sleeping mat, not caring that the thin layer of hay offered little protection from the
packed earthen floor. She would scold the trickster god along
with her mother. They would shout through the open window,
ensuring their words were directed toward the heavens.

"You made a mistake, Yissa God!" they would shout. "Take
us back to where we belong!"

Only much later did she realize that Mama's version of the
story acted as a balm to soothe the uncertainty and fear that
coated the town of Duskmere like a dense, heavy fog. Nobody
was immune to it, not even the children.

On festival days, which were few and far between, everyone
would gather in the town square. Shops would turn their lanterns high, though the oil cost them dearly, and illuminate the
blankets that families laid upon the ground. Hands would wrap

around chipped, steaming clay mugs filled with spiced cider, and people would listen to the elders' stories of malevolent gods.

Their stories differed from the tale Lore's mama told her. She liked these less, for they made her cower, clutching Baba's sleeve. These versions claimed that their ancestors had angered a powerful god, Brokyr. In retaliation, and to humble the humans, he had pulled them through a void, taken them from their rightful world, and banished them to a land of suffering.

According to the elders, the Cursed Crossing was not a mistake but a punishment.

This was usually where the elders would chime in about the importance of prayer, of hard work, and of being humble while keeping one's eyes on the stars. One day, they would be returned to their rightful land, they claimed.

Lore would close her eyes tight and pray as fervently as she could. She wanted to be part of the first generation to leave their banishment and return to Shahassa, the motherland.

Then, the mood would shift, someone would sing a lighthearted ballad, and less devastating stories would be told until the children's eyes grew heavy; they would soon fall asleep on their babas' shoulders. Young lovers would slip away, their hands clasped tight against the cold.

But that had been years ago. Now, on the nights when Lore put the children to bed at the shelter, she would close her eyes and think back to Mama's stories. It was those versions that she recounted to the little ones as she smoothed their hair and blew out candles. She shared tales of too much wine and tricks and, most importantly, of hope, though she held very little of it herself.

Lore didn't tell the children that surely no god or goddess was going to save them. The only person she told this to was Grey.

"What makes you think the elders are right and the answers lie in the stars?" her oldest friend asked, his brow furrowed as he worked at mending his warmest pair of pants.

"There are many legends, but they all have one thing in common: the sky. That's why we look through the skyglass on our eighth nameday. It's why our church has no roof. The answers lie there, I'm sure of it," Lore replied. She was pouring hot wax into molds. She had spent the last year perfecting the scent of her juniper and sage candles and never tired of making them.

"Well, you know what I think," Grey said, his raspy voice muffled by the thread between his teeth. He tied off the last stitch.

"That the answers are to be found outside Duskmere?"

"Why else aren't we allowed to leave?" he asked, raising the trousers to inspect them.

"Because the fae are cruel?" she suggested.

He couldn't argue with her there.

"I just don't see how the answers could be out there if we're the only humans in Alytheria," she continued. "Most of our history was lost in the crossing between worlds. We won't find it in this one."

"That's not what you used to believe. You were the one who put this in my head—this need to escape and to search out there for answers."

Lore shrugged. "I told you. My feelings have changed. There isn't any point in trying to leave Duskmere. That's a child's dream."

The words tasted of ash and Lore had to glance away as she began to trim the wicks on the batch of candles that had already set. She was no longer a child. There was no leaving Duskmere. For hundreds of years, they'd been confined to the town because the Alytherian fae would never let them leave.

Believing otherwise was a waste of time.

"Well, why won't you tell me what changed? Aging out of the shelter, packing a bag, and scouring the world for answers used to be all you would talk about. You used to beg me to come with you."

"That was a long time ago. Now I have to be here to help

Aunty and Uncle—they're getting much too old to take care of all fifteen children."

"You're telling me you're content to stay here? To live above the apothecary until you eventually move back into the shelter and take Eshe and Salim's place?" Grey's voice was exasperated. They had had this conversation before, and he already knew her answer.

"There is honor in caring for those who cannot care for themselves, Grey. And besides, I love it here."

The apothecary they were sitting in was small, with an even smaller second floor, due to the slant of the roof. Boxes were heaped around, obscuring their view of most everything. But through an open door, she could just make out her cramped room. It contained everything she owned: her sleeping mat, one crooked wooden shelf that held her clothes and journals, and a stack of books that she'd loved too much to sell. The rest of the space was the studio where Aunty Eshe and Lore made candles, salves, remedies, tinctures, and soap. It was where she devoured stories and copied them out, letter by letter, to sell in the apothecary during her free time. And though books were a luxury, people still cherished and purchased them when they could afford to.

Grey was sitting on a laughably small stool better suited to a child, with his long legs crossed before him and his broad shoulders squeezed in between two shelves filled with herbs and empty jars.

"I hate it when you lie to me," he said at last. There was a note of defeat in his voice.

Lore frowned, stung. If she couldn't admit the truth to herself, why would she admit it to Grey? She couldn't tell him that she still believed the answers were out there, somewhere beyond the barrier surrounding their town. Or that, at night, she still dreamed of leaving Duskmere and solving the great mystery of how her people came to be trapped in these lands.

She couldn't tell Grey she had another, secret, explanation—that it had not been the wrath of an angry god, nor the blunder of an inept one that brought them here. Instead, it was the one thing that surrounded them, that they, as humans, could never possess.

Magic.

She shoved the thought away.

"It's almost time for me to open the shop. Don't you have work to do?" she asked as she busied herself with the last of the candlewicks.

"We could still do it. We could leave together. I've been practicing with—"

"Your sword is no match for the sentries' arrows," Lore snapped, the words coming out harsher than she intended.

The sentries, members of the Alytherian army, didn't usually cross the barrier. They guarded Duskmere from outside, wearing their signature blue stripes across their tunics, which signaled to all their rank and that they took pride in shooting down any human who tried to leave.

For a moment, she was freshly eighteen again and back in that dark forest. Her pack was stuffed with everything precious to her. A knee pressed against her back, so hard that she couldn't pull in any breath. There was a fist in her hair and a cruel voice, hissing, "What are you doing out at night? And where are you going with that bag?"

She had thought she'd known fear—thought years of food scarcity and deprivation had taught her the meaning of the word—but nothing had prepared her for that. For the terror of being caught past the barrier.

She would never forget the smell of the sentry's blade—the bitter scent had burned her nostrils. She later learned, while Aunty Eshe set leeches on her wounds with a practiced hand, that the sentries' weapons were coated in a substance that slowed the healing process, to make sure that, where the sentries cut, it would scar.

Grey drew her back to the present with a gentle cuff on the shoulder. He was more family than friend; the man knew her better than anyone, and he recognized when her mood had soured. She wouldn't indulge in the fantasy of escape with him any longer.

She'd changed her tune and expectations that night in the woods three years ago.

"I'll be late for work if I don't leave soon." Grey gestured at the pants he'd just mended for the umpteenth time. "And if I arrive early, maybe I'll finally be able to afford a new pair." He gave a dramatic sigh and pushed one hand through his hair—a tell for whenever he was remotely frustrated. As always, his black, silky hair fell back into his face in waves.

Meanwhile, all Lore had to do was look at her curls wrong and they would break free of their coils and try their hardest to imitate a cloud.

"I hope so. Those are starting to resemble one of your mom's quilts," Lore said with a straight face.

Grey pulled the pants to his chest protectively as he headed toward the stairs. "I'll have you know I happen to like the quilted look!"

She followed him down the spiral staircase that led to the shop. "Don't we all?" She pulled at the skirt of her simple cotton dress; she'd had to let the seams out twice now. The dress had grown up with her and was also beginning to resemble a quilt.

Their goodbye was brief. She would meet him tonight after she closed the shop and checked on the little ones at the shelter. They'd eat dinner at his house with his mother and little sister, and then they would head to one of their usual haunts—either the Burgs' tavern or the lake. This was her life, and for the most part, she was content.

When she closed the door behind him and flipped the sign to "Open," she knew it wouldn't be long before customers arrived. Emalie would be there to pick up the soap order for her family's shop, and Mai, a midwife, would arrive within the hour to re-stock her herbs.

A busy shift made the hours pass quickly. It was well into the afternoon when she realized Lex would soon be arriving to pick up the day's deliveries. Once Lore moved out of the shelter, Lex had taken her place as the eldest. Now fifteen, he oversaw deliveries for the apothecary.

When the door swung open, the familiar tinkle of the bell cascaded through the shop. Lore opened her mouth to tease Lex for running late as always, but her words caught in her throat.

Two figures were standing just inside the doorway. The warm glow of the oil lamps cast flickering shadows over their inhumanly sharp cheekbones, making their faces look hollow. They wore mirrored looks of disdain as they studied the space, which felt all the smaller for their presence.

Fae.

Lore's mouth went dry, and she felt as if she could taste their power. Magic rolled off them in waves, permeating the room and her mind, and seeping into her pores, heavy with the promise of violence.

CHAPTER 2

From the moment they could toddle, human children were taught to hide when the dark fae ventured down from their mountain keep and stepped through the tree line that surrounded Duskmere.

It was unusual for the elite order of Alytherians to be in Duskmere at all. It was unheard of that they should be in the apothecary.

And yet, here they were.

Lore froze like a deer about to be shot through the heart with an arrow. Her heartbeat roared in her ears and her lungs ached for air. She wanted to look away from the depthless void of the male's irises, but found it impossible.

It wasn't until he raised an artfully manicured brow and made a comment under his breath to his companion that Lore's body remembered how to work. She inhaled in relief, gulping the sweet, dusty air. The pair had seen her and hadn't immediately ended her life.

Their tunics were lined with exquisite, delicate lace, and both blouses were adorned with embroidery. The colors of the threads were unbelievably vibrant; Lore couldn't imagine what flower or animal could provide pigments that rich. Surely it was something poisonous, as anything that colorful probably needn't worry about being eaten.

Their clothes dripped with wealth. It was another oddity, as the wealthy didn't come to Duskmere. The only fae who came around were the sentries and the taxers. And even then, the sentries rarely crossed the border into Duskmere and the taxers' visits were expected, planned like clockwork at the same time every season to bleed the humans' coffers dry.

Lore's eyes snapped to the female as she leaned forward to sniff a candle. Long, silky braids dripped like syrup down her smooth, brown shoulders. The noble's nose wrinkled like she'd smelled dog shit instead of warm amber and honey. That candle had been poured just the week before. The female's eyes narrowed at the crowded tables and sagging wooden shelves, eventually lingering on Lore's frayed boots. Her painted lips pulled up into a sneer.

A lick of shame burned through Lore's sternum. She glanced away, sidestepped stacks of handwritten books, crates of glass bottles filled with perfumes, and a cupboard bursting with dried herbs and fragrant berries, trying to ignore the heaviness of the male's eyes following her every move.

"Welcome, my lord, my lady. How may I be of service?" Lore asked, hating how much her voice shook. Had she addressed them correctly? She bowed her head, waiting for them to reply.

"We're looking for the owner of this establishment," the male finally said. His words were unhurried and spoken with a tone that commanded attention.

"My aunt and uncle own this shop, my lord, but they're on the other side of town by the vineyard."

"The other side of town?" The male sounded disappointed and more than a little annoyed.

Lore glanced through her lashes. His eyes combed the place, as if her aunt and uncle would suddenly pop out of a cupboard with whatever item he sought.

What could he possibly want from here that he didn't have in abundance out there?

"I am happy to take you to them," she added.

The female reached out, tugging on the male's sleeve. "You dragged me on this fool's errand when we could have sent an attendant. The human you seek isn't even here. Don't tell me you expect me to walk farther through these stinking, muddy streets." The female's words were ugly, but the lyrical timbre of her voice was a song.

She tugged on the male's sleeve again, and Lore's eyes snagged on her nails. They were long, filed into sharp points, and painted the same color as her delicate slippers. Small embedded gems sparkled.

Lore fisted her hands. Her own unpainted nails bit into the flesh of her palms—she used the pain to distract herself from speaking her thoughts aloud. *If we didn't have to give almost all our earnings to the Alytherians, then maybe we humans could pave our streets.*

The male ignored his companion, his eyes still flitting around the shop.

"Perhaps I can help you find something?" Lore motioned toward the low table near the door. Every inch of the scuffed wood was covered in salves, candles, soaps made from goat's milk, and bottles of wine from her uncle's vineyard. Without this shop, Aunty Eshe and Uncle Salim wouldn't have had the resources to care for the fifteen children at the orphanage.

The female's eyes lit up. "While we are here, we should choose a present for Row."

The male grimaced.

"Oh, don't look that way," she continued. "It will be the perfect thing. He's always been fascinated with them."

"We have many gifts if he is interested in us humans." Lore had to swallow back bile as she said "interested"—as if humans were little different than a newly discovered bird with peculiar feathering.

As if they were little more than creatures to be examined.

Lore walked the length of the shop and plucked a book from a shelf. It was an adventure novel, a copy of a copy, written by a person who had never been to Duskmere nor heard of the nightmare of the place. The original book had come over with the humans in the crossing.

Lore caressed the cloth binding. She had spent weeks copying each word, finding a sort of catharsis in crafting the pages. In binding the books.

Unfortunately, frivolities such as books weren't something most people could afford, so she rarely had cause to do so.

Lore eyed their clothing again, and an idea began to form. It was reckless, dangerous, and terrible all around, but she barreled on. "This is the last copy of a book that came from our homeland," she lied. "It's quite pricey, but it would be a perfect gift." Lore stilled her features, trying not to look terrified by what she'd just done.

Lying to a fae? Did she *want* to die?

"Pricey? How much?" The beautiful woman arched a brow, disdain evident on her face, but she still withdrew a coin purse from a hidden pocket.

Lore named the price—high enough to cover new boots for both sets of twins *and* the new flooring they needed in the cellar at the shelter.

"That costs more than my shoes, human." She turned to the male and grumbled, "Which have been ruined from walking through these filthy streets."

Lore shrugged. "Perhaps another option, then. A bottle of wine, perhaps?" She began to slide the book back onto the shelf, treating it with far more care than she had when she'd shelved it last month.

The female opened her mouth to retort—probably to eviscerate Lore with a single word or something equally terrible.

The male cut her off. "We'll take it."

Something deep in his eyes briefly glittered.

Was it mischief? Lore couldn't tell.

The female looked shocked, then delighted. "It's a gift, so wrap it up. If you know how to, that is."

Lore had to hide her sigh of relief as she walked to the counter. She crouched unnecessarily low so she could rub out the chalk marking of the real price, which was a fraction of what she'd told them.

By the time she wrapped the gift in fabric, tied it with an extra-large ribbon—because of course she knew how to gift wrap—and the coin had been exchanged, Lore was already thinking of how pleased Aunty would be. And furious if she knew Lore had willingly tricked the Alytherians.

"These books here . . . some of the titles are in Alytherian. How did you come by them?" the male asked.

Lore bit her lip. "My aunt and I trade with the merchants when they come. Then we translate them to our common language and sell them in our store. Some of the townsfolk like to collect the originals as well, so we put them up for sale."

"You help your aunt with the translations?" His voice was coated with surprise.

"Yes, my lord. I have since I was little." Lore held his gaze, a lick of pride raising her chin.

"I thought humans too dimwitted to write in our language, but I see now that I must have been mistaken." It was casual cruelty in the highest form.

Lore dared not reply. Her feelings wouldn't matter to him, anyway.

He broke off the look first, dismissing her and snuffing her pride out like a candle.

The woman frowned at her companion. "Are we done here? Can we go back? My clothes are starting to stink like them."

The male placed his hand on the female's lower back, leading her toward the door. "We can pause our search. I might have found what I'm looking for, after all."

They left, and the door swung shut behind him.

Lore slid down against the counter, laughing, half from the hysteria—that she had, somehow, survived her first encounter with noble Alytherians unscathed—and half from the weight of the coin in her hands. She'd never held a purse this heavy in her life.

She could take a copper and donate it to the elders. In appreciation, they might let Lore look through the skyglass and track the movement of the stars at service that weekend. Baba used to say the stars sang a song that only she could hear, and she knew the words rang true. When she looked through the skyglass, she swore she could hear a ballad spun from stardust, with the sweet promise of home.

She tucked the coin into the purse on her belt with shaking hands, then reached into the pocket of her apron for the small, rounded stone with a gap in its center. It was shaped like the crescent moon. The curved hole, just big enough to peer through, had reminded Grey of Lore.

"For the girl whose eyes always stray to the moon," he had said as he pressed the rock into her palm.

Her thumb found the crescent-shaped hole in the stone's center and circled it, a nervous habit she'd picked up years ago. The cool touch of the stone settled her racing heart.

She returned to work. She cleaned, helped Lex compile his delivery order once he finally arrived, and finished shelving items while keeping an eye on the changing shadows, ready for the day to end so she could race to tell Grey about the noble fae and her brush with death.

She might exaggerate the tale a little, but Grey loved a good story.

At last, it was time to close the shop. Lore began to tally the day's coin when she heard a loud noise. The floor trembled, as if a thousand people were stomping their feet outside. Lore reached out, stilling a rattling stack of coppers.

The earth began to shake. To sway.

The ground moved back and forth.

The shelves began to roll and tip. Books tumbled from the tall shelves. Tinctures crashed to the floor, shattering into a thousand pieces and releasing so much perfume that Lore had to turn away, gagging.

She pushed the chair out of the way and dove beneath the desk, just in time to see bits of the ceiling rain down. She knelt, covering her head with her arms, and squeezed her eyes shut. Her teeth chattered so hard from the vibrations of the earth that she bit her tongue, tasting blood. She prayed to the goddess that the desk would hold if the roof caved in above her.

She prayed, as she did every day in one form or another, to survive.

CHAPTER 3

L ight, thick with dust, streamed in through the splintered
ceiling, illuminating utter chaos.

As quickly as it had started, the phenomenon was over,
but the apothecary was in ruins. Lore brushed some dust off her
face and hissed in pain. There were small shards of glass embedded in her cheek, and when she pulled her fingers away, they were
slick with blood.

She gripped the front of her tunic and used it to cover her
mouth from the dust. It took minutes to crawl toward the door;
her leather boots kept slipping on the loose pages from torn and
battered books.

From the silence, shouts emerged, filtering in from the outside. One voice she recognized better than her own.

"Lore!" Grey shouted. His call was followed by loud thuds
against the front door, as if he were shoving against it.

"I'm here!" Lore called back as she climbed over the remains of
a bookshelf, ripped open the door, and gripped him in a tight hug.

He held her to him for a moment before he pulled away to
look at her, eyes scanning her for injury and lingering on her
cheek. When he saw she was relatively all right, he reached out
and tugged gently on one of her dust-covered curls.

The familiar gesture helped settle the panic growing in Lore's chest.

She scanned him, then sighed in relief; he looked shaken but unhurt. His familiar, kind, dark eyes were imbued with warmth, even though he was covered in so much dust it had streaked into a sort of paste on his nose and forehead.

"What *was* that, Grey?"

He grabbed her hand, speaking as he pulled her out of the apothecary. "An earthshake of some kind. You're lucky you made it out with only a few scratches. The shop looks a lot worse from outside. I didn't know what I would find when I made it through the door." He exhaled a shaky breath, squeezing her hand.

Lore licked her lips, tasting blood and dust. She followed Grey outside, stumbling behind him. Her vision blurred as they kept walking and tears sprang to her eyes.

Grey said she'd been lucky.

He was right.

Her worst nightmares couldn't have prepared her for the devastation around her. The buildings on the street were almost flattened, and her stomach turned when she thought of anyone who might have been caught inside. Shops and houses had expelled bricks and wood out into the streets. Black smoke billowed up into the cloudless sky, while far too few neighbors used water from the closest well on the growing flames.

There should be more people out . . . there shouldn't be so few of them fighting to preserve this heap of rubble. Lore's legs trembled beneath her.

"Your family?" she asked.

She glanced at the row of houses across the pond behind the apothecary. It was just a few minutes' walk from the shop, which was how she had met Grey. He was at the shop almost as much as she was when they were children.

Grey's house was usually swathed in perpetual shade from

the tall trees that surrounded it. On a good day, she could hardly see it from the shop. But where there should have been branches reaching up toward the sky, the trees had split during the shake and fallen.

"They're fine. Ara is shaken, but you know my mom and Aunt Xio—they'll cheer her up in no time. Though I can't say the same for our house."

Lore didn't know what to say to comfort him, so she cursed, instead. Grey, his mom, and his sister lived in a small house with his aunt and her four daughters. It wasn't much, but it was all they had since his father and uncle—along with her own—had died in the uprising all those years ago. It was not as though they could afford to just build a new home.

"And the shelter?" Lore choked out, though how could he know? Grey's house was in town, close to the apothecary. The shelter was not.

They raced through the field toward the small cluster of buildings. The closer they drew and the more she saw of the shelter, the harder it was to process what had really happened. Every window was shattered, and the corner of the west side had caved in completely.

She sped up, tears blurring her vision.

Please, let them be all right.

Please, let them be all right.

Please.

Lore cried out when she saw the huddled children in the now exposed playroom.

Aunty Eshe rushed to meet her, pulling her into a tight embrace. Lore inhaled her scent of jasmine, sweat, and relief. "Are—"

"Yes, yes, all accounted for. You were the only one missing."

Lore slipped from Aunty Eshe's arms and sank to the ground, sobbing in relief. Suddenly, the kids were piling atop her, hugging her, and crying with her. Touching each of their faces in

turn, she chuckled as they all started to yell, telling her a different version of the same tale. For them, the earthshake was just an
exciting event that had happened, and they'd already forgotten
how scary it was. The realization that their home would not be
whole anytime soon had not yet hit them.

Her eyes turned to Uncle Salim, who knew, as she did, what
this meant for them. In a matter of moments, their lives had
changed irrevocably.

The earthshake had leveled the winery, same as the shop.

They would no longer be able to support the children.

Uncle Salim was surrounded by a pile of glass. His broom
was frozen mid-sweep. Curly salt-and-pepper hair was plastered
to his dusty face. His leather gloves were caked in dirt, and tears
streamed down his cheeks, mixing with the blood that had trick-
led from a head wound on his brow. Lore noted a nasty gash on
his elbow, which steadily dripped blood onto the earth.

Katu offered her a piece of clean linen from the medical bag.
He was newly twelve, with flaming locks of red hair, mischievous
green eyes, and a pale face filled with freckles—he was also usually the *first* to cause trouble. But even he was missing his usual
crooked grin. He seemed determined to be as responsible as possible today.

She squeezed his shoulder in thanks and took the linen
from him.

She turned back to her uncle, stepping into the space he'd
cleared around him. "I'm so sorry." She swabbed his wound
with alcohol and wrapped the cloth around his elbow. When she
could retrieve clean water, she would clean the wound, but for
now, she just needed to staunch the bleeding.

Uncle Salim wiped the back of a glove across his cheek,
smearing the dust into grime. He nodded distractedly, crying
silently, even as he bent to sweep up more chunks of brick, clay,
and glass.

He needed to rest, but, after twelve years of being his ward, Lore knew that he wouldn't until this space was clear of dangerous debris. He would always put the children first.

Lore turned back to the kids and sat before Milo, pulling him onto her lap, the last of the children to come in for a hug. He'd held back until the swarm of excited children had thinned. She squeezed his shaking shoulders and held him tight. Even though he was six years old, Milo still hadn't uttered a word and was often prone to fits at even the smallest change in his routine.

How was he going to get through this?

The other young children were laughing and jumping over the larger pieces of rubble. They were already turning this devastation into a game, trying to make the best of a horrible situation, as they'd always had to do.

But Lore thought there was a new look behind their eyes, one of fear and uncertainty.

. . . Except it wasn't new, was it? All of the children had arrived at the shelter with that same look after their worlds had been turned upside down by the tragic events that had brought them there.

It may not be new, but it was a look she hadn't seen for a while. Salim, Eshe, and, in the last few years, Lore, had tried to mend the children's heartbreak. She hadn't realized they'd been successful until she saw the sorrow return to their faces.

She sighed into Milo's thick, dusty coils. Another loss to add to their long list.

"I've got to get back to my mother—I just needed to make sure you and the kids were all right," Grey said softly.

"I would come with you but . . ." She motioned to Milo on her lap and the view around them.

"I know. It's all right." He knelt next to her, laying his hand on her shaking shoulder. She hadn't realized she was trembling until his touch stilled her. "It's all right," he said again.

But Lore was having a hard time understanding him. Her eyes stung from unshed tears. Her lungs ached for dust-free air.

She was back in that room with Mama, begging her not to leave, to please stay. And Baba was sitting in the corner with his head in his hands, and she knew that she'd lost him before he'd ever really left her.

A blink and she was standing in front of two strangers. Despite their kind eyes and warm arms, she didn't want them. She wanted Mama and Baba. And then she was back in the apothecary with the power of two fae flooding her senses and she couldn't move, couldn't breathe, and the world was shaking, the ceiling was falling all around her—

Milo reached out and placed both of his small hands on her cheeks before grabbing one of her flyaway curls and slowly twisting it around his finger—a comfort for him and now, in this moment, a comfort for her, tethering her to him.

She drew in a shaky breath, panic subsiding for the moment. She would take strength from Milo and give him some in turn.

She turned back to Grey, covering his hand with her own. "I'm fine," she said. But then she corrected herself—she never did like to lie to him. "I'll *be* fine. Head back home, Grey. After the kids are taken care of, I'll try to come by to check in on your place."

Grey nodded and stood, attempting and failing to brush the dust from his pants. It would take multiple washings before his trousers looked clean again. He gave her one last worried smile before he picked his way carefully through the cracked courtyard and slipped into the dawning night.

It took hours to clear the debris from the main dormitory. The six oldest kids were set to shaking out the bedding, sweeping, minding the younger children, or scrounging up food and water from the one still-intact well.

It was while she was settling the kids in with some bread and cheese that the outside sounds of a village on fire quieted. But although the last of the fires had been extinguished, the night sky was darkened further by the billowing smoke, pitching them into a nightmarish haze.

She finished feeding the kids, cleaned them of dust, dressed them in fresh clothes, and got them to sleep on their shared mats, clutching each other. She knew she couldn't risk navigating the streets at night given all the debris that likely still filled them, so she would go to Grey's first thing in the morning.

Lore counted the sleeping little ones before realizing that Milo was missing. She turned quickly, eyes searching the dormitory, and smiled. He was curled up on the pallet she'd scavenged and put in the corner for herself.

She slid beneath the blanket beside the small boy. He was sleeping so peacefully that Lore could almost forget this day had been a waking nightmare. As she lay down, exhaustion took over, and she was asleep before her head touched the mat.

)⟩)●(⟨(

As usual, Lore woke up before the sun with a weight on her chest and lead in her stomach. Her head pounded, signaling a migraine. She massaged her jaw, trying to ease the tension there, and blinked until the tears dried in her eyes.

Another dream about her parents.

She extracted herself from Milo's octopus grip and looked out one of the broken windows at the town. A small part of her had hoped that she would find that the day before had been a nightmare.

It wasn't.

By the time she was ready to face the devastation, the sun was just peeking over the horizon. It illuminated the vineyard, highlighting entire rows of trees that had been uprooted, flooded, and lost to the jagged cracks that spread across the field. Beyond that, where the edge of the town center used to stand, were many missing buildings. It was as if they'd once been drawn with a stylus and then erased by a careless rag, leaving scattered remnants across the ground.

She placed her rock into the pocket of her dress before sneaking out so she didn't disturb the sleeping kids. She wanted to check in with her aunt and uncle before heading to Grey's place. After checking Eshe's office—which was also in ruins—and the kitchen, which was mostly intact, thank the goddess, she went to the courtyard.

She stopped short. Two fae wearing the black and gold uniforms of the Wyndlin Castle guard and the realm to the south of their town were in the courtyard.

She crept across the cracked earth, skirting around a fallen tree. Aunty Eshe was nowhere to be found, nor was Uncle Salim. The children would wake up soon, and she needed to make sure none of them crossed paths with the two guards—one tall, with a sword on his hip, and the other short, with a bow and arrows.

She stepped toward the guards hesitantly. "Are you lost?" she asked.

"Excuse me?" the taller guard snarled.

Lore took an involuntary step backward.

The taller guard didn't bother reaching for the sword sheathed at his hip. He didn't need any weapon other than himself to split her from navel to neck. Instead, he reached out a taloned finger and raked it through her curls. The feeling of his hand made her shudder, and the guard smirked at this, revealing sharp teeth. He all but purred with satisfaction at her display of fear.

And she was, truly, terrified. She abruptly realized that despite the disgust the fae the afternoon before had treated her with, they had been civil.

These guards would not extend the same courtesy.

Suddenly the guard barked a laugh, wound his hand farther into her hair, and yanked hard, tossing her to the ground.

Lore didn't give them the satisfaction of crying out, though her body screamed in pain as she collided with the stone. Stunned, she leaned back on her hands and stared up at them.

"Don't you kneel when speaking to your superiors, human?" the shorter one crooned.

Her heart was in her throat, pounding with fear and choking her up. But she wouldn't, *couldn't* bring herself to bow. She struggled to her feet.

Their smiles grew. After all, what fun was prey that gave up so easily?

"How may I be of service?" she managed.

"We have come to escort the owner of the apothecary to Wyndlin Castle. Bring her to us," the tall one said, dark eyes flashing dangerously.

Lore almost choked on air. Escort? As in leave? As in walk past the tree line?

Lore shut her mouth, which was hanging open. She couldn't fathom what they were saying. If she brought Aunty Eshe to the fae, she would have to go. Uncle Salim would never be able to put this place back together, rebuild their businesses, and take care of the kids on his own. Not to mention, these fae clearly had no qualms about hurting humans.

She couldn't allow such harm to befall Aunty Eshe. She was the glue that held this entire shelter together. Uncle Salim was the heart, but Aunty was the driving force. If anyone was going to travel into the unknown and make this dangerous trip, it should be herself. The children would be okay without her, but they wouldn't survive if Aunty or Uncle left.

Yes, the kids needed Eshe more than they needed Lore.

"I'm the owner of the apothecary," she choked out. She hoped they couldn't smell a lie.

"Does she seem a bit young to you?" the one with the bow and arrows asked the other. His demeanor had changed in the few moments she had taken to consider her circumstances. He no longer looked at her, instead looking bored and indifferent as he stared at his claws.

That was how mercurial the fae were.

That was how easy it was for him to decide whether she was worth toying with or worth killing.

"He said we can bring the owner or her ward," he drawled. "I do not care which one it is." He looked at Lore. "Come."

Who said?

"Can I make my goodbyes?" Lore took a hesitant step backward, preparing to run back to the shelter.

"I think not."

But her family wouldn't know where she went. If she didn't return—and there was a good chance she would not—they would never know what had happened to her.

She couldn't catch her breath. It felt like clamps had seized her lungs.

She opened her mouth to beg or plead, when the guard's hand flashed out, wrapping around her arm in a cruel grip.

"Don't make us repeat ourselves, human."

Lore stepped back, trying to tug her arm free. Tears sprang to her eyes at the tightness of his grip. His fingernails dug into her skin harder.

"We said, it's time to go—"

He was interrupted by Milo. The boy, clad only in his sleeping tunic, ran full speed into the taller of the dark fae, tiny fists flying.

"Milo!" Lore could barely get his name out; her heart was in her throat.

She stepped forward at the same time Aunty Eshe did. She must've seen him run out. They both grabbed for the boy, trying to get to him before—

The fae sneered, piercing eyes boring into the boy. With a

flick of his other wrist, he knocked Milo away and into a small pile of stones. Milo cried out as he hit the ground.

"Milo!" She finally tore free from the guard and knelt, scooping the boy up before he could try to attack the fae again. She held him tightly and rubbed soothing circles on his back while examining him for injuries. His body might be a little sore from the fall, but, ultimately, he would be okay. She squeezed him gently until his panting stopped and a tiny, scraped hand reached up to twist one of her curls around his small finger.

Lore whispered in his ear, voice thick with unshed tears. "Milo, I'll be back soon. You be good and listen to Aunty. She needs your help, all right? I love you."

She handed him directly to Aunty Eshe, whispering, "I'll be back soon. Check under my mattress for the earnings from the apothecary." Her aunt nodded, her eyes wide with fear for Lore, but she had had more run-ins with the guards than Lore had. Aunty Eshe knew you didn't argue with them, didn't question them, or hold them up. She nodded and cradled a squirming Milo.

Lore backed away, not daring to look at the two guards so they wouldn't see the fury that burned in her. What kind of person shoves a child?

Then again, she supposed they weren't people at all. The Alytherians were fae.

Instead of looking at them, she kept her eyes on Milo as she walked away, willing him to stay and be strong.

When they stepped through the forest, passing by the sentries stationed in this zone, she turned back once. Aunty stood there still, her mouth moving while she rocked Milo. Lore didn't need to hear her to know that she would be singing softly, likely something she'd sung to Lore when she herself had been a scared child.

Lore turned back, sending a prayer to the goddess above that this wouldn't be the last time she saw her loved ones.

))) ● (((

The deeper into the forest they ventured, the darker it became.

Her resolve melted away, allowing the fear to rush back in. She shouldn't be here, this deep in the forest. More than anything, she wanted to sprint as fast as her legs would take her until she was back in Duskmere.

It might not be safe, but at least it was home. At least it was something familiar.

The leaves themselves seemed to whisper, *Go home, go home, go home.*

Barely any light reached the ground through the thick canopy of leaves. Though Lore distrusted the guards, she trailed close behind them, her legs struggling to keep up with their long strides. She swore she could feel the breath of a hungry beast waiting just beyond the shadows and could see the gleam of monstrous eyes tracking her every move.

She'd felt this before.

Lore had grown up surrounded by sentries. One of them had murdered her father in front of her and laughed when he realized that his sharp jab to her father's temple hadn't just shut him up—it had killed him.

She'd had to run and hide from sentries her entire life and had been forced to lower her eyes when in their view. Her whole existence had felt like she was dying a slow death by a thousand cuts. So, she'd tried to run from Duskmere. There had to be somewhere the sentries were not, after all.

At least, that's what she'd thought.

But she hadn't made it far into the woods before the fear of the unknown began to choke her and cloud her mind. And then a sentry had found her, anyway. And that's when she'd gotten the scar below her breast. He'd taken his time carving into her. He'd delighted in it, knowing that she'd be forced to bear the mark for a lifetime.

She resisted the urge to press on the spot that even now seemed to burn. The phantom pain came to her anytime she saw it, thought of it, or accidentally brushed against it.

The memory of that night in the woods was overwhelming her, mixing with her present terror. She thought if she didn't turn back now, the beating of her heart might stop all together.

She couldn't catch her breath.

Lore slowed her steps, dragging her feet. She could hardly get the fae to listen to her. She had to go—she'd volunteered for this. She could do it. The guards would keep her safe . . . well, from everything save from themselves. They weren't like that sentry from that night; they needed something from her after all.

Her eyes swelled with tears, and a whimper escaped her. For a second, she believed she would die in the forest. Something was going to eat her, or she would fall and break her leg, and nobody would come looking for her.

The forest itself was evil. It would consume her. Devour her. Swallow her whole like a monster with a gaping maw in one of her nightmares.

Suddenly, something changed. The bloodcurdling fear that had been pulsing through her dissipated. Her chest relaxed and the beads of sweat collecting on her brow dried up. Her jaw and fists unclenched, too. The all-consuming urge to turn back that was warring within her, the pressing need to be close to the guards and the false sense of protection their presence provided—despite knowing neither of them would actually lift their swords to *protect* her—just stopped. The fear dissipated.

She heard the trill of birdsong. The soft, almost imperceptible footfalls of the guards as they continued their pace. The trees here differed from the ones on the edge of Duskmere. They were older, more spread out. Rather than imposing giants working in league with the guards, these trees had an almost calming aura to them.

The guards were paying her no mind, seemingly unaware of the change in thinking Lore had just undergone. She turned around and walked a few paces back, retracing her footsteps.

All at once, that fear invaded her senses again. Her stomach heaved with it, her heartbeat roared in her ears, and she had to consciously fight the urge to panic and run blindly through the woods until she was back in Duskmere.

She turned with difficulty and walked three more paces. Her fear vanished again.

The fear—the panic—was false. A spell. Some disgusting magic, no doubt placed here centuries ago by the Alytherians to stop the humans from leaving.

Lore's eyes filled with tears. Not from sadness, but anger. How *dare* they?

"Do not fall behind, human!"

Genuine fear shot through Lore's stomach at the guard's order. She recalled his grip around her arm and the way he had cast her to the ground.

The guards had gotten too far ahead of her. She quickened her steps and rearranged her features. They could never know that she was aware of the spell.

If they knew she had that knowledge, she would never be allowed to return home.

CHAPTER 4

B y early evening, Lore's feet ached in her too-small boots, and the meager strip of dried fruit the guards had given her left her stomach rumbling from hunger. Despite all of that, it was uncertainty that caused unease to settle in the pit of her belly as she stepped into an Alytherian city.

Lore kept seeing flashes of Duskmere every time she blinked: the crumpled ceiling in the shop, the Burgs' tavern on fire, the kids' terrified faces as they tried so hard to be brave. Less than a full day's walk from here, her entire world had fallen apart because of an earth-shattering force. Life as they knew it was gone forever.

Yet in this city, there wasn't a single brick out of place. Every beautiful house was intact and the fae in them were living a life untouched by the desolation that had shaken her town.

The bitter taste of resentment burned her throat. Was this what magic could do? It could induce a fear so palpable she was still shaking with the memory of it, and it could keep an entire city standing despite the movement of the very earth beneath it?

With each step she took through the main street toward the looming castle that rose above all else, she felt more like she was walking into a daydream, though she had only just left a nightmare behind. Lore reached up with shaking hands, trying to smooth her unruly curls, but stopped as she caught sight of her grimy hands and dirty fingernails. She hadn't had a chance to wash up during their journey at all, other than to clean the wounds on her cheek. She'd been too tired to care.

But now she cared. It seemed that on every street, beautifully dressed fae of all ages stopped to look at her. Fae children, eyes wide, asked their mothers if she really, truly, was a *human*. She watched their little mouths form the word, some with awe, some with disgust.

Her eyes flicked away as her nails bit into her palms. She wished that she was wearing her Starday best. She wished that her hair was combed and smoothed into shining ringlets.

Instead, she looked exactly like what she imagined their false, preconceived notions of how humans *would* look. She wanted to stop and tell them that her world had just fallen apart once again, that the rip in her tunic and the dust in her hair were from *helping* children not so unlike them. Tears of frustration stung her eyes, but still she held her chin up, even while avoiding their gazes.

Her courage faltered. She regretted every step she took away from Duskmere.

Let this be quick. Let whatever they need take only a moment. Let me be back home in time to kiss little Milo goodnight, maybe sit by the lake with Grey.

))) ● (((

It wasn't long before Lore saw the castle up close. A fortress at the highest point of the kingdom, it was built of stone and its towers and turrets seemed to pierce the sky itself. Even from the streets far below, she could see that its surrounding walls were thick and sturdy— anyone would be foolish to attack it where it sat perched on high, overseeing Alytheria.

It took hours to reach the castle, and by the time the guards led her through what appeared to be a heavily guarded side entrance, across deserted castle grounds, and bid her wait outside a closed door, she was so tired from the trek she forgot to be afraid.

She slumped to the floor, grateful that this part of the castle had a lush carpet spanning the length of the corridor. As the plush fabric cushioned her, she wished to remove her boots and survey the damage, suspecting that she would find bloody blisters and skin rubbed raw. But she resisted the urge.

She had walked the last few leagues with the pain; she could last another hour or so.

She looked at the guard, the short one with the bow and arrows, who was standing nearby, watching her. She supposed he had been left to ensure she didn't try to pry the sconces off the wall or shove the nearby silver candlesticks up her tunic. She wanted to glare at him, but knew she couldn't risk it. Instead, she glanced at his boots. They looked so well made. She bet he felt like he was walking on a cloud all the time.

She sprang to her feet when the door swung open, wincing as she did so. Yes, definitely burst blisters. She peered inside the room.

"Is this the human that owns the shop with the books for sale?" an aging male asked from where he sat behind a grand wooden desk.

"Lord High Steward, this is she."

"I see. She seems to be younger than we expected."

Lore exhaled a shaky breath. She hated when men spoke about her like she wasn't there. She had grown used to it from adults after her parents had died—outside of her aunt and uncle—but such a conversation being carried out by fae was uncharted territory, so she didn't say a word. Instead, she stood across from the fae, looking as stoic as she could, praying to the goddess that this was all the questioning he would do about her identity. If they discovered she didn't own the apothecary, there was no knowing how they might punish her.

The steward, a fae with a silver braid so long it was tied in several knots yet still hung down to coil on a decorative cloth on the floor, leaned toward her and steepled his aged hands. He was the oldest fae Lore had ever seen, though his brown eyes still shone, clear and piercing. His pointed ears were adorned with jewels, his fingers with rings. A pendant with the royal crest hung on a large chain, resting against his exquisite robes.

Someone wealthy, important, but still a servant of the royal family.

"I have a proposition for you." His voice was smooth and didn't betray his advanced age like the wrinkles between his brow did. His teeth were sharp, *too sharp*, and the hair on the back of her neck stood up at the sight of them. "Sit down," he said.

Suppressing her body's natural response of wanting to re-main as far away from the male as possible, she sat. "What can I do for you . . . ?" She trailed off, unsure of how to address him.

He didn't respond. His eyes bore into her own until she looked away.

She studied the ornate walls of his study. They were carved and painted with every flower that could possibly exist in the world. The petals and stems were pressed with gold leaf, which shone in the fading twilight filtering through the enormous win-dows behind him. The floors were made from a polished stone that gleamed, reflecting the colors of the mural on the ceiling. It was a painting of the sky on a sunny day, colored with a blue so rich and saturated it made her eyes water. Though she took in all this beauty, she didn't miss how the fae's lip curled in disgust when he looked at her.

Finally, he answered. "You may address me as Chief Steward Vinelake. As to my proposition, we have a library here that has been in this castle for longer than you can probably comprehend.

It houses books and scrolls that are very important to the crown. One thousand years ago, an enchantment was placed on the room so no Alytherian creature could enter it. However . . ." He leaned forward, placing his hands flat on his desk.

Lore couldn't help but lean back, maintaining the distance between them.

"Your kind isn't from Alytheria, nor even from our world, *Raelysh*." He said this like it was news to her and not the sole reason human lives were so miserable. "When Lord Syrelle learned your village—what does your kind call it, Dustmere—"

"*Duskmere*," she ground out through her teeth.

He continued as if she hadn't spoken, "—had an apothecary and books, he had an idea." Here, a zealous light shone through his eyes. "What if a human could pass through the doors un-harmed?"

Uneasy shivers rose up Lore's spine.

"The library is in shambles. We need someone to clean the space."

Lore wanted to laugh. *They just want a servant. Then why demand the owner of the apothecary—*

"You can read Alytherian, yes?"

"I can." *Oh, this is why.*

"Good. We want you to clean up the library, but your main focus will be organizing the tomes and artifacts within, meticulously logging and categorizing each and every book, scroll, and pamphlet you find. At the end of every week, you will provide me with a list, and I will let you know if I wish you to bring any of them to me. Of course, you will be compensated for your time. We'll send you home with enough coin to rebuild your shop and more. We'll throw in a horse too. I've heard those are quite rare."

So, they *did* know that Duskmere had been destroyed. They just hadn't bothered to help.

Wait. Lore's eyes widened. Spend all day in a library? One probably filled with fae relics, history, medical, and alchemical texts? One that nobody had set foot into for millennia? Lore pinched her leg to make sure she wasn't dreaming.

This could be the answer to their problems. She might even learn where humans came from.

"You theorize that I will be unharmed when entering the library, but if you're wrong, will I be killed?" she asked.

"We have every reason to believe that you will be unharmed."

It wasn't an answer to her question, but access to the books within the library could be incredibly beneficial. There was so much humans didn't know about the outside world, information that was purposefully withheld from them.

Even so, if his theory was wrong, she was gambling with her life; she better make it worth her while.

"I will risk my life, but I won't do it for *just* coin and a single horse."

Anger flashed across the steward's face.

"You're lucky my patron is offering you anything at all, human, and yet you wish to negotiate?"

Lore wanted to tell him and his mysterious patron to shove the offer somewhere private, but the steward seemed like he would have her executed for such a slight. Though he had appeared respectful initially, it was clear he believed he was lowering himself by speaking to her.

"What is this about negotiation?"

Lore startled, her head whipping around. She recognized that voice; she'd heard it just yesterday.

Sure enough, the fae from the apothecary was stepping into the steward's office. Only, the male looked different. His face was the same: same sharp jaw, manicured brow, full lips, smooth, dewy brown skin, but he had . . .

"Wings?"

She hadn't meant to say that out loud, but the shock of seeing wings that had definitely not been sprouting from his shoulder blades yesterday loosened her tongue.

The male continued into the room until he stood beside the steward's desk. Once again, that power radiated from him. Lore could *feel* the magnitude of his magic.

"Lord Syrelle, I was just telling her that—"

"Hush."

The steward's mouth snapped closed.

"I would like to hear what she has to say," Lord Syrelle said.

There was that fear again. It was impossible not to want to shrink back from his presence. And now, dressed as he was in a black cloak, with trousers, boots, and black, eagle-like wings that brushed the floor, he looked beyond intimidating.

Lore had to clear her throat three times before she remembered how to speak. "I would love to help," she eventually managed. "But as it is, the only good coin does us is paying taxes and tithes. Without trade, it's just pretty, but useless, metal. If you were to send supplies along with skilled masons and healers to Duskmere to help with the devastation from the earthshake . . ."

She trailed off. *Goddess, his eyes are intense.* They gazed into her soul, as if demanding she spill her secrets.

Lore swallowed. She could do this. And anyway, she didn't truly have a choice, did she? She tore her eyes from the lord and back to the steward. He was a fraction as terrifying as the winged beast at her side.

"If you can promise me that your people will help Duskmere recover," she said, "then I will risk my life for your theory."

The steward said nothing, gaze darting between her and his master.

Sweat dripped down Lore's back as she held her breath. Was she stupid to even try to negotiate?

"You have a deal. I'll send our finest healers, masons, and

more than enough supplies. But you must start your work in the library today."

Lore relaxed, gulping in air. "Show me the way and I will start right n—" She flinched backward, scurrying into the corner of the room in her haste to get away from the lord's suddenly outstretched hand. "I would appreciate it if you would keep your distance, my lord," she choked out.

Lord Syrelle dropped his hand to his side. He searched her face, assessing. He was always assessing. Lore wanted to squirm beneath his inquisitive gaze. "I apologize for my rude behavior, but I have to ask . . . am I really so terrifying?"

Yes. "No, my lord. I was just surprised, is all."

He made a disappointed sound. "That won't do," he murmured. Then, louder, "I appreciate your support in this. The library means a lot to my family."

Lore could only nod in response. Her tongue felt like it had swelled up in her mouth. Her throat was dry.

The winged fae walked toward the door, giving her a wide berth. His feathers shimmered with light. He called to the steward. "Show her to the library after you've discussed the rules with her."

"Yes, my lord." As the door closed behind him, the steward barked at her, "Sit down, will you?"

Lore's cheeks burned as she returned to her chair.

"I can show you the library and then you will be taken to your quarters. However, we have some rules you must agree to before we can move forward."

"Of course. What are they?"

"You aren't to read any of the texts, at least not beyond what is necessary to organize them. If you find any particularly . . . interesting tomes, scrolls, or grimoires, they are to be brought to me right away. *Especially* if they appear to be *spelled*. In addition, you aren't to discuss the books you find in there with anyone but me or Lord Syrelle."

Lore nodded, curls bouncing around her face. Seemed reasonable. "Understood. No reading in the library and bring you anything that seems spelled with magic. When do I get the coin?"

Chief Steward Vinelake's smile grew. "As soon as the task is finished. As you will see, it is quite a . . . monumental task. As for the coin, you will not need any while you reside here—the servants' quarters, dining hall, and baths should provide all you will need."

"Chief Steward, with respect, I was brought here without a moment's notice. I wasn't able to bring clothing or supplies. Might I get paid a small sum every few days so I might purchase what I need? Assuming this work cannot be completed in a day."

The steward's eyes flashed with annoyance, but he consented with a nod. "I think this shall take you some time. Despite my protests, I believe it unwise to permit a human to remain outside of Duskmere for so long, and in such close quarters with your betters, but it seems you are likely to spend the winter here."

Lore sat up straight. *The winter?* They hadn't even celebrated the autumn equinox yet. She ignored his comments about permitting a human to remain outside of Duskmere. She wasn't surprised in the least that this was his thought process, nor that he wasn't ashamed to let her know it. Lore remained quiet—he hadn't actually answered her question.

Chief Steward Vinelake relented with a sneer. "Fine. I'll alert the treasury." He raised one long finger. "The royal family is not here this season, but you will use the servants' passageways at all times. You are to remain in your quarters when you aren't eating, bathing, or in the library. That means no attending festivals or exploring the grounds. I expect you to be working every day.

I will permit you a short break on the mornings the market is here to acquire any items you may need. But if I find you are slacking, I will send you home. Through the forest."

A perversion of a smile broke out across his face.

"Without an escort."

CHAPTER 5

Lore surveyed the Alytherian Royal Library with the chief steward through glass windows inlaid in thick metal doors, though "door" didn't seem like an adequate word for what these were. They rose before Lore from floor to ceiling, towering so high above her that, even when she craned her neck all the way, she couldn't see their tops.

Each door was embossed with a beautiful picture, one depicting the night sky dripping down from above, as constellations swirled above a cascade of mountains. A forest scene flowed up from the bottom. Trees had been fashioned in such a way that the flickering light of the torches seemed to make their leaves sway in a breeze. Animals gallivanted through the woods, and two adolescents lounged near the tree, one writing on a scroll while the other read aloud from a book.

Ancient glass panes were inlaid in the center of each door, the glass warped and rippled by time. Through the windows she could see bits and pieces of the library. It was pure chaos. Gargantuan stone shelves rose up to the ceiling, and long ladders on wheels climbed up each shelf. The floor had disappeared beneath the books that covered every inch, as if they had chosen to leap from their shelves to their deaths rather than go unread.

Every. Single. Tome.

Lore didn't know if she wanted to laugh or cry at the state of the library. She whispered a quick prayer of gratitude to the stars that the shelves were, for the most part, all standing. After a millennium without care, she thought they would have crumbled to dust. Lore had never seen a library before, but the sheer number of books filled her with excitement. She'd read about libraries in her stories, but to see one before her, even in its current state of chaos, was magical. She wished more than anything that Duskmere could have a library, one filled not just with fae texts but human stories as well. There was a time when they weren't permitted to write their own stories—it was only in her lifetime that they had been allowed to keep and write their own books, and it wasn't often that anyone had the time or energy to do so. It would take many lifetimes to fill a library of this size with their own stories, but how incredible a feat it would be.

Amid the amazement, dread crept in. How was she to pick these books up, organize them, and put them back in their respective places by herself? It would take a team of at least thirty people to do so in a remotely reasonable time frame. Then again, someone with magic could probably do it in a day.

Or at least, she thought they could. She knew little about what limits magic had. The Alytherians didn't like it when humans even acknowledged their alluring abilities, let alone learn about them. It was their best-kept secret.

Lore jumped when Chief Steward Vinelake cleared his throat beside her. His face was an emotionless void. "Evening meal is after high bells. We will send someone to collect you today, but tomorrow you will have to find your own way. When you find any books of interest, do not remove them from the library yourself. We have tasked two younglings to your detail. They can notify me, and I will meet you at the doors to retrieve them." The steward retreated to the other end of the hall.

Lore focused on slowing her breathing and unclenching her jaw.

The Alytherians had never lifted a hand to help the humans. As she saw it, they were the reason it had been so hard for her people to even clothe or feed their families. And here she was, about to risk her life for their curiosity. Nevertheless, them sending aid and supplies to Duskmere would be worth it.

The chief steward and the guards were irritating and scary, yes, but just thinking of all that she could do for the people she loved made her hands itch to get working. Eventually, the task would be finished, and she would be on her way home with a fat purse and a tale to tell. Or maybe one she could write herself. *She* could write the first story to be stored in a library of their own.

Still, she was a little apprehensive about walking through the doors. She hadn't failed to notice that Chief Steward Vinelake hadn't dared even step near the entrance. He may have appeared nonchalant, but he kept far back from the library, not risking the consequences of the spell.

She just needed to reach out, grab the ornate handle, and *pull*. Lore cursed. Her hands did not want to follow orders.

She focused on breathing again. Be calm. Just enter the library. It's just a regular door. A regular room.

She heard a noise behind her and jumped. Someone was coming.

She turned sharply. But it was just two children peering wide-eyed at her from around a marble statue. A chill rose up Lore's back. In the torchlight of the corridor, one of the younglings' large eyes glinted like those of the cats back home.

They were probably just curious. This entire part of the castle appeared to be abandoned, as if it were a dead limb they had amputated long before. She imagined the two had never seen anyone go near the library before, let alone prepare to enter it.

She let out a breath, steadying her resolve. "You can do this," she muttered.

The steward had said the wards wouldn't hurt a human. She was a human. *Just open the doors. They're just doors. Regular doors.*

She might feel nothing at all when she passed through.

She also might be incinerated on the spot.

She glanced to where he stood on the other end of the hall, his face void of emotion. Did he care if she survived this? She was sure he would feel no sorrow if she was killed by the spell; his only emotion would probably be irritation that his mission had failed.

The bronze handle was ice cold under her fingertips, and she felt a slight shock where she touched the metal. It wasn't painful, just annoying. After a moment, the handle warmed. She wrapped her fingers around it and pulled.

The door didn't budge.

Were they wrong? Was she locked out, too?

She wanted to vomit at the thought of *almost* having all that coin and all that information, only for it to be stripped from her grasp before she'd even had a chance to try to earn it.

Then she had a thought and couldn't help but laugh to herself.

Instead of pulling, she pushed.

The doors glided open as if light as a feather, though they were made of metal. Enchanted, then.

She entered the stale air of a room that had been untouched by any living creature for more than a thousand years. She waited a beat, her breath held, and squeezed her eyes shut. Just in case the spell was delayed. Maybe her death wouldn't be instantaneous—it would be slower, more painful. She could be poisoned by the air instead of smitten by lightning.

After a few moments she breathed a sigh of relief and opened her eyes. She was alive. Her body felt the same. She took another step into the library.

Dust kicked up around her, dancing in the low light that filtered in through the row of clerestory windows near the ceiling. Lore frowned; it would not be enough light. Today was sunny, but if she faced a cloudy day, the library would be so dark she would scarcely be able to see her hand in front of her face. She would need candles—lots of them—to light the darkness that pressed in from the ends of the stacks and all the way to the ceiling.

Lore shuddered, averting her gaze from the shadows. When she looked into that darkness, it felt a little like the darkness was looking back.

She ventured farther in, but stayed close to the well-lit areas, browsing the endless rows of shelves. Not all of them were as empty as she had initially thought, and books were not all they housed. There were jars, boxes, and various other objects covered in so much dust she couldn't tell what they were.

It wasn't unlike her beloved apothecary.

She wandered, uncovering alcoves, seating areas, and rooms for study; one room was filled with equipment that the scholars must have used to bind, copy, or mend the books. What she could do with all this equipment back home.

She wandered over to a door and pulled it open to find a broom closet filled with cleaning supplies. Another door led to a room that housed candles, matches, and extra rugs. There were even some old garments, aprons, robes, and a few faded guard uniforms.

One closet held weapons. Lore quickly closed that one.

Once she explored each room, she pulled up an old chair and sat down with a huff before immediately sneezing from the sudden cloud of dust.

Well, she'd found the candles, but she would probably need

a cloth to cover her nose, gloves, and another hundred cloths to wipe the tomes down with.

And coffee.

She would need lots of coffee.

Rapid staccato knocks interrupted Lore's exploration of the library, and she was glad for it. The sun had dipped below the horizon and the library had quickly gone from thrilling to chilling. She pushed the doors open and peeked out to find a tall female wearing a green uniform with the royal emblem sewn into the corner.

The woman retreated, holding a broom in her hand with the handle pointing toward the doors. Apparently, she hadn't wanted to get close enough to knock with her hand, so she had improvised.

The scene was comical. Lore couldn't help but smile a little.

The female stood up straight, lowering the broom to the floor. "I'm Elra. I've been told to show you to the dining hall for dinner, after which you will head to your room for the night." Her tone was curt, stiff, and dismissive.

Lore's smile fell.

Not long after, she sat by herself in a large dining hall. Elra had made it painfully clear that, although she'd been assigned to show Lore where to go, she had no intention of remaining in her presence a second longer than she needed to. The moment Lore had her food, Elra scurried over to a few other uniformed females and ignored her.

The servants' hall was large but simple. Food was piled high at a table in one corner. Guards and servants in various uniforms filed in in twos or threes, filled their plates, and sat at the unadorned wooden tables.

Though the food wasn't fancy, it was flavorful and hot. Lore wasted no time in sopping up the last remnants of her mutton stew with a roll of freshly baked bread bigger than her fist. Her goblet was filled with a thick cider that tasted a little *too* strong, forcing her to sip it sparingly. She didn't want to find herself drunk on her first day. She would need her wits about her, where the fae were concerned.

Nobody sat at her table. The other servants made it clear she wasn't welcome to sit with them on their dinner break.

Lore suspected it had nothing to do with the layers of grime caked on her from the earthshake, the road, and the library, and everything to do with the fact that she was a human. At least her hands were clean; despite Elra giving her only a few moments to wash up, she'd managed to scrub them raw.

Lore stood, filled another bowl with stew from a great cauldron on the table, and grabbed three more rolls.

She sat back down at her table, brushing off the stares with another bite of steaming stew, and had to stifle a groan as the savory taste of the broth, coupled with the sweet fattiness of the mutton, burst over her tongue. Not to mention, the stew was *filled* with vegetables she had never tasted before. The rolls were hot and soft as a cloud, with fresh butter melted on top.

She ate more butter in that one meal than she probably had in her entire lifetime. Even if they served this same meal every night she was here, she didn't think she'd ever grow tired of it.

A slight wave of guilt coursed through her. She wished more than anything that she could share this meal with Milo and the other kids. It wasn't fair that they were probably eating plain rice while she got all of this. But, when she came back with the promised coin, she could buy them food that tasted like this too.

If the food for the servants tasted this good, the royalty must eat like the old gods.

She used her third roll to sop up the very last of the stew in her bowl and looked around. What did she do with her empty bowl and the still mostly full cup of cider? She eyed trash bins and a large bucket filled with other soiled dishes; no doubt there were scullery maids who took care of these dishes.

She spotted a fae male dropping his bowl off at the exact moment she stood to do the same. She hesitated, immediately itching to pull the rock from her tunic pocket. Should she wait until he walked away? So far, she hadn't suffered any rude comments from the fae who worked here, not to her face at least, but she also hadn't gone near any of them either.

She sat, placing the bowl and cup back on the table, watching the fae from the corner of her eye. *Thistle and Sage.* He was just hanging out by the waste bin like a trash goblin. Was he waiting for her to come up there so he could mess with her?

The fae wore a guard's uniform, same as the two fae who had brought her here, but with one main difference: this guard wore the blue stripes of a sentry. She searched the male's face; had she seen him before on the outskirts of Duskmere?

The guard was tall and slim, his skin a gorgeous reddish-brown that looked a shade darker than Lore's own. A thin scar bisected his eyebrow; she followed the line of it, past a lovely, wide nose, and a very full, even more lovely, bottom lip. There was an odd juxtaposition between the beauty of the sentries and their cruelty. A children's rhyme detailing just that came unbidden to her, and she had to stop herself from humming it.

She might have recognized his uniform as that of a sentry, but after some more inspection, she was sure she had never seen this guard before. She would've remembered a face that magnificent. Then her eyes snagged on a patch where his tunic had been mended, and his boots, though freshly shined, were worn. Not high ranking enough to warrant a new uniform then. His black, wooly hair was pulled up into a loose topknot, and it wove around two brown antlers that stretched toward the low ceiling of the dining hall. Wooden ornaments on the tips of his ears matched the rich color of his antlers.

She glanced around the room again, grimacing. It was the only bin. She looked back at him, and unease shot through her. The male was looking right at her, his eyes burning with fury.

Lore jumped, knocking over her cider. The sweet liquid shot across the table, and she sprang to her feet with a curse at the same moment a youngling wearing the garb of a scullery maid hurried over with a cloth.

Lore reached out to grab the cloth from the child. "Oh, thank you—let me—"

The child stumbled back with a squeak, a look of horror on her face when she realized who, or rather what, exactly was reaching for the rag.

"Oh, it's okay. I'll clean this up," said the youngling, whose voice came out in a squeak. She seemed genuinely frightened of Lore, who had spent her entire life in terror of the young maid's kind.

"Joji, come away from there at once!" Another servant ordered the child away from Lore.

Lore stepped backward, away from the mess dripping onto the floor and the youngling. Twisting her hands, she looked around at all the fae. Everyone had ceased their conversations. Some had stood up, glowering at Lore.

She hadn't meant to scare the child or to make a mess.

"Disgusting human, what is she doing here with—?"

"It's wrong, she shouldn't be permitted—"

"Think of the children, her kind is known to be violent and rash, what if she hurts—"

"Who allowed it out—"

The voices came from every corner of the room, the castle staff no longer concealing their conversations. Suddenly, she wanted to be home so badly. Her eyes burned with unshed tears.

"Thank you. I'm so sorry," she said to the room, shame burning through her as she clumsily snatched up her bowl and now-empty cup, glancing back to the waste bin. The guard was nowhere to be seen. Thank all the stars in the dark sea. Lore dropped off the soiled dishes and looked around for Elra, but the maidservant was nowhere in sight. She'd left her.

Wasn't she supposed to take her from here to her quarters?

A feeling of dread washed over Lore. She had absolutely no clue where her quarters were. Here she was, trying to stay under the radar, eat her food, do her job, and yet it was clear to her now that she would need to thicken her skin to get through this ordeal. Easier said than done.

Because really, all she wanted to do was scream.

Lore clenched her fists, trying to ground herself with the sharp pain of her nails biting into her palms, but it didn't work. She could feel the stares burning into her like hot coals. Her chest tightened, constricting. She was beginning to panic, and the burning threat of tears increased.

She wouldn't cry here.

She would rather sleep in the library than stay in the dining hall another second.

Lore turned and stumbled out of the hall, trying to retrace her steps. She turned down a hallway that looked familiar. The servants' corridors were dark and unadorned, but she was sure she remembered the turns that Elra had taken while leading her to the dining hall.

Or should she have gone the other way at the last fork?

Her breaths were shallow, erratic. A choked laugh escaped her—she was definitely lost. The strangled sound bounced around the red stone walls of the hallway.

She kept walking, trying to ignore her panic by counting the torches, though they did little to illuminate the space, leaving the rust-colored hallway mostly in menacing shadows.

Fae eyes just probably didn't need as much light as her human eyes did. That was why it was so dark . . . and creepy.

Right?

Lore shuffled along, trailing her hand along the cool, rough stone of the castle walls.

Finally, she saw a young-looking maidservant carrying a bundle of sheets in her arms. Lore opened her mouth to call out, but, before she could, the girl disappeared through a door.

Desperate, she tried the door, then raised a hand to knock when it didn't budge. Her hand froze. Hadn't the steward said he would be furious if she disturbed anyone staying in the castle?

She dropped her hand and continued down the twisting hallways. There was nobody to ask for help and she was surely going to be eaten by some monster if she continued to wander through this creeping darkness. Thistle and Sage, how she wished she was home.

CHAPTER 6

"Y ou know, if you continue along that corridor, you'll eventually end up in the dungeons. They're quite a dreary place to visit—unless you're into dampness and foul smells."

Lore started at the accented, deep timbre of a male's voice coming from behind her. Turning, she pressed her back to the red earth of the wall and took in the fae before her.

It was the same guard who had lingered by the trash bins in the dining hall, watching her. In this light, his almond-shaped eyes seemed the color of onyx, matching his black hair. His antlers almost brushed the low ceiling.

Lore became acutely aware of every one of those layers of dust and grime coating her. She sniffed and thought she could, in fact, smell something foul wafting from the direction she'd just been headed.

"I . . ." She cleared her throat. "I'm looking for my quarters. The maidservant, Elra, disappeared after bringing me to the dining hall and, well, I thought I would have run into her by now."

"Elra is rarely where she ought to be. I don't know how she still has her position here." The guard took a step toward her, sliding his hands into his pockets. "But I am more concerned about why you are wandering the halls like a lost little puppy."

"I wasn't—"

"Should I alert the steward about you sneaking around the halls?"

Fear crawled up Lore's back. "I'm not sneaking! I'm trying to find my way back to the library, or actually, to—"

The guard cut her off. "You shouldn't be in the library at this hour. You should be in your room."

If he had let her finish. "I was looking for the library or Elra, so she could show me to my room."

The guard rolled his eyes and sighed, like he was making a massive sacrifice. "Follow me," he said.

Panic flared in Lore's chest as her gaze fell to the blue stripes on his uniform. He could take her anywhere and she would have no way of knowing if it was the right direction.

But, then again, the dungeons definitely weren't where she wanted to go either.

Why would he be so kind as to take her to her quarters? Everyone else had been . . . a slew of unpleasant adjectives ran through her head. And earlier, he'd been glaring at her so furiously, too. "Follow you where, exactly?"

His mouth quirked, a hint of a dimple appearing on either cheek. "Do you not know how to follow orders?"

Lore wanted to glare at him, but she stilled her features and waited a beat, hoping he would answer her question.

"Hmm." The thoughtful sound rumbled from his broad chest. "I'm a castle guard. It would be remiss of my duties to let an outsider wander unescorted through the castle. And anyway, I've nothing better to do than show a little mouse to a safe place."

"I am *not* a rodent!" Lore hissed. Anger writhed through her. She knew the Alytherians viewed her as less than them, but to be compared to a mouse?

"No, you are not a rodent. But you are small, weak, and you

work in the library—a place a mouse would love to be. Are you going to follow me or not, Mouse?"

She clenched her fists, bit the retort on the tip of her tongue, and gave him a slight nod.

"Maybe you *aren't* as dim as you appear." He turned, walking in the opposite direction of where he claimed the dungeons were.

"What gives you the right to call me dim?" Lore mouthed to his back.

"You would have to be dim to voluntarily explore this area of the castle at night."

Lore jumped. How had he seen her? She needed to bite her tongue. But some strange brand of courage seemed to have gripped her, and she said, rather stupidly, "It's not like I thought to myself, 'Hmm, I shall explore the dungeons today.'"

"Exactly. You didn't seem to *think* at all. This way." He turned left.

She felt uneasy following him so blindly, but the thought of finding herself alone once again in the maze of low corridors was worse than enduring the company of a sentry.

Eventually, he led her to a different low-lit corridor with considerably more signs of life. This one had doors with symbols carved on them. He stopped at a blue door with a swirling symbol on it: three swirls connected by one line.

"It's this one. I would suggest you not do any more 'exploring.'" The disbelief was obvious in his tone. "There are some in this castle who would like to know what a little mouse such as yourself tastes like."

She supposed she should thank him, even though the thought made her stomach turn. "Well, thanks," she gritted out.

"Try not to sound so appreciative."

I'll do that, she thought, *just as soon as you try not to sound like such a prick.*

The guard's cold eyes flitted over her face like he knew what she was thinking. She stilled her features, putting on a blank mask.

He didn't know. Couldn't know. Because if he really knew her thoughts, he would have broken her jaw for her insolence by now.

"Now, do what you're told and go to your room."

It was a dismissal.

Without a word, Lore pressed down on the latch and pushed the door open. Relief coursed through her when she saw that she had, indeed, been led to a small room.

When she turned back to the guard, he was already halfway down the corridor, his hands still in his pockets.

Maybe he was on his way to find another waste bin to lurk by.

Lore stepped into a sparsely furnished room. A small bed stood against one wall, with a thin pillow and an even thinner quilt adorning it. Next to the foot of the bed frame was a wardrobe that held two pale green tunics, two pairs of thick tights, underclothes, and a worn pair of boots. The only other furniture was a small chair and table in the corner with a single candle and flint.

Her door had a lock on the inside. She latched it. Checked that the lock worked. It did. She removed her boots with a pained hiss and sunk onto the lumpy mattress. It was stuffed with hay, not unlike her bed at home. She thought she might be too anxious to sleep, but it was amazing what the body could do when faced with two days of terror. Lore was asleep before her head hit the pillow.

Lore was startled awake by a pounding.

She stumbled to the door, then hesitated, not knowing what she would find on the other side. She prayed it wouldn't be the steward—she honestly hoped to never see him again.

The knock came again, more persistent this time. She didn't have a choice. She cracked the door open to find the antlered guard who had led her to her room last night. He was wearing the same scowl as the evening before.

"You should be ready to go." His words were clipped.

It would've been nice if he had told her what time to be ready. He could have mentioned it at any point last night.

"I'm sorry," she bit out. "I didn't know what time to be ready." She eyed the guard's twin swords, which were slung low on his narrow hips.

He hadn't been wearing those last night.

Any courage she'd rallied abruptly fled.

"All the same, I expect you to be ready when I knock tomorrow. Hurry, if you wish to visit the washroom."

Her mind snagged on one word. "Wait, tomorrow?" What happened to Elra?

"I'll be in charge of you for now, unfortunately."

Unfortunately, indeed.

Lore couldn't help but close the door forcefully in the male's face. She hadn't particularly liked the maidservant—especially given Elra had abandoned her during dinner—but this guard certainly wasn't an improvement.

She quickly made her bed before grabbing a tunic and underclothes from the wardrobe. Clutching them to her chest, she followed the guard to the washroom, which was blissfully empty.

How late had she slept? She decided she didn't care as she sank into the steaming water of the bath. A moan escaped her lips. The hot water swirled around her, loosening her fatigued muscles and washing away the dust and grime caked on her skin.

How had she survived this long without a bath?

Her cheeks burned when she thought about the fae who was standing outside the washroom, waiting for her. She had probably looked and smelled frightening. But what did she care what a sentry thought about her? They were the worst kind of fae.

Lore noted two wooden bowls on the ledge of the bathing tub—one filled with shaved bits of soap and another with herbs and flowers floating in what looked like oil. She grabbed a few shavings and rubbed her body down. Once she rinsed the suds off, she moved to her hair, then immediately groaned.

Knots.

Her hair was in knots.

With disappointment, she realized there wasn't any cream for her hair, meaning that it would be extra frizzy today. Trying to tame her hair as best she could, she finger-combed her knotted curls, then pulled them to the side to braid them loosely.

She sniffed the floral mixture: cinnamon, something else she couldn't place . . . pear? No, something caramelized.

It smelled divine.

She rubbed the mixture under her arms and along her throat before rinsing. The leftover herbs and petals swirled in a current straight into a grate to be whisked away to who knew where.

When you have magic, even the servants bathe like royalty.

She wished she could relax in the bath forever, but she had work to do. She grimaced and got out of the water, then hurriedly dressed. A quick glance at the looking glass cemented what she already knew.

She needed to organize this library and get home before her hair knotted past the point of no return.

CHAPTER 7

W hen she exited the baths, the guard remained quiet, walking ahead of her as they headed toward the library. His long legs ate up the distance with ease. Lore made sure to pay attention to the twists and turns—she didn't plan on getting lost again.

Two servant boys sitting outside the large double doors of the library hopped up at their approach, greeting the guard first and introducing themselves as Tarun and Libb. The two curious boys from yesterday.

The guard shook both of their little hands. "Are you Rotha's boy?" He asked Tarun, the taller of the two.

"Yes, my lord. Rotha's my mom."

"I thought you might be. You look just like her. I'm Asher. I'll be on this one's detail from now on, so you boys let me know if you see or hear anything, all right? Come to me, first."

"Yes, my lord. Of course." Tarun stood tall with pride and grinned, clearly tickled at the important job he'd been given.

"I'm no lord, Tarun. Asher is just fine."

"You can count on us," Libb said.

Lore, however, was not grinning. Asher, was it? He seemed to be of the mind that she was up to something or, at the very least, not to be trusted.

Which, she *was* technically hoping to earn more than just the help of a few Alytherians and some coin. But it wasn't like she was a thief or anything. She just wanted to gain some knowledge, something that should have been freely shared with them.

She turned her back on Asher and spoke directly to the boys. Tarun had budding antlers just pushing through his tight coils, and his voice cracked when he spoke. Alternatively, Libb didn't have any antlers, though his pointed ears ended in tufts of fur, and he had a furred, spotted tail idly swishing behind him.

She made a mental note to learn the difference between the fae. She knew a little. The ones who hailed from Alytheria and came to Duskmere demanding all their coin were known as dark fae. Everyone she'd seen at the castle so far seemed to hail from Alytheria.

So, if they were dark fae, did that mean there were light fae? Hopefully, that was just one of the many questions that would be answered within the library.

"Tarun, right? I have a list for you boys today. Are you ready to do some work?"

They both nodded—Tarun eagerly and Libb shyly and subdued. Surprisingly, they were treating her with what felt an awful lot like respect.

"Okay, good," she continued. "I'll need parchment, a quill and ink, cream for my hair, and a stack of rags for cleaning—as many as you can carry." She looked at them for understanding.

"When you have the materials, bring them to me. I don't want you going near the library doors—your loss would be felt by more than just your families. All of us would feel it," said Asher, his voice losing its cheer and becoming oddly serious.

"Our mothers have already lectured us about the dangers of the library sir, we know." Tarun's voice was grave.

"Good. Now off you go."

Both boys nodded again, and with the slightest tilt of their curly heads, they disappeared down the corridor. The little one walked on his tippy toes, just like Milo.

Lore frowned. She doubted they would be successful in all but the quill and ink, but she'd had to try.

The guard, Asher, sat on the floor on the opposite side of the library entrance. It seemed he wasn't going to take his chances with the cursed library, either.

"Don't you have somewhere else to be?" Lore placed her hands on her hips. She felt emboldened by him sitting across the corridor while she was close to the forbidden library.

Asher gazed up at her. "I am exactly where I am supposed to be. Get to work. I've been ordered to let them know if you appear to be wasting time."

Lore made an irritated noise and turned on her heel.

Stepping through the library doors, Lore was met again by the damp, musty smell of decaying parchment and ancient dust. She decided to brush off the dismissive guard and focus on the task at hand. Goddess knew she had plenty to keep her busy.

But the smell was strong, and some fresh air would do wonders for the place. If she could climb onto a shelf, she may be able to un-latch and open one of the windows lining the tops of the shelves on the far back wall. It looked to be a bright, warm day outside, which would be perfect for airing out an old, damp—possibly haunted— library.

She was irritated by the guard outside, but she had to admit it was nice to know that *someone* would notice if she was suddenly killed by a disgruntled spirit.

She pushed a wooden ladder up against the back shelves. It had been worn smooth from the hands and feet of long-dead scholars and scribes. The first rung groaned under her weight, but when she bounced a little bit on it, testing if it could hold her weight, it held. She began a slow, cautious climb. When she reached the top, she pulled herself up onto the stone shelf to kneel before one of the large windows.

She gasped at the view. Towering trees with vines twisted together like braids danced in the breeze. There was a large pond with a stream that disappeared into the grounds. Sunlight glinted on the dappled mosaics and bushes with purple berry–lined paths of red brick. One young couple was picnicking in the shade of a tree as red and gold leaves tumbled in the breeze around them.

A small fox lounged on a thick branch in a tree to Lore's right, lulled to sleep by the serenity of the garden. Its paw twitched in its sleep, no doubt dreaming of chasing a plump rabbit.

As had been the case with the city, nothing was amiss here. How much progress had the masons made back home by now? Even one magic-gifted fae who was willing to help could do so much good. How much damage had the fires caused before being put out? How many families were now without homes and any source of coin?

How many lives had been lost?

Lore's stomach turned at the thought that she wasn't there to help. She wanted to be with her family and her community, helping to rebuild the only home she'd ever known. Instead, she was in a castle, filled with creatures who viewed her entire species as dirt beneath their feet.

But she *was* helping her people. Or trying to, at least. And that meant she had to do her job in this dusty library.

Lore reached out to a window and tried to lift it. It didn't budge. She climbed farther onto the ledge to try another window. She gritted her teeth and heaved again, knuckles turning pale, but the window remained shut.

The first three windows she tried were stuck firm with dirt, grime, and thick vines, but the fourth opened with a groan, letting in the aroma of ripe berries and freshly turned earth. She inhaled, sipping the air and filling her lungs up with its sweetness. She managed to open two more windows before climbing down the creaky ladder.

While Lore surveyed the library once more, trying to find a sensible place to start, she thought of home. She'd never gone this long without tracking the stars. She couldn't believe that just a few days ago she'd been hoping to look through the skyglass and now she was leagues away from it.

Lore had had the honor of looking through *Ziara*, the great skyglass, for the first time on her eighth nameday. She'd been terrified as she slipped out of the pew and walked the dimly lit and seemingly endless path up to the front of the open-air church.

She'd held her breath with every step and hadn't let it out until she'd closed one eye—just like she'd practiced all the previous week—and looked through the eyepiece with a relieved giggle. So afraid that she wouldn't see anything or that, somehow, the eyepiece would black out for her, as if she wasn't worthy of the light of the stars.

But her giggle had been swallowed by a gasp because what she'd beheld was like nothing she'd ever seen before. Countless stars lit up her view and swirling trails of stardust glowed before her, winking a greeting that was surely meant just for her.

She had felt like she could almost hear the stars welcoming her on her honorable nameday. Lore's eyes had glistened as she stepped back, tearing her gaze from the heavens in order to complete the ritual that all children in Duskmere completed on their eighth nameday. Though her eyes had glistened and her heart had beat loudly in her ears, she had tilted her chin up and belted the words for all to hear.

I, Lore Alemeyu, vow to always keep my gaze to the heavens. I will search and search so that I might be the one to lead my people home to Shahassa, where we belong.

Lore's grin had broken across her face as the sounds of clapping and cheering reached her ears.

Her parents had been the loudest of them all.

Lore decided to start in the library's atrium.

There weren't any books in the atrium. Instead, there were just a few scrolls that had somehow managed to find themselves far from their home, smaller boxed shelves, already bogged down by rolls of parchment. The scrolls were heavier than she thought they should be for their size, yellowed with age and tied with different colored ribbons.

She would sort them by color for now and decide later if the ribbons indicated a labeling system or not. The colors had faded, but not as much as she would have expected.

In any other situation, the guard would have been right about one thing—mice typically loved libraries because they used the paper and cloth for their nests. In theory, everything in the library should have been gnawed through by rodents, but that wasn't the case. The scrolls that were still rolled and tied were dusty and showed signs of aging, but not a *millennium's* worth of aging.

She did not have an explanation for this, so she chalked it up to magic. For what else could slow the aging of an entire library and keep even the smallest rodents from eating everything they could sink their teeth into?

Was it the same spell that kept everyone else out? Maybe if a mouse tried to enter, it, too, would be obliterated.

When she had stacked and sorted the scrolls, she swept, revealing an intricately tiled floor beneath the layers of dust. Someone had taken a lot of care to design this library only for it to be shut away. What would the architect think of the state of the library now?

She moved on to a small shelf just to the right of the atrium, which only held a few books. Here, she was in view of the door, so she cleared finely spun spiderwebs from shelves, dusted, and wiped the books without opening any of them. She wasn't sure if Asher, the guard, could see her or not. She didn't want him reporting to the steward that she was reading any of the books.

She moved on from shelf to shelf while staying close to the atrium, where the guard could presumably see her through the windows. Once she was sure he'd seen how thorough and careful she was being—assuming he was watching—she slipped over to a shelf that was hidden from view and cleared a space just wide enough for her to sit and settled down to start sorting.

From this vantage point, it seemed as if the stacks stretched above her for eternity. She had to admit, being surrounded by books was a dream come true. She glanced back toward the door, checking again that the guard couldn't see her from this angle.

She seemed to be in the clear.

Her stomach flipped with a nervous excitement as she opened the first tome in the Alytherian Royal Library.

The book itself was nondescript—a simple faded green cloth binding covered the tome, and inside appeared to be a collection of children's tales that were not so different from the tales Lore herself had grown up with and now told to the little ones at the shelter. Each tale had an obstacle or three to overcome and all ended with a moral. Be kind to your neighbors, help those weaker than you, never trust a weasel for they will trick you and take all your food. It seemed as though the Alytherians needed these stories, for maybe they wouldn't be so inherently awful.

Lore placed the book in a pile for nursery tales and logged the title in the notebook that Tarun and Libb had brought her. She continued to the next book, this one appearing to be an ordinary novel. The turning of pages and the scratching of her quill were the only sounds in the library.

CHAPTER 8

ays later, when Asher's knock came at the door to her bedroom, Lore was retying the blue ribbon in her hair for the third time. She tightened the knot with a frustrated huff and poked three curls that had already sprung free back into their cloth prison. She gave one last look in the small, cracked looking glass and decided that, without the proper creams and oils for her hair, managing her riotous curls would be an impossible endeavor.

She swung the door open, scowling at the guard.

"Not having a good morning?" he asked.

"No." Lore slipped past him after closing the door behind her and started heading toward the library. She walked a few steps before realizing Asher wasn't with her. She paused.

Asher hadn't moved from outside her door.

"Aren't you coming with me today?" In the last week she'd come to picture Asher as her shadow. He showed up every morning to walk her to the library, the dining hall, or the baths, before ultimately depositing her in her room in the evening. Then he'd do it all again the next day.

But Asher didn't have the aura of a shadow today. She tilted her head, waiting for an answer, but instead of giving one, he leaned against her closed door and casually pulled a small leather pouch from within his jacket. He flicked his wrist, shaking it, and the sweet sound of clinking coins tumbled through the air.

"Is that for me?" She stepped toward him, her hand reaching for the little purse.

"This was given to me yesterday during my nightly report on your progress." He dropped the pleated cloth into her outstretched hand.

"Thank you." She tucked it into her pocket.

He pushed off the door in one fluid movement, his long legs carrying him past her in just one step. He was walking the opposite way from the library.

Lore frowned. "Why are you heading that way?"

"I thought since you have the coin, we could head to the market before the library."

Market day already? Lore hurried to catch up with him. Asher's curls gleamed in the jumping torchlight. Meanwhile, she could feel hers frizzing around her head, already escaping the ribbon she'd just tied. She pushed a few stray curls back beneath the ribbon, but it was futile. Fortunately, her anticipation for the market outweighed her annoyance with her hair.

Asher nodded to the guards posted at the western exit of the castle as they passed through and into the garden.

The market here had no similarities to the one back home. The one in Duskmere was a paltry show in comparison. Here, hundreds of vendors must have shown up before dawn to claim their spots. Some were setting up ornate tents spelled to keep warm despite the biting autumn wind, and their owners invited anyone who showed any interest inside to see their wares and escape the morning's winds. Others had wooden stalls, and others still sold out of covered wagons, opening the backs wide and setting up tables that dripped with gorgeous jewelry, clothing, rugs, quills, personalized stationery, and a thousand other things Lore longed for.

Lore and Asher had to weave their way through throngs of fae. She'd never been around so many people in her life, nor so much variety. Her eyes flitted from one sight to the next. At one stall, a male and female loudly advertised their wares in gravelly voices—they were selling candles they claimed burned for a lifetime. Another one sold daggers, their hilts gilt with precious metals and encrusted with jewels.

Back home, families would mill around the market, browsing at their leisure, often bartering rather than exchanging coins. The wagons would be filled with produce, pelts, mead, clay pottery, and other simple wares. The apothecary's table had boasted the most variety of them all, with their goat's milk soaps, wines, poultices, and perfumes.

Here, anything Lore could imagine—and more—was available, if only you had the coin to pay for it.

As the breeze shifted, the smell of something warm and sweet wafted toward them. Inhaling deeply, she followed the scent and found her way to a section dedicated entirely to vendors selling hot, freshly cooked food.

Tables had been set up and a stage erected so a small ensemble could play on elaborately carved instruments. A female stood at the center of the stage, wearing a gauzy gown of deep purple despite the crisp wind. She crooned a song, her eyes closed, her face filled with emotion.

Lore marveled that she could hear the haunting melody from across the large bazaar; the woman's voice must be magic.

Lore sniffed again, no longer smelling the sugary sweet scent of honey. A spicy aroma enveloped her senses and her mouth watered instead. "What is that?"

She hadn't realized she'd said it out loud until Asher pointed to a small stall adorned with an intricate pattern. The vendor, a beautiful female with pale skin and pin-straight ink-black hair, waved, her eyes brightening with recognition.

"Asher! If it isn't my favorite member of the Alytherian army," she said. "It's been a while. Have you come for your usual?"

Asher slipped from his spot just behind Lore and strolled up to the stall. "Xuong, I haven't seen your booth here in too long."

The female leaned on the counter, her body language at ease. "I thought to try my hand at being a traveling merchant, but it wasn't worth the expense. Do you know how many people in Viba call my food too spicy? Too spicy! Can you believe it? I had to add milk to the curry for them. Once the flood season ended and the roads were safe again, I headed back here as quickly as I could. It's nice to be back where the people appreciate flavor."

"I've missed your pies, though I'm sorry to hear your traveling wasn't a success. I know how much you've wanted to expand your empire."

She laughed, throwing her head back with mirth. "Since when can anyone call two carts an empire?"

Asher smiled. "It's quality over quantity." He eyed the menu and Lore followed his gaze. The food available that day was written on paper in a beautiful, swirling script that had been secured to a board. "I'll take two of the usuals today, please. I'm on duty."

Xuong's eyes flicked to Lore curiously. Lore, for her part, continued to quietly observe. She had never seen Asher so at ease. Even when he ate with the other guards in the dining hall, he was usually quiet and reserved.

"I had heard you'd been put on guard duty. Is she really one of them?" Xuong lowered her voice, though Lore could still hear her.

Lore braced herself to hear an insult or two, even though the Alytherian sounded more curious than anything.

Asher straightened. "Just the usual, Xuong. Thank you."

"Relax! I'm not going to make your job any harder than it is."

She busied herself wrapping a few small food items with beeswax-lined paper. "I wonder why she's here. There are so many rumors. You should hear some of them."

Lore sensed that she was hoping Asher would take the bait and divulge the reason Lore was there. It seemed as if Xuong might trade in gossip as well as spicy curry.

"I'm sure I've heard them." Asher slid a glance back to Lore.

Lore wished she could just go, though she knew she would be in trouble if she separated from her guard.

Asher continued, "I guarantee the real reason she is here is not nearly as interesting as the mildest rumor."

"Well, that's too bad. It's been so long since anything exciting happened here."

"As a part of the king's army, I prefer it that way."

Xuong laughed. "Ah, I suppose you would, you big bore. I miss the younger you, though. The one with the wild spirit before they made you a guard."

"Mhmm." Asher dropped a few coins onto the counter and picked up the wrapped pies. "Thanks, Xu. I'll see you next time."

"See you, Asher." Xuong waved at Lore, a big grin on her face.

Lore didn't know whether to smile back or not, so she just waved and turned on her heel, her insides all mixed up.

Lore wound through the crowd toward a collection of clothing stalls she'd spied earlier. It took Asher only a few moments to catch up to her, his long strides eating up the distance easily. With his uniform and the swords on his hips, he had an easier time navigating the tide of shoppers.

Asher pushed one of the beeswax wrappers into her hand. She brought the wrapping up to her nose and sniffed. Her stomach growled at the spiced scent wafting up at her. She unwrapped the layers and found five small, strange-looking delicacies. The dough was smooth and round on the bottom but pinched together at the top, keeping whatever the contents were tucked away inside.

She watched Asher as he picked one up and bit into it. He slurped a bit to make sure none of the juices escaped. Lore picked one up and bit into it as well.

Marinated meat, both sweet and spicy, burst into her mouth. There were vegetables too: shredded carrot, sweet caramelized onion, and something else she couldn't place, all cooked to perfection, and she hurried and slurped too, lest the broth dribble down her chin. She moaned as the spiciness alighted across her tongue and quickly pushed the rest of the piece into her mouth, chewing contentedly with her eyes closed.

She popped another one in her mouth, this time not bothering to bite it in half. Goddess, this one seemed even better than the first. The smooth, almost sweet outside contrasted so well with the spicy tang of the meat.

She popped a third in. *Is this heaven?*

"Slow down. They're not going anywhere."

Lore's eyes flashed open. Goddess, she'd forgotten that she was surrounded by people, one of them being Asher. She smiled even though her mouth was filled with delicate meat pie. "They're so good. What are they?"

"Xuong calls them dumplings. These are my favorites."

"Dumplings? I love them. Should we get more?" Lore looked longingly at the two dumplings left. She could probably eat these for every meal and never grow tired of them.

"Here, have mine. I had a large breakfast, anyway." Asher thrust his four dumplings toward her.

"Are you sure?" she asked, as she grabbed his wrapping, quickly combining their dumplings.

He raised an eyebrow. "You seem to enjoy them even more than I do, which I hadn't known was possible."

She popped one into her mouth with another small moan of delight.

Lore's cheeks warmed. She couldn't help it. She loved food and rejoiced when she had the chance to try new flavors. Especially because back home, her diet usually consisted of the same foods again and again unless it was a feast day.

She remembered her manners. "Thank you. They're quite delicious."

Asher's lip quirked at the corner, his dimple appearing. "It's nothing. You need to eat before we head to the library, anyway."

He was odd for a sentry. An enigma. She couldn't figure him out.

Lore stepped around a female holding the leash of a small dog with a fuchsia bow and popped another dumpling in her mouth. "What are some of the rumors circulating about why I'm here? It seemed like Xuong had heard quite a few," Lore said.

"I assure you. You don't want to know."

Lore popped another dumpling into her mouth, surprised to find it was the last one. She chewed, thinking, then asked, "Why not just tell Xuong I'm here to work in the library?"

Asher looked away, wiping his hands on a cloth square he'd pulled from a hidden pocket in his uniform. "I'm actually under strict orders to not discuss why you are here and to make sure that you don't get close to anyone."

Of course. The steward would make sure that even though she *could* go to the market, she would still be isolated. And Asher would make sure that his orders were followed.

She pressed on farther into the market, the loneliness that had been eating at her the last few days suddenly blanketing her again.

"Though, I think you would like Xuong," Asher said suddenly. "I've known her since I was a child. She grew up at the castle as well. Her mother and father both work in the kitchen."

Lore stumbled. She hadn't expected him to say anything else. She gripped the conversational thread like a lifeline. "So that's where she got her talent from?"

"Yes. I suppose it must run in the family." His eyes roamed over her face briefly, seemingly searching for something.

She couldn't imagine what. She wiped her mouth, making sure she didn't have any broth on her lips or chin, and continued toward a row of stalls filled with clothing for sale.

The pair fell back into their usual silence.

Lore spied a vendor selling gleaming boots, gold-spun tunics, and dainty shoes similar to the ones that the female Alytherian noble had worn to the apothecary the day of the earthshake. Lore had never seen a pair of shoes so lovely and yet, here were dozens of them in every color.

Lore eyed the price and rolled her eyes. That fae female had lied about the book costing more than her shoes. She frowned. She hadn't seen her since that day in the apothecary. Maybe, like the other royals, she was gone from the castle for the cold months.

She moved on to the next vendor. This one sold decorative maps. Duskmere wasn't on any of them. One day, she vowed, their town would be marked by a star on every map.

Lore moved on, spying another clothing stall, this one with more practical and affordable choices.

She left the clothing stall with wool leggings, her first-ever pair of *new* boots, a few extra underclothes, and a black cloak that she might have splurged on a little bit. It was so soft and had lavender thread stitched throughout. Lavender pigment was so rare back home that she had never been able to afford cloth or thread of that color before.

She stopped by another stall to purchase cream and oils for her hair, more luxurious than anything she could have made at home. Just as she was reaching for her purse, Asher touched the back of her hand, the pressure feather light. Warmth spread from where his hand brushed hers and her stomach clenched as moth wings suddenly awoke, flapping inside her.

Asher had never touched her before.

He leaned in and softly said, "These look fancy, but most of the bottles are filled with air, not cream or oil. They will leave your curls dry and brittle at the end of the day. You'll want to try those over there. I think you'll be happier with the results."

Lore followed his gaze to a small cart farther down the walkway. When she lowered her hand from her purse, Asher withdrew his own and stepped back to his usual spot behind her.

Lore didn't want to think of the disappointment that coursed through her at the loss of his presence.

Two females owned the cart that Asher had indicated, and Lore was happy to see that not only was there more product in each bottle, as Asher had said, but she also got into a spirited and good-natured haggling discussion with the females. It was reminiscent of shopping back home. At the end of it, they even included a small woven basket for her to carry her purchases in for a single copper. For those brief moments, Lore hadn't been painfully aware that as a human, she didn't belong here. She walked away from them with a tightness in her throat and the urge to cry at the normalcy of it all.

Goods secured, Lore continued to an as-yet-unexplored part of the market. She was happy to continue shopping in silence, but there was something bothering her. Something she probably shouldn't voice out loud. And yet, exhilaration was still thrumming through her from her haggling session, and she was riding that high.

"There is something I can't quite wrap my head around, Asher. You willingly put on those vile blue stripes of your uniform every morning, and yet, you buy me damned delicious dumplings. And you encourage me to try a certain set of creams for my hair, ones that you think would make me 'happier.' I can't seem to grasp how all these things can be true of one person."

Asher blinked, surprise and then distrust flashing across his face. "I thought you would have realized that this isn't my uniform."

Lore stilled, her eyebrows knitting together in confusion. What did *that* mean?

He looked around, seemingly remembering that they were in a crowd of people. "Follow me." He led her to an alcove that held a small stone garden with a trellis and a bath for birds. Only then did he continue. "I only wear this because I volunteered to be on your detail. A *real* sentry would have relished the opportunity to—"

"I know what they would have done," Lore hissed. What did he mean by a "real sentry"? "Is this some twisted plan of the steward's? Send a sentry and have you win my trust? Trick me for some vile reason I can't even begin to understand?"

Lore froze. Goddess, what was she saying?

When he turned her in, she would be executed for her insolence.

But he didn't react as she'd expected. He turned away. "I'm a castle guard from a low-tiered deerclan. A grounder. When I saw you being led into the castle, you looked so lost, and I knew they would eat that up. That something terrible would happen to you if one of them had been assigned to you." Asher looked away, almost embarrassed. "So, I traded in my regular guard's uniform for this one and volunteered."

Lore didn't know what to believe.

Should she trust that Asher had really volunteered to be on her detail to protect her? As far as she knew, there had never been even one iota of evidence that an Alytherian would go out of their way for a human, let alone be on guard duty.

Then again, the fae male standing before her seemed sincere, and she knew the ring of truth when she heard it. Gratitude swelled within her; if this was true, then Asher had done her a great kindness.

She clamped it down. The last thing she needed to do was put her faith in the guard whose job it was to watch her every move and report back to the very person who held the well-being of her entire community in his scaly hands.

So she went back to her instincts, the ones she'd been honing her entire life when confronted with a sentry.

She lied.

"I believe you. I suppose I should thank you, then?"

"No, that's not wh—"

"Because you're right. My time here could have been a lot worse than it is. So, thank you, but let's not speak of this again." She looked around at the bustling marketplace. No one seemed to pay them any mind, but that didn't mean she wanted anyone to overhear this conversation. Nobody needed to see them conversing this much. "What do you say we head to the library?"

Asher's eyes shuttered and his face, which had seemed so animated before, became devoid of all emotion, like he knew she was lying.

But thankfully, he didn't say another word. He just stepped behind her, taking his usual place as her shadow.

)) ● (((

The steward was waiting for them in the hall by the library the next day. Lore kept as far back as she could from him, but still, the way his eyes roamed over her face made her feel small and inadequate. She glanced to Asher, who seemed unphased by the appearance of the steward. She relaxed a little.

"You aren't working fast enough. Why haven't you sent any tomes or scrolls to me?"

Lore wanted to bite back that this was a monumental task he had assigned her. He'd said it himself when they'd met! Instead, she said, "I haven't found any books of note. Children's books, novels, countless mundane ledgers of kitchen supply orders from a thousand years ago, scientific texts—"

He latched on to an idea. "Scientific texts? Anything to do with astronomy?"

Lore frowned. "Astronomy? What is that?"

She didn't think it was possible, but Steward Vinelake's face managed to pull itself into an even more condescending expression. "Don't you have schooling where you are from? I'm shocked you can even read."

Lore let the insults roll off her back like water. She couldn't give a single fuck what this shit stain thought of her. She raised her chin and held her tongue. She wouldn't answer him if all he was going to do was insult her instead of explaining what it was that he needed. All she had to do today was more of the same she'd been doing. She could stand out here all day, what did she care if she delayed more cleaning and organizing?

Asher answered, his voice soft as he spoke to her. "Astronomy is the science of the night sky. The tracking of the stars and so forth." His tone was kind but his expression as he looked at the steward was filled with an open distain that Lore herself wished she could wear.

Lore had been mapping the stars since her eighth year of life. Almost everyone from Duskmere knew that the answers to their lineage, the truth of their history, would be answered by searching the skies. It was through *Ziara*, their sacred skyglass, that the elders communed with the gods and goddesses. The sky was where they sought answers to their most important questions: the truth of their lineage, their stolen history. Lore probably knew more about the skies above them than he. The steward was too busy looking down on everyone to look up and marvel.

Lore couldn't keep the annoyance from her tone. "I've found a few maps of the stars, but they're outdated of course—the night sky doesn't match our own—so I categorized and shelved them. I'll collect them and have the boys bring them to you right away."

"Good. And look harder, maybe I wasn't clear with you, but my master has some specific texts in mind that he wants. I must implore you to broaden your search and bring anything to us that has to do with magic—or astronomy."

"I'll narrow my search." *You big cow.*

He turned to leave, but tossed over his shoulder as he shuffled away, his long robes trailing behind him, "Next week is the equinox. Be sure to stay clear of the festival—we will have lords and ladies on the castle grounds to celebrate. I don't want them disobliged by your presence."

Lore clenched her jaw. The longer she was here the harder it was to bite her tongue. Fuck him for wanting her to hide. For implying that her very existence was loathsome. She was proud of who she was, of *what* she was. With every snide, insulting comment, Lore's fear was being replaced by rage. One of these days she was going to haul back and punch one of these fae assholes right in the jaw and nobody would be able to fault her for it.

The moment the steward's big head was out of sight, Lore let off a string of expletives.

Asher raised an eyebrow, shocked, and then broke out into a fit of laughter. Lore was about to give him the finger when she erupted into laughter, too. She bent over, placing her hands on her knees, trying to catch her breath.

"Breathe, Lore. It will be all right," Asher said, his own shoulders shaking with mirth.

"I bet you didn't know a lady could curse like that, huh?" Lore peeked at him, even while wiping a tear from her eye. Laughing too hard always made her eyes water.

Asher looked around, that eyebrow of his arching up in mock surprise.

"I don't see any ladies here. Just a little mouse with a shockingly filthy mouth."

Lore scowled. "You're just jealous because you have the manners of a grandma. You wish you could curse like me."

"If I'm assigned to you much longer, I don't see how I'll possibly manage to keep my decorum."

"Courtesies are overrated. That's why I don't bother with them." Lore headed farther into the corridor, Asher in step beside her.

"I'm curious, what kind of books *have* you found in the library? I've seen you reading."

Lore looked at him sharply, but his expression was playful. "Nothing of what the steward or that high and mighty Lord Syrelle are looking for. Honestly, though, I did find a book yesterday that was hard to put down. It was my favorite type of story."

"And what's that?"

The two were standing in front of the library's entrance now. Lore hesitated, wondering if she should be truthful. She could make a quip about a bit of romance being all she needed to please her, which wouldn't exactly be a lie. She searched his eyes, biting her lip, and decided to tell Asher the truth. "My favorite stories are the ones I can escape into. The ones where I can leave behind this bleak existence and be somebody else, even if just for a little while. Someone braver than me. Someone with the power to change their circumstances."

"I know that feeling well. That wanting to be someone else. Somewhere else." Asher's words had the ring of truth to them. What in his life would he wish to change. His low station? His position? There was so little that she knew about him. If she had more time, maybe she could learn about him. She opened her mouth to ask when Tarun and Libb came racing around the corner, howling and skipping as they ran.

"Lore, Lore, we have a present for you!"

"A present for me? What could it possibly be?"

Tarun and Libb smiled at each other, their youthful glow filling Lore with warmth. Libb, no longer the shy youngling she'd met on her second day here, pulled a wrapped parcel from behind his back and thrust it into Lore's hands.

She opened it and withdrew a garland strung with dried apples, pinecones, and bright yellow leaves from a walnut tree.

"It's for the autumn equinox next week. We thought you could wear it in your hair, or maybe around your waist."

Lore smiled. That was sweet of them. She was sure they didn't know that she had been forbidden from attending. "This is beautiful. Did you make it yourself?"

"I made it," Tarun announced, puffing his chest out in pride, before remembering, "Well, Libb helped. A bit."

Libb scowled, refusing to be outdone. "Tarun didn't even know how to slice the apples! His mom babies him. She still won't let him use a sharp knife." The younger boy declared, "I cut every single one myself and dried them out over our hearth."

Now that Lore looked a little closer she could see that the apples were indeed cut by a child—they were uneven and some were hacked to bits.

Tarun stomped his foot, forgetting that he was trying to appear more mature than he was. "It's not my fault that my mom is so overprotective! I've told her time and again . . ."

Lore eyed Asher from where he stood behind the boys, his laughter barely suppressed.

"Boys, boys! It's lovely. You did a wonderful job, and I can't tell you how much this kindness means to me. I shall treasure it." She brought it to her nose and inhaled the smell of autumn before draping it over her hair and tying the garland in a bow at the base of her neck.

"How do I look?"

"Like a princess," Libb pronounced with all the surety of a little boy.

"Beautiful," Tarun said, suddenly the shy one, as his cheeks turned a darling shade of pink.

At that, Asher had to cover his bark of laughter with a cough so as not to hurt the boys' feelings.

"Okay, that's enough. Run along now and check back in an hour or so to see if this princess needs anything." The boys did as Asher said, racing back the way they had just come, arguing over who had done more in the creation of their gift.

"I think you have yourself two admirers, Mouse."

"It's nice that someone in this gods forsaken place appreciates what I have to offer." Lore tossed her hair back and checked her nails in an exaggerated fashion before sighing. "I've wasted enough of the morning. You heard the steward; I need to increase my pace in finding a collection of books that nobody knows what they're called, how many there are, or even what they look like."

"Good luck."

"Thanks. I'll need all the luck I can get."

Lore closed the door behind her and looked around. The vastness of the library was daunting again. How was she to compile every book on the stars for the steward?

One book at a time, she supposed.

Lore spoke out loud in a gruff, disdainful way, mimicking Steward Vinelake's voice, "Astronomy." The word rang through the library, echoing back to her.

And then she changed her tone, walking past the atrium and heading toward the west end of the library. "Astronomy," she said, calling back to Asher's kind intonation.

Then she said it a third time, as the tips of her fingers brushed across the stone edge of a shelf. "A. stron. o. my," she sounded the word out joyfully. To have a distinctive descriptor for what she loved to do was quite wondrous.

Suddenly, her head cocked to the side. A pulsing sound was coming from somewhere. *Odd.*

She walked ahead, gingerly, her heartbeat racing. The sound was getting louder the farther she walked to the west. She investigated further until she figured out the source. It was coming from the end of a bookshelf, toward the far wall. She would have to enter the stacks now if she wanted to locate the exact source of the sound.

She hesitated for a moment before taking a halting step into the rows of books. This was an area she had yet to sort through. Hardly any of the books had fallen from the shelves, and at a glance they all seemed relatively organized. She'd been saving this spot as a little treat for a later date when she would need to spend the day cataloguing but might not be in the mood to do any heavy lifting.

Curious, Lore moved farther in, the sound growing louder.

When she reached the source, she gasped.

A number of the books on either side of her had begun to *quiver* as if, well, it didn't make any sense, but it was as if they were *excited*.

She tilted her head again, honing in on a muffled sound emanating from a few of the individual books. Lore leaned in close to one, straining her ears, and focused on just one sound, trying to block out the others. After a moment the sound became clear, and she realized with a start that the book was calling to her, a tinny sound, repeating "astronomy," again and again. The book was mimicking her own voice in a way, conveying perfectly that wondrous feeling she herself had imbued into the word.

"*The Stargazers Companion*," Lore read one of the wiggling titles aloud. She read the title of the book next to it, which was vibrating as well: "*Tenecia Jobari's Celestial Observations*," Lore said to the stacks. Another tome, this one higher up on the shelf, was jostling so hard it was about to wriggle itself right off the shelf and onto Lore's face. She rose up on her tippy toes to take a closer look. This one didn't have a title on its spine, but the picture of a circle with tapered points jutting from its edges made it perfectly clear what the contents of the book would pertain to. *Stars.* Lore had the feeling this one was begging to be opened by her.

"All right, all right, I'll open you, just don't leap out onto my face, please." As if hearing her, it calmed its jostling down, just a little.

She gripped the tome, so thick her hand could barely fit around its spine, and withdrew it from its place. Lore had barely parted the edges of the book before it thrust itself wide, the pages fluttering as if on a phantom wind. Lore yelped, so surprised she almost dropped the thing.

After a few moments of flipping through artfully drawn illustrations of constellations, the books settled down until silence rang all through the library.

Well, she needed more, didn't she? Lore said again, out loud to the library, "astronomy." And the same books as before began vibrating, the sound of their whispers reverberating throughout the library.

Lore repeated this process, moving from stack to stack, until she'd retrieved each and every fussing book.

In the end, she slumped on the floor, slightly out of breath, and gazed in awe at the neatly piled towers before her. She'd collected everything in the library that pertained to celestial bodies. A total of two hundred sixty-eight books, fourteen scrolls, and twelve maps to have brought to the steward.

The morning of the autumn equinox, Lore sat in the servants' dining hall, frowning. There was a small stain on the hem of her servant's tunic—it was shaped exactly like a leaf, stem and all. She rubbed it with her thumb, though she assumed the stain was probably almost as old as the tunic itself. She doubted anyone had noticed it, especially since it was so much smaller than the black royal crest of Wyndlin Castle that was emblazoned on the front *and* back of her outfit.

Overkill, if you asked her.

She hated that she bore their crest as if she belonged to them. She wanted to rip this tunic off. She picked at the crest, though it was sewn on with a stitch so thick it would require a dagger to break.

She didn't know what to do. She'd already finished her meal and the thought of heading back to the library to continue working by herself—on today of all days—made the food in her stomach turn to lead.

She shouldn't be here, alone in this gargantuan castle, without a single person to celebrate the autumn equinox with.

The autumn equinox marked the day when the nights became longer than the days. It had always been a significant day for her people and the most enjoyable festival of the year.

That was what bothered her—she should have been home, with Grey, stringing leaf wreaths and garlands and eating sizzling spiced apples and star-shaped oat cookies to celebrate the longer nights. They should have been speculating over who would be chosen to track the movement of the wandering stars that evening.

She imagined what the community would be doing now. If they had managed to rebuild the Burgs' tavern, then she imagined that Emalie, their daughter, would be directing the other young folks to open all the windows and doors wide. Everyone would be working together to remove the tables and chairs and spread them out in the courtyard, so that the tavern's wooden patio could be used for a dance space.

Thane, the blacksmith, would have put his hammer down and would be tuning his instruments. The man could play *everything*. Aunty Eshe would be tidying the children: brushing and braiding their hair and making sure they looked their best for the festival.

Acrid heat pooled within Lore's chest when she thought of the conversation she'd had with the chief steward, when he'd forbidden her from attending the festivities.

She stopped picking at the crest and slumped against the table, dropping her head onto her arms. Resigning herself to an autumn equinox spent alone, Lore sniffed back tears.

She could smell the food already being prepared in the kitchens. No wonder the only thing they served for breakfast was yesterday's bread and a small portion of butter. They were already preparing the feasts for that evening.

Though the humans' more intimate affair would have been preferable, she did not doubt that the spread served tonight would be like nothing she'd ever seen—or tasted—before. Her mouth watered at the prospect.

If she couldn't be with her loved ones, there had to be a way to sneak in and steal a plate from the fae, if only so she could eat it alone in her room. She'd be out of the way, as requested.

But she wasn't going to miss out completely. She looked toward the kitchen. She picked up her tray and walked over to peek inside. *Double* the usual confectioners were hard at work. She could see at least six fae decorating *just* the tarts. There were seven more dusting, icing, and glazing what appeared to be dozens of different flavors of cookies. It put her oat cookies to shame, but she would trade all the feasts in the world to have those oat cookies with Grey.

Lore twirled a stray curl around her finger, biting her lip to hold back her grin. Yeah, there was no way she was missing out on these cookies.

On the way out of the servant's hall, she swiped a clean bowl from the counter.

)) ● (((

The sun had already set by the time Lore had figured out her plan. She fluffed her curls over her very human ears and slipped her new cloak over her shoulders. Lore placed the stolen bowl into the pocket of the cloak and peeked her head out of the door. The hallway was empty, so she slipped out and closed her door.

The warm kitchen was empty aside from three boys fanning the flames of the largest oven. She sent a silent prayer of thanks up to the stars and the goddess of sweets that the desserts hadn't all been removed to the royal banquet hall yet. She knew it wouldn't be long before they were, though, so she didn't have time to browse. Quickly scooping a few of the smallest tarts, she then grabbed a handful of cookies and was out the door before the boys noticed.

Now, all she had to do was make it through the servant's dining hall and downstairs to her room without running into—

Lore swore while staring straight ahead at a tart—she suspected lemon, given its terribly bright yellow jelly—stuck firmly to the front of an otherwise immaculate guard uniform.

The tart slid down the front of the guard's pressed coat, painfully slow, and landed with a muffled thud back into her bowl.

Oh stars, thistle, and sage.

This was probably her doom.

What did the fae do with thieves?

Her gaze slowly slid up from the sticky lemon jelly clinging to the gleaming golden buttons of the uniform, to a vaguely familiar chin, to the guard's smirk, two prominent dimples, and piercing onyx eyes.

Relief shot through her. Asher.

Lore's lips pursed, and she decided to ignore his raised eyebrow.

"I recognize that garland. Tsk tsk. Just like a little mouse to be thieving pastries from the crown. Turns out I was right all along." His voice shook with what she thought was poorly restrained laughter.

Lore sniffed, stepping back half a step—sage, he was tall. She glared, shaking her head. Wild curls flew around her face. She put on a shocked expression. "I would never. I was told to bring these—er—cookies to . . ." She trailed off.

At what point would she have been ordered to bring cookies anywhere? Why hadn't she included an alibi in her plan?

His smirk deepened into a mischievous grin. "Mmm-hmm," he whispered conspiratorially. "I know exactly where a thief like you can enjoy their spoils. Come with me." The guard turned, walking toward the door.

Lore hesitated, confusion shooting through her. It was almost like he was two different fae males: the one who wouldn't speak to her while on duty and the one he allowed her to glimpse so rarely.

She stepped reluctantly after him. "If you take me to the dungeons, I swear . . ."

He turned; his eyebrow raised again. He pushed his hands through his thick hair, tapping one of his antlers, the same way someone else might crack their knuckles or chew their lip. It seemed to be a habit of his.

"You'll what, exactly?" He turned away once more and quickened his pace. "Just follow me, thief."

Lore huffed, but followed him, nonetheless, clutching the bowl to her chest. She ought to be afraid, but something in his playful tone put her at ease. Besides, what else was she going to do—sit by herself in her room all night? Wallow in lonesome self-pity while eating every single cookie she'd nabbed?

"Where are you bringing me?" She had to raise her voice a little, given the distance between them, and quickened her pace.

His long legs had carried him out of the dining hall and far into the corridor already. He paused for a moment, turning to her, and she almost bumped right into him again.

"Let us start over for tonight," he said. "Let's pretend that this is our first meeting. I am not your guard. You are not my charge." He tilted his head a smidge, midnight eyes sparkling in the torchlight of the corridor, and reached out a large hand, palm up. "I'm Asher Gylthrae. It's a pleasure to formally meet you."

She would play along. Pretend he hadn't been her constant guard for weeks now. "Seeing as you refused to give me your name when we first ran into each other by the dungeons, I believe it's your fault we haven't formally met yet," she chided.

His smirk grew, as if taking delight in her standoffishness, but he kept his hand outstretched. Lore reached out with one hand, shaking his. His fingers were calloused, and the muscle of his arm flexed against the sleeve of his uniform. By looking at his broad shoulders, she had already gleaned that he must be very skilled with the twin swords he wore low on his hips.

Asher Gylthrae.

He brushed his calloused thumb against her palm, sending lightning up her wrist. Her core warmed and her stomach tumbled around as if moths had suddenly taken flight.

"Again, true, little mouse. I suppose I owe you an apology for my standoffish behavior," he replied.

"Lore Alemeyu." She tightened her fingers on his hand, her lips widening into a smile. "And I don't think that constitutes as an apology."

Asher dropped her hand, grinning. "I said I owe you one, not that I'd give one," he said over his shoulder as he turned and headed back down the corridor.

She shouldn't trust this guard and yet . . . she snorted as he led her through the twisting corridors and out through a side entrance to one of the garden paths.

When they pushed through the door, her breath caught in her throat. Chilly, ice-kissed air brushed against her face, blowing her curls around. She glanced every which way, drinking in the sights.

Though this looked to be one of the castle's smaller gardens—at least compared to the one she had seen through the window in the library—it had still been completely transformed for the festival. Lit paper lanterns hanging on string were wrapped around tree trunks and branches, were bobbing in the fountains, and were artfully placed in patterns around shrubs. Candles floated along the pathways, clearly magicked. Heaps of pumpkins and gourds in every autumnal shade imaginable were stacked in elaborate displays.

Fae roamed, and though their attire was usually beautiful, tonight they had outdone themselves. Dresses made of delicate fabric shimmered in the lantern light like the incandescent wings of beetles. They had drinks in hand and were smiling, something Lore had rarely seen in the fae. They all were clearly enjoying the festival. Some danced together to lilting music; the band was playing a slow tune that reminded Lore of the wind dancing through autumn leaves. But where that tune yielded to the autumn night, another in the distance tried to keep up with the wind in a jovial race.

Lore realized there wasn't just one band, but various forms of entertainment sprinkled throughout the grounds. A juggler here, a storyteller there, and, farther down one path, she could see a small theater troupe putting on a performance.

"Not much farther," Asher murmured.

Suddenly remembering that she was forbidden from being here, she took a small step back toward the door, toward the safety of her room. She might be alone in there, but at least it was where she was supposed to be.

But Asher was there, silhouetted against the lantern-lit garden.

For a moment, he looked like he was standing in the night sky among the stars, a constellation come to life. And when he reached out to take her hand, a pleasant thrill ignited inside her.

Asher didn't lead them out into the grounds. Instead, he turned, and they slipped down an unlit path to the side. After a few steps, he halted and, with a quick look around to see if they were being watched, he reached his other hand into a hedge, pushing vines aside to reveal a door. It seemed ancient, carved from petrified wood that had warped since it was first put there. He pressed down hard on the handle, and, with a pop, the door opened. He pushed it open an inch and turned to face her, leaning his back against the door.

"Now, Lore, before I let you into this extremely confidential location, you must swear to never reveal what you see to anyone." The mischievous smirk danced across his lips again, but she had a feeling he wasn't joking. Whatever he was about to show her was his secret place.

Lore couldn't hold back her grin. How long had it been since she'd done anything playful like this? Even with Grey, life had become more and more about taking care of others, with fewer stolen moments just for themselves.

She put her free hand over her heart. "I swear to the stars themselves I shall reveal this location to no one. Not even the King of Alytheria himself."

Asher nodded, eyes sparkling and dimples showing. "Good. Now there *is* an entry fee; you must give me something. But not just anything." He brought his own hand up to his chest and tapped it three times. "It must be something that you cherish and hold close to your heart."

Lore narrowed her eyes before laughing. "I've got the perfect thing." She handed him the ruined lemon tart. Technically, she *was* holding it close to her heart.

"Hmm, I suppose it shall suffice," he teased. With a grin, he popped the whole pastry into his mouth, his cheeks puffing up like a chipmunk's.

Again, Lore couldn't help but giggle. His bloated cheeks and impish grin were utterly endearing. He leaned back, opening the door just enough for them to slip through.

She entered a garden.

It was impossibly overgrown for it to be on castle grounds, especially since, in the other gardens, there wasn't so much as a leaf out of place. But here was a secret wonder in all its wild, untamed beauty. Inside, although there were no floating candles or perfectly manicured hedges in the shapes of great beasts, her breath hitched just as it had done when she'd seen the festival in full swing. At the garden's center stood an ancient tree with an old swing hanging from one of its proud branches.

She craned her neck, looking around for the bubbling brook she could hear nearby, but she wasn't able to find it.

The garden path itself had long ago been reclaimed by the plants, as had the statues and benches. The tree's branches covered the entire expanse of the garden like a canopy, but moonlight filtered through the gaps and pale night-blooming flowers reflected it back in every color.

She tore her gaze away for a moment and caught Asher's starlit eyes. "This was worth the price of my payment," she said.

His laugh warmed her from the inside out. "I thought it would be. I stumbled upon this garden as a child during a game of hide-and-seek. Needless to say, my brother didn't find me that round."

"I bet. This is the perfect hiding place." Lore frowned. "It seems a shame though, a garden like this would be perfect for children to play in. I wonder why it was lost to time."

"A shame, indeed." Asher's tone was mournful. Surprised, Lore glanced at him just in time to see a dark cloud pass over his face, so briefly she almost missed it.

"Oh, what's that?" Lore asked, changing the subject. She set her bowl of sweets down and picked her way to the ornately carved swing. Flecks of gold paint peeked through the vines that had curled around the seat and up the twin ropes.

Lore tugged on the rope and frowned; too bad. There was no way it would hold her weight.

"It will hold."

Lore glanced up, startled to see Asher by her side, munching on another pastry—a cookie this time. He'd crossed the garden without a sound.

Fae. Always so quiet.

Now it was Lore's turn to raise an eyebrow. "This swing looks older than our village elder."

"This swing is *definitely* older than your village elder. All the same, it will hold." He reached out and tugged the rope as well. "Though you can see its age, it would have been spelled to never break while someone is on it."

Lore tilted her head. He said that as if magic was something to be expected and taken for granted. She was curious about magic, which was such an integral part of his life—of all the fae's lives—but was a complete mystery to her.

"Don't these spells . . . expire?"

Asher chuckled with a shake of his head, licking dusted sugar off his thumb. Then he bit into another cookie he'd grabbed.

"Hey, don't eat them all! I risked my life for those cookies."

He didn't have the decency to even pretend to feel guilty as he took another bite.

"Sit on the swing and I'll give you one." He waved one of her cookies in the air while continuing. "Some spells expire, some are faulty, but you can trust this particular magic."

Lore looked at him again—really looked. She'd seen him as tall, fierce, and too dedicated to his duties for his own good. But, at this moment, holding a bowl of stolen cookies and looking at her in earnest, it seemed he truly wanted her to see the good in magic, as he did.

She wanted to tell him that it wasn't that she didn't see the wonder in magic, but it was that she knew, too well, how beautiful having magic could be.

And how ugly it was that she didn't.

Even so, those cookies were hers and she wasn't going to let him eat them all.

"Asher, give me my cookies first and then I'll sit on your beloved swing." She hummed with moths' wings again at the feel of his name upon her tongue.

He grinned, expression brightening. It was as if every smile until then had been half-hearted, but now that she'd said his name, they'd doubled in intensity.

Lore's heart skipped a beat. She wouldn't—no, couldn't get used to his beauty. His brown skin, moisturized with fragrant oils, and his sharp cheekbones reflecting a hint of the moon's light needed to alienate her. That thick, wooly hair and those brown antlers that reached through his topknot and up toward the stars should remind her of their differences, although she couldn't help but wonder if they were as smooth as they looked. She needed to ignore how his full lips—especially the bottom one that she'd tried not to notice—jutted out into a slight pout when he was deep in thought, waiting for her outside the library. She definitely needed to shy away from his black eyes that always seemed to shift and move, like a midnight storm with flecks of lightning, rutilant with gold.

That was what she needed to do.

Instead, she took the offered cookies, noting that only a few remained, and sat cautiously on the swing, holding her breath. It seemed like it would hold. Slowly, she let her toes lift off the soft moss and reached one hand up, gripping the ancient rope to her right.

Asher moved behind her, placing a hand just above hers on the rope so the side of his hand rested against the edge of her own. She was quickly overwhelmed by the smell of him: blackberries and cedarwood, swirling with the tart lemon and the sweetness of sugar. He placed his other hand on the small of her back, and her heartbeat pounded in her ears.

He can't hear that, can he?

He pushed gently, as if he knew she was still hesitant to trust the magic.

Lore closed her eyes, tilting her head up just a bit. The breeze felt cool on her flushed face. The moonlight of the autumn equinox, marking the start of their sacred long nights, filtered through the leaves and scattered like sunlight across a lake's surface behind her eyelids.

When she opened her eyes, she spotted a fox sitting at the edge of the garden wall. Its bright, keen eyes followed her back and forth, back and forth.

CHAPTER 9

The following day, Asher greeted Lore with a smile. Instead of melting into her shadow and walking behind her, he fell into step beside her. Lore hadn't known which Asher would pick her up for another day in the library. The moody guard who eyed her with suspicion, or the guard who shared his dumplings, who traded secrets for cookies.

"May I ask you a question?"

Lore resisted the urge to say childishly: *You just did.* "Only if it won't make me dislike you again."

Asher frowned. "It shouldn't. But now I don't know."

"Well, now *I'm* curious, so you must ask your question."

"What made you risk your life? Watching you walk into the library my first day, I almost had to look away. It seemed like a dream to see someone passing through those doors. You didn't even hesitate."

Lore smirked. "You didn't see me the first time I entered the library, that's why. I was so scared I thought the doors were locked because I kept pulling on them when I needed to push."

Asher smiled. "But still . . . ?"

Lore thought before she answered. Just because the two were being friendly didn't mean he had any right to her story. They passed a scullery attendant in the hall and Lore averted her gaze, lest she see a sneer on their face.

"One of your lords made a deal with me that I couldn't refuse." Literally. "He sent aid to my village in exchange for my . . . work here in the library."

"That's admirable."

"Well, don't you risk your life being a soldier? In exchange for your village?"

Asher's eyes flashed with something dark for a moment. "What I do is not the same."

Lore didn't press the subject, though she wanted to. If the humans were allowed to have a militia of sorts, would she join it? Yes. Absolutely. She would join as a healer and help protect Duskmere. If only they were allowed.

)) ● ((

Lore decided to work in the alcove beneath the open windows.

She carefully arranged the books on either side of her, so as not to step on them and damage them further. Then, she began to sort them by salvageable and unsalvageable, as she had done every day. She wouldn't throw any away until she talked to Chief Steward Vinelake.

These all appeared to be research and medical books. They were old and heavy, with lots of diagrams of fae anatomy and plants of this world that could help heal. As she flipped through the pages, she noticed there were no human diagrams. Then again, there wouldn't be. This library had been locked to the outside world before the appearance of the human race on Raelysh.

Lore would wager the healers back home would kill for a chance to read one of these books. The healing properties of the plants surrounding the village were incredible, but often it took lots of trial and error before the healers deduced how best to use them and in what quantities. And those were just the few they had learned to use; judging by these books, there were clearly so many more that they didn't know about.

She made a mental note to peruse some of the information before she left and try to take notes. Maybe she could take something useful other than coin home with her. Especially as she hadn't yet come across any magical texts. The chief steward had hinted at the library being full of them, but she'd seen none.

She picked up another medical text—this one discussed the different fins of merpeople who apparently lived off the coast of each corner of the continent—before adding it to the general medical stack.

The sun was setting, and she'd just completed organizing one of the tall shelves when she heard whispering from the shadows. A shiver went down her spine and chills burst across her flesh. When the astronomy books had answered her requests it was in response to her speaking out loud. Since then she'd used that trick a few more times to find similar subjects. But she was sure she hadn't spoken a word today.

Whatever this was, was unbidden. The sound was soft, like a breath almost. But one on the back of her neck. Lore whipped her head around, but of course, she was alone.

She set down the book that she was holding and strained her ears, trying to make out the words in the whispers.

The hair on Lore's arms stood up and she couldn't shake the feeling that she wasn't alone.

Lore stood and tiptoed out of the stack. Her head cocked to one side as she tried to make out the direction of the voices. She looked around for a weapon and grabbed a candlestick with an unlit candle. It was heavy and, she suspected, made of solid brass. If Lore was fast enough, she could do real damage with it.

She knew she should leave and tell the boys and Asher to fetch Chief Steward Vinelake. *He* would be interested in learning that she wasn't alone in there. It seemed there were other creatures that could get through the wards.

But she found herself drawn to the voices, and the thought of getting help flitted from her as though the idea had never crossed her mind.

Despite the initial fear the voices had induced, Lore soon realized that their tones were pleasant, inviting rather than malicious. It made her distrust them even more.

She walked toward the whispers, picking her way over the tomes and scrolls still scattered in this area of the library. She moved carefully, her candlestick in hand. Despite her boots, her steps were near silent on the marble floor.

The voices were getting louder, and the hair on the back of her neck stood up when she smelled an earthy scent, wild and untamed like an animal that had lived its whole life in the heart of a forest. But there was a sweeter note beneath it, that of a delicate rose, freshly bloomed and lovingly cultivated.

She clenched her jaw when she realized where the sound was coming from—the dark stack in the far back corner, the one Lore had avoided all this time because the sunlight couldn't reach it and none of the candles in the area seemed to react to her flint. Any light she brought with her from elsewhere in the library went out in a mysterious gust of wind as she approached the corner.

That had been enough to keep her away.

Today, though, she reached out with her candlestick and lit the closest candle to her, one with a wood wick that crackled and popped when it ignited. Odd. She had tried to light this exact candle a few days before and it had refused to even spark.

The space around her began to brighten, though the shadows didn't dissipate. Now she could understand the words. She realized it was not multiple words, but one said by many voices altogether. Some were deep, some young, old, both masculine and feminine, or neither.

Just one word, again and again.

Lore.

Her name.

There were voices whispering her name. She knew she should stop, drop the candlestick and run as fast as she could toward the iron doors, and get out of this library forever. But she didn't want to. She wanted to find out where the smell and voices were coming from; the scent was both exciting and familiar, as if she'd known it in her childhood or in her dreams.

Wild sage and roses. It called to her.

Memories from her childhood fluttered through her, of sitting at Mama's feet, helping her tie string around bundles of sage, then, later, threading plant fibers together to make a basket. Her mama's patient voice directed where to place each strand. Then, a separate memory of her baba's laughter as he held her tiny, chubby hand and dabbed Mama's perfume on her wrist. She distinctly remembered the sound of her sneezing as the scent of rose rushed through her.

She stepped into the darkness and the shadows melted away with her memories.

She was in a small alcove. There was a couch against the far wall and two chairs on either side of an end table stacked high with books. Where bookshelves should have been were floor-to-ceiling tapestries, embroidered with stories.

One depicted a small child underwater, with her thick curling hair fanning around her earth-brown face and wide-open eyes. Beneath the child, thin green plants stretched up to the water's surface. On another tapestry, a monstrous creature sat in a field of wildflowers. Though it looked like a beast with massive fangs and claws and spiked, webbed wings along its back, it had a look of utter peace on its face. A third tapestry showed two fae sitting in a hollowed-out tree holding hands with their eyes closed in meditation or prayer.

With a shudder of unease, she realized there was a teapot and a steaming cup of tea on the end table, as if someone had just served it. Although the voices were louder and clearer now, she couldn't see anyone filling the seats or to whom the solitary teacup belonged.

Her eyes snagged on a lone tome laying open on the floor. It looked as if it had been abruptly discarded, as if someone had stood up from the chair and the book had dropped from their lap. As soon as her eyes found the book, the whispers stopped.

Her ears rang in the sudden silence.

What was this magic? She was in the library, but not in the library at all. It was a study of some kind, though there were no doors or windows. In fact, behind her, where she had just come from, was another tapestry, this one of a garden scene. A stag stood in the center, head down as it grazed on berries. Though it appeared to be eating with contentment, its coat had been nicked by small cuts from the thorns of nearby rose bushes. From these wounds, droplets of ruby-red blood fell. Where the drops spilled on the ground, yet more roses bloomed.

She reached her hand out to touch a petal and her fingertips slid through the tapestry as if it were air. An illusion, then; there wasn't truly a tapestry here. And she knew at once that if she walked through it, she would be back in the library.

Feeling a little more at ease knowing she could get back to the library should she wish, she turned back to the room, kneeled on the thick carpet, and dug her fingers into the fabric. This, however, didn't feel like an illusion. It was the softest rug she had ever felt, making this a perfect spot to lie and sleep the day away.

Instead, Lore picked up the tome on the floor, turning it this way and that.

It was marvelous. The binding was cloth, similar to the tapestries. In the center of the cover, the phases of the moon were expertly stitched in shimmering silver thread. It started with a crescent moon, then below, a waxing moon, with the full moon in the center, only for the pattern to start over again in reverse, ending with a mirrored crescent moon at the bottom.

Lore ran her hands over the full moon, marveling at the likeness. Surrounding the moons was a circle of vines with small flowering buds. Moon moths circled the flowers in perpetual flight. The back was solid black cloth.

Lore held the tome. It was heavy and solid, heavier than a normal book, and, instead of being cool from disuse, the book radiated a slight warmth. It warmed her cold hands and calmed her soul in a way nothing ever had before.

She sniffed the edges of the book.

This was what smelled of roses and wild sage.

Her hands were steady, but her breath hitched as she opened the tome.

Lore's shoulders slumped. Blank. She quickly thumbed through the pages—empty.

All of them, empty.

Within a breath, the room around her melted away, and she found herself kneeling on the hard marble floor of the library. Her head felt cloudy and as if it wasn't attached to her body. She inhaled deeply, pulling in the regular dusty library air, but couldn't quite manage to catch her breath.

Gone was the tea set, the plush carpet, and the tapestries, and yet, her hands gripped the book so hard her brown knuckles were almost white.

She felt an odd sense of relief that the book hadn't disappeared with the rest of the illusion because the book was proof that the room had been real enough, an illusion cast by some advanced magical spell, yes, but it was not a delusion.

With shaking hands, Lore tucked the tome behind a stack of books detailing the flora and fauna of Alytheria. She would be back for it later. For now, she needed to get out of this library, get her bearings, and catch her breath.

She knew she should call to the boys and have them send for the steward at once. That this was probably one of the books they were looking for. But Lore couldn't make herself do it. Whatever had just transpired had been for her, and her alone. She would think about it before turning the tome over to the steward or Lord Syrelle.

If she waited a day or two they would be none the wiser.

She just needed to take a break from the library. To eat and process whatever had just happened. Then she could decide what to do.

)) ◗ ● ◖ ((

Though Lore's head was still cloudy, and her hands still had a slight tremor from the events in the library, she had to hide her grin when Asher placed his plate across from her in the dining hall and sat. She had eaten alone since arriving; no fae had sat with her, and she'd had enough of this forced isolation.

Back home, the only time Lore spent alone was during the quiet mornings at the apothecary, when she made her tinctures or potted her salves—especially when she potted her salves. No amount of rosemary was going to hide the smell of most of them.

She was used to either being out with Grey, Aunty Eshe in the shop, or any number of kids at the shelter. Now, she was spending all her time alone, trapped in her room or sorting books. She couldn't have traded her coin for a smile from these people. Save Asher, who'd smiled at her last night in the garden.

That seemed like a dream. Had she imagined it, along with the voices saying her name in the library? No, because here he was, plopping down in front of her like they were old friends.

Though he wasn't smiling today. He ran his hand through his hair, tapping one antler three times with his index finger. With a slight thrill in her stomach, she noticed his bottom lip was doing the pouty thing.

Was it as soft as it looked?

"Afternoon, Lore. How is your task coming along?" He bit into his wrap like it was going to escape if he didn't eat it immediately.

Lore arched an eyebrow. Asher ate his food with a certain ferociousness that, well, she had to admit was *somehow* equal parts charming and alarming.

She finished chewing her reasonable-size bite before replying. "It's monumental. I need a crew of eight at least, but since it's just me . . . the fact it's coming along at all is a miracle, I suppose."

She wanted to tell him about the empty book she had found earlier and about the strange room that was there and not there at all. About the fact that even half a bell later she was still light-headed and swore she could smell the lingering scent of the wild sage and rose. Could feel the plush rug just out of reach of her fingertips. That she had been terrified she was losing her mind because she didn't know much about magic, but she hadn't thought a spell could create something so . . . *real*.

It was one thing for a spell to manipulate her emotions like the one around Duskmere—which had successfully kept her people trapped there for centuries by inciting raw terror—but to be able to see something? Feel it?

That was a different beast altogether.

At the same time, she didn't want to alarm him and risk losing this opportunity to learn more. Asher would be obligated to report it to his superior, who would then tell Chief Steward Vinelake, and then she wouldn't have any answers at all. And more than that, the choice to bring them the book herself would be taken away from her, and she didn't quite understand why she couldn't let that happen, but she couldn't.

If she gave up the book, it would be because she *chose* to.

She was surprised, honestly. For weeks she had been scouring the library for a magical text, and now that she'd found one, even an empty one, she hesitated to bring it to the very people who were paying her to find it.

But in the back of her mind a voice was whispering to her, wondering at her surprise. Hadn't she always wanted magic? Isn't that why she was searching the library? Yes, to aid in the rebuilding of Duskmere as payment, but mostly to find some magic that she could keep for herself. Hadn't this been exactly what she'd been looking for?

No, she wouldn't give up the book yet, or tell anyone about that secret room.

She wanted to understand how magic could be that powerful and how it could transport you to a different place. Or at least make it look, smell, and feel like one had been transported to a different place. That book was the closest she'd gotten to a magical text and she wasn't going to give it up that fast.

She closed her eyes, sipping her hot coffee with a sigh.

"You love that drink, don't you?"

She opened her eyes to see Asher peering at her over what was left of his wrap. It wasn't much. The poor wrap hadn't stood a chance against the fae male.

"Coffee? Yes, we humans need it to survive, or we will wither away to nothing."

He raised his eyebrow speculatively. She was starting to like that eyebrow, the particular arch of it, questioning her, teasing her.

Lore hid her smile behind her clay mug. "No, it's true. Without a daily dose of coffee, I would surely die."

His eyebrows narrowed. "You're jesting."

She laughed into her cup. "Yes, I'm jesting. I just don't see how you don't drink coffee."

He took a large gulp of his iced herbal tea and shrugged. There were literal leaves floating around in it and Lore had to resist the urge to stick out her tongue in mock disgust.

"Coffee makes me jittery, so this is enough for me."

"Right. Well, I'm glad you have your cold leaf water then. I'll enjoy my creamy cup of joy."

There—a small smile from him. His eyes seemed to sparkle a little more when he smiled.

Then it disappeared again as he turned serious. "I'm leaving for a bit. I don't know how long, but don't stray too far from your quarters while I'm away, okay? Remember what I said about the other sentries?"

"I remember." She hadn't believed him then. She'd thought it had been a trick of some sort. She knew now that it wasn't. Comparing Asher to the male fae who had scarred her . . .

She withheld a shudder.

"Good." A pause, a little bit of sparkle returning to his eyes. "And don't steal from the kitchens anymore, hmm? You make a terrible thief."

Was that concern behind the mirth in his eyes?

"First of all, if I wanted to be a thief, I would excel at it!" She eyed him. "You said you would be gone for 'a bit.' How long is that?"

He shrugged. "They tell me when to go, and I go. I don't ask questions."

She looked at his uniform. Gone was the sentry blue. Today he wore the black of the castle guard. Of the army.

"What happened to the sentry uniform?"

He frowned. "My mission isn't to watch you right now, so I put my regular uniform back on."

She placed her mug on the table, fear coursing through her,

appetite lost. She was almost scared to ask. "Will you be replaced by an actual sentry?"

What if it was someone she recognized? Someone she'd even had a run-in with before? The memory of a sharp knife flashed in her mind. A burning scar. Baba's pained expression: the last one he would ever make.

Asher shook his head. "I've told my commander that you've never stepped a toe out of line. She's decided not to waste a sentry on one single human. I don't like the idea of nobody protecting you, but I like the idea of one of the sentries watching you even less. It's no secret how they treat humans."

Relief coursed through her. He didn't have to do that, and yet, he had.

It was then that she had to admit it, even if only to herself— she didn't like the idea of being in this place without Asher guarding her, either. She'd gotten used to his quiet presence. And, after last night, she thought they might even be friends, or on their way to becoming friends.

Friends with a fae. Grey would never believe her.

"Where are you going?"

"South." He spoke the word with finality.

Her shoulders relaxed. Duskmere was north. She knew that much. The thought of a unit being deployed anywhere near Duskmere frightened her.

He stood to leave but hesitated for a moment, like he wanted to say something more. In the end, he tipped his head in goodbye and left, dropping his tray off on the way out the door.

Lore downed the last of her coffee, dumped her tray in the bin, and headed back to the library.

She needed answers about that book and that room, and she wasn't going to find them in the dining hall.

It would also serve as a great distraction while Asher was away.

Two weeks later, Asher still hadn't returned from the south. His word regarding her good behavior must have been trusted, however, because no other sentries showed up in his place. Lore hadn't wanted to risk that happening, so she'd done as she was told. No more nighttime trips to the kitchen or sneaking out to festivals where she wasn't wanted.

She spent every waking moment in the library.

She'd been here for weeks and hadn't found anything else that even hinted at where magic came from or how one acquired it. Nor had she found any books with spells, just that one book that still smelled like sage and roses, but was, unfortunately, devoid of any spells. Or anything at all. She'd even tried that "astronomy" trick, but no matter what word she used for "magic" no books made themselves known.

She was starting to suspect someone had cleared them out long ago. If they had ever existed.

Today, when Lore headed back to the library after the mid-day meal, Tarun and Libb were sitting in the corridor, playing a game involving small shiny rocks and a flat board with smooth, shallow holes whittled into it.

It was a game she wasn't familiar with. Just like everything else in this place.

Earlier that day, she'd found a book on the distinctive clans within Alytheria. At first glance Lore had almost dismissed it. The book itself was primarily a meticulously kept ledger of the lineages of the clans in power from before the library's curse. She'd flipped through the book to determine which pile it should go in, when something caught her eye. In the margins, scribbled between family trees, marriage documents, and records of birth, she began to see what an integral part clans played here . . . and that the main thing that determined where one landed in the social hierarchy all came down to whether one was born with antlers like Asher and Tarun or a spotted tail and tufted ears like Libb. There were hundreds of clans, but none so revered as the winged class. Dark fae born with wings were rare and usually associated with the royal line.

So, Lord Syrelle, the winged fae who had made the deal with her, likely wasn't just nobility, but *royalty*.

The book touched a bit on light fae, which did, in fact, exist. The light fae, who lived south of Alytheria, lived longer than the dark fae, had pointier ears, and didn't have clans or animalistic features. She'd found maps of the continent of Raelysh in the back of the book and studied them greedily, hungry for all the knowledge she and her people had been denied for decades. She tried to commit it all to memory.

She learned that the light fae inhabited Rywandall, in the southern part of the continent. The dark fae and light fae could produce offspring, but it was rare, and the mixed younglings were usually ostracized. Each group of fae took so much pride in their lineage that, oftentimes, marriages were arranged so the offspring would carry on their particular trait.

It appeared that those with wings had always ruled Alytheria and a family of flyers wouldn't want to have a child who couldn't fly with them—likely an inconvenience, although she suspected that, more importantly, having a non-flyer offspring would hurt their social standing. Lore couldn't imagine ostracizing a child just because they were different, and she didn't know anyone who would. Not back home, anyway.

Especially since she'd learned that producing younglings at all was rare. Most dark fae had only, at most, two children in their entire long lifetimes, and they oftentimes had those children many years apart. The elder child could be eighty years older than their sibling.

It was hard to even grasp an age difference like that; it seemed more likely to be the gap between grandparent and grandchild. She'd scanned the passage again. Despite the low birth rate, Alytheria was a powerful kingdom and was equal in size to Rywandall, at least geographically. But how about population wise? The book didn't say. And anyway, according to the book, Alytheria and Rywandall were fierce allies. Outdated information, as to be expected considering how old it was, because Lore overheard a few of the staff discussing turmoil in the south. There were reports that the light fae were gathering troops and forming alliances with the sirens from Olan, an island off Rywandall's southern coast. There were talks of closing the borders, but it hadn't happened yet, as far as she knew.

For now, Alytheria had increased guard presence along the border and added new posts in some of the smaller entry points and port cities. She just hoped that didn't mean that the crown would raise the taxes on her people back home. If they weren't already broken, Alytheria being at war would do it.

She also couldn't help but worry for Asher a little bit. Though being stationed at Wyndlin Castle seemed dull, at least it had been safe. She didn't know what things looked like for the soldiers who were patrolling the borders. She didn't want to think about how often she looked to the doors in the dining hall searching for a familiar pair of antlers and a pouty bottom lip.

Lore sighed, slipping from her train of thought as she reached Tarun and Libb. She kneeled by the boys, smiling. They were sweet younglings, and so helpful. She felt bad that they had to work with her all day, every day.

"Is there anything we can collect for you?" Tarun asked.

"Why don't you take the evening off? I shouldn't need anything."

They grinned at each other as they scooped up their game pieces and tore off down the corridor. No doubt they had a million other places they would rather be instead of hanging outside a cursed library.

They could be older than her, officially, but that wouldn't really matter; they acted just like the human kids back home, full of mischief and excitement.

What were they doing right now? Were they comfortable? Warm? She didn't think she could ever get used to not knowing the answers to these questions. She had never been away from some of them for longer than a day, not since the littlest was born, crying into the sky and angry at the world for taking them from the safety of the womb.

She remembered the feel of Milo's little hands in hers, gripping her fingers so tightly despite being so small, so new. She'd just turned fifteen, but assisting Aunty Eshe in deliveries wasn't new to her. Milo's mother had been young and one of eight children herself. Her family had chosen not to take him in when she passed. When Milo was born, he was thrust into Lore's hands, squalling and covered in his mother's blood, while Aunty tried to save her.

When his mother's weak cries grew silent, Lore knew that the baby would be one of her responsibilities. She bathed him and wrapped him in a warm blanket, singing a song that her mother had sung to her on nights when the moon had disappeared and the dark appeared to creep into her window.

Lore stood from the cold stone of the corridor, long after the sound of the boys' footsteps had stopped echoing, and stepped into the library.

Later, Lore pressed her sweaty forehead to the inside of her bedroom door and latched the lock. She sank to the floor and tried to calm her ragged breathing.

She had made it—all the way from the library, past the warded doors, and to her room with the magical sage and roses book.

And nobody knew she had it.

She pulled the blank book from beneath her tunic, rubbing her thumb over the stitched moons and the ring of florals and moths. She set it carefully on her frayed quilt and took down her hair, massaging her scalp. She hoped the slight headache she'd gotten from restraining her thick hair would dissipate. If only Aunty Eshe was here to help her clear out the library while giving her all the gossip of their neighbors and, more importantly, braiding her hair.

It would be nice to not have to worry about her thick curls *every* morning.

Absently, Lore felt the purse at her hip. She'd also finally been paid again, a small sum.

Lore grabbed the quill and ink from her bedside table, sat, and opened the blank book. She flipped through the thick pages, all blank except for the bits of twigs and flora pressed into the rough parchment. She liked that; it reminded her of the books at home, as she'd made the paper herself for a lot of them.

She brought the book up to her nose, inhaling the scent. She loved that smell.

Carefully, she wrote her name at the top of the first page in her most careful script.

Lore Alemeyu.

She waited a moment, holding her breath. When the book didn't suddenly sprout wings and fly away, nor curse her with some terrible disfigurement, she laughed, feeling a bit silly. Nothing out of the ordinary had happened since the day she'd found it, and she had almost convinced herself that the separate room, plush rug, and warm tea had all been her imagination, little more than a combination of isolation and lack of sleep.

She began writing down her thoughts, her worries, and her

wishes. It was a relief to write in a journal once more, just as she had done back at the shelter. It was as if some semblance of normalcy had returned.

She wrote about Grey's easy and loud laugh, Milo's quirky habits, and the rubble that was all that was left of her room above the apothecary. She described Asher's pouty bottom lip and how seeing it made her heart skip a beat. She wrote about her fear for her community and the uncertainty that every single person she knew faced right now.

She made a list of everything she would buy with the coin she was earning and her wishes for priceless things, such as safety and security, the apothecary to be rebuilt, and for things to go back to how they once were.

And then she crossed that out and wrote her most secret desire. The one she'd buried for three years—the desire to leave, explore, and find magic of her own before going back to settle down and run the apothecary.

The sun had dipped well below the horizon by the time she placed her quill down and stretched the muscles in her hand. She hung up her tunic and stood in her shift. She missed her home, but she needed to be strong for those she loved. She needed to be strong so she could build a better world for all of them.

The next morning, she woke up and did it all again. And again.

With Asher gone, the days bled into each other. She spent every day in the dusty library, organizing tome after tome, shelf by shelf. She'd never felt so utterly alone. At the end of each day, she was so exhausted from hours filled with lifting heavy tomes, sweeping, and mopping each aisle, that she could scarcely keep her eyes open when she arrived in her room.

When she took breaks, she sat in a little nook she'd made for herself in the library. It was composed of a chair, a small table, and a rug she'd found in one of the many closets. She would curl up in one of the chairs, perusing a tome. Though Vinelake had told her not to read any of the books beyond what was necessary to discern where to put them in the library or to log them in the book that, by now, was filled with pages and pages of titles and descriptions, she knew that no one would be any the wiser if she flipped through them a bit.

After all, how was anyone to get into the library to know?

The more books she picked up, the more she learned. Though she was too wary of Steward Vinelake to read any from cover to cover, she left the library every day knowing more than when she'd walked in that morning.

Today, while taking a break for coffee, she'd chosen a short book on a small species of water sprites that lived in a collection of lakes in the west. They were fascinating. Their life cycles and habits were so different from her own. In another life, she imagined she could have been like the author of this tome, traveling from territory to territory and learning all there was to know about the people that inhabited them: their customs, religion, and diet.

Outside, the garden was covered in snow, which Lore could only glimpse through the windows. These days, she spent all day in the library, even taking her meals there, and only coming out to bathe and sleep.

Sometimes, Lore would climb up to the windows, cracking one open and leaving food out for the fox that lived in the west garden. She was so lonely in Asher's absence that she was determined to make at least one friend here.

As the days passed and he still didn't return, she couldn't lie to herself any longer. She considered him a friend, and his absence was directly feeding into her loneliness.

The fox hadn't let her pet it yet, always grabbing the food tentatively, eyes never leaving her own. As soon as it had a good grip on the food, it would race back down to its hedge in the garden. Its sienna-colored coat gleamed even in the shade of the canopy made by the branches and leaves of the giant tree that stretched to the library windows.

The afternoon sun illuminated Lore's favorite desk. Lore set down her quill and closed her eyes, letting the bright sunlight filter through her lids, warming her skin. She was almost done logging every book she'd set to for the day when a pounding sound came from the door. Lore—who had begun to feel like she was the only one to exist in the entire world while shut away in the library—startled, her hand flew out and knocked into her pot of ink. She almost didn't grab the bottle before its contents spilled across the log book. It would have erased days of ledgers. Lore cursed and placed it back onto the desk with a sigh of relief, just as another knock rang through the library.

Was it Asher returned?

Lore fluffed out her curls and smoothed the cream-colored apron she'd begun wearing over her uniform. It had a gorgeous frill at the bottom and deep pockets for Lore's supplies, but more conveniently, it covered the Wyndlin crest, which Lore despised. She hurried over to the door and swung it open, only for her excitement to flee from her body immediately.

"Oh, hello, Elra."

"Gods, you are slow. I thought I was going to have to knock a third time. You've been summoned to the high steward's office. Bring your log book." Elra clutched her broom in such a tight grip, Lore thought she was planning on using it as a weapon against, well, she didn't know what. Did Elra think Lore was hiding flesh-eating monsters inside the library and they were going to break free and devour her at any moment?

"I'll just grab the log and be out in a moment."

"Hurry. You've kept him waiting long enough, girl."

Lore scratched her eyebrow with her middle finger.

Elra pretended not to notice the insult.

Lore closed the library door behind her and hurried to grab the log book. Was this about the sage and roses book? There was no way that it would be about that. Besides, she'd been writing in it for days and it had proved to be little more than a journal— even the smell had dissipated. Lore's worries about whether or not to turn it in had long since stopped plaguing her.

Unless someone had gone into her room and found it? But no, her hiding place was a good one. She kept the journal stuck to the bottom of her wardrobe with putty she'd purchased at the market. Even if someone swept underneath it or managed to move the beastly thing, the book would remain out of sight. Besides, if they actually suspected Lore had smuggled out a magical book and was keeping it for her own use then it wouldn't be a maidservant who came to fetch her, but a whole host of guards.

Elra was halfway down the hallway by the time Lore returned to the door with the log book. Lore swore before jogging to catch up with the maid. Who was fast.

No doubt counting every moment before she could be free of Lore's presence . . . *Well, same, Elra, same.* But Lore had to take two strides for every one of hers and she was a little out of breath when they finally stopped outside the steward's office. Elra knocked gently, her hands free after she deposited the broom into a closet Lore had never noticed before.

At her knock the door swung open from the inside and Lore was surprised to see Lord Syrelle on the other side of it. She hadn't seen him since her first day at the castle, almost two months ago. Lore had to stop herself from retreating a step. His presence was just so . . . *large.* And it wasn't because the lord physically towered over her, or because his broad shoulders strained at the seams in the arms of his black dress shirt. It was his *magic.* The sheer power that emanated from within him was palpable.

And Lore noticed, because it was impossible not to, that his wings were not sprouting from his back today. The male could quite literally magic away entire parts of his body. Lore wished more than anything she could ask where they went. Were they there, just glamoured away, or was his magic so powerful he could actually bring them out when it pleased him and . . . and squirrel them away when it didn't?

But of course, Lore *couldn't* ask him.

Elra, on the other hand, had also been surprised at his presence and had folded herself into a curtsy so low, she was bent in half entirely, and yet still somehow managed to glance up at the lord through her, wow, quite long eyelashes. Lore almost let a laugh escape her lips. She honestly didn't think Elra knew *how* to smile and yet, here she was, acting the demure lady for Lord Syrelle.

Syrelle, on the other hand, hadn't even noticed Elra.

"Please, come in." He stepped backward to let Lore enter. "I hope you don't mind being taken from your work without notice, but I thought you could use a break. I have refreshments."

Indeed, he did. Set upon a table was a whole spread. A decanter filled with burgundy wine, elaborately decorated cakes, finger sandwiches. A small bowl filled with fruit.

"Is all this . . . for me?" Lore relaxed as much as she was able. If they knew about the journal, they wouldn't be offering her finger sandwiches as a snack. More likely, her fingers would probably *be* the snack for the horrible beast that, a few days before in typical Libb and Tarun fashion, the boys claimed lived beneath the castle. Libb had sworn they kept a dragon in the dungeons for when the prisoners became unruly. Though Tarun had been convinced it was not a dragon at all but a worm the size of a greenhouse. A worm with three heads that fought over which one would get to eat the prisoners' toes. Lore shuddered at the thought. She was ninety percent sure they had been mistaken.

Syrelle smiled. "I've just returned from a trip to the Sunshine Isles, and I was hoping to pick your brain a bit about what you've discovered in the library during my absence. I thought you would appreciate something to graze on during our discussion."

"I . . . yes, thank you." Where were the Sunshine Isles? Lore hadn't seen them on a map, but it sounded lovely. Especially because winter had decided it was here to stay and anywhere called the Sunshine Isles ought to be warm and sunny year round. If not, it was named by a cretin.

"Fresian, will you please pour each of us a glass of wine?"

The steward startled from where he sat behind his desk.

The steward's first name was *Fresian*? For some reason Lore was surprised that the steward's first name wasn't *High Lord*.

The steward sputtered, his face flushing with indignation. "I—sir, you want me to pour her wine? Surely, I can call the maid-servant back to—"

"Steward, are you so above your station that you cannot pour my guest and me a glass of wine?"

The steward snapped his mouth shut like a toad and walked stiffly toward the table.

Lore decided that she wouldn't thank him when he thrust the wine into her hands. Instead, she nodded her thanks to Lord Syrelle and drank deeply from the crystal chalice. She had missed wine, and this was spiced. Her favorite.

"How do you like it? This is from my personal collection." Lord Syrelle drank a small sip.

"It's lovely. Almost as delicious as my uncle Salim's spiced wine." Lore swirled the glass, admiring the robust liquid. "Is that cinnamon, anise, and orange peel?" she asked.

Syrelle raised an eyebrow in amusement. "That it is." He took a sip himself before remarking, "If your uncle's wine is indeed better, I'll have to order a case of it for my own collection."

"My uncle would be pleased to fulfill that order." Lore swallowed another mouthful before asking, "Do you have news of Duskmere, my lord?"

"Please, call me Syrelle," he insisted before sliding a plate of sandwiches toward Lore. "And yes, I do. I've just had a report from a courier this morning. The masons and healers I sent have been hard at work rebuilding your town."

Good. Then all this work and isolation was worth it. Lore took a bite of a sandwich and melted a little bit. Roasted chicken breast, lettuce, tomato, perfectly caramelized onion, thick slices of brie, and tangy vinaigrette on a buttery croissant. Was this what the gods ate? Possibly. Lore devoured the sandwich and promptly grabbed another.

Syrelle, she noticed, was taking small, polite bites. His restraint was impressive. The steward wasn't eating at all—instead he looked at Lore with open contempt.

"That's great news. Thank you." Lore put down her sandwich, though she wanted to eat them all. Maybe she could smuggle some out in her apron? "What would you like to know about my work so far? I've been supplying the steward with weekly updates as requested."

"Yes, we are just concerned that you haven't found any magical texts yet. We have it on good authority that there were quite a few in the library on the day it was closed off. Have you been checking every area?"

"She's lazy, my lord. I suspect the girl does not wish to go back to that hovel of a town and is delaying her work here on purpose," the steward hissed.

"*The girl*, Steward, would rather be anywhere than here," Lore replied to the steward before he could continue bad mouthing her to Lord Syrelle. She directed the rest of her reply to Lord Syrelle, "I am working diligently, but the library is quite massive. Admittedly, there are some places I have yet to search." Because they're dark. No matter how many candles she lit in some areas, the darkness persisted. It made her skin crawl and she could swear she could hear whispering coming from within the stacks.

"Fresian, from the look of this log book, she has been working tirelessly." Syrelle had a way of speaking that made the steward visibly wilt in his chair. Lore raised her chin a little in pride. *See, you old goat. I have been working hard.* Syrelle tapped on the desk idly. "Lore, will you do me a favor and start on those areas tomorrow? We are looking for a collection of magical texts . . . and I must admit I am growing anxious to have them."

"Absolutely. I'll start on them first thing tomorrow."

"Wonderful. And please, if there is anything you can think of to make the work more efficient do not hesitate to send word to the steward. He knows how important this is to me and to our king."

"I will, my lord."

"Do you remember the way back or shall I call the maidservant to guide you?"

Lore drained the rest of her wine—no point in wasting such delicious spirits—and stood up. "I know the way, thank you. I'll send word the moment I find anything."

"Would you like to take some of this food with you? I've heard you are no longer eating in the servants' dining hall."

For someone who supposedly just returned from sunshine land, he sure was keeping tabs on her.

Yes. "No, thank you."

Syrelle smirked, light amusement playing across his features. There was something nagging Lore about his eyes. Something she didn't often see in the fae.

"I'll have your little helpers bring the leftover food to you in a bit. I'm sure Tarun and Libb would love to." She was surprised that nobility knew the names of the boys assigned to attend her. They were part of the lower class.

"I'll be sure to share with them. They will appreciate the snacks."

"I look forward to your updates," he said, dismissing her.

Despite being exhausted from spending more time in the library during the day, she still took the time to write down everything she'd learned. It was clear that Syrelle expected results soon and Lore hadn't any to give. Anxiety was beginning to gnaw at her. What if she never did find any magic books? What if she explored every nook and cranny and came up empty? Lore hadn't realized until this afternoon what that could mean for herself and Duskmere. They hadn't said that she would be blamed if nothing was found, but then again, why wouldn't they blame her?

Lore sat on her small bed, wrapped in her quilt, journaling about everything she could remember from the passage on sprites she'd read that morning. She wasn't sure how the knowledge of the far-off clan could help her people, but she was determined to write everything down. When she shared this with the elders back home, they would no doubt find more helpful information in this knowledge than she could alone.

Lore's back twinged and she shifted position, trying to alleviate the tight muscles. Just as she moved, the clouds cleared from the sky and moonlight filtered in through the window, its tendrils casting everything in silver. The light spilled across her bed, and she gasped.

Where the moonlight touched the book, it exploded with starlight. A thousand stars of every color filled the open pages and erased her words. In their place were now constellations swirling across the pages.

She stood up, holding the book. Her entire room was cast in the swirling of the night sky.

Once again, she found herself in the study. An illusion again, though this time she could feel the cold stone of her room beneath her bare feet instead of the carpet.

"Where am I?" she asked, the words escaping in a breathless whisper. "What is this?"

"What would you give us for the power to Know?" The voice came from beside her, behind her, and within her. It was her own voice and no voice she'd ever heard before.

"Know what?"

"To Know. We see that you have a yearning for answers. We can give them to you."

Lore's breath hitched. "What would it cost me? I haven't much to give." She didn't have *anything* to give, really.

"We don't ask for much. Just be ours and we will be yours."

"Be . . . yours? Who—or what—are you?"

"Would you like to know how to capture the moonlight and wield it for yourself? How about which mushrooms will give you the strength of a hundred men, and which will put one hundred to sleep with just one taste? To never be subjected to the dark again? Would you like to know if your loved ones are safe all those miles away? We will be the best parts of you and you the best parts of us. All you must do is take us from this place."

Lore's mind reeled. "Show me something so I know you speak the truth."

The room around her changed, wavering and shimmering. Though she could feel the cold stone of Wyndlin Castle beneath her feet, she was simultaneously in the sky, floating above the ruins of a village.

She cried out at what she saw—they weren't just ruins. It was Duskmere.

Half of the town had burned to the ground. In the other half, buildings were still toppled and she saw people sleeping in the streets. They were dirty. Hungry. Freezing in the icy autumnal night.

She recognized some of them before the view changed.

She found herself inside the shelter and the number of children had tripled. Aunty Eshe slept sitting up in a chair in the dormitory, a baby Lore didn't recognize asleep in her arms. Dried salty tear tracks marked her cheeks. She muttered restlessly.

Suddenly, the scene changed again, and she could see the town square, or where it should have been. All the shops and buildings surrounding it had collapsed. Their meeting place was no more. It didn't make sense. If the fae had truly sent masons, supplies, and help, then this area should have been cleared by now and well on to rebuilding.

"What is this? What are you showing me? I told you to show me something true." Lore sank to her knees.

"Take away their stability and they cannot fight back."

"Take it away? Who took it away?"

"Take us from this place and we will give you what you seek."

And then she was alone, hands and knees pressed against the rough floor. She leaned forward, pushing her forehead against the cool stone, and let out a soft sob.

She had hoped her people would be rebuilding. She'd trusted that the fae would have sent builders and healers. Not only had they broken their deal, but they had obviously made the situation much worse. And Syrelle had sat across from her just a few hours before and lied to her face. Promising her that things were much improved. He'd given her wine and food and Lore had fallen for his lies, even working longer hours this evening, searching for any sign of magic. For him. For Alytheria.

The same Alytherians who demanded a certain amount every quarter and then demanded more than they could pay, all while forbidding them to trade with anyone else. The Alytherians who would do anything to keep her people from being whole.

And now, looking at her people, she knew they had been broken.

Perhaps the earthshake wasn't just a natural occurrence. Perhaps something or someone had caused it, someone who gained from the tragedy of her people.

Hadn't they been through enough? They already had their world stolen from them and had their history ripped from their hands. They had had to fight tooth and nail for what little they had. And in the span of a few moments, once again they had to start from scratch.

Goddess, had Asher known the true cause of the earthshake?

She fisted her hands and stood. She grabbed the tome, noticing that every word of hope and bit of knowledge she had collected was gone, as if the book itself had devoured them.

The pages were as empty as the day she had found it.

She dressed quickly. It was cold outside, but she couldn't stay here. She packed all of her clothes—thankful that she had new boots—the coin she'd earned so far, and the tome. Take the book from the castle grounds and whatever was contained within it would give her what she sought? What she wanted above all else was magic, sovereignty, and a life worth living.

She would have it.

She probably should stop and think; in every tale she'd ever heard, and even the ones she'd spun herself, if a deal was too good to be true, it was exactly that.

But she didn't have time to waffle.

She needed to get home.

CHAPTER 10

L ore?"

Lore stopped in her tracks, feet sliding on the ground of the garden pathway, slick with frost. She slowly turned around.

There was Asher, in full guard's uniform, with his sword pointed firmly at her throat.

He'd been gone for weeks. When had he returned?

"Asher." His name was a prayer on her lips, but his blade didn't waver even a centimeter.

If he called for another guard, she would be searched. When they discovered the stolen book, she would surely be executed.

She had jokingly asked what would happen to her if she was caught stealing cookies, but she had been raised in terror of the sentries her entire life. She knew they wouldn't hesitate to execute a thieving human.

His tumultuous black eyes burned in the dark, and she realized she had never seen him look truly furious before. She had thought she'd seen a glimpse of anger when they'd first locked eyes in the dining hall, but it was nothing compared to this. Suddenly, he looked less like the person she remembered and more like a predator.

What was he even doing here? Had he been here the whole time? Watching her still, but without her knowledge? His teeth were bared, and she realized how sharp his canines actually were. Sharper than those of any human. His antlers were no longer alluring; instead, they were frightening weapons that could be used to gouge her, rather than a mere mark of being a fae.

Had she really wanted to touch them the last time they'd spoken? Had she really wondered what his lips tasted like? Had she truly spent the last few weeks with her eyes set on the doors of the dining hall, waiting for him to walk through with a small smile and a complaint about the few weeks away?

"Please." She tried to sound strong, but her voice was a whimper. She had never been more scared in her life, not even when the sentries had caught her.

He looked at her, stricken, having already noted her cloak and bag. He knew she was running away. "They'll kill you, Lore. I must . . . but how can I . . ." His voice trailed off, thick with fury. He glanced around frantically, as if looking for a way out of the impossible predicament he found himself in.

Lore stood perfectly still, holding her breath. Her life was in his hands.

A single tear dropped from her eye in sync with the lowering of his sword. He slid it back into the scabbard at his hip.

"If I let you go, they will kill me. If I turn you in, they will kill you. What would you have me do? What have you done to me, Lore?"

Her name wasn't a prayer on his lips as his had been on hers. It was a curse, one she had placed on him, no less.

"Let me explain."

"We don't have time. Go back to your room. Now." He spoke through clenched teeth.

"I can't." She shook her head, willing more tears not to spill.

"Go. It is your only option if you wish to live."

"No." She tilted her chin up and pushed her shoulders back. She wasn't less than him and she wouldn't act as though she was. She wouldn't be beaten into the belief that she was. She may have temporarily forgotten who and what Asher was, but the memory of cold steel against her throat had cleared her of any romantic notions.

He was a dark fae and she a human.

She certainly didn't owe him—or any of the fae, for that matter—allegiance. She needed to go back to her own people.

Suddenly, he tensed and turned his back to her, both swords drawn this time. It took Lore a moment to realize that he'd put himself between her and two guards patrolling the grounds. She hadn't even heard them approach.

"What is this? Who is there? The garden is closed at night."

"Yes, sir. I was just explaining this to the lady," Asher said.

"Hey, you . . . wait a minute, is that the human?"

"What are you doing out at night? Where are you going with that bag?"

Lore flinched, stumbling back a step, and suddenly she was back in that dark forest. Nineteen, with her bag. A cruel hiss in her ear: *What are you doing out at night? And where are you going with that bag?*

"I, I . . ." Lore stuttered.

The taller soldier cut her off, sneering at Asher. "Gylthrae, you should have taken her into custody immediately. You will report to me as soon as your shift is over. As for the human, it looks like she was trying to escape." He pulled a small knife from his boot. "Come with us. I want to see what's in that bag. I'm sure there are valuables in there."

This couldn't be happening. Not again.

Asher was still between her and the two guards. "Let me take her back to her quarters, sir. I can search her there."

"And let you have all the fun? Stand down, soldier, we will handle this human scum."

Lore bristled. It had been a while since a fae had spoken to her with such evident disdain. She'd almost forgotten that this was really what they thought of her.

She expected Asher to move aside and let them through.

But Asher hadn't moved. He was as still as a statue.

"I'm telling you to let me handle it."

The speaking guard visibly bristled. "Who are you to give me demands, Lower? I am your superior. You will do as I say."

Asher steeled his jaw, a muscle ticking in his temple. "Lore, go back to your room."

Lore made as if to take a step, but the guard barked laughter. The sound was cold, cruel, and haughty. She froze with fear, not daring to move a muscle.

"Not only do you defy me, but you do it to protect this unnatural spawn of demons? Her kind were cast away by the very demons that made them, and yet you would defend her from your own kind?"

"Lore, go," Asher said through clenched teeth.

"Handel, I bet he has lain with her. That's why he's risking everything to defend her." The other guard spoke for the first time, venom and disgust coating his words.

The first guard's eyes widened in mock outrage, though the vile delight in his eyes showed that he was enjoying toying with them. "Gylthrae, you know it's a death sentence for one of our kind to lie with one of them." His mouth twitched into a malicious grin. "Stand down, soldier. We are taking you both in."

The blood drained from Lore's face. She would rather die than go through what their sick minds promised to put her through. She hadn't been aware that it was a death sentence for the sentries who were with humans. She just knew that when the fae forced themselves on humans, it was never the human's choice, and the humans didn't live to tell the tale.

This was it. This was the moment Asher would end his hesitation and follow their orders.

A gust of wind rustled the leaves beside her, and she closed her eyes against the sudden onslaught of leaves. When she opened them, Asher had become a blur of movement.

He disarmed the tall soldier by knocking the hilt of his sword out of his hand. He immediately brought his own sword up to block the other soldier as it swung in a powerful arc straight toward his throat.

He was fighting two against one. He was fighting for her.

Though he was younger and faster than these two higher-ranking officers, they had more experience, and it didn't take long before they overpowered him. He bent low, rolling away to put as much distance between them as he could.

Asher plucked a sprouted plant that had pushed its way through the path and whispered a word, one Lore couldn't hear. Suddenly, vines sprouted from the small plant in his hand, splitting into two and wrapping around his swords. Sharp thorns of hardened wood sprouted from the vines. *Magic.*

Lore swore, backing away from the fight.

Asher went on the offensive again, jumping forward with both swords raised and targeting the taller of the guards first. At the last minute, the guard twisted, narrowly avoiding losing his neck, but Asher's blades still tore into his chest. Blood erupted from the freshly cut wounds made worse by the spikes from Asher's earth magic. The spikes seemed to grow and pierce deeper into the flesh, even as his swords pulled free.

The hurt guard cried out, falling back, while the other launched himself at Asher, his sword cutting through the air. Asher parried the blow at the last second, barely protecting his face.

Lore looked around when she heard the shouts of other soldiers running toward them. Clearly, the sound of swords clashing was so loud in the quiet garden it must have drawn their attention. When she looked back, Asher was on one knee, swords straining against both guards' blades. Somehow, the one with the shredded chest had gotten back up and was still battling. She could see the other guards now as they ran full speed from the castle, so incredibly fast.

Glancing back to Asher, she saw a cut along his shoulder and his uniform was darkening with his own blood.

This would be it. They would overtake him. It would be his end, and, shortly after, hers would come too.

Lore cried out and dove into her bag, finding the tome she had shoved to the bottom for safekeeping. She threw it open. The moonlight ignited its pages.

"I accept. I'm taking you from here, but you must help me do it. Help me escape with Asher!" she shouted at the book. Her voice was hoarse with fear.

Suddenly, she was bathed in silver moonlight. It spooled out of her in shimmering waves to race up the guards' legs, over their arms, and down their throats. Both guards dropped their swords and began clawing at their necks, gurgling as they choked on the thick, viscous light.

Asher hadn't moved. He kneeled in shock, staring at the two men who, only a breath ago, had been ready to end his life.

Lore shouldered her bag and pressed the still open book to her chest; she could feel power pulsing from the pages through the fabric of her cloak, soaking into her body. Then she grabbed Asher's arm, careful to avoid the wounded shoulder, and tugged. They had to go!

They raced from the garden path and into the shadows. Her mind reeled at the vision of the two guards, their throats bleeding from where they tried to claw at the light.

She had done that. That horrible, powerful, awful thing had been done by her. She flinched, pushing the guilt down.

She couldn't—*wouldn't*—think about that now.

Asher was silent, but he followed as she guided him through the garden. Wherever they stepped, the shadows rose to meet them. The moonlight was no longer drawn to her. The book knew somehow that they did not need light, now. It had gone dark the moment they'd turned to flee, though the pages still pulsed against her chest with magic.

They were invisible in their shroud of darkness, invisible as they scaled a tree, invisible as they climbed over the garden wall, and invisible as they entered the woods.

CHAPTER 11

The pair didn't stop running until Lore was sure her lungs would burst. Though Asher could have run farther and faster, he'd kept pace with her, sometimes placing a guiding hand on her back when she tried to slow down or when the moonlight disappeared completely and rendered her human eyes useless.

They finally emerged from the woods at the edge of a cliff, and Lore suddenly realized she was seeing the sea for the first time. Before them was ocean, stretching as far as the eyes could see. Even this high up, she could hear its power. Tumultuous waves churned below her, the sound mixing with the roar of blood in her ears until it was deafening.

She followed Asher down the rocky cliff face, barely keeping a grip on the slick salt-sprayed rocks. She slipped twice, slicing her thigh on a jagged piece of rock the second time.

Her tears mingled with the salty spray of the unforgiving winter ocean.

She was tired of crying.

By the time they climbed into a small cavern carved into the rock, still far above the rocky shore, Lore's tunic and leggings were soaked through. Her curls clung to her cheeks, and her lips were numb.

She couldn't feel her hands.

She collapsed onto the ground, tucked her knees against her chest, and blew on her fingers, trying to coax warmth back into them. Soft moonlight filtered into the cave, yet she could barely make out Asher piling wood at the back of the cave.

"Where did th-that wo-wood come from?" She rubbed her hands together, still numb.

"Me." He picked up a piece of flint and, in a flash, slashed it on the floor. Sparks ignited the wood.

Lore stood and walked to the glorious fire, certain it was the most beautiful thing she had ever seen. No doubt it was more beautiful than her first glimpse of the ocean.

She sucked in a breath as she sat down. The cut on her thigh stung. She reached out toward the flames, holding her fingers as close as she dared. They were starting to ache, but she only sighed as the pins and needles of feeling returned. She risked a glance at Asher.

He sat across from her on the other side of the fire, hands propped up on either knee, head thrown back and resting against the cavern wall. His eyes were closed. The shadows cast by the flames played across his features, dancing along his sharp cheekbones and full bottom lip. They didn't reach his hair though, and his antlers looked inky black in this light.

If he hadn't been radiating complete and total rage in the angry, solid set of his jaw and if his face hadn't been smeared with dirt and blood, he would almost look at peace.

"Why did you bring wood here?"

He opened his eyes and Lore couldn't help but flinch at the fury shining through them. They were molten lava in the firelight and his teeth were bared in a silent growl. Again, she was reminded of how sharp his canines were, how decidedly not human they were.

He wasn't human.

He also, apparently, wasn't up to talking.

Lore didn't blame him. Because of her, he had almost been killed and had lost his position and his home. He'd lost everything he knew, and it was her fault.

Lore lay down. The cave was heating up now and there was less smoke on the floor. She hugged her pack to her. A stray thought came to her—that she should change out of her wet clothes and into the spare ones in her bag.

But she couldn't will her arms to move even if she had wanted to.

$$))) ● ((($$

Lore was startled awake by a nudge from Asher.

"Wha—" She blinked, trying to adjust to the dimly lit cave now that the fire had burned down to embers.

Asher crouched on one knee beside her, holding a wet cloth in one hand and a few leaves in the other. He looked pointedly at her thigh. Though he clearly still wasn't speaking to her, and he maintained an aura of anger, his eyebrows were pulled down in concern.

"Oh, yeah. I need to clean this." She looked at her thick leggings. They were too tight to roll up past the wound on her thigh, meaning they would have to come down.

She stood, wincing as blinding pain tore through her when she put weight on her leg.

Asher lowered his eyes and reached beneath her short servant's tunic. Slowly, he hooked his fingers into the band of her leggings, tugging downward and shimmying them past her hips and her butt. She hissed as dried blood and fresh scabs pulled away with the ripped fabric, but he pulled until they could see her wound.

The gash was deep and angry.

Asher remained kneeling in front of her, assessing. He was so tall that this was the first time she had ever seen the top of his head or his antlers this close.

Slowly, he pressed the rag onto the cut and started brushing it with small strokes, removing the rest of the blood. It hurt, but she was able to stay upright. She ached to reach out and rest her hand on his shoulder for support, but suspected the gesture wouldn't be welcome.

When the wound was clear of the old blood and began weeping anew, he picked up some leaves he'd set aside and put them in his mouth, chewing them.

Lore couldn't look away from his lips even if she'd wanted to.

He pulled the wad from his mouth and set it against her wound. Where the leaves touched the cut flesh, flame ignited. She cried out, instinctively reaching out to grab his shoulder. He reached up with one hand and held her wrist, pressing her hand against him, providing comfort.

For a moment, she felt his touch more than the burning sensation.

He leaned closer to her, blowing onto her thigh.

Suddenly, the fire licking her flesh went out and a coolness spread through her leg, followed by numbness. She couldn't feel any pain at all.

When she relaxed, evening her weight onto both feet, Asher dropped her wrist and ripped a small, thin strip from his undershirt before wrapping it around her thigh. There was a section missing from the other side of his shirt as well; that must have been where the cloth he'd cleaned her wound had come from. But where had he found the fresh water? Had he climbed back up the cliff face to search?

Where his deft fingers brushed her thigh, goosebumps rose. She could feel her heart rate spike, the blood rushing through her ears.

Just as quickly as he had appeared beside her, he finished his task, stood, and moved back to the other side of the fire. He hadn't spoken a word to her, yet she was sure she now owed him even more.

She lay down, scooting closer to the embers. She closed her eyes and prayed to the stars that she wouldn't see those guards' faces in her dreams.

But she had a feeling their silent screams would haunt her anyway.

))) ● (((

Sleep brought Lore no relief. Again and again, the guards' pan-icked, choking faces appeared in her dreams. Their frantic ex-pressions were seared into her mind by the time the sun shone through the entrance of the cave.

Lore woke with a start, her muscles protesting as she sat up. She sucked in a sharp breath; her entire body was sore, from the bottom of her feet to the muscles in her jaw. Shifting her thigh was hardly painful, though. The leaves Asher had put on her wound the night before seemed to still be working.

She surveyed the dim cave. The ceiling was low, and it really wasn't very big. It somehow looked smaller in the daytime than it had the night before. The fire had died down completely in the night and the cold breeze blowing in the mouth of the cave raised goosebumps on her arms.

Asher was nowhere in sight.

Had he left her there? Changed his mind, realized his mis-take in saving her, and went to turn her in to the guard?

She pulled herself to her feet, wincing with every step toward the mouth of the cave. When she reached the entrance, she gasped. As far as the eye could see, there were rolling blue waves with caps of white.

Duskmere was landlocked—they relied on a small lake for fish and an even smaller river and a few wells for their freshwater. As far as she knew, nobody in her lifetime had seen the ocean. It was beyond the boundary, which they were not permitted to cross. She had had no idea they were only a few days' walk from this magnificent force.

They didn't even know they could be out here in the summers, swimming or fishing. Her ancestors could have built boats and escaped the tyranny of Alytheria.

In that moment, she hated this continent they were stranded on.

No, not the continent. The creatures that inhabit it. The ones who had made her and her people's lives so impossibly difficult when they need not be.

She sat on the edge of the cliff and peered down. Directly below her were jagged rocks. The ocean crashed relentlessly against them, as if it couldn't stand being obstructed. As if it wanted to devour the very continent she stood upon.

Goddess.

If she hadn't caught herself last night, she would have fallen to her death. Suddenly, the wound on her thigh seemed painless in comparison to what could have been. Her pain seemed like such a small price to pay for managing to escape the dark fae and the harm she had inflicted upon those guards.

The memory of them choked her up. She turned away from the jagged rocks and the tumultuous ocean, putting her face in her hands. What was she going to do? If Asher had actually left to turn her in, she didn't think there was anything she could do to stay alive, and certainly nothing she could do to return to Duskmere.

The fae would find her, and they would end her life without a second thought. What was an unruly human to them but a nuisance or something to be ended and brushed aside, like a spider in a bedroom? And would the people she loved also be disposed of so dismissively? Would they suffer for the choices she had made? From what the book had shown her, they were already suffering.

She had risked everything to help them, but in the end she may have only doomed them.

Her fingers dug against her flesh, nails biting into her skin with a sharpness that should startle her. Instead, it was all she clung to. Her throat tightened, as if the air she breathed traveled through a pinhole and she could scarcely bring enough in to keep herself conscious. Her body was trembling, and she could feel the tremors of her chest, the uneven rising and falling as her breaths grew shakier.

The children—her chest collapsed inward, followed by a few short, sharp risings as she tried to inhale, to no avail—*Aunty Eshe, Uncle Salim*. Her fingers curled deeper against her skin, the pain the only thing still grounding her—*Grey and his family*— she sobbed, but the breath was choked coming out of her, sounding more like the cry of a wounded animal than a human sound. *All of them, all the people of Duskmere!*

She crumpled to her knees.

And what about her? She had scarcely spared herself a thought. A thought of her own future seemed futile. It seemed useless to eat up what precious time she had left with thoughts of the impossible.

Curling forward, she pressed her forehead to her legs. Even through her thick leggings, she could feel the sharp bite of the rock beneath her. But the pain was a reminder that it was not over yet. As the numbness devoured her, she knew that there was still more to endure, if only so she could make the world a better place.

She couldn't do that if she gave up now.

Lore closed her eyes and let go of the tightness that held her body. She relaxed her shoulders, which had hunched around her ears, and took a deep breath. It was difficult to pull enough air in at first, but eventually, she filled her lungs. She pressed her hands to her chest, trying to ease the tightness in it.

Breathe in. Breathe out. Breathe in. Breathe out.

As she thought the words, she heard them in the low rumble of Uncle Salim's voice, as if he were whispering in her ear. This was a simple technique he'd used with her since she was little and had woken up from nightmares, certain she was drowning. He wasn't there to say them now, but the wind blowing her wild curls back from her face could've almost been her uncle's hand, brushing them aside so they didn't stick to her tear-stained cheeks.

Her chest ached at the thought of having him by her side. She was tired of missing people and scared of needing them. It had been a long time since she had lost her parents, but now that she was separated from those at the shelter, she started to wonder if this was all her life would ever be: loving people only to eventually lose them.

Would she forever be forced to only imagine their touches in the caress of the ocean breeze and their voice in the whisper of the wind?

Still, for all her anguish, she persisted through the breathing exercise. When her heartbeat had slowed and she felt like she could fill her lungs fully with air again, she rose from where she had fallen and limped back into the cave, head held high.

She would help no one if she continued to kneel before the world and its relentless onslaught, so like the ocean against the cliffs. She would seek her salvation and that of those she loved, instead.

And she knew exactly where to start looking for it.

Inside the cave, she unlatched her backpack and pulled out the book. Sitting back down, she opened the pages, which remained blank in the dark cave.

She closed her eyes and whispered, "Are you here?"

Though she had long treasured books and felt proud of the ones she had made at the apothecary, she felt silly talking out loud to one.

Her heart twisted as she again considered the possibility that Asher had abandoned her.

Now was not the time.

She peeked one eye open, peering at the book. No voice sounded, and no words appeared on the page. She tried again, squeezing her eyes shut and thinking rather than speaking this time.

Are you here?

Still no response. She closed the book and opened it again, this time with more force.

Nothing.

The empty book stared back at her, looking completely normal. Looking as if it hadn't cast the midnight sky across her room, shown her the terrible fate of Duskmere, or given her the power to protect Asher from those guards.

She tried again, this time meditating with the book in her hands, turning over her wish to have it speak again and again in her mind like a smooth pebble. She wanted to know what accepting this deal really meant.

Back in the garden, during those last moments of the fight with those guards, she'd been so panicked she would have agreed to any bargain that might allow her to save Duskmere. Now, she wanted to understand the silvery light that had filled up her entire being and shot from her hands.

Thinking of it, she could swear that she felt an emptiness in her chest where that power, that force, had been. And she was certain now that that space had always been there, but she just hadn't known it. She hadn't known that there was something missing, so she had not sought it out. But that power had filled her up in a way she hadn't known she'd needed. Craved, even.

When she opened her eyes, she saw nothing on the pages but instead spied movement outside the cave's mouth. Asher was climbing back down the cliff face—alone.

Even as relief coursed through her, a thread of guilt wound around her heart for thinking the worst of Asher, especially after he had risked his life for her. She tried to distract herself by studying his careful, measured movements but couldn't help but roll her eyes.

He made descending the near-vertical cliff face look easy.

Asher grabbed a ledge in the rock and swung into the cave, the powerful muscles of his arms flexing where he had rolled up his sleeves. He landed on his feet with the grace of a, well, fae. He wasn't even out of breath.

What it must be to be fae.

She searched his face for any sign of how he was feeling today, but Asher avoided her gaze. He turned his face away from her, obscuring it in shadow, and that thread of guilt tightened as she thought of all she had cost him.

Still, he approached and handed her something wrapped in dark green leaves. She unfolded them and her stomach growled when she saw the white meat inside. She looked at him with a question in her eyes.

"Eat. It's fish." The right corner of his mouth almost turned up, like he wanted to be amused by her skepticism, but was still wary of her. He had every right to be.

Lore sniffed it, then studied it. Judging by the slight translucent quality of the meat, it seemed to be raw. He had sprinkled it with some fragrant herbs, including one she'd never smelled before, that were earthy and tangy.

She was apprehensive about eating raw fish, but didn't want to seem ungrateful. Also, she was just happy that he'd finally spoken to her, even if it was just to bark an order.

She took a tentative bite. The fish was richer than she had ever known fish to be before, with fat veins through it. But where fatty meat in Duskmere was often chewy, here it all but melted in her mouth. The herbs weren't just earthy, they also had a delicious spicy bite that lingered on her tongue, warming her up. She quickly devoured the piece.

As she ate, Asher lowered himself beside her with much less caution than she had. Apparently, being on a cliff face with a steep drop to the ocean didn't faze him.

Asher sighed, pulling his topknot free of the ribbon that held it in place and setting his hair free. He worked his fingertips back through his thick curls, flicking his wrist in an effortless movement to gather them back up, then tied it back into his bun, all while staring out to sea. The texture of his curls was tighter than hers, but his hair was still so long, and it looked so soft.

Once he finished with his hair, he dropped his hands into his lap, clasping them loosely, and turned to her.

Lore's cheeks warmed, and she averted her gaze, suddenly wishing he was still unable to look at her. The mouth of the cave wasn't very big, and they were actually quite close. She was aware of the warmth radiating from his leg, which sat a mere inch from hers. His shoulder brushed her, but she couldn't bring herself to lean away. If anything, she was fighting the urge to fold herself against him to see if, when his strong arms wrapped around her, she would feel the most impossible thing of all.

Safe.

"We need to talk. Or, rather, you need to explain. I thought humans didn't have magic. And yet, last night, you took down two trained guards with . . . some type of light that burst out of your body."

He looked confused and a little angry, but mostly he looked like he didn't trust her. She could read it in the slight arch of his eyebrow and in the way he leaned away from her.

Lore thought for a moment, trying to find the best way to explain something to him that she wasn't even sure she understood yet. "We don't. Humans can't do magic. But, while working in the library, I found this book, or, well—" She bit her lip. "This book found me."

Asher raised his eyebrow farther, distrust still filling his eyes.

"Hear me out, all right? This book—" She held it up for him to see while keeping a tight grip on it. She feared it would somehow slip from her hands and fall to the ocean below. Then everything she'd done truly would have been for nothing. "This book called to me by name while I was working in the library. It knew my name. And it called me again when I opened it up. Which, now that I think about it, sounds totally deranged."

She bit her lip, looking away from his distrustful eyes and back out at the ocean. It was easier to face the heaving, destructive force beneath her than that look from him.

"I thought it was blank at first. I started using it as a journal, writing random thoughts throughout, stupid bits of poetry, and my anger every day . . ."

She stopped herself, not feeling like talking to a fae about how much harder the humans had it. He would never understand.

"And then last night, the book showed me that it wasn't blank. It soaked up all my words and reflected the moonlight back to me. And it—it spoke again, after weeks of staying silent. It wanted to work together. It said it could give me power, as long as I accepted its deal."

She glanced back at Asher now. His look of distrust had completely melted away to one of certainty that she was completely mad. She didn't blame him for thinking that.

"I didn't trust it at first, thinking it must be a trick, or maybe a punishment for sneaking the book out of the library and not giving it to Steward Vinelake like I'd promised. So, I asked it to show me something. To prove to me that it could do what it said it could and make me powerful. And it showed me Duskmere. My people are hurting right now, far worse than when I left them. I hadn't thought that possible, especially since the steward and his lord promised to send them aid. But what the book showed was that everything they promised me was a lie."

Lore began tearing the leaves from the meal into pieces as she continued, if only to hide the tremor of her hands.

"There are so many more children at the shelter now. It's where I'm from, a place kids in Duskmere go when they . . . when their parents have joined their ancestors in the beyond."

She avoided his gaze, not wanting to see the pity that surely clouded his face now. She had known that look on many faces throughout her life, but it always elicited the same response from her: heartache and bitterness.

"I don't understand what happened to their parents. Why have the numbers of orphaned children quadrupled? Perhaps the earth-shake? But surely not so many—not so many are dead from that." Lore looked up from where she was clenching the remaining leaves in her fists, her knuckles white. "I need to be with them, Asher. I can help them if only I can understand this book and its power."

She held her breath, looking to Asher and searching his gaze. She was relieved that she didn't see distrust or pity, but the ut-terly blank expression that had taken over his face was not much better.

"How do you know it's real? It could be a trick," he said at last.

She lifted her chin, looking him in the eye. "I can feel that it is true. I knew it from the moment I agreed to the deal. This book cannot lie to me, nor I to it."

"So, you are connected to the book? Show me. Show me that light."

"I can't. I've been trying to get the book to talk to me and show me its secrets all morning. I think . . . I think it only works at night when the moon is high."

Asher nodded, going along with what she was saying. Whether he truly believed her or not, she could not say. His blank expression was a veil, hiding his true emotions.

"Okay. I will help you get home, but we can't go straight there. Chief Steward Vinelake will have soldiers looking for you, assuming you are headed home. We'll need to buy enough time for him to call back his soldiers. We can go south first. I have friends who might be able to help us."

))) ● (((

Unsurprisingly, it took Lore far longer to climb the cliff than it took Asher. Although her leg still hurt, it felt better. That wasn't the problem. Now that it was day, Lore could see the jagged rocks that spelled death below her and forcing her limbs to move was difficult, due to sheer terror.

Asher went first, showing her which indentations in the rock were best and which roots could hold their weight. When they finally reached the top of the cliff, Lore's arms were screaming from the exertion. Asher, ahead of her, leaned down, grabbed her by the wrist, and hauled her up. She muttered her gratitude, but they didn't waste any more time or breath before heading south.

Asher had returned to his brooding, and Lore fell behind the silent fae. She was in awe that he didn't make a single sound or get scratched by a single branch. It was as if the trees themselves bowed out of his way, the earth welcomed his footfalls willingly, and the leaves on the bushes turned silent when he brushed them.

Meanwhile, Lore's every step snapped a twig or crunched dry leaves. The branches seemed to reach out at her hair, snagging in her curls, and leaving leaves behind out of spite.

When the two finally came upon the packed red dirt of a road, she wanted to cry from happiness. No more rocks waiting to twist her ankle or spiderwebs to dodge.

Lore pulled her scarf up around her face, covering her hair and ears. Most of the individuals they would pass likely would have never seen a human and she would stand out. Only the tip of her nose and the glint of her dark brown eyes peeked out of the blue scarf and, as long as she kept her eyes downturned and didn't get too close to anyone, nobody should notice that she was human. Though she was significantly shorter than the dark fae, her research in the library had shown that she was the average height of many of the other creatures traveling the trade road.

Asher was smart and knew his homeland well; he'd had them exit the woods in a busy location, one filled with all manner of creatures. Some, like Asher, looked almost human, save for their larger eyes, pointed ears, and animal characteristics. Others were as different from Lore as Lore was from a bunny. There were blue creatures with saltwater dripping down from their seaweed-like hair to pool at their feet. Some were even stranger still, flying above them with giant membranous wings that twinkled in the sunlight, casting rainbows on hers and Asher's cheeks. Others with feathered wings pulled flags behind them, boasting advertisements for lodging and eateries in the sprawling city before them, Veyesh.

And what a city it was. It made the city surrounding Wyndlin Castle seem like a cozy village. Wooden gates carved from tree trunks towered before her. She craned her neck up and up . . . then still farther up, but couldn't see where the canopy ended and the sky began.

"Close your mouth. You look like the fish I caught this morning."

Lore slammed her jaw shut, cheeks warming. She stilled her features, trying to mimic the business-as-usual attitude of the crowd as they crossed a giant bridge. She had a wild urge to run to the edge and throw something down into the river below, to watch it float within the powerful current beneath her, but that would draw too much attention. Nobody around her seemed fazed by the sight of the rushing water, meandering through the gates and going about their day.

Thoughts of the river scattered when two flying dark fae in familiar Alytherian black and gold uniforms glided down to the gate, their pearly wings shimmering in the sun. They conferred with the gate guards for a moment, halting the procession into the city.

The guards, upon closer inspection, seemed to be stopping people at random to check merchant's wares and search families. Lore noted from where she stood in line that some coin tended to wink in the light when travelers were stopped. The dark fae with the ability of flight seemed to be the only ones not targeted for these searches; instead, they were allowed to skip ahead of the line as the guards bowed their heads and waved them through the gates.

While there were plenty of children riding on wagons and running throughout the line, some holding on to their parent's skirt, their tiny, pointed wings fluttering behind them, there weren't many dark fae children.

But she had other things to worry about than the offspring of the dark fae as the line between them and the gate dwindled. Lore's palms began to sweat. There was no doubt the guards were on alert for two fugitives on the run. And, if by some miracle the guards had not been looking for them, and a simple bribe would be all they needed, Lore wouldn't even know what the asking price was, or how to go about bribing a guard.

"Asher, I'm worried," Lore whispered to him, quelling the urge to reach out and grab his hand. His stony silence since they left the cave had made it clear how angry he was with her.

"I have a plan," he said, his tone clipped, as the last group between them and the gate were admitted past the checkpoint.

They stepped forward as a guard, an aging female peering down at a clipboard, asked them to state their purpose in the city, her voice bored. Asher began to spin a tale when she glanced up and noticed Lore's hood. She cut him off. "Girl, draw back your hood, we need to see your face," she ordered.

With shaking hands Lore reached up to her hood and gripped the smooth edges of the fabric, but she made no move to draw it back. Even if, by some miracle, the guards hadn't realized they were fugitives, one look at her human ears and they would know. Lore and Asher would be detained and imprisoned.

The guard squinted her eyes in suspicion at Lore's hesitation and repeated her order. If Lore didn't follow her directive she would call out to the other guards, and they would remove Lore's hood for her. She froze, not knowing what to do. It was too late to turn and run. They should have hidden in the woods longer and come up with a different plan. If she had known that there would be a checkpoint, she wouldn't have followed Asher outside the dense forest.

Lore's heart pounded in her chest as she glanced at him. Asher had said he had a plan, but now he wasn't looking at her or even the guard, who was growing increasingly impatient. Instead, his gaze was fixed on the river behind them. The guard opened her mouth to call to two patrols on the other side of the gate, who were questioning a woman leading an animal so laden with packs and parcels that Lore couldn't even tell what kind of animal it was.

Lore glared at the back of Asher's head, willing him to make something happen, when she saw him flick his wrist toward the river.

Crack! Crack! Crack!

Lore ducked her head in instinct as a deafening series of cracks reverberated through her body from the direction of the river. Birds by the hundreds erupted in flight from every direction, their frantic cries overwhelming the roar of the river and city sounds wafting through the gate.

Lore, along with everyone in the vicinity, looked toward the river. Gasps rang out as it dawned on the crowd just what was transpiring. A massive tree, one of many that lined the edge of the roaring river, had begun to splinter as visible shock waves rippled through its trunk.

For one single moment, not a soul outside the gates of Veyesh drew a breath as they gazed on in terror. The thick, gnarled roots of the tree had begun to pull free from the earth as the tree began to sway.

Though it was the shortest tree growing along the bank of the river, the circumference of the trunk appeared to be the size of Lore's childhood room. If it fell backward, it would crush a portion of the city wall and decimate the buildings behind it. The shingled roofs and smoking chimneys that rose above the wall would come crashing down, killing anyone inside the buildings or in the surrounding streets.

If it fell toward the bridge, it would crush the overpass, and anyone on the bridge who wasn't pulverized beneath the tree, or its expansive branches, would be dropped into the deadly river below. If the water didn't kill them, the crumbling bridge would.

The people watched in horror as the tree tipped closer and closer to the bridge. Some began to scream and run; others froze in place, unable to move from fear. A few people began to pray, crying to their gods for help.

Asher was muttering under his breath, his brows pulled together in concentration, his gaze on the swaying tree.

"Asher, oh gods, don't let it—"

With an eerie groan, the bark itself seeming to scream a death rattle, its ancient roots ripped from the earth, and the tree capsized.

The tree did not fall at an angle onto the bridge, nor toward the wall. Instead, it fell parallel to the bridge, and pitched onto the river.

The force from the gargantuan tree caused a wave of water from the deep river to erupt into the air. A wave swept up and over the bridge so swiftly, nobody had a chance to escape before they were swept off their feet by a current of frothing water. Horses reared onto their hind legs, their hooves kicking into the air in panic, before running wildly. Parents scooped up their children and scrambled out of their way as the mad beasts dragged their wagons and carts in every direction, wares spilling out into the water behind them.

Lore's hood was forgotten as the guard, along with her brethren, abandoned their posts, rushing toward the chaotic scene on the bridge, shouting orders for the merchants and families to restrain their horses.

They slipped into the city, unnoticed.

CHAPTER 12

The Siren's Song Inn smelled like sautéed onions and Katu's socks.

These two very separate but distinct smells made Lore's stomach churn, while simultaneously making her miss the days when her biggest obstacle was convincing Katu—newly twelve and with a hatred for bathing—to wash his feet before they stank up the boy's room.

Still, when she'd read the inn's name on the signpost, she'd really thought it was going to be . . . cleaner.

Her boots stuck to the floor and made an audible sound with each step. While Asher talked about acquiring a room to an adorably petite pixie—large eyes, locs piled in an elaborate bun, and dragonfly wings that twinkled in the lamplight—at the bar, Lore surveyed the room. Though the round tables filling the wide dining room weren't empty, there wasn't anyone in an official royal uniform, and Lore felt herself relax.

Still, the travelers sitting down to their evening meals didn't seem like the safest of boarding companions, either. In one corner, giant creatures who looked like they had been carved from rocks drew attention where they sat. They were the noisiest group in the large pub—as she watched, one called loudly for more ale, while the others cheered and thrust their various weapons into the air. The weapons were rusted, and it seemed like one cut from them would cause you to die from infection rather than blood loss.

In the middle of the inn, lone travelers were scattered here and there. One particularly sinister-looking fellow sat with his back to the wall while an equally angry-looking mutt perched at his feet. They bared their teeth when Lore looked over, and she shuddered; the tips of both his and the mutt's teeth ended in needlelike points.

In the opposite corner sat a family. The female appeared to be a dryad. Lore eyed her discreetly, excitement thrumming through her. She'd read about dryads in one of the books from the library. The female was tall and slender, and her skin was a gorgeous sage green. Her hair flowed around her shoulders and her dress was sunflower yellow with lace sleeves. Her assumed husband was also a dryad, though his family tree appeared to be a different variety. Where the female's skin was smooth and green like that of a young sapling, his had the look of tree bark. He was brown and tall, with leaves that escaped his cap and brushed the tops of his ears.

Two children were with them, each one a small version of one of the parents. Judging by the fine cut of their clothes, they seemed too wealthy to be in a rough inn like this, and it seemed the mother agreed. She pushed her food around her plate, clenching her utensils in a viselike grip, hissing at her husband about dragging her and the children on the dangerous road with him to sell his wares.

The mention of danger caused Lore to turn back to her own companion, only to find him smiling as the pixie giggled and twirled a long lilac loc around a finger. Asher was leaning on the bar, murmuring something to her in low tones.

Lore felt her cheeks get hot. "Ahem. Ash—if you could give me the key? I'm in need of a hot bath and a bed."

Asher ignored her and continued speaking quietly. The pixie tossed her head back and laughed, a tinkling that sounded like bells.

Lore was debating between casually smacking him with her backpack or giving him a swift kick to the shin when he straightened, gave a nod, and scooped a brass key off the counter.

"Come on," Asher said to her, breezing by her without so much as a glance. Still, at least he was speaking to her; she was beginning to think he was going to give her the silent treatment forever.

Lore stopped in the doorway to their room, which was so small the one bed filled up almost the entire floor. She stumbled in, dropping her pack on the bed and sitting beside it while untying her scarf. "I can't believe you were flirting at a time like this," she groused, then froze.

Shit. She hadn't meant to say that out loud.

Asher raised an eyebrow, face expressionless.

"I just thought we weren't supposed to be drawing attention to ourselves," she added, trying to cover up her blunder. She willed her cheeks not to heat up.

Asher kicked off his boots and sat at the head of the bed, leaning against the wooden headboard. He rubbed his face roughly, then pushed his hair back and looked at her. "I had to haggle for a reasonable price. We didn't have enough to cover the room and an evening meal." His tone was clipped.

Lore felt her cheeks burn a second time. What business was it of hers if he was flirting, anyway? She had no right to say anything.

"Oh." She didn't want to admit that what she'd said was unfair, but knew she ought to. Yet at the same time, if she started apologizing now, would she ever stop? She had uprooted his life and turned his world upside down. Even when she made it home to Duskmere and he was rid of her, his life would never be the same. He could never return to being a castle guard.

He gave a slight nod, face once again buried in his large hands. Lore felt the acid burn at the back of her throat and her stomach clench. He looked defeated.

It was all because of her.

Lore cleared her throat. "So, what's our cover story?"

Asher looked like he almost wanted to smile. "I told them we're married. Let's just hope they don't ask too many questions."

The thought of being married to Asher was shoved into a box in her mind, never to be considered again. She tried to keep her voice light. "We'll be fine, as long as you can pretend like you don't hate me for the next two days." Asher hadn't said more than two words to her since the cave.

"Yeah, if I can manage that, I think I'll have found a new life calling. Then I'll be able to join a traveling theater troupe, at least." His laugh sounded hollow.

Lore tried not to let the hurt show. "Look, Asher . . . I didn't know you were on guard at that gate. I didn't even know you were at the castle! Last time I saw you was weeks ago. I know you've broken orders, defected, lost your home, and . . . and I know you are now on the run. And I know that's all because of me."

She wanted to look away, but she owed him this much, at least.

"I'm sure you're wishing I had never been brought to the castle in the first place, but I lost things too, Asher. The shop, my home, and my entire village is in chaos. I didn't ask to be born human or to be trapped in Duskmere like a prisoner without simple rights awarded to every other creature in this land. I didn't have a choice. Going to the castle was never a choice, not really. It was something I had to do if I wanted to stay alive." She blinked, trying to force the threat of tears away. "I keep expecting to wake up from this horrific nightmare I'm having, but instead, every day I wake up to this."

She waved her hands to indicate the room, him, the disaster that had become their lives in the last two days.

"And I'm just trying to get back to my people, Asher. Like you and like me, they are just victims of circumstance. They don't deserve to live like this, and I think—for the first time in my life—I can do something to change things for them. I want to help my people stop surviving and start living."

Asher remained silent, staring at her.

Suddenly she was sick of this—of all that had been happening to her against her will and of the guilt eating at her insides and hollowing her out. And she decided, just then, that she was especially tired of Asher's sulking, no matter how justified it may be.

"If you hate me so much, why are you still here?" She was surprised to find that she was shouting, but she didn't care. "Why not just leave me? You don't have to be here. I didn't ask you to be! In fact, you should just leave!" She reached out to shove him. "I don't need you here just to—"

He caught her wrist before she could shove him, his hand moving faster than her eyes could track. He growled, a low, guttural sound, and pulled her to him as he stood. He grabbed her chin with his other thumb and finger and tipped her head up.

She parted her lips, wanting to continue yelling, but she suddenly forgot how to form words.

His teeth were bared, and his breath came out in quick, uneven pants. They were so close; she could feel the pounding of his heart against her chest and see the flecks of sienna and gold in his black irises. Some quiet part of her whispered, *No wonder they look like molten lava.*

She tried to pull back and slip out of his grip to continue yelling at him, but his calloused fingers tightened on her jaw—

And suddenly his mouth was on hers.

Every thought flew out of her head but one: *He tastes like blackberries and honey.*

His hand was no longer on her chin but wound tightly in her hair, while his other was at her back, pulling her closer. Without conscious thought, her own hands tangled in his tunic, flattening against his chest. She slid them up to his jaw and felt his stubble, startled to realize that, for the first time since she'd first seen him in the dining hall weeks ago, he hadn't shaved.

She needed more of his taste. She grabbed his bottom lip between her teeth and nibbled, unable to stop a moan escaping her.

At her moan, he growled again, deepening the kiss. His tongue entered her mouth, tentative at first—then more insistent, hungry.

She was on fire.

It seemed that, like her, that little bit of a taste wasn't enough. His hand left her hair, and he grabbed her thighs, lifting her like she weighed nothing. She wrapped her legs around his hips, needing this—needing to be closer.

Asher took a step forward and suddenly, she was pressed up against the wall. He deepened the kiss, pressing his hips into her core. She moaned into his mouth as she pressed back into him.

He tore his mouth from hers.

She almost cried out in protest, but his lips were back on her in a moment, tasting her neck. She moaned when he nibbled the sensitive skin there—his sharp canines were quick to find that perfect line between pleasure and pain.

She needed to feel his skin. They weren't close enough.

She opened her eyes and looked at the bed. But, as if he'd sensed the direction of her thoughts, he stilled, coming to his senses.

She was afraid he would back up and drop her, but he didn't. Instead, he leaned into her, pressing his weight against her and nuzzling into her neck and curls, breathing in her scent.

Their breathing was loud and ragged in the silent room.

"I'm sorry." His words were soft, muffled by her hair. His breath was warm against her neck, and it sent a shiver of pleasure straight to her core. He pulled back, just a little, and leaned his forehead to hers. "I'm sorry, Lore," he repeated, clearer this time.

Her name sounded so lovely on his lips.

She started to speak, but he cut her off with the lightest of kisses. "Wait, just let me—" He extricated her legs from around him and set her on her feet, but he didn't let go of her. Instead, he gently cupped her cheek in his hand—so different from the rough way he'd grabbed her hair only moments before.

Lore wouldn't mind going back to that roughness, but she managed to keep that thought silent as she let Asher gather his words.

He eventually continued, voice hoarse and thick with emotion. "I hate what's been done to your people and to you. I've just been pissed at the situation—I had another three months of required service to the crown, and then I would've been done. Finally, I would be able to walk my own path. I could put this shit behind me and stop bowing to my betters." He said "betters" like it put a bad taste in his mouth. "I've acted like an ass to you."

She blinked in surprise. His mouth quirked.

"But the truth is, I'm still here because I *want* to help you. To be honest, the thought of leaving you on your own never once crossed my mind."

Lore's cheeks heated. Gods, if she were honest with herself, she had been scared shitless that he would've taken her up on the words she'd said in anger and bailed on her.

He only had three months left, and he threw it all away for her.

She thought back to when she first saw him in the sentry uniform, thinking he was one of them. But really, he had been forced to join and, just three months shy of gaining his freedom, he'd chosen to help a human girl, all because he believed in her.

Suddenly, Lore felt sick. She wriggled free of his grip and slipped into the washroom, shutting the door behind her. She leaned against it and bit her finger, stifling a sob.

She would figure out a way to repay him. She would find a way to relieve him of the burden she had become. She didn't know how. In truth, she wasn't sure of anything at all.

After Lore bathed and had a chance to properly brush her hair—there had been a truly alarming number of twigs and leaves in it—she washed her clothes, hung them up to dry, and changed into clean trousers and a loose tunic.

The routine motions served to calm her, and she finally had a clearer head.

Asher emerged from the bathing room wearing nothing but the black pants of his uniform. Her gaze lingered on the low-slung pants, and the V of muscles there. Her core clenched, and she thought of the feel of his mouth on hers and of his grip on her thighs.

But she looked away. She would find a way to fix what she'd broken in his life.

She didn't deserve his kindness, nor his touch.

The first step to fixing anything would be to determine their next steps. Asher had removed his uniform jacket as soon as they left the cave, which solved the problem of him being easily identified, though not much else. Most importantly, they were going to have to figure out this coin situation. They only had a small amount of it and had spent a good chunk of it on this inn.

They had a lot to figure out.

Lore handed him a bowl of lamb stew and a chunk of bread she'd gotten from the pixie at the bar while Asher had bathed. The bread may have been a little stale and the stew a little greasy, but at least it was hot, and the bowls were large enough to fill their bellies.

Outside the small window in their room, a storm raged, and Lore was just happy that they weren't sleeping outside. She probably wouldn't have survived, as the temperature had dropped significantly since that morning in the cave.

"Asher, I think I've got an idea on how we can make enough coin and travel south without being detained."

"Yeah? How?" he asked through a mouthful of potatoes. He was inhaling his stew, his usual ferocious appetite intact, and Lore felt a stirring of hope that, though everything had changed between them, at least this one thing was the same.

Lore set her empty bowl on the floor, suddenly nervous about telling him her plan. But maybe, just maybe, it could work.

))) ● (((

That night, Asher disappeared after dinner to sell his two army-issued swords. Lore had scooted as far to one side of the lumpy bed as possible, planning to wait up for his return, but she'd fallen asleep the moment her head had hit the pillow, only to wake up to the sound of birdsong out the window that morning.

Asher was asleep next to her on top of the blanket, his pillow stuffed in between them.

He slept with his brow unfurrowed and the wrinkles she'd grown used to seeing on his forehead had smoothed. She hadn't seen him like this since the autumn equinox—before she had gotten them into this mess. She thought of him pushing her on the swing. He had grown at ease with her and had even seemed to enjoy being around her over the weeks.

Her eyes trailed to his lips. She wanted to taste them again. Devour him and never come up for air. But they had bigger problems to worry about—Lore being sidetracked by kisses was the last thing she needed right now.

Still, it was nice to see that relaxation in him again, even if only while he was sleeping.

He lay on his back, broad chest rising and falling. His brown cheeks were slightly flushed, and a thick curl fell across his forehead. Lore couldn't help inhaling his scent of blackberries and night-blooming jasmine before quickly hopping up.

She didn't need him waking up to her smelling him.

Eventually, he woke up, and they hurried to get dressed and leave the room.

She pulled on her boots and slipped downstairs, sighing with relief when she saw the family of dryads had decided to break their fast before heading out on the road—she hadn't missed them.

She and Asher sat at the neighboring table, eating their porridge and toast. Lore's stomach roiled with nerves, but their next meal was uncertain, so she forced down every bite while listening to the merchant's conversation.

"We should head to Dartmith's Estate as soon as we finish eating. He's expecting us to head out with the caravan immediately. As you know, there have been double the robberies and assaults in the last month."

"I just can't believe how dangerous it's become on the road."

Lore took another bite, keeping the merchants in her vision. Thus, she was able to see the moment the wife noticed them.

Just as she'd hoped.

Lore knew what the wife was seeing: Asher, wearing a black long-sleeved tunic, buttoned up to his throat. His hair was pulled up into a loose topknot that allowed a few curly tendrils to escape and frame his pointed ears. Beside him sat a new jacket with his new swords resting on top of it—although they were not quite as sharp as his two army-issued swords, they looked impressive.

She spared a moment to wonder how the sale of his swords had gone. They both knew he couldn't carry his old ones around anymore, lest he be identified as a defector immediately. She wondered how much he'd gotten for them and his uniform, realizing it was likely treason to sell them. She hoped the person he'd sold them to was discreet and paid well.

Lore fingered the lace collar that she'd buttoned all the way up to her throat. The tunic she now wore was a lovely shade of purple. She hoped they looked the part—that of a clean, well-off couple, who looked strong and capable of protecting a certain merchant and their family, rather than exactly what they were. A pair of fugitives on the run.

"Are you ready?" she asked.

Asher stood, pushing away from the table. They both pretended not to be listening to the whispering couple next to them, but Lore had to hide her squeal of excitement when she heard the husband call out.

His voice was low and gruff. "Excuse me, sir. Madam."

They both turned to the merchant family, pleasant smiles on their faces.

"Excuse me," the man continued, once he had their attention. "I wouldn't want to intrude but, might you be looking for a temporary venture? We are traveling with some wares and we are looking to hire a personal guard. Short term. Just for our next journey."

His wife spoke up. "Yes, and we noticed that you two were traveling as well. Might you travel with us? We can pay, of course, and provide an evening meal."

Lore and Asher looked at each other, pretending to consider it. Asher replied, "When are you leaving and which way are you heading? We are due in Camella in two days' time."

"Oh, perfect! Yes, we are heading to Lolabrock, so it won't be out of your way at all. We're leaving in a moment, isn't that right, dear?" The dryad looked to her husband.

"That's right. What do you say?"

Asher grinned. "Well, if we are heading the same way, then I surely couldn't let you travel this road alone. We shall meet you out front in a few moments. My wife and I just need to grab our things."

With a slight bow of their heads, they took their leave upstairs.

Lore waited until they were in their room, door firmly shut, before exclaiming, "I can't believe it worked!"

CHAPTER 13

As soon as they made it through the city gates and left behind the majority of the traffic, Lore felt as if a weight had lifted from her chest. The guards, who had been stopping and questioning almost everyone traveling, hadn't even looked at the merchants. With their gorgeous carriage and fine clothes, they had been waved through without a second glance.

Now Lore sat on the back of the wagon, feet dangling off the edge, studying her book. It was a beautiful day: sunny and with a light breeze. The forest thinned along the southern road, and they'd begun passing farms and orchards. She couldn't believe the size of the land these farmers owned. As far as she could see were rows of trees, oblivious to the season, heavy with fruit.

She wanted to fill wagons to the brim and bring them to her people.

Lore turned back to the book. She'd kept quiet since the merchants had asked about her odd accent. She had quickly spun a lie about being raised by an aunt from a faraway city she remembered seeing in one of the tomes at the library.

The children were asleep in the carriage and Asher was riding up front with the merchant, taking his turn at the reins.

Lore ran her fingers down the pages, which were still blank.

The voices didn't speak to her and didn't explain what that strange light or power had been.

She closed the book with a sigh, tucking it back into her sack.

She'd try again tonight.

$$)) \blacktriangleright \bullet \blacktriangleleft ((	$$

They stopped for the evening just after sundown. Lore watered and brushed the horses while Asher and Vyncent—the merchant—built a fire and dealt with securing the wagon and carriage.

The merchants had four horses. There were only a handful of them in Lore's entire village, and this one family owned *four*. She didn't have much experience with the beasts, but she knew enough to brush them in the direction of their coat and avoid getting behind them. She'd seen a man get kicked by one when she was little and had never forgotten the sight.

She was currently brushing a light brown mare with a white patch in the shape of a star on its face. Lore liked these creatures with their long manes and curious eyes. This one kept nuzzling her hand, likely looking for a carrot or an apple.

"I haven't got one for you, silly girl." She laughed and stroked the mare's strong neck with the brush.

"Fern is always looking for treats. Never full, that one."

Lore looked down. One of the merchant's children, Posie, was standing beside her, petting the other mare's nose.

"Well, she and I are the same, then," Lore said. "I feel like I'm always looking for treats myself."

The girl smiled. Her smile was sweet and missing more than one baby tooth, but it felt rare, like she didn't show it to just anyone.

"Do you always travel with your parents when they have merch to sell?" Lore asked, running her fingers through Fern's black mane and untangling a few knots.

"No, never. We usually stay home with Mother, but folks have been going missing. Well, not folks—" Her voice dropped to a whisper. "Don't tell my brother, but younglings have been disappearing. Well, dark fae younglings. But Mother said we can't be too sure dryads aren't next. She didn't want him to leave us, but Father couldn't miss the market. So, here we are."

"Wow. That is quite scary." Missing fae children? Lore fought off a shiver.

"It is. But my mom told me because I'm the eldest and have to look after my little brother, Jene." She turned her chin up, puffing her chest out with pride.

"I'm sure you can do just that. You seem like a great big sister."

The girl nodded before running off to find her little brother. After a meal of cold sandwiches, the Pineray family locked themselves in their carriage for the night. Asher and Lore sat by the fire on borrowed bedrolls. Tonight, she would sleep under the sky. The wind would be her lullaby and the stars her guardians.

Asher sat across from her, sharpening one of his swords. His muscles rippled beneath his light jacket and his eyebrows were pulled into his usual scowl. Lore would give a thousand coin to know what he was thinking at this moment.

"Draw a picture. I'm sure it will last longer." The hint of a smirk danced along his lips and a dimple almost showed itself.

Lore's cheeks heated. Caught.

She raised her eyebrow, hoping he couldn't see her blush in the low firelight. "And immortalize your constant frown? No, thanks." But surely there was something better she could do with her time than stare at a brooding fae.

She rummaged through her pack again, pulling out the tome. She had basically signed her life away and who knew what else to this blank book, and it hadn't made a peep since the night of her escape. No visions. Not even a random joke to pass the time.

She flipped open the book and almost threw it when she realized it was no longer empty. Instead, where the moonlight was shining between the thinner branches above and striking the pages, words and diagrams appeared.

"Moonlight. The key *is* moonlight," Lore whispered, lightly touching the aged paper.

An illustrated plant was drawn on the page now. It showed a thin stem with branches extending in every direction, rounded leaves the color of overripe strawberries hanging from the stems, and tiny budding flowers that were scattered throughout the leaves. Cramped lettering written in a foreign tongue appeared beside the roots, stems, flowers, and seeds. It seemed to her to detail the different times of year to pick this plant and, if the diagrams with the seasons drawn beside it were what Lore thought they were, when the best time to harvest them would be.

Or maybe to plant them. She couldn't be sure because she couldn't read it.

The next page showed a recipe for—Lore brought the book closer, squinting her eyes in the low light—some kind of sleeping or calming tonic. She recognized two of the words written in a curling script at the top of the page, as they were Alytherian. The next page showed another recipe for an elixir with a drawing of a dragon in the corner.

She rubbed her finger over its wings. Did this have something to do with the elixir, or was it a doodle, drawn by a student whose mind wandered during a lecture, or maybe a powerful magic user who dreamed of riding dragons?

Lore's blood sang with excitement. She may only be able to pick out one or two words from the diagrams, but at least the book—no, grimoire—had revealed them at last. As she flipped through the pages, she saw that her book was not just a magical book, but one in which someone had inscribed magic spells, potions, and elixirs.

"Lore. Get down." Asher's voice cut through her revelation. His command was quiet, yet filled with steel.

She didn't give a moment's thought about *why*—she just *did*.

She dropped as a dagger flew over her head. Not even a moment later, she heard a sharp whistle above her and cursed as another dagger flew above her, thrown by Asher.

A sickening squelch and a cry of pain let her know he hadn't missed.

On instinct, Lore took the tome and shoved it into her pack before pushing it behind her.

A deep voice shouted toward them from the tree line. "I'm going to kill ye for that one."

Lore looked at Asher. He stood by the fire, feet set apart and twin swords now in his hands. His stony face showed no emotion.

Though her blood pounded in her ears, Lore couldn't help but think how right the swords looked in Asher's hands, as if they were extensions of his body rather than mere tools.

He stalked forward and hopped over the fallen log Lore had been sitting on, one sword raised and the other behind him, readied if he should need it.

A stranger appeared from the shadowed tree line, running toward Asher with his own sword raised. Asher, twin antlers gleaming in the moonlight and jaw set in determination, blocked the intruder's swing with a practiced arc of his own. Their blades met with such force that the stranger cursed and staggered backward. His broadsword, one that required two hands, quivered. When Asher struck again, his movements lightning quick, the stranger retreated another step.

"Asher—behind you!" Lore yelled out, jumping to her feet as another male stepped out of the shadows, aiming his sword at Asher's back.

She gritted her teeth, calling out to that moonlit power and hoping it would flow through her and out toward Asher, protecting him. But nothing happened. Where she hoped to feel that power fill her up and explode from within her, she felt nothing, as if she were trying to fish water from a dried-up well.

Thankfully, Asher reacted to her warning and sidestepped the arc of the third male's sword, so gracefully it looked more like a dance. While turning, Asher slashed behind him with his second sword, slicing the third interloper across the thigh.

The male roared as he dropped to one knee, hands pushed to the ribbon cut to try to stop the bubbling blood that gushed through his fingers.

Asher didn't pause. He leaped closer and slammed his hilt into the temple of the kneeling fae, turning back to the second before the third one fell face first into the earth.

The second had recovered and raised his sword again, teeth bared in the moonlight and eyes red with fury. Asher, baring his teeth in return, swung both swords this time, keeping one high to block the sword and shoving the other through his opponent's arm and right through his heart. The fae was dead before he could register what had happened.

Asher pulled his sword free, wiping it on the fallen fae's vest. His breathing was ragged. He spared a quick glance at Lore but wouldn't meet her gaze.

Lore looked around at the campsite, hands clenched tightly to her tunic as she swallowed back bile. Bodies seemed to be piling up before her. Before she'd set foot outside of Duskmere, if someone had asked her if the fae could even be mortally wounded she would have answered that they probably couldn't. They'd seemed invincible. Impossible to wound, let alone *kill*.

But now she could see that she would have been very wrong.

She glanced back to Asher, who was kneeling on the ground, his fingers digging into the dirt as if looking for comfort in the soil. His mouth moved as if whispering a prayer.

Lore's mind spun. Mere moments ago, she'd been sitting by

the fire, and now the campsite stank of blood and death. She tried to play the encounter back.

Three bandits had attacked—one went down immediately with Asher's expert throw of the dagger and another now lay knocked out on the ground, with Asher standing over him and tying him up with rope.

How is he always prepared?

Asher grabbed a stick and used it with the rope to tie a tourniquet around the fae's thigh. The third lay dead where he'd dropped, still clutching his sword.

So much death, and yet her power still hadn't come back to her. The moon was high. She blinked back frustrated tears. She was tired of feeling so small and helpless.

On the other side of the clearing, the merchants were still asleep in their wagon, with no idea that they had almost been robbed—or worse. Were these bandits after their money, supplies, or the two younglings? She supposed they would find out when the one who remained alive woke and could be questioned.

Still, what had the girl said before? Fae younglings had gone missing of late.

Those two children could have been kidnapped and Lore would've been no help.

She kneeled, pulling the grimoire from her pack. This time, when she opened the book, she shivered at the familiar tingle that ran through her fingertips and up her arms. She slid her thumb over the rough pages of the parchment.

She sat back on her heels, angling the book so the moonlight fell on it. Sketches of weapons—two daggers side by side with an arrow between them—appeared on the page. The second dagger was on fire. Below the image was one of a sword that appeared to be made of ice. But what good would an ice sword be?

Suddenly the page changed before her eyes, the ink bleeding together and reforming into new pictures, faster than she could register. Words appeared and disappeared in languages she couldn't read. A ringing filled her ears, and she could hear her blood rushing in time with her heartbeat.

Lore closed the book.

She pushed the escaped hair from her unraveled scarf out of her face, immediately panicking. *My ears!* Her hands flew to the exposed appendages, and she glanced around wildly, only to calm when she remembered the rest of the camp was still asleep.

She had too many thoughts racing through her head to read the book right now. It seemed like it was trying to answer all her questions at once. She placed the book on the grass beside her, put her hands on her knees, and closed her eyes, willing her breathing to slow and her mind to clear. She thought back to meditating with Uncle Salim, his deep timbre encouraging her to empty her mind.

It wasn't long before the ringing stopped and the tightness in her chest eased.

A light brush to her cheek brought her back to the present. Calloused fingers, trained to fight and kill, but so *so* gentle when brushing her cheek felt like a calming tonic. She inhaled, smelling Asher's scent of blackberry, smoke, and the faint hint of metal from handling his swords before opening her eyes and looking at the dark fae who had saved her life.

Again.

Asher sat on the log beside her, long legs stretched out toward the low flames of the fire, swords at his feet. He held a cloth and sharpening stone in his hand.

"Are you all right? I've cleared the camp of the bodies. The one still alive is tied to a tree outside of hearing distance from the camp." Lore must have looked scared, because Asher hurried to continue. "He won't be able to escape those knots. Trust me." Asher handed her a piece of dried jerky with a smirk. "Eat this. You'll feel better."

She took the jerky, ignoring the flecks of blood on his wrist and sleeve. "Thank you."

"It's just a bit of jerky."

"Not for that. I mean, yes, thank you for the jerky." She waved the strip of meat in the air. "But I mean, thank you for saving my life. Again. And the lives of the entire camp from those assholes."

Asher looked uncomfortable with her gratitude, giving a slight nod.

Lore took a bite of the jerky, hoping that eating would calm her nerves and make her forget that there were dead bodies near the camp. That there was a bandit tied up somewhere. That she'd just seen a creature stabbed through his heart.

It didn't work, but she knew what might.

"I called on the magic," she blurted into the silence, "but nothing happened. Last time I used it, it saturated my entire mind and body until it erupted out of me. Tonight, it was like there was *nothing* there. Like my body had never known magic. If you hadn't seen it yourself, I would almost think I had made it up."

Asher's brows knit together. "It appears you've a lot more to learn from your book before you can rely on it. My mother used to say that worthwhile things don't come easy."

Lore took a deep breath, kneading the stone Grey had given her with one hand and munching on the jerky with the other.

"I've figured out how to read it, sort of." She bit her lip, thinking about the different pages she'd seen by the light of the moon. "But when I open the book, different pages appear each time. I haven't managed to see the same page twice yet. And, well." She glanced to the wagon, making sure the door was still closed and that the merchants showed no signs of waking. With a lower voice, she said, "The book hasn't spoken to me again. Not since that night with the guards at Wyndlin Castle."

Asher sat across from her, having switched from cleaning his swords to sharpening them. "Maybe it requires more from you.

Maybe you're required to give more of yourself before it will help again. To be honest, I've never heard of a magical object 'speaking' before, though, so I have no idea."

The ring of the sharpening stone on the sword echoed through the camp. Asher kept his eyes trained on her.

"Usually, when something is infused with magic, it is to be wielded—like fire on a sword, or a protection or anti-theft charm, or even a spell meant to increase an object's resistance to breaking. When I encourage a flower to bloom, I impose my will on the flower and force it to bloom. I've never heard of a spell that could make an object have a will of its own."

Lore wanted to ask him more about his own magic, but this was the first time he'd ever brought it up. Something told her she needed to let him tell her about it at his own pace. Still thinking, she idly placed the rock back in the pocket of her trousers and curled a stray bit of hair around her finger.

"I thought that this book was rare, but I didn't realize it was 'one of a kind' rare. Wait—" She glanced toward where Asher had come back in from the woods. "Do you think they might not have been here to rob the merchants? What if they were after the book? After me?"

"The thought crossed my mind." Asher nodded with a grimace. "I'll go question him now. See what he has to say."

Lore avoided his gaze. They needed to know why he was there, but that didn't mean she wanted to see how Asher would make him talk. Her stomach knotted, and she felt sick.

But it wasn't fair to leave this up to just Asher, though. After all, she'd stolen the grimoire and gotten them into this mess.

Lore pushed up from the ground, clenching her jaw and steeling her stomach. She thought of Milo, Grey, Uncle, and Aunty. She needed to do this for them.

She followed Asher into the forest.

Their captive sat on the ground, hands tied behind his back, straining against another rope that secured him to a tree. His eyes were dulled from pain and his golden hair, matted with sweat, fell in front of his face.

"Why did you attack us?" Asher held the tip of one of his swords to the fae's throat.

The fae barred his canines before spitting rust-colored fluid on the ground. This close, Lore could see that he had scales on his cheeks and that his jaw was wider than the usual fae. She was reminded of the lizards that scuttled through the garden at the shelter.

Asher flicked his wrist, cutting a very shallow X into the fae's throat. Blood dripped from it instantly, landing on the fae's tunic. "Who sent you? Tell us and I'll let you live."

"Swear on it." His voice was a hiss, emphasizing the S sound in "swear."

Lore stepped forward. "We swear it. When we pack up camp, we will leave you here alive."

The male looked at Lore for the first time, eyes blazing with hatred. "I was sent for you, the human who stole from our kingdom. You don't deserve to set foot on our soil, let alone possess our sacred tomes."

Lore's stomach clenched. She wanted to throw up. The heat of shame burned behind her sternum and the sharp taste of hate coated her tongue. But she kept her face still, avoiding Asher's gaze. "What were you planning on doing with me once you captured me? What were your orders?"

The fae laughed, an oily, guttural sound that made Lore recoil. "Capture you? We were to kill you, as slowly and as painfully as we wanted. He told us we could take our time, as long as we had possession of the book."

"Who sent you?"

The fae leaned back against the tree, his breathing ragged and shallow. "I don't know. Truly, I don't. He came to me and didn't reveal his face or his name. Just handed over a heavy purse filled with coin and a story of a filthy human thief."

Asher stepped forward, raising his sword, but Lore stopped him.

"I know who it was. The chief steward from the castle, or his lord. The one who hired me." Lore's voice was a whisper. Was her life worth so little to them?

Asher looked at her sharply. "You knew the steward was after you?"

"No!" Lore touched his arm, turning him so he was looking at her. "I didn't, but it makes sense now. He told me if I found anything that appeared magical to give it straight to him, and nobody else. When I initially removed the book from the library, I didn't know it had magic, I swear, or I would have given it to him. Although it was weird how I found it, once I opened it and saw it was just a blank book, I figured it was normal. I had no reason to hide it or try to take it. Humans can't do magic, and this was just a blank book, I thought. But the day I found out what the book was, was the same day I found out what was happening at home." Lore bit her lip. "That night, I decided to leave, and I brought the grimoire with me."

"Okay, this is good. Now we know that they are after us for more than just you running away and me being a deserter. We can plan accordingly." He turned back to the fae. "Did you say you had a purse full of coin?" Asher's tone was cool, like shards of ice.

The fae gritted his teeth, then slumped, resigned. "It's in my boot." He shook his left boot a little, and they heard the muffled sound of coins clinking together.

Asher kneeled, keeping his sword trained at the fae's throat, just in case he tried anything. In one swift motion, he reached into the boot, withdrawing a leather pouch. He stood, tucking the pouch into his jacket pocket, and raised his sword again.

Lore blanched. "Asher, no—"

He slit the fae's throat with one more rapid movement.

She moved forward instinctively, needing to do *something*, but Asher grabbed her, turning her face away and pulling her close against his chest. She shuddered at the choking sounds coming from the dying fae.

"But we swore," she said into his chest. She fisted her hands into the thick, rough cloth of his tunic.

"No, *you* swore. I couldn't let him leave. He would have tracked us and been more prepared to attack us a second time. And next time, I might not be enough to save you. I couldn't allow him to live." Asher threaded his fingers through her hair, careful of her curls.

Lore closed her eyes, letting Asher's scent calm her—his familiar blackberry and cedarwood. The smell of his leathers. The slight tang of sweat. She listened to the sounds from the camp that drifted through the trees, noting the crackling fire and the horses kicking at the ground.

The assassin had gone silent, and relief flooded her body; the sounds of him choking on his lifeblood had been so like those of the guards back at the castle.

"I need to hide these bodies," Asher said. "It will be dawn soon and the merchants will be up."

"Oh, right." She opened her eyes and stepped back from Asher, instantly missing his warmth.

With a flick of his wrist, Asher cut the ropes that secured the fae to the tree. Kneeling, he touched the leaf of a low vine creeping along the forest floor, closed his eyes, and forced the vine to grow beneath his hands. The small vine thickened, curling, and wrapped around the fae's boots before creeping over the rest of him. More vines popped up from the ground, loosening the dirt, and the body began to sink into the earth.

As Asher used his magic, Lore swore she could feel it in the air—something like a slight buzzing, like that of a bee flying too close. Her nose filled with the scent of growing things.

Lore picked her way carefully through the woods and back to the campsite, feeling every bit of the winter's chill. It permeated her quilted tunic and settled into her bones, joined by the knowledge that those fae had intended to hurt her badly for nothing more than coin, and a false sense of superiority.

Yet she still had to choke back bile at the thought of their bodies just behind her in the trees, and at the gaping slit in the fae's throat.

When she got back to her pack, she crouched and retrieved the book again. She pushed all thoughts from her head but one.

"Show me something to ward the camp from anyone who wishes us harm," she called aloud, angling the book into the moonlight.

The book complied this time, and her fingertips tingled with the magic within it. A recipe appeared on the page, filled with detailed diagrams and drawings.

Lore gathered all that she needed: dirt from the campsite floor, a handful of pine needles, and a piece of her hair. She yanked the coiled strand from her scalp, stretching it between her fingers.

She chanted the words, a poem in a language she didn't know but could somehow read, tossing the pine needles into the flames first, followed by the sprinkles of dirt from their campsite floor, and finishing by dropping her hair into the fire last. The flames roared up, and the heat licked at her hand for a moment as the fire changed from orange to a pale lavender color.

She felt something within her—a connection extending from the grimoire to her chest and then casting out toward the fire. The connection pulled taut before splitting thousands of times into a web that sank into the ground all throughout the clearing.

It rushed out in front of her and beside her, running through the trees until it even enveloped Asher, who was kneeling on the ground with his forehead pressed to the earth in meditation.

She didn't know how she had this knowledge without being able to see him, but it came to her as an undeniable, certain feeling.

A tingle from the tips of her toes spread up to her hairline, and she knew the spell was done. She'd cast a spell.

Magic.

She'd done magic.

CHAPTER 14

As dawn spread its light through the trees, Lore and Asher sat by the fire. Lore added coffee to the pot of boiling water over the low flames. Frost blanketed the world around them, and Lore marveled at the beauty that was a forest awakening.

"Teach me to use a sword and dagger," she was saying. "I'm a quick study, I promise." Lore grinned into her cup of black coffee. She longed for a dollop of fresh cream—which she'd gotten used to at the castle—but she was still delighted by the fragrant nutty flavor of the coffee and the warmth of the ceramic mug between her hands.

Asher didn't grin back. In fact, he frowned into his tea. "You want me to teach you to use a sword? Lo, I'm no teacher. I've never had to teach anyone in my life, and I'm afraid I'll probably be too hard on you."

Lore's insides thrilled when he said "Lo."

She raised her chin, meeting his gaze. "So *be* hard on me. I'm not asking you to tutor me to dance. I want to be able to protect myself, so you don't have to. I never want to feel that helpless again. Ever."

Their gazes locked, his molten onyx to her rich brown. They

only broke their gaze when he removed his dagger from its hiding place in his boot.

"We will start with the dagger. Come on."

A few moments later, she stood with him, surrounded by trees and the morning songs of birds. The sunrays glinted off stray highlights in his wooly hair, showcasing reddish tones she hadn't noticed before.

Asher stood with his feet shoulder length apart, knees slightly bent, and the dagger between them pointed at her. Lore mimicked his stance, wishing she had a dagger of her own.

"You'll start with the dagger because you can hide it in your boots. Realistically, you'll probably be fighting with this more than a sword. Largely because if we start with the sword right now, you likely won't be able to lift anything tomorrow."

Lore blew a stray curl out of her eyes and nodded. She'd already been struggling with the heavy tomes in the library; she knew she had to work on her strength.

"Now, there are a few important things about the dagger. If an opponent gets too close and you aren't able to stick them with it, they might be able to wrestle it away and kill you with your own weapon. We want to avoid this, so I'm going to show you where to stab to drop someone instantly. Another thing—make sure you don't leave the dagger in them either. Once you've stabbed, you'll want to pull it back out. They'll bleed out faster that way *and* you won't be leaving your weapon behind."

Asher lowered his dagger, stepping close. He brushed his hand lightly on her throat, just above her collarbone. Her pulse quickened at the feather-light touch of his thumb. "Make sure to stab your assailant here."

Her mouth went very dry. She longed for the wild mint water that'd been infusing all night.

He brought his hand down to her sternum. "Or here."

Her heartbeat quickened.

His hand dropped to her lower hip, and he tightened his grip, rubbing a small circle with his thumb. "Here." He took a half step closer, sliding his hand to her back and pressing lightly. "Or here."

Lore bit her lip. *Stars, he smells good.* His usual blackberry and cedarwood scent had mixed with the smell of smoke from sleeping next to the fire.

Asher reached up and brushed that stubborn, stray curl away from her face, tucking it behind her ear. His hand lingered there for a moment before tracing his thumb lightly down her face, following the curve of her jaw. His eyes smoldered like banked coals as they dipped from her eyes down to her lips.

Gods, his touch ignited something inside her, that desire within him calling to her own. Her pulse quickened and her breath hitched. Would he close the distance between them?

Suddenly, he stepped back, the moment broken.

"Okay, show me what I just showed you."

Lore felt dizzy from his closeness, but she stepped forward, pointing to each spot on his body, all the while trying to control her breathing. She stepped back when she was done.

"Good. Now I'm going to give you the dagger and I'm going to show you the ideal way to grip it." Asher flipped the knife around with a fluid flick of his wrist. She grabbed the hilt, but he shook his head. "Put your thumb here and grip it like this, see? And when you think of your dagger, think of it like an extension of your own arm. When you thrust, put your entire body into it, not just your arms. Make sure to maintain your center of gravity. Watch."

He grabbed the blade back and mimicked a series of thrusts, jabs, blocks, and slices. The dagger really did look like an extension of his arm. When he was done, he handed the knife back to her.

She mimicked the grip he'd shown her, but the dagger didn't feel like an extension of her arm—it felt foreign and dangerous. The edge glinted in the sunlight when she mimicked his moves.

Stars. She felt silly and sent a silent prayer up that she didn't look as ridiculous as she felt.

To his credit, Asher didn't laugh. He pushed her arm down, bringing it toward him a little. "Not terrible, but here, see? Widen your stance." He nudged her left foot forward and tapped her arm lightly. "Be firm. Your arms are like soggy noodles." A pause as she adjusted. "That's better," he said.

Lore went through the motions again, this time tightening the muscles in her core and focusing on the technique. She did it again. And again.

After a few more repetitions, he produced a slim belt and poked a new hole in it before handing it to her. She secured it around her waist before they started working on her drawing the dagger. Then, he blindfolded her and had her draw her dagger using nothing but the muscle memory of where it lay against her hip.

They did this until she was sure she would be drawing the thing in her dreams at night.

By the time they had finished training, the sun was high enough in the sky that it was time to secure the horses to the wagons. The merchants were up, fed, and ready to head out when they returned to the campsite.

Lore was surprised when Asher told her to secure the dagger at her waist and carry it for the day. Its presence at her hip was both comforting and alarming.

How much she had changed.

CHAPTER 15

T hey reached the city at the base of the Canaan Mountains two days later. Once they passed the gates, Asher hoped they wouldn't have to worry about the king's guard any longer; this far south was Rywandall territory, and the people gave allegiance to Queen Riella and her consort.

The farewell with the merchants was brief, consisting of a quick exchange of some coins, well wishes to the little ones, and a swift departure. As they separated from the family, Lore nervously checked and rechecked the knot on her headscarf. She was sure a human had never been this far south, not ever, and if her presence was revealed, the news would surely make itself known to Wyndlin Castle and the chief steward.

Lore was filled with both trepidation and excitement.

The city itself was different from the last one. Here, the houses were built higher and farther apart. Many had decorative walls and tall iron gates that showed picturesque courtyards. Some even had fountains and ponds. The roads weren't built from packed earth, but instead with red brick placed so evenly she couldn't even imagine the skill of the stonemasons. Despite the smell of frost in the air and the puff of cloud that accompanied each of their breaths, flowers still grew in gardens and hung lusciously from windowsills and balconies.

Lore closed her eyes, breathing in. She couldn't smell any of the usual putrid aromas that came with people living in close quarters—no horse dung, rotting garbage, sweaty unwashed villagers, or chicken coops like back home. Instead, she just smelled an overpowering floral scent with undertones of the upcoming frost.

They wove through markets selling colorful spices, hand-carved toys for children, cooked meats, and freshly baked bread. Lore kept her eyes lowered, afraid to speak to any of the vendors for fear of them recognizing her for what she was.

Some stalls were loaded down with fruit: grapes so plump they looked like you would barely have to squeeze one between thumb and finger for it to burst and apples so big and shiny they reflected the lantern light. None of the fruits had a single bruise or wormhole in them.

Other stalls were filled with different types of dried sausages, some covered thickly in spices while others swam in sweet-smelling sauces.

Lore's mouth watered.

Asher stopped and purchased two pieces of meat on a stick. He handed one to her and kept the other for himself.

When she bit into it, she had to stifle her groan of pleasure. The meat was so tender, it practically fell off the stick. When she finished, she licked the sticky sweet and spicy sauce from her fingers and barely resisted the urge to lick the poker clean.

Lore walked past young light fae couples with linked arms and younglings shopping with their parents, begging for toys. She spied a young tree nymph perusing flowers, maybe to woo a lover or place on their kitchen table. Everyone walked so slowly, as if they didn't have a care in the world.

She'd never imagined anything like this place. Not even in her dreams had she imagined such idle decadence.

A few streets past the market, the houses began to change. They were no longer three or four stories tall; instead, they started to shrink. They now had fewer flowers, more weeds, and ill-looking shrubs. The pedestrians sped up or slowed to a crawl. There was a male dark fae asleep in the road, ass in the dirt, bottle in hand, snoring loudly.

Lore felt more at home here than in the wealthier district but, still, she put her hands on her dagger, thumb running over the smooth leather and the embroidered design.

The streets grew muddier, the buildings more decrepit.

Finally, Asher paused with a sigh. "We're here. I thought for a minute I wouldn't be able to find it. I haven't been here since—" A dark cloud overtook his face before he shook it off. "Well, it's been a long time."

They walked toward a tavern, but instead of going through the worn front door, Lore was surprised when he kept walking, headed toward the dark alley on the side. She followed him up a set of crooked stairs to a cramped landing. Cigar butts littered the patio, spilling out of a broken flowerpot in the corner.

Before Asher could knock, the most beautiful light fae Lore had ever laid eyes on threw the door open with a grin. She had none of the animalistic characteristics of the dark fae, despite her large eyes. Her cheekbones were high, sharpened by the light that fell on them. Black hair dripped down her back in beautiful spun locs. Her rich brown skin was done up with makeup and her eyelids were artfully painted with glittering oranges, pinks, and reds. Kohl lined the lids of her eyes, ending in a point sharper than Lore's dagger. Her gold dress was made from a fabric that was sewn with a thousand glittering stones—even her dainty shoes were painted with a shining pigmented gold. She looked like a walking sunset.

Lore had to pick her jaw up off the floor.

"Asher!" Despite her slight frame, the light fae picked him up in a bear hug.

Lore was surprised to see how defined her arms were. Muscles rippled with movement. Elegant and buff? This female was intimidating, but Lore couldn't help laughing at the sight of Asher being picked up by the small female.

Asher extracted himself from her grip, grinning with his dimples on full display. "Isla, is your father here?" His voice was filled with affection.

Isla shook her head. "He's working tonight and won't be home until after shutdown. Who is this tiny thing?" Isla's voice was breathless, somehow making her already stunning and mysterious self even more attractive.

The female peeked around Asher and looked at Lore with surprise. She peered at her curiously, tilted her head a little and blinked her doe eyes slowly.

Goddess, her eyes were the exact gold of her dress. Lore could hardly breathe. Isla was so beautiful. Lore looked down and away, scuffing her boot into the worn wood of the balcony, pushing stray cigar butts aside.

What was a creature like her doing amidst cigar butts and muddy streets?

"I'll introduce you later. Mind if we come in?" Asher asked.

"Of course! Come on in," Isla said, backing away from the door.

As they entered, it really hit her that they weren't in the castle anymore. The small apartment above the tavern was, well, lived in. Old scrolls were stacked to the ceiling in one corner. A broken lamp sat on a broken chair next to a sagging couch, and more junk littered the surrounding floor. Lore peered to the other side of the room. The kitchen was filled with mismatched dishes that had crusted food on them.

Alongside the junk, there were plants everywhere—hanging from the ceiling, filling the table, and on a row of shelves against the back wall.

"Oh, don't mind the mess. I'll be cleaning up soon!" Isla's voice had risen an octave, and she wrung her hands in embarrassment.

Lore fixed her expression; she was being so incredibly rude and judgmental, just like the fae had been when they'd walked into the apothecary. What gave her the right? She supposed she had always assumed everyone outside Duskmere lived in luxury. Her cheeks warmed at her naivety.

Isla continued, breathless words rushing out of her like a stream. "I only arrived about one bell ago—perfect timing, huh, Ash? My father has always been too busy to keep a tidy house. Not since my mom left, you know. That's where I come in! I show up every year or so and do a deep clean, but it always looks the same when I come back." She beamed at Asher while bouncing on the balls of her feet.

Lore had a feeling she wasn't still very often.

Asher was at ease here. He placed his hands in his pockets. "Quite serendipitous timing, then. I thought you were at the academy. Shouldn't courses be in session?"

"I'm taking the winter off." She didn't volunteer any more information, instead saying, "Why haven't we seen you in so long?" Before he could answer, Isla was already on to her next thought. "Who is she, Ash? You've never brought a girl before. Father isn't going to shut up about it." She turned to Lore again. "You're so small. It's adorable, honestly."

Lore couldn't hide her scowl. Sure, she was short—even by human standards—but she didn't think it needed to be pointed out by everyone she met.

"What's your name?" Isla asked.

"Lore."

Isla grabbed her hand, shaking it warmly. "What's your family name, Lore?"

"I . . . uh . . ." *Shit.*

"We've got to speak with your father, Isla," Asher butted in, stepping slightly in front of Lore and saving her from having to answer.

Isla narrowed her eyes but didn't press the matter. She clearly noted that Asher hadn't answered the question either.

Lore got the feeling Isla didn't miss much, but instead of prying, Isla just nodded and dropped the topic.

Lore sighed with relief. At least she would now have time to think up a cover story.

CHAPTER 16

The pub wasn't an improvement on the cramped apartment upstairs. Both places were obviously owned by the same person.

Small, mismatched tables were scattered about the sparsely inhabited bar. There wasn't a single matching chair—which might have made the place feel somewhat cozy and sweet—and every table shined with a sticky, oily sheen.

A tall fae male stood behind the bar, scowling as he worked. His long hair, locked like Isla's, was plaited into twin braids that fell down his back. They swayed behind him as he chopped fruit with expert speed. Instead of wearing a cloth tunic like everyone else in the bar, his was made of gleaming leather.

Lore examined the design that crawled up the front of his tunic, following it up to a high collar that was clasped with a shining, blood-red brooch. Even from across the room, she could see the angry set of his jaw, which did not distract from the simple fact that he was beautiful.

He was as beautiful as Isla and, she noticed, his eyes had a similar shape and his nose the same curve as Isla's.

Her brother, maybe?

Like Isla, Lore noticed that he didn't have any type of animal features, unless you counted the sheer predatory power radiating from him. He was, without a doubt, the most striking fae male she'd ever seen, though in the same way a wolf was striking—absolutely beautiful to look at but able to rip your throat out on a whim.

His dark eyes lit with recognition when he spied Asher, but he didn't smile in greeting. His scowl and the furrow between his perfectly shaped eyebrows seemed only to deepen.

Isla glanced back and laughed when she saw Lore's alarmed face. "Don't mind my twin, hun. That's just his face."

Lore scooted behind Asher and farther from the male. How could someone that predatory have shared a womb with the walking sunshine that was Isla?

Lore glanced toward Asher and wasn't surprised to see that Isla's brother's cold reception hadn't bothered him. They continued past the bar to a small door at the back, which was likely where their father worked.

The door opened into a closet-size office that held a small desk covered in towering paperwork surrounded by barrels filled with spirits.

Lore had time for a momentary glance at an older, scruffier version of the angry male from the bar when Asher leaned close and said, "Why don't you get a drink? I'll discuss business."

He went into the office, closing the door behind him, leaving Lore standing outside with an equally startled Isla.

"Well, that was rude." Lore hadn't meant to say it out loud, but, oh well. It was true.

Isla laughed, looking at her with a mischievous gleam in her eye. "Asher has always been private."

"Has he?" Lore frowned. She'd gotten the impression that Asher and Isla had been very close, and that Isla seemed to know him very well.

"Come on. We can go meet my brother. I'm sure he'll love

you," Isla said through a laugh that seemed to imply to Lore that her brother was, in fact, not going to love her.

Lore followed the glittering woman, slightly mesmerized by how her inky black locs gleamed with threads of gold and artfully carved wooden beads.

Isla sat on a stool at the bar and Lore plopped herself on one between Isla and a wood nymph. The nymph's hair sprouted from her head in plant-like ropes, each one studded with beads carved from bone. The nymph didn't return Lore's smile, and she tried not to shrink at the dismissal.

Isla snagged her attention by shouting, "Hey, asshole! I'll have a lavender and sage tonic. My new friend will have . . ." She glanced to Lore, waiting for her preferred drink.

"The same." Lore tried to appear like she ordered drinks all the time.

Back home, there had been only one tavern. Men and women alike had gone to the tavern to relax after working in their shops, the fields, or the quarry. They took comfort in their solidarity and joy in one another's company.

It was this feeling, not the ale that tasted more like dirty river water, that had brought her to the tavern with Grey or Uncle Salim now and again. The memories of her townsfolk's increasing joyousness as they drank and laughed formed a knot in her throat. She pushed those thoughts deep down.

She wouldn't—couldn't—think of Duskmere right now.

"Why don't you come back here and make it yourself?" Isla's brother said. "I didn't even want to come back to this forsaken town and yet, somehow, I'm the one working the bar."

The male's voice came out as a deep purr that made Lore think of an ice-cold river, one that would pull you under to its darkest depths if you dared dip a toe in. It stood in sharp contrast to his sister's voice, which was that of a babbling brook.

"Hush, just gimme these two drinks and then I'll be heading

upstairs to tackle Father's kitchen. Unless you want to switch?" She raised an eyebrow.

Isla's brother was tellingly silent.

"Now, Lore, don't expect these drinks to be any good with him behind the bar. But they *will* be *strong*. Oh, and I forgot to introduce you two! This"—she gestured toward Lore with both hands—"is Lore. She's a friend of our dear Asher! Lore, this is—"

"I don't care to meet anyone who came with *him*." Isla's brother continued to busy himself behind the bar, pointedly not looking at Lore.

"Well, if you don't wish to be introduced, I'll just have to guess your name," Lore said, fed up with being dismissed. "Twins, hmm? What goes along with Isla? Cape? Peninsula?"

Isla's brother glared at her, and she had to resist the urge to shrink under the weight of his gaze. To lower her eyes and cower. His gaze was colossal and cruel. He didn't have to bare his teeth at her. His gaze alone seemed deadly enough.

"My name is Finndryl Theaon Hwraeth. I am named after my great grandfather, the *savior* of Freya Isle. I'm sure you've heard of him."

Lore hadn't. Of course, she hadn't. If they knew where she was from, they would understand that. "I have not." Lore steepled her hands in front of her, returning his glare. She noted Isla's curious expression when she denied knowing of their grandfather.

"Are you denying this just to—" Finndryl started in on her, apparently deciding instantly that she was a liar.

"It's a long, tragic tale anyway—" Isla butted in.

His eyes flicked to Isla. "Isla, your cavalier—"

"—that isn't one to tell over drinks, Finn. You can bore her with how our family name was unjustly tarnished some other time."

Finndryl sneered, sharp canines glistening even in the low lamplight of the bar. He dropped the glass he was holding into the sink, where it shattered, before walking away to angrily clean the bit of counter farthest from them.

Isla stood and hopped up onto the counter.

"Don't mind my brother, Lore. He's just angry that I convinced him to travel all the way up here. He's all bark and no bite, truly. I'll make our drinks and at least"—she raised her voice—"now they will actually taste good."

Finn didn't look up from his self-imposed task.

A moment later, Lore was clutching a fizzing, light-purple drink. She took a small sip through the wooden straw and struggled to keep herself from falling off the stool.

It wasn't like anything she'd ever had before. It tasted exactly how lavender smelled in spring after a long winter without flowers, when the sun was warm, but the breeze was cool, and you could cry from contentment.

It was like that, but somehow *better*.

Lore smiled, allowing herself to enjoy this moment of contentedness, right before pulling another large sip through the straw.

)) ● (((

By the time Asher finished the meeting with the twins' father, Lore was on her third lavender and sage tonic, and Isla was on her fifth.

Her head felt light, her thoughts flitted about like butterflies, and she was having a hard time catching them. When Asher appeared, she realized any hint of annoyance she'd felt toward him for shutting her out of the office had dissipated. Now, all she wanted was to shut him in a dark room with her and make sure that they had absolutely no clothes between them.

Why hadn't they kissed since that day at the inn? It had seemed like pretending it had never happened was the right thing to do, but now she couldn't think of a single good reason not to carry on where they'd last let off.

She opened her mouth to tell him this, but hiccupped instead. She and Isla fell into a fit of giggles.

Asher narrowed his eyes, picked up her half-empty drink, and sniffed. "Are you drunk?"

"No!" She swatted his arm. Then she and Isla started giggling again. She hopped off the stool and immediately stumbled, so she fell against Asher's chest. She couldn't stop herself from nuzzling into him and giving his firm chest a light pet. She loved his blackberry smell.

She wanted to eat him up.

"Ash, why—" *Hiccup.* "—haven't you—" *Hiccup.*

Before she could finish her question, the world had started to spin.

Asher stepped back, keeping his hands on her shoulders. He bent to her level and lifted her chin up a bit. "Come on. Let's get you upstairs. Gryph said we can stay here as long as we need."

"Who is—" *Hiccup.* "—Gryph?"

"My father. Come on, Lore!" Isla exclaimed.

Suddenly, Asher's warm hands weren't on her shoulders and she was being whisked away, pulled outside the tavern behind a glittering Isla. The wind blew against Lore's hot cheeks, and though she knew it was probably blistering cold, she couldn't feel it.

"Isla, wait! I don't remember there being so many stairs!"

Isla laughed again, doubling back to take Lore's hand to pull her up the stairs.

Once inside the apartment, Isla went to the kitchen. Lore thought she might've been going in there to start on the dishes as she'd promised her brother, but, instead, Isla danced back out of the kitchen holding three glasses and a bottle of what looked like whiskey.

Lore plopped onto the couch in the hopes that the world would stop spinning if she was seated.

"Isla, haven't you had enough?" Asher asked, lowering himself next to Lore.

She hadn't realized he'd slipped in behind them.

"C'mon, Asher! We haven't drunk together since we went camping in the Wilds." Isla swirled the glass a little.

The warm amber liquid *did* look extra yummy in the lamplight.

Lore raised an eyebrow. Asher had sounded so disapproving, but he still reached out for the glass.

"Yeah, and I seem to remember a certain someone being dared to walk on coals and actually doing it."

Isla didn't seem to have it in her to look embarrassed. "You're just pissy because you didn't have the balls, and I did."

Asher laughed then, a full and carefree sound. Lore's core clenched at the sound of it.

"Isla, if you remember correctly, I was dared to walk on my hands across the coals and I did, right before doing—"

"A backflip!" Isla finished. "I forgot you were deranged, Asher." Through a fit of giggles, Isla handed Lore a glass half-filled with the amber liquid she'd grabbed from the kitchen.

Lore had had whiskey before, though it had been made by humans for humans. She raised the glass to her nose and gave it a sniff before immediately pulling the glass away. Her eyes watered from the strength of the alcohol but she wasn't about to be rude and turn her nose up at Isla's offer.

Just as she was raising the glass back to her lips, Asher lightly put a hand on hers. "This whiskey probably won't be like the whiskey you're used to."

Lore noticed Isla's eyes narrow at this, probably wondering what kind of whiskey she would be familiar with if not this whiskey. Asher wouldn't have brought them here if he didn't trust

Isla and her family, right? And Lore wasn't sure when it had happened but, she trusted Asher inherently.

And she wanted to trust Isla, too.

Lore set the glass down, not wanting to know what would happen if she drank the liquor. She removed the scarf that had been holding back her wild curls and hiding her very human ears, fluffed her curls out, and then wrangled them into a sorry excuse of a bun on top of her head.

Isla stilled, staring at Lore's rounded ears. "You're the one they're looking for. The human who deigned to leave their village. The one the northern king will pay to get back."

The carefree mood from a moment ago filled with tension.

Lore didn't say anything. What was there to say? Still, she couldn't leave it like that.

She opened her mouth to respond, but just then, the door opened, letting in a rush of winter air, heavy with the promise of snow. Finndryl walked in, setting down a bag on an end table, and stilled, probably feeling all their eyes on him.

Lore didn't move. It was one thing to put her faith in Isla—the kind fae who had treated her as a friend from the moment they met—but Finndryl was another story.

His eyes grazed over Lore, snagging a moment on her ears, but the aloof fae didn't say anything. Instead, he moved farther in and headed down the hallway.

"Don't worry," Isla said into the silence. "Finn would never turn anyone in. He hates the Alytherians as much as you probably do. All he wanted was to join the guard along with Asher, but they wouldn't let him. We're half–light fae and half–dark fae, and although he takes after our dark fae side, they still wouldn't let a halfling into the army." Lore nodded, apprehensive. The appearance of Isla's brother had shifted the mood further and Lore sobered up, the haze of drink clearing. Lore may have been far from home, but her thoughts needn't be. If there was one thing

Asher had helped her to learn over the last few days, it was that she couldn't do this on her own. And maybe she didn't have to.

She might as well try to glean information from those around her who were willing to share what they knew. Reaching over to her backpack, she pulled out her book. "Asher, open the curtains."

He leaned back, stretching his long arms to the window, and pulled one frayed curtain aside. Lore eyed the delicious bit of skin that appeared where his shirt rode up, distracted by how his lower abs rippled in the low light.

Focus, she told herself. She scooted over an inch, twisting so the closed grimoire sat in the moonlight. She ran her fingers lightly over the stitched moons, lingering on the waxing crescent, which was her favorite. Then she lightly brushed her fingertips over the flowers and vines that surrounded the moons.

Whoever had designed this book had seemed to make it just for her, because she could gaze upon it for hours and never grow tired of its beauty.

"Okay, Isla. I'm going to show you something, something I don't even understand myself." Lore flipped the book open. At first the pages were blank, like always, until the moonlight illuminated the aged pages and ink bled into existence.

Lore flipped through the pages, showing Isla glimpses of recipes and diagrams as she told her the story of how she'd come to be in possession of the grimoire.

))◐((

When her story led to the present, Lore lowered the book onto the woven rug beneath her.

Isla reached out a hand, gold-painted nails gleaming in the flickering lamplight, and squeezed Lore's hand. "Thank you for sharing your truth with me, Lore. I guess I didn't have any idea what your people have gone through. I'm embarrassed to say this, but I'd never actually thought about it. Humans just seemed like an interesting anecdote in Raelysh's long history. I never gave your kind much thought."

Lore already knew this, but the burning anger that normally accompanied this realization didn't blaze into life at Isla's words.

"I honestly didn't realize that you all couldn't leave—what was your town called again? Duskmere?" At Lore's nod, she squeezed Lore's hand again. Isla wasn't afraid to show affection, that was for sure; she appeared to grant her love freely and openly.

Lore envied her that. She was always second-guessing herself.

"I just want to apologize again, that I didn't realize," Isla continued. "I thought Duskmere must have been a paradise, and that's why you didn't leave. I didn't realize it was basically a prison. I'm determined to help however I can. Finndryl will, too—he just doesn't know it yet!"

Lore muttered an awkward "Thank you." She didn't know how to handle Isla's intense look of pity or Asher's searching gaze, knowing how upset she got when she thought of Duskmere and her people's circumstances.

Out of the corner of her eye, she noticed the grimoire had started to fill with ink. A picture appeared, one of hands reaching up, detached from a body. But then she realized each hand was different—the first drawing showed the whole hand and wrist, the next drawing was just the hand, as if something invisible had swallowed up the wrist, and the last drawing was just fingertips.

Beneath it was a script she couldn't quite read. She pulled her hand from Isla's, picked up the book, and brought it closer to her face, squinting to try to see the messy scrawl better. She had the oddest feeling, as if she could almost read the words. It was similar to the feeling when she knew a word but couldn't remember it at that exact moment, when it was on the tip of her tongue.

Was this a more powerful spell than the protection one she had cast over the campsite? Was that why there was so much more script and vague diagrams?

"Can you read this?" She showed the pages to Asher and Isla.

They both shook their heads. Asher took a swig of his whiskey before answering, his Adam's apple bobbing.

How is he attractive even when swallowing a drink?

"I can see what looks like a disappearing hand, I guess? But the words don't mean anything to me. It might be Old Alytherian?" Asher said. "I think I recognize the characters, but I never learned how to read it. I don't know anyone who can."

"Can I call my brother to come look? He reads a lot, so he might know!"

"Okay. But let's just see if he can read it. He doesn't need to know the story behind the book. If that's okay?"

Lore didn't feel comfortable telling Finndryl her life story just yet; she still felt raw from exposing so much of herself to Isla. Being so honest felt like she'd been burned, and her skin was new and extra sensitive. Not to mention, Finndryl hadn't exactly been welcoming. She couldn't imagine he would share Isla's compassionate response.

Lore reached into her pocket, pulled out Grey's stone, and kneaded it with her thumb.

Isla threw her head back and yelled for her brother. All three peered down the dim hallway just as Finndryl shouted back a loud "No!"

Isla threw up her hands. "He is the worst! Lore, never have a twin."

"Chances are slim I will ever acquire a twin," she said.

"Good point. Let me go get this grump."

Isla grabbed the bottle of whiskey before stomping down the hallway, possibly to go smack her brother with it, or else to pour it on his head and light him on fire.

"Should we intervene and possibly save Finndryl?" Lore asked Asher, a smile dancing on her lips.

His eyes glittered in the low light, and he smiled before downing the last of the whiskey in his glass. "Eh, he'll survive. He's faced far worse at the hands of Isla—this is small potatoes."

"She's quite the character, isn't she?" Lore asked.

"That's an understatement. Everything Isla does, she does it with her entire being, whether it's attempting to cook—and I do mean attempting—or being your friend. It makes her fiercely loyal. She's one of the best people you could ever have on your side."

Lore nodded. She felt like she could tell that, even just from the last few hours she'd spent with Isla. It felt like she'd known the fae for years, and Lore wasn't used to connecting with someone so quickly. Everyone she'd ever known up until the last few months she *had* known for years. She had never felt such an instantaneous connection with anyone.

Lore met Asher's gaze as he sprawled on the couch. He seemed utterly at ease in his friend's home. His brown cheeks were rosy from the whiskey, and she was certain it was the first time she'd ever seen him flushed, even when they'd been out in the cold.

It was utterly endearing.

His eyes dropped to her lips for just a moment. Lore squirmed, pressing her thighs together against the ache building between them.

Could she bite his pouty bottom lip before Isla and Finndryl came back?

Lore might feel comfortable around Isla, but she didn't feel confident enough to do what she wanted—which was to climb into Asher's lap and wrap her arms around his neck, pull him to her, and taste the whiskey on his tongue.

His eyes, which had momentarily turned to her, dropped back to her lips, and he smirked. When his dimple appeared, that was it. Who cared if anyone saw them? She wanted him.

And Lore was tired of not getting what she wanted.

Just as Lore leaned forward, someone cleared their throat. Loudly.

Isla might not have had it in her to look embarrassed—in fact, she looked more amused than anything—but Lore did. She felt her face warm and knew her cheeks would be a darker shade of brown than usual and that her freckles would stand out a little less.

"Oh, Finn! You're here!" Lore exclaimed, her voice awkwardly high. He was glowering at the floor next to Isla, who was wiggling her eyebrows lasciviously. "We, um, just wanted to see if you could read this," Lore said.

Lore shoved the open book toward Finn, willing to do anything to distract everyone in the room from the very heated look she'd just shared with Asher.

"Finndryl," Finndryl said, his voice deep, low, and underscored with a warning.

Lore frowned; gaze drawn back to Asher. His eyes were molten lava in the flickering lamplight. His bottom lip looked so *soft*. "What's that, Finn?" she asked.

"My name is Finndryl. Only my friends call me Finn." He grabbed the book from her outstretched hands.

Lore finally ripped her gaze from Asher. "Oh, right. Sorry, Finndryl." Now her cheeks burned for a different reason.

He was so rude, even as he started studying the tome.

Lore glanced at Isla as she sat. The light fae rolled her eyes at her twin and took a swig straight from the whiskey bottle. When she saw Lore looking at her, she mouthed, "Sorry. He's an ass."

Lore grinned, feeling a little better knowing she wasn't the only one who thought so.

After a moment, Finndryl sat next to Isla, stretching his long legs out before him, and placed the book carefully on the floor in front of Lore. The four of them now formed a little circle, with the half-empty whiskey bottle and book in the middle.

"Well, Isla woke me up for nothing. I can't read this, though I recognize some of the characters. They're related to Old Alytherian, but my guess is they predate it. Some of the words are quite similar to what I was taught at school, but I'd only be hazarding a guess if I tried to translate it. I don't know what your book is trying to tell you."

"Really?" Isla asked, surprise dragging out the word.

"Yes. Really."

Damn. Disappointment coated Lore's tongue. "All right. Thank you anyway."

"What is that in your hand?" Finn asked suddenly, his voice sharp.

For a moment, Lore wasn't sure what he was referring to, but then she felt the smooth stone between her thumb and finger. She'd forgotten she was holding it. "Oh, this? It was a gift from an old friend. I guess it's become kind of a comfort to me. I always have it on me."

"I think that's an Adder Stone. They're extremely rare now, and very valuable."

"Really?" Lore held up her stone, glancing at each of them through the hole. She noticed something odd—there was a green light shimmering around the door behind Finn. She tilted the stone and noticed the windows had the same green glow.

"What do you see?" Finndryl's irritated expression had shifted into, well, not excitement, but perhaps mild interest bordering on curiosity.

"I see a greenish light around your door and windows."

Isla let out a squeal of delight, startling them all. "They're real, then! Those would be our protection spells! My father paid a lot for those. For someone who owns a pub, which is an inherently social place, he really doesn't like or trust people. The traveler he paid seemed untrustworthy, and I never understood why my father trusted him." She bounced in her seat. "What do you see when you look at your book?"

Lore angled the stone until its hole faced the pages of the book. She held her breath as she looked through, focusing on the strange characters. Excitement thrummed through her. If the Adder Stone showed her the spells in the house, could it translate her book, too?

After a brief moment, Lore's shoulders fell in disappointment. "Still the same characters. I can't read them."

She wanted so badly for Grey's gift to be the answer to all her problems. It would have made understanding what she was dealing with so much easier. It was still helpful though, if it could show her spells, and she would need to always keep it on her. It was just like Grey to give her something that could help her, even when he couldn't be there himself.

She placed the stone back into her tunic pocket and reached for the whiskey bottle instead, despite Asher's raised brow.

She didn't care, though. If she couldn't read the book tonight, she might as well drink to drown her disappointment.

CHAPTER 17

The sun burned red through Lore's eyelids, and she turned her face away, pressing into the sheets.

She groaned. Her sheets protested, pulling against her.

Lore leaned back, opening one eye, and immediately scooted backward into the couch cushions. Those hadn't been sheets—she had been snuggling into the back of an incredibly gorgeous fae, one who was in nothing but a slip.

Lore pushed up from where she was lying sandwiched between the couch cushions and Isla, looking around the living room. Asher was sprawled on the floor beside the sofa, head on a book, arm thrown over his eyes, and breathing evenly in his sleep.

She looked up and noted that Finndryl wasn't asleep. Instead, he was sitting at the kitchen table, pouring tea and reading a book. He didn't even glance toward her, though he must have known she was awake from her clumsy movements.

Lore raised an eyebrow. Nobody needed that much concentration when pouring tea. *He's still being an ass, then.*

Lore climbed over Isla, trying not to wake her. She swayed on her feet a little and winced at the dull thudding behind her eyes. She was relieved that she was still in her clothes from the day before and not in her underthings like Isla.

Come to think of it, why *was* she snuggled up with Isla and not Asher? She'd had every intention of kissing him into oblivion last night.

Lore frowned. She actually didn't remember anything past her third swig of the bottle, after Finndryl had made a snarky comment to Asher about . . . something. She couldn't quite remember what. Finndryl had then gone back to his room, anger radiating from him like a dark cloud.

Asher had brushed it off with a shrug and an amused glint in his eye.

Lore squinted at the wall, as if it would tell her the events of the previous night. Well, she couldn't remember, but she thought they had played a drinking game? She vaguely recalled relishing the burn of the whiskey every time she missed the cup with the coin.

She must have fallen asleep on the couch at some point.

Where was the washroom?

She opened her mouth to ask Finndryl, but before she did, he pointed down the hallway behind him, still not looking up from his book. Lore nodded in silent thanks—she didn't think she could form coherent words at the moment. She began picking her way over the empty bottle of whiskey, glasses, and the still sleeping Asher on the floor.

When she returned from the washroom, feeling mostly refreshed, she passed a sleepy-looking Gryph. At last, she got a look at Isla and Finndryl's father. The dark fae was tall and strong, with arms like tree trunks and hands so large she figured he could crush his enemies' skulls one-handed if that was something he was into. He *did* look like casual skull-crushing might have been a hobby in his youth.

Gryph turned, revealing his wild, unkempt beard, and his even-wilder-than-Lore's curly hair, which had strands of silver that gleamed in the gray light filtering through the window. Despite his threatening size, she noticed laugh lines surrounding his eyes and that his mouth was already set into a grin.

He looked intimidating, but he radiated warmth.

"I've been wanting to meet a human for so long. Though I have to say, I didn't realize your kind was so small when you are full grown."

Lore couldn't help but laugh. "Most aren't. I'm definitely on the small side for a human."

He eyed her up and down again. "You look like you require breakfast. I was planning on heading down to the Exile to whip up some food before I open for the day. I'll feed you."

"The Exile?"

"Come on. I'll show you." He raised his voice, clearly not caring that Isla and Asher were still asleep just behind him. "And Finn, you come, too! It's almost time for your shift!"

Lore hid her smirk when she noticed Finndryl's perpetual frown deepen. He grabbed a leaf to mark his place in his book before standing up and sliding his boots on. Lore, too, donned her boots and scarf, wrapping the latter tightly over her ears, and followed Gryph's massive frame out the door.

Once outside, she stopped to look around. When they had arrived last night, it had been dark, with no lanterns to light the street. But now, in the gray light of morning, she could see that their stairs led down to a small stone and dirt courtyard with a single tree in the middle that reached up toward the sky. Narrow alleyways branched out in different directions, all lined by apartments.

Gryph's dwelling was also on an alley, with another two-story building beside it and more across the way. The buildings were made from stone, and some looked worse for wear, showing off stone that was covered in moss or that had chipped away. The roofs sagged with age, many of them missing shingles. Smoke rose from chimneys as people warmed up their breakfast or morning tea inside their homes, and below in the courtyard, children played under the watchful eyes of their parents. Snippets of conversation carried on the wind in languages Lore had never heard before.

Here, there weren't just dark fae. There was a small boy, wrestling a tree nymph child by the tree. The boy was careful of his two small tusks; even from a distance Lore could see that they ended in two sharp points. An orc child, she thought. She'd read about them in the library.

Old men sat on their sagging wooden balconies smoking pipes and playing board games.

Lore felt a sharp pang of nostalgia for home. This wasn't like Wyndlin Castle, where the servants stayed out of sight in dark corridors, while the royalty lived like . . . well royalty, in abundant extravagance.

Behind the row of dwellings was a steep drop-off into a forest. This early, and on such an overcast day, Lore couldn't see far into it at all—thick tendrils of fog curled between the trees, blanketing the edge of the hill and reaching toward the balcony Lore leaned against. Most would probably be wary of the dark forest, but she felt that the forest was somehow calling to her.

Perhaps the lonely forest recognized the lonely ache that permeated her core.

She tucked the longing for home away, burying the ache, and followed Gryph and Finndryl down the narrow stairs.

The Exile was, apparently, the pub below their residence, the one that Gryph owned. Its true name, which was carved into a wooden sign above a simple image of a dragon in flight, was the Dragon's Exile.

Lore avoided walking directly beneath the sign; it was hanging crookedly by a single hook that did not look secure. That was an accident waiting to happen.

Gryph pulled a set of keys from his inner coat pocket but didn't try to unlock the pub quite yet, as someone had fallen asleep on the stairs, blocking the door. Gryph nudged him with his boot. "Aye, Flix. Wake up. I told ye you can't be sleeping out here. I don't run an inn."

Flix opened bloodshot eyes and smiled at Gryph. He was missing more than a few teeth and Lore could smell him from where she stood a few paces behind Finndryl, who didn't appear to be surprised by this exchange.

"Gryph, good morning! I, uh, didn't sleep here. I just came early."

"Riiight." Gryph drew out the word, emphasizing his disbelief. "You need to go home to your children, Flix. Wash up and then come back. I'll be open all day, just like I always am."

Flix stood slowly, then stepped out of the way. Lore spied his dirt-stained, wrinkled hands and how they shook with small tremors.

"You're right, you're right," Flix said. "Jus' gonna have one drink and then I'll head home. Great idea." His words petered off in unintelligible mumbling.

Gryph shook his head but didn't bar him from entering behind him.

Lore had a feeling this was a conversation they had had plenty of times, and Gryph hadn't really expected it to go any other way. Lore didn't know the dark fae's—Flix's—story, but there were a few like that back at home. They drank way too much and neglected their partners and children, driven by the same haunted look that lurked in Flix's eyes.

The pub was dark, as the sky, thick with clouds, barely let in any light. Lore thought she smelled rain lingering in the air, refreshing the stale scent it had held the night before. Gryph went straight to the bar and grabbed a box of long matches to light the candles in the wall sconces.

Flix grabbed a seat at the bar, placing his head in his hands as he waited for one of them to pour him a drink and ease his hangover. Finndryl disappeared through a door at the end of the bar that Lore hadn't noticed the night before.

She hoped it was a kitchen. Her stomach growled and unlike Flix, what Lore needed to ease her hangover was food and lots of it. She followed Finndryl through the door.

Her hunch proved correct, and she entered a large kitchen. A huge brick oven stood in the center of the room, with brick arches on all four sides. In the center of the oven was a massive iron pot suspended from the ceiling above a bed of coal. Beside the oven stood a long wooden table, perfect for preparing food. On the table was an old, well-loved cutting board, a pan for frying, and an iron kettle.

Behind the table was a small bundle of firewood. Along one wall hung cooking knives, more pans, a few dried herbs, and a small piece of dried meat. On the table beneath the herbs was a small, half-eaten wheel of cheese and some dried potatoes with buds growing out of them. The wall farthest away from Lore was lined with more barrels of spirits—some large, some small. High up near the ceiling, long narrow windows let light in, and Lore could see dust dancing in the rays.

She immediately decided she loved this room. It reminded her of home and of Eshe cooking for the children.

Finndryl grabbed a few logs and some smaller sticks. He set them onto the coals of the banked fire before cranking a lever built into one of the brick arches around the cookstove. His muscles strained against the sleeves of his tunic. The giant cook pot rose toward the ceiling and, once it was high enough, he struck a match, coaxing the flames to ignite the fresh logs.

Lore grabbed a kettle from the table, checked it was clean, and walked over to the water tap to fill it. Tea would do all of them good, and even from the doorway, she could tell some of the herbs hanging up were dandelion leaves, which were perfect for tea. She rummaged through the small apothecary chest sitting on the table and found a few dried lavender buds and a small honeycomb wrapped in cloth.

It wasn't coffee, but tea was better than nothing. She stirred the leaves and herbs into the kettle and placed the large pot onto the coals.

Finn had disappeared without a word. Lore peeked out of the door toward the bar where Gryph was sitting, sharing some mead with Flix. Apparently, Gryph's invitation to breakfast hadn't actually meant that he would be cooking it anytime soon.

Just fine. Lore washed her hands, along with one of the knives from the wall, and started chopping the small potatoes, removing the buds and any dark spots as she went. She'd cooked most evenings back at home. She wondered how the little ones were doing as she moved onto an onion. Especially Milo—he was going to be so big when she saw him next.

She pushed that thought away as she scooped the chopped potatoes and onion into a pan. She didn't know when she was going to see any of them next; she wasn't even sure exactly how long she'd been away already. She opened drawers looking for oil, salt, and rosemary, but found none. This meal wouldn't be her best, but it would fill them up and hopefully soak up some of the spirits.

Nausea boiled up in her throat and she paused to let it pass. She was never drinking again.

She set the pan over the coals and sautéed the potatoes and onions, wishing she had oil when they kept sticking to the pan. She sipped her tea, wishing it were coffee, before adding a little water and covering the pan with a lid.

She sipped the tea again before making a face and setting it on the nearby table. There wasn't anything with which to create a makeshift strainer, so there were quite a few dandelion leaves floating around the chipped clay mug.

She set to grating the little bit of cheese she found. The innate saltiness in the cheese would help, but this meal was going to be bland. She pulled the pan over to a corner without flame and covered the potatoes with cheese. They looked a little burned, but she hadn't had a lot to work with.

Just as she was wiping her hands on an apron she'd found, Finndryl walked in, long legs carrying him to the oven in a few strides. "What are you burning in here?" He sniffed, nose scrunching up.

Rude. "I'm cooking breakfast. If this place had a decent supply of oil and food, it wouldn't have burned at all."

Finndryl didn't reply. Apparently, the few words he had said to her were already too many.

Well, if he didn't want to eat her food, she wasn't going to make him. She grabbed three plates from a cupboard and piled them high with potatoes and onions. She wished again she had a few eggs she could have fried to place on top. And a chili or five for some spice, but this would have to do. She and Asher wouldn't be here for long—soon she would be back home anyway, and then she wouldn't have to think about this place.

Lore balanced all three plates with ease. Growing up in the shelter, she was used to carrying as many as possible out to the table, what with there being so many mouths to feed. She pushed the door open with her hip. Gryph grinned from ear to ear when she placed it in front of him, not batting an eye at the few burned potatoes on his plate, and thanked her with a simple "Thanks, love."

"Thank you so much, miss. I was mighty hungry." Flix now had a big grin on his face, too. He was apparently in better spirits now that he'd had the hair of the dog and was working on his second ale.

"Good. I'm glad to hear it. Eat every bite, okay?" She frowned a bit. Hopefully, his children at home had plenty of food.

Lore walked over to an empty table so she could eat. She drowned out Gryph's and Flix's chatter as she spooned potatoes into her mouth. While Asher's idea to travel south and play for time was a good one, she really needed to figure out how she was going to get back to Duskmere without being captured. Every minute spent away from home was another minute her people went without knowing that they were in danger.

She should have brought the grimoire down; she needed to spend these few days of safety figuring out how it worked and how to use it. The more access to magic the book had, the better her chances of getting home and telling everyone the truth— that the danger in the woods was a spell, and that, with the help of the book, they could end the control the Alytherians held over them.

She scarfed down the rest of her food. She would do the dishes, then come out here and wipe these tables. After all, she owed Gryph for his kindness. He was technically harboring a thief and a runaway soldier. She owed him and the twins for giving her and Asher a place to lay low and get their bearings.

She couldn't pay them with coin, so she might as well do something for the family by leaving the tavern cleaner than when she'd arrived. And she wouldn't let herself get distracted by any more drinking, games, or Asher's dimples and pouty bottom lip.

She had a mission that was already taking too damn long.

By the time Lore had washed the dishes, scrubbed every table in the pub, and mopped the floors, her back ached, her hands were raw, and her fingers had pruned. She stood back with her hands on her hips and surveyed her work.

Every surface in the pub gleamed.

Lore wrung the rags out and hung them up to dry above the sink, returning the old mop and bucket to the small closet in the kitchen, while making sure to avoid the spiders and their thick cobwebs that lined the space.

As she walked up the steps toward the main room, she made a mental note to mention the state of the pub to Finndryl if he said anything else about her cooking. As if she'd summoned him, she found him standing behind the bar, leaning against the shelf that held the bottles of spirits, with his arms crossed and a scowl on his face.

She was pretty sure he was annoyed that she had given his portion of the potatoes to Flix, but at least Flix had been grateful to have them.

Lore averted her eyes from the scowling fae. She needed to bathe and change into fresh clothes. Isla was way taller than her, but Lore would worship at her feet if she had clean clothes Lore could wear.

"Wait, before you head out, Gryph wanted me to give this to you. For all this." Finndryl spoke to her for the first time since he'd insulted her cooking that morning, gesturing with his long fingers toward the sparkling tables.

Lore couldn't help but notice that he called his father by his first name, as if he were holding him at arm's length. And she recalled him saying to Isla yesterday that he hadn't even wanted to come home.

In a blink, Finndryl skirted the bar to stand in front of her. The black pants he wore fit him like a glove, outlining his strong thighs perfectly. He was *fast*.

And close. Close enough that she could now see how long his lashes were. His dark eyes were haunted and deep, like swirling pools that could drown a girl if she wasn't careful.

"What is it?" Lore wasn't sure if it was his proximity or the lingering hangover that was clouding her thought process.

He unhooked a coin purse from his leather belt and dropped it into her outstretched hand. She was startled back to her senses by the weight of it. "I can't take this. It's the least I could do since your father is letting us stay here."

His eyes narrowed when she said *us*. What was his problem with Asher?

"Look, if you don't want it, then take it up with Gryph. It matters not either way." Dislike radiated off him like a storm cloud heavy with the promise of rain, and the shadows seemed just a little darker where he stood.

What was his magical affinity? She hadn't seen him so much as light a fire with magic or sweep away dirt with a gust of wind.

She looked at the coin purse in her hand, then opened her mouth to thank Finndryl, but he was gone. The door leading to the kitchen swung forcefully in his wake.

She hefted the coin purse one last time before slipping it into her pack.

She knew exactly what to do with it.

CHAPTER 18

By the time Lore stepped outside, the sun had broken through the clouds and was drying up the damp courtyard. She shook off the unpleasant exchange with Finndryl, letting the sun warm her face and soak into her skin. She would try to steer clear of him for the next few days.

Lore found Isla cleaning the cramped kitchen upstairs, finishing the task she'd given herself the day before. Asher was standing in the living room, a watering can in one hand and a duster in the other.

Lore smiled. He had a fuzzball in his hair.

"I figured if you were cleaning downstairs, the least we could do is help out up here." He grinned at her, and her chest filled with warmth, washing away the last of that negative exchange with Finndryl downstairs.

She reached up and pulled the fuzzball out of his bun, flicking it away.

"Hey, I was saving that for later."

"Mmhmm. I'm sure you can find another to replace it."

"Lore!" Isla came bounding out of the kitchen and pulled her into a tight hug.

Lore gladly returned it. "Isla! Just the lady I wanted to see. I am in desperate need of a wash. You don't happen to have a spare tunic I could borrow, do you?"

Isla looked down at Lore; she was more than a head taller and her shoulders were broad where Lore's were small. It didn't seem like she would let that stop her. "I should have some clothes in a trunk somewhere from when I was younger. As you can see, my father doesn't get rid of much."

Lore very well *could* see, but over the day, the mess had grown on her. The apartment wasn't dirty—it was cozy. The older male really liked his books and plants.

She should bring plants downstairs to the pub. It would help the ambiance.

"Would you mind checking for me?" she asked. "And then afterward, I was wondering if you could take me to the nearest food market. The kitchen is empty downstairs, outside of the whiskey."

"I'll set some clothes in the bathing room for you. It shouldn't take me long to find something."

Isla and Lore walked arm in arm, each with a woven basket tucked into the crook of their arms. Though the sun had made its appearance, it had been weeks since Asher and Lore had celebrated the autumnal equinox alone in that hidden garden, and now its bright light did little to combat the blustery wind. The beautiful fallen leaves of early autumn were gone, and they'd taken their satisfying crunch with them.

The pair trudged through the soggy brown leaves of almost-winter and avoided puddles left over from that morning's rain. Each held a cup of coffee with dollops of molten chocolate and thick, fresh cream swirled in. The heaven in a cup was topped with a peppermint candy, and Lore wanted to moan with every sip she took of the sweet, minty drink.

Despite the thick fabric of the simple dress, knitted sweater, and woolen stockings Isla had found for Lore, the wind bit right through to her skin. That aside, she'd been delighted when she'd seen what Isla had scrounged up.

The dress was plain, but the belt Isla had given her was made from exquisite leather that had been braided in an intricate pattern. It was long, and Lore slid her dagger's holster into it. Tied to the belt were three small pouches, perfect for foraging or collecting. Lore had tucked her coin purse in one and her Adder Stone in another. The third was left empty for possibilities.

Lore and Isla decided to take a loop of the market before making any purchases, giving them a chance to check out all the prices. The vendors here were no less cutthroat than any market Lore had been to; all shouted out their prices and deals and tried hollering louder than everyone else. Their stalls were bursting with cabbages, turnips, carrots, and squashes of every color.

"Why doesn't your father use the kitchen in the tavern? I'm sure he knows he could double or triple his business if he served food *and* mead instead of using it as a storage space."

Lore scooted around an orc she'd seen hanging up her laundry this morning. She was haggling with a vendor over the price of cinnamon sticks while her son clutched her skirts, clearly overwhelmed by the noise.

"When we were little, the Exile was more of an eatery than a pub. Finndryl and I spent more time playing on the kitchen floor while our mother cooked than we did upstairs at home. We cut our teeth on ladles and learned to count by sorting beans. My mom made the best pumpkin soup in the whole town." Isla's eyes looked far away, past the market and into her memories. The light fae's eyes glistened. "People came from all over Hazel Grove just to eat a bowl of it on the autumn equinox. Back then, my father was so proud of the Dragon's Exile. But when my mother left and took us with her, he let the cooks go and closed the kitchen for good. He stopped really caring after that, and—well, you've seen the place."

"I have. I got up close and personal with it today. It needs some love, that's for sure." Lore frowned. Now she was unsure if she should go ahead with her plan for the coin Gryph had given her. She'd told Isla her plan to bring food back to cook in the kitchen—was she overstepping?

But Isla squeezed her arm in a comforting gesture. "I could tell my father loved that the kitchen was being used again. It's been a long time since my mom left and I think he's finally accepted that she's not coming back. It's time for him to move on and start caring again. That's another reason I decided to come up here for a few weeks—to help him with the Exile."

"Good, then let's purchase some provisions and get out of this wind. I smell snow." She was just turning to Isla to ask if she preferred beef or mutton stew when she saw them.

Three sentries in black uniforms with blue stripes.

Suddenly, the sweet chocolate on her tongue turned to ash. Her legs froze and her chest constricted, so tight she thought her heart would burst.

They had found her. Somehow, they had found her. They would hurt Isla for being with her, and it would be all her fault. She and Asher had thought they wouldn't come this far south.

They'd been wrong. And Lore had been stupid to leave the safety of Gryph's home.

But wait, maybe they hadn't seen her yet. The guards weren't paying her any mind, meandering through the market. She could leave right now and slip away.

"What is it? Lore, what is going on?" Isla's sharp voice cut through Lore's fear just as a gust of winter wind tore through the market, snatching Lore's scarf from her head and exposing her ears to the sentry looking right at her.

"Run." Lore's voice came out choked as she dropped her basket, grabbed Isla's hand, and sprinted toward the first side street she saw. But there were so many people shopping now, and customers seemed to be everywhere. Stalls were popping up where she could've sworn there weren't any before.

Lore had to drop Isla's hand to skirt around a wood nymph's jewelry stand, but she wasn't fast enough, and she knocked into it. A sharp pain shot through her hip, making her cry out. She winced again at the crunch of a beautiful shell necklace beneath her boot.

If she survived and made it out of here alive, she would come back and pay the cursing owner of the stall.

Lore glanced back. The guards were gaining on her. They were so much faster than her. She cursed her short, human legs. In a few more breaths, they would be close enough to grab her.

She dropped, crawling beneath a vendor's stall, and bolted into an alley. She didn't know how she would get away, considering they could probably smell her fear and would follow her trail.

"Hey, stop her! She's wanted by the royal guard!"

She could barely hear their cries over the sound of the blood roaring in her ears, and yet they sounded so close. She thought her lungs might seize up from fear and the exertion of running, but she kept sprinting from one alley to the next. She didn't dare turn around for long to see if they were closing in on her. She just pushed forward, running without knowing where she was going.

It wasn't until she found a row of backyards, all connected by rotting wooden fences, that she realized she'd lost Isla. Panic came over her. Had the light fae been captured? Had they hurt her? Lore knew she would never forgive herself if harm befell her new friend.

But she couldn't do anything to help her, not against the fae. Besides, her hip smarted from where she'd run into the stall and now her palm hurt. She must have scraped it on the wooden fence. Plus, the likelihood of Isla being caught was slim. She knew this village better than the visiting sentries, and she was fast and light on her feet. She would lose them easily.

Lore tore through the backyards, dodging wooden horses meant for children, hanging laundry, and shrubs. To her right were the woods. Maybe she could lose them through there? She glanced back and saw one of the guards kicking the wooden fence and breaking it apart easily.

They were so close.

She turned sharply and, instead of finding her way to the next yard, took a running leap. Clinging to the top of the fence, she used all her might, praying to the hidden stars above as she heaved herself up. She flailed with her feet and launched herself over the fence.

She had thought—or rather had hoped—that there would be a soft patch of moss that would break her fall, but instead there was a steep, jagged granite slope leading to a drop-off. She'd seen the trees on the other side of the fence but had grossly underestimated their height. Their roots were not even with the ground of the backyards she'd just left; instead, they stretched out far below her.

She skidded down the slope, feet first, trying not to pitch forward. She was falling fast, and she didn't want to tumble head-first. Twisting her body, she tried to slow her fall by grabbing onto a root or anything, but the ground was too steep and the wet leaves and moss too slippery to hold on to.

She was gaining too much momentum.

She cried out in agony as she slipped, her shoulder digging into a sharp rock before her weight pulled her farther down the slope. She could hear the voices of the guards.

Shit, they were following her. If this fall didn't kill her, then the guards would.

Finally, she made it to the bottom of the slope and immediately started crawling through a clump of roots. She managed to get through them and bolted. The trees here were spread out, but up ahead the trees were younger, closer together, and there were more bushes. She would have a better chance of hiding there.

She cursed herself for going to the market. She wasn't here to explore. She was in hiding.

Why did she take the risk?

Lore ran, trying to quiet her panting, though her lungs were on fire. She stepped only on soft moss, trying to avoid any fallen leaves or twigs that might crunch beneath her feet.

With every step into the forest, there was less sunlight, and she could swear the forest was whispering to her. A hush of voices mixed in with the sound of the wind in the trees. She followed the voices deeper into the forest, where almost no sunlight showed through the thick canopy.

Here the ground was moist, covered as it was in a thick layer of moss. Orange mushrooms grew in thick patches along the tree bark and ferns as tall as her reached up toward the sky. The smell of greenery and damp earth filled her, utterly intoxicating.

This far into the forest, she couldn't see the sun, so she prayed to the trees towering above her, the soft earth beneath her feet, and the rolling fog drifting in.

Save me.

Hide me.

Please.

CHAPTER 19

She squinted into the fog and the surrounding darkness. Despite it being harder to see, she increased her speed. Branches pulled at her hair less than before, no longer twisting in her curls and snagging them. The roots beneath her boots no longer tripped her up. Instead, they almost seemed to move out of her way. The crunch of twigs lessened, too.

She was now moving through the forest silently, like a ghost or a forest creature herself.

Still, no matter how quickly she moved, no matter how silent her footfalls, the guards' shouts grew louder. Their disgusting words coated her, violating her ears.

"Come on, girl, we just want to play," they called. "Won't you play with us?" They laughed, hardly even out of breath.

They knew what she knew, that in just a few heartbeats, she would be found.

Fear ricocheted through her, and she could swear the scar beneath her breast burned. She'd been here, two years before.

She stopped for a moment, slipping behind a tree. She pressed her fingertips into the rough bark, grounding herself as she pulled in ragged breaths. Her lungs were on fire. Running wasn't working; just as it hadn't before.

But she wasn't going down without a fight. Maybe she could scar one of them herself before he took her weapon.

She leaned against the rough bark of the tree and unlatched her dagger from her borrowed belt. She gripped the hilt, trying to remember all the places Asher had told her to aim for: the kidney, the neck, the eyes, and the lower back.

The sun briefly broke through the canopy and the outline of a guard coming up on the tree appeared. She clenched her teeth, trying to remember to breathe. Hopefully, she had the element of surprise.

It was now or never. She stepped out, lunging with her dagger.

She cursed as the guard grabbed her wrist in a bruising grip, twisting it back. She cried out as her hand spasmed, and her only weapon fell to the ground. He pressed his other hand to her mouth, shoving her back against the tree. Her cry was muffled, and his grip was firm enough that she couldn't turn her head at all.

She tried to inhale, eyes darting in a panic, and prepared to bring her knee up to slam it into his groin—

"Stop fighting me, Lore, and do what I say. The guards will be here any second."

"Finndryl?" Her cry was muffled by his hand. How did he find her?

When he saw the recognition in her eyes, he released his grip on her wrist and pulled his hand away from her mouth. He leaned toward her, his breath tickling her jaw. "Grab your dagger and be ready to fight. There are three of them. I should be able to take them down, but just in case, be ready. Do you know how to use that dagger?"

Lore nodded, though she wasn't sure if she could count the one practice session she'd had with Asher as knowing how.

"Good girl. They're here." And with that, Finndryl pushed away from the tree, turned in the air twice while withdrawing a sword from where it was sheathed on his back, swung it wide, and removed the head of one of the guards from his shoulders.

Lore froze in shock and horror as she watched the body of the guard fall to his knees before slumping sideways. The head spun in a circle on the moss. But she could still feel Finndryl's breath on her cheek and smell his spiced bourbon scent, as his words filtered back to her.

She kneeled, grabbed her dagger from where it had dropped, and held it ready.

The second guard was more prepared than the first. He blocked Finndryl's sword, the impact ringing through the air before being swallowed by the fog. Not dissuaded, the guard withdrew a dagger from his own belt and tried to shove it into Finndryl's side.

Lore cried out a warning, but Finndryl was prepared. He jumped out of reach and swung out his leg, knocking the guard onto his back. Before the guard could roll out of the way or stand back up, Finndryl's sword had slid into his chest, parting it like butter.

He withdrew his sword, and a fountain of blood watered the ground in its wake.

But hadn't Finndryl said there was a third guard?

Lore looked around wildly but didn't see anyone else. Suddenly, her head was yanked painfully to the side and the point of a dagger was pressed into her rib cage, angled up toward her heart. She swore.

"Let me go, you piece of shit!"

He ignored her, squeezing her tighter and whispering in her ear, rank breath making her want to gag. "Don't move or I'll pierce your heart right now," he said.

Lore stilled, trying her hardest to pull air into her lungs without moving too much. She was either going to pass out from sheer panic or burst into tears. She willed her eyes to stop roving around and instead looked at Finndryl.

"You killed them. You killed my friends." The guard behind her sounded choked up, perhaps with sadness from losing his friends.

But Lore suspected it was mostly anger, outrage, or disbelief. They were supposed to be capturing a human girl. She imagined none of them had woken up this morning thinking it would be their last.

"Yes, I did." Finndryl's voice was quiet as he spoke. "And I'll kill you for touching her."

Shivers rose up Lore's back. She could feel the guard's wild, racing heartbeat and realized he was scared. The hunter had suddenly become the prey.

"D-don't come any closer or I'll end her right here. This is official, royal business. I have a letter I can show you. We—I mean, I—am sanctioned to capture her. Let me take her and you'll be free to go. No one else has to get hurt."

Finndryl smiled. It was the first smile she'd ever seen on him. His sharp canines gleamed even in the low light of the forest. His grin was feral, reminiscent of a cougar playing with its prey right before crushing its head beneath its paws.

Fear shot through her. Finndryl was absolutely terrifying.

Finndryl looked away from the guard and his eyes landed on Lore's. She felt a fire roar within her the moment their gazes met. Warmth pooled in her belly even as her blood sang with fear. She knew what he wanted from her.

"Let me see this letter, then," he said.

Just as the sentry opened his mouth to reply, Lore threw her head back, smashing her skull as hard as she could into the guard's face. The sentry plunged his sword painfully into her side, splitting her skin and scraping against her rib.

She jerked away from the searing pain and dropped, rolling to the ground.

By the time she sat up, hand pressed to her side where the blade had cut her, the guard's blood was pumping into the moss on the forest floor, mixing with his friends'.

Finndryl stood over him, casually wiping his blade on his thigh once more, like murdering guards who were on "official royal business" was normal for him.

She wasn't sure she'd ever been more terrified.

$$))) \bullet ((($$

Lore quickly backed up before the spreading pool of blood could reach her and soak into Isla's dress, ruining it further. She stood with a grunt, pressing her hand to her side. The wound stung, but she wasn't bleeding too badly. She would pack it with moss and cinch her belt a little higher.

She glanced at Finndryl where he stood, eyeing her wound.

"I'll be fine. Nothing a few days of taking it easy won't heal. Though it will scar. They always do when they get you with one of their knives." She was babbling. Shock, probably.

She noticed that the only blood on him was the guard's blood he'd wiped on his thigh.

"I don't remember asking."

Right. She'd forgotten for a moment that Finndryl was an ass.

Nevertheless, she would be dead, or worse, without him. "Thank you. For, you know, saving me." Lore walked over to a fallen tree and plopped against it. She picked some moss off the log and gently began pulling up her dress so she could look at the wound better. She didn't think it would still be bleeding too much.

Finndryl glanced away, putting his sword back in its sheath on his back. He grunted a reply to her thanks.

Lore willed herself to focus on gathering moss and to ignore the sliver of deep brown skin that showed above his belt when he reached his arm up to sheathe his sword.

How did he lift a sword that size with one arm?

Apparently, the few words he'd spoken were more than he could handle. But still, she had to ask, "How did you find me?"

Finndryl didn't reply, and she thought maybe he hadn't heard her until he glanced back at her when she hissed. She thought this moss would make her wound feel better, but it was still burning. In fact, her side was on fire. She felt like someone was holding a torch to it and the wound was still bleeding freely.

Poison.

Suddenly, Finndryl was crouched in front of her. She tried to pull her dress down, but Finndryl wasn't having that.

"Don't be ridiculous. Something is wrong. Let me see." He removed her hand from where she'd pressed the moss against her side and nudged her dress up a little higher. His frown deepened when the moss came away bright red, not a hint of its original green.

Lore swayed a little where she sat, feeling lightheaded. Fear tore through her, sharp and burning. Her pulse pounded in her ears.

"Take a deep breath. I can hear your heart pounding. If this is, indeed, poison, you need to slow your heart rate. The slower the better. That's right, slow breath in. Then do the same when you release it. I passed a stream back there, so I'm going to lift you up and take you to it, all right?"

"All right." Her reply came out as a hoarse whisper. Suddenly her mouth and throat were so dry she could barely swallow, let alone form words.

In one swift movement, Finndryl slid one arm beneath her

knees, while the other supported her back. She tried not to, but she couldn't help letting her head rest on his chest.

The world was fuzzy. The only thing keeping her awake was the fire in her side. It burned with every step they took toward the stream. He was trying to be careful, but she thought he must know how fast he had to go if he were going to get her there in time.

In time. The thought rocketed through her, but she refused to think about what would happen if he didn't reach the stream soon.

She must have dozed off, because the next thing she knew she was screaming, woken by a burning she'd never known before. She thrashed, trying to push whatever demon was causing this torment away from her, but the monster wouldn't budge.

She cried out again. It felt like liquid fire was soaring through her veins, burning her up from the inside. This was it. This was her end.

A firm hand held her down, and no matter how much she pushed or clawed at it, it wouldn't let her go free. She'd never known pain like this. She thought she would go mad before this fire finished consuming her body.

She cried out again as the fire increased in heat, though a moment ago she would have thought that impossible. She ground her teeth against the searing pain, praying for it to end.

Before she could pull air into her lungs to scream again, the fire eased and went out. She felt a moment of peace as a sweet coolness washed over her side. She whimpered.

Was she dead?

She opened her eyes and noticed a male fae rinsing his mouth out, again and again, then spitting back into the rushing water. She had a moment to be confused before her world turned black and she slept the deep sleep of the dead.

CHAPTER 20

*L*ore dreamed of a stone house on the edge of a forbidden wood and a flower crown.

She remembered plucking each flower, splitting the stems, and twining them together. It wasn't easy for her small, chubby fingers. Mama could weave a crown in a blink, but it took all of Lore's concentration to thread the stems together without damaging the soft, delicate petals or breaking the stems.

Still, she worked diligently, only picking the most beautiful blossoms and making sure each was secure before moving on to the next. As she sat among the flowers, she wondered . . .

Are the woods really calling to me or is it just my imagination, like Mama says?

If it was her imagination, why did she often sleepwalk to the edge of the woods? Her parents had had to move the lock up high, so she couldn't open the door in the middle of the night.

She was forbidden from entering the woods—everyone knew that to enter them was to call to death.

But even as Lore sat among the fragrant flowers and her face was warmed by the sunlight, her feet itched to take her past the tree line so she could walk among the ancient trees of the wildwood.

She longed to meet the monsters that lived there. To learn their tales and tell their stories, but she never dared disobey her parents.

She ignored the call of the shadows among the trees, and she worked. The dancing lights that collected in the shadows weren't real. Mama said she had to stop pretending to see them. So, she ignored them, instead plucking, splitting, and weaving.

Later, when she placed a completed crown triumphantly atop Mama's curls, the smile she was gifted filled Lore with a warmth she would ache for every day of her life, long after she'd grown into a woman and could make crowns in a blink as well.

)) ● ((

Lore's eyelids fluttered as she woke in the low light. A candle flickered nearby, illuminating a room she'd never seen before. She flexed her jaw; she'd been clenching her teeth in her sleep again. She winced at the slight movement.

Actually, she was in way too much pain for it to just be a case of a bad dream. Her entire body ached like she'd been tossed down a mountain.

Someone was squeezing her hand, and she followed the limb to the person's face.

Asher.

Asher was squeezing her hand.

"How do you feel?"

Asher flickered in and out of focus; his face was mostly shadows, like those in the forest calling to her.

Wait, no. That had been a dream. Her mind felt fuzzy, sluggish.

Asher's eyebrows pulled together, and she noticed the deep lines between his thick brows had returned. She wanted to reach up and smooth the worried lines away, but her arms wouldn't obey her commands.

He leaned over her, tucking her wild curls away from her face. "How are you feeling, little mouse?"

"I feel like I was tossed down a mountain by a giant. Then run over by a horse and carriage for good measure." Her voice was raspy. She sounded like her old neighbor, the one who always had a lit pipe puffing out of the corner of her lips.

Asher grimaced, the concerned look on his face growing, but he moved away from her. He pulled the tattered quilt up to her chin, tucked it in, and whispered, "You need to rest. You've been through a lot."

"No, it's fine. I'm being dramatic." She tried to sit up to put him at ease, but she found she didn't have the strength. The effort alone almost made her black out again. "Where is Finndryl?"

Asher stiffened beside her. "He's downstairs at the Exile. We told him to take the night off, but he said, 'The house is too crowded.' Prick."

Lore had so many questions for Finndryl. She closed her eyes, thinking back to that morning—how had he found her so deep in the woods? She'd left him, sulking in the tavern, to go to the market with Isla.

But then, when she was about to be captured or violently murdered, he had shown up in the middle of the forest, murdered three royal guards to save her, sucked poison out of her—risking his own life—washed her wound, and apparently, probably, carried her all the way back to his home.

She wanted to ask Asher to call for Finndryl, but her questions would have to wait.

The world faded again.

She was shaken awake some time later. Her teeth were chattering, and the room was still going in and out of focus.

Asher and Isla were both crouched over her.

"Lore, honey, wake up a moment." Isla's usual cheery self was subdued.

Lore hadn't thought it was possible, given how perfect Isla's skin was, but there were bags under her eyes. They were somehow still attractive, making her look like the haunted heroine of a romance novel.

"Here, drink this. You need your strength." She tipped a shallow bowl of broth to Lore's lips.

She drank as much as she could, finding herself famished and thirstier than she had been in her entire life.

Beside Isla, Asher held her hand. "Lore." He squeezed her fingers and swallowed, taking a moment to collect his thoughts.

Whatever he's about to say, I'm not going to like it.

"Isla and I are leaving in a bit. The town is crawling with sentries. Some of them are the wolf clan—dark fae with wolfen attributes—and they almost always find what they are looking for. We want to draw them away. At this moment, you are . . . not well enough to move and we heard they're searching people's homes." He swallowed again, gaze darting away. "We can't risk you being found, so Isla is going to wear your scarves and tunic, take your pack, and pretend to be you. We are going to lead them away, farther south."

"Absolutely not. What if they catch you?"

Now Asher smiled. It was merely a shadow of his usual grin, but Lore appreciated the effort.

"Trust me, they won't. As soon as we lead them away, we'll lose them, no problem. I'll have Isla with me—the best tracker and the best archer this side of the Tallylah River."

Still, Lore wanted to throw up the broth at the idea of them risking their lives for her while she stayed behind. How many more lives was she going to ruin before she returned to Duskmere?

"It's fine, Lore. I left the academy and came up to see my father because I was bored. I wanted to find an adventure, and guess what?" Isla moved in closer, as if she were about to share a secret. "I found it, thanks to you. We won't let them catch you, okay? I just hope you can survive my brother's general doom and gloom personality. Stay safe, Lore. We will see you before the next moon has cycled through."

"Thank you. Both of you. Come back, okay? Don't leave me here forever." Her voice broke on the last word. She'd meant it as a weak attempt at humor, but it showed itself for the plea that it was.

"Never." Asher leaned in, pressing the lightest of kisses to her lips.

And then they were gone.

Lore slept, dreaming once more of a flower crown and the dancing wisps that gleamed luminescent in the shadows, calling to her.

CHAPTER 21

I t took three days for Lore to shake the fever dreams.

She woke every few hours to steaming broth on the table next to the bed and Finndryl's broad shoulders disappearing through the door.

From there, it took three more days for her head to clear of clouds and the wound on her side to knit together enough that she didn't faint from pain every time she shifted in the bed. In that time, the uniformed guards cleared out of the town—at least, according to a hushed conversation she'd heard between Gryph and Finndryl.

Lore thought there might still be some like the first trio Chief Steward Vinelake had sent after her: regular males with a penchant for violence and a lust for coin. She wanted to tell them about those men, but she couldn't make her voice work, and instead she fell into a nightmare, one where Asher hadn't been there with her in that camp and they'd caught her, only to rip the grimoire from her and stab it with poison-tipped swords.

She'd woken up screaming, only to quickly fall back asleep to a soft touch on her brow and murmured words of comfort.

Finndryl had been a silent presence in the room, a shadow in her fever dreams, a gentle, cool hand on her forehead. He was the nudge of the bowl to her parched, cracked lips. But, despite his comfort, Lore kept screaming herself awake.

The pain and the fevered dreams were too much.

So, Finndryl began to read her stories from his books. Wild tales of fighting dragons and sailing across monster-ridden seas for lost treasure.

She would listen, eyes closed and teeth gritted from the fierce pain, but his stories helped.

He read when dressing Lore's wound, as she gulped whiskey in the hopes that it would lessen the sensation that her side was on fire.

Once, in a rare moment when her head wasn't pounding, she caught him sleeping. He'd fallen asleep in the chair with his head on the bed, his locs escaping their tie.

The book, she noted through a haze, was a text on alchemical theories.

Lore realized he was making the stories up himself. She marveled at the fact that this fae—who never wanted to talk—seemed to have endless tales within him that he could spin effortlessly. If she was honest with herself, his tales were the only thing that were getting her through the fever and the pain.

By the seventh day, she'd burned off every ounce of poison and every bit of fever.

She woke up feeling mostly new.

Not even a day later, she realized that if Finndryl and Gryph wouldn't let her out of the twins' room, she would give herself up to the royal guard just to escape. So, they compromised, and Lore found herself downstairs in the Exile, making the mutton stew she'd planned the week before.

She missed Isla and was sad the other fae couldn't be there to try it. Gryph had gone to the market for her this time, fetching everything from a list she'd written back before she'd been poisoned and her body had gone into shock.

Lore heaped another serving of stew into a chipped wooden bowl and handed it to a scowling Finndryl. Now that she was awake, he was back to being the worst.

Didn't change the fact that he'd saved her life, though.

Lore had almost given up on getting answers from him when she overheard him complaining to his father about Lore still being there. He'd yelled something about "not wanting to babysit."

Lore gripped the wooden cup. She didn't *need* to be babysat, and she wished they would stop fussing over her so. The truth was, she was stir-crazy and guilty and the two emotions were eating her alive.

At least Gryph had a large collection of novels she could use to try to pass the time. She had to wonder why Finndryl had chosen to make up those stories while she was sick. He could have easily read from the extensive collection of adventure novels in the apartment.

She wished she could ask him, but when she'd brought it up to him a few days before, trying to tentatively thank him, Finndryl had shut down, refusing to acknowledge that he'd done anything of the sort.

She couldn't wait to dive into her current read about a dark fae prince who moonlit as an assassin, despite his secret heart of gold. Lore couldn't wait to see which princess he ended up with. Which she would find out when the kitchen closed in—she glanced at the clock on the wall—two bells.

In fact, she thought she might actually sleep tonight after spending all day in charge of the Exile's kitchen. She'd had to toss most of the breakfast she made; she had overestimated how many people would show up to a tavern that early. But by the afternoon, word had gotten out that the Exile was serving food again, and the roast tenderloin she'd cooked went fast, along with the crusty bread and gravy she'd made.

Lore wiped sweat from her brow. Although it was snowing

for the third day in a row outside, the kitchen was steaming hot from the cookfires going all day. Gryph and Finndryl had had to move the spirits they'd stored in the kitchen down to the cellar, lest they spoil in the heat.

At one point, she peeked her head out the door and noticed Finndryl sopping up all the gravy on his plate with his bread and licking each of his fingers when he was done. He could dislike her all he wanted—after all, she did take his room from him and put his family in danger—but he couldn't pretend to not like her food.

She counted it as a win.

Lore finished drying the large pot, sweating just from the effort it had taken to clean the thing. She slid the hook back into place on the large pot, ready for another day of cooking tomorrow, then started mopping the floors.

By the time she was standing in the middle of a sparkling kitchen, she heard the last of the patrons saying goodbye to a grumpy Finn. Good. While he cleaned up in the main room, she would be able to escape and do something for herself.

She had a choice. She could go upstairs to the small room and read that book about the assassin . . . or she could sneak out the back door of the Exile's kitchen.

Previously blocked with barrels of whiskey, the door had been uncovered when Gryph and Finndryl had moved the barrels. The kitchen was mostly underground, with skinny windows near the ceiling that sat at ground level. Stairs led up to the excavated door.

Clearly, it hadn't been used in forever; the hinges were rusted shut. But she'd oiled them up and now, when she used all her strength, she could force the door open enough to squeeze through.

It opened right up to the forest in their backyard, the one that Isla had called the Wilds. If Lore was here and Asher and Isla were out there risking their lives for her, she needed to do something.

If there was no way to translate the knowledge contained in her grimoire, then she would have to be creative. Flipping through the pages inside hadn't given her any answers. Yet, when she was outside at the campsite with Asher, she'd been able to understand the book so clearly.

Maybe, if she took the grimoire into the woods, she might be able to replicate the ease with which she comprehended the protection spell.

She'd been wrestling with this decision all day. Leaving the tavern was a huge risk, and an insult to everyone who had gone out of their way to protect her. Asher and Isla were *still* risking everything for her right now. Not only that, but it would put Gryph and Finndryl at an even greater peril if she were discovered.

But the only way to actually make a difference, to *incite* change and make their risk worth it, was for her to learn how to use the grimoire.

She would be careful. She would only go directly into the Wilds and only at night. She wouldn't go far.

She didn't bother asking anyone, knowing that everyone would tell her no.

$$)) \,) \bullet\, (\,(\,($$

Lore walked carefully toward the tree line, accompanied by the grimoire—tucked into her belt—and a small candle stub to light her way. The trees in this area of the forest were pillars, so tall they seemed to hold up the night sky itself.

The moment she passed the first tree, the world around her fell silent and her heart beat softly in her ears. A song of hope came to her, whispering about *home, home, home.*

Is this what it feels like to be in a home of one's own?

Lore couldn't remember what it felt like in her own home with her parents, unless she was dreaming. But when that happened, she would wake with salt tracks on her cheeks and a sore jaw from clenching her teeth. Her sense of home had always been tainted with longing.

She shook off those feelings and focused on the hushed reverence of the Wilds. It was different from the forest surrounding Wyndlin Castle, and also different from the trees surrounding Duskmere.

That forest was dark and ominous, spelled with such hateful, dark magic.

Instead, this wildwood seemed older and welcoming. Every step she took into the slumbering wood sent a thrill through her. Lore had never been alone in the woods at night before, but she felt safe here. Safer than she had felt since those last days before the autumn equinox, when she'd been in the apothecary amongst her many treasures.

But still, she wanted to remember this moment—a first. One of those few *important* firsts, like when she lost her first tooth and knew, even as a child, that somehow one chapter in her life had ended. Or when she'd started her monthly bleeds.

She still felt every bit like that lost girl, angry that her body had seemed to betray her for the first time. But in the next moment, she felt ancient for all she'd been through, weighed down by responsibility and the burden of living after losing so many loved ones.

Lore walked, careful not to go so far that she wouldn't find her way out, but despite her caution, she felt like someone was guiding her. She could swear she heard a humming that overshadowed the beat of *home, home, home.*

It sounded like, *We will protect you, child.*

Whatever was guiding her was gentle in its nudges—quietly telling her to turn here and follow *this* game trail while avoiding another path that screamed danger.

Soon, she began to see floating light in pockets along the trail. These lights seemed to shimmer like moonlight on water, winking in and out like starlight in the midnight skies. The farther she walked into the woods, the thicker and more substantial that light became.

Excitement thrummed up her spine and her steps quickened. She'd seen these lights before, back when she was a child. Only then, she couldn't have known what this was.

Magic. Raw magic, collected in spots. She suddenly knew her grimoire was infused with this raw magic. It positively pulsed with it, shimmering with a thousand colors and iridescent with power.

The light was brightest within a thicket of hazel trees. In its center was a small clearing overrun with clovers covered in a thick layer of frost. The small flowers blanketed the ground and in their middle, pushing their way through, was a circle of bright red mushrooms with white spots so vivid they gleamed in the rays of moonlight.

It seemed to Lore like a temple for the moon.

Lore knew this was where she would finally learn of her calling, for she had felt it for most of her life, ever since her mother burned up from the fever. The only rudimentary knowledge of her town healer meant she hadn't known what to give her mother to bring the fever down successfully, and it had cost Lore's family everything.

Lore knew she had the heart of a healer, but knowing which herbs, infusions, and salves would work was a different matter.

She'd needed a teacher, and she'd finally found one in the grimoire and the wildwood itself.

Lore kneeled in the middle of the circle of mushrooms and opened her grimoire with shaking hands. Here in the clearing, the moonlight reached the forest floor, lighting the pages just as they had that first time in her small room at the castle.

Only now, the magic amassed within the book seemed to call to the magic around her.

The glowing spots within the shadows began to swirl. Even the mushrooms and clovers seemed to vibrate with the magic. Lore breathed in deeply—the fungi surrounding her smelled like rain and the clovers had a sweet, vanilla smell. Lore wished she could bottle the scent.

When she touched the grimoire, the light soared from it, seeping into her like thick honey. Although the light was vivid and bright, it was cool to the touch. Comforting.

Lore brought her hand up in front of her face, turning it this way and that, marveling at the light staining her fingers like spilled ink, if ink were made of starlight.

The thicket of trees surrounding her seemed to sigh with contentment and the leaves shook with glee.

Lore laughed, the sound echoing through the wildwood. She plucked a single clover and placed it on the rough page of the grimoire. She watched, wide-eyed, as diagrams appeared before her. She saw that in the spring, the clover would sprout flowers. She saw a hand plucking the flowers and boiling them in water to make tea, and that a salve could be made from the leaves to treat ailments of the skin.

Despite that, the words surrounding the illustrations were in the old dialect and she could not decipher them.

Lore woke up to do it all again. And again.

Once word spread about food being served at the Exile, the small tavern was now filled twice a day. Lore was thankful for it. The chopping, washing, cutting, and cooking kept her so busy she almost didn't think about Asher and Isla risking their lives for her. She almost didn't think about the fact that another week had gone by with no word from them. She almost didn't wonder if they were captured or lying dead somewhere because of her.

When she brought up her worries to Gryph, he just laughed them off. He had complete faith in Isla to do whatever she put her mind to. Finndryl . . . well, he felt the same about his twin, and he claimed Asher was too stubborn to ever let anything really bad happen to him.

But Finndryl hadn't been there when those two guards were going to cut Asher down like he was nothing. In those few moments back at the castle, Asher would have died were it not for the book. No amount of stubbornness would have saved him.

She wanted to have the same confidence that they did, but she didn't. So, she cooked and cleaned and kept herself distracted. And when she wasn't in the kitchen, she was out in the forest, poring over the book and searching for anything that could help them.

Despite not being able to read the book, she *was* learning. She thought she might have discovered a way to help Asher and Isla, even if she couldn't be with them. The spell was similar to the one she'd used in the camp to protect their perimeter, only this one would protect them from enemy eyes.

She knew the herbs required for the spell from the drawings. She searched the ground, the trees, under stones, and in the wet earth beside a river until she could match them to the pictures in the book. The diagrams of flora were drawn with such care, they seemed almost lifelike. She gathered everything she needed and mixed it all into an incense.

When she lit it and spoke the words of the spell out loud, she infused her intentions into the smoke, even while stumbling over the foreign words. She did this spell every evening until she felt the magic catch and grow. She didn't know if that meant the spell had worked, but she hoped her protection reached Asher and Isla, wherever they were.

With the increase in business, Gryph's spirits were up. He would pop into the kitchen when he wasn't busy behind the bar to help her serve, do paperwork, or grab something to eat or drink for himself. No matter what it was, he always had a kind word for Lore.

She soon learned that, like herself, he never stopped. He was always busy, always moving—and if she thought that might have something to do with not wanting to think about his pain, just like herself, she never breathed a word.

Unsurprisingly, while Gryph might have taken a liking to Lore, Finndryl's mood remained unchanged. He was still surly, always glaring at her when he had to come back for more food or to get ingredients to stock the bar.

Lore began to think that she'd imagined his kindness when she'd been injured. He wouldn't know kindness if it hit him in the face.

))) ● (((

After another two weeks, when Lore's wound no longer needed to be dressed or cleaned, she walked farther into the woods than she ever had before. With more mobility, she could gather more plants and add them to her growing collection. The kitchen had become half kitchen and half storeroom at this point, and it had begun to remind her of their kitchen at the shelter back home. Back in Duskmere, there had always been a half-finished project laying around on the counter, drying herbs hanging from the rafters, or a simmering poultice or three on the stove.

One evening, she climbed a tree, trying to reach a vine that only bloomed at night. The milky white flower had a glowing center, one that shimmered and swirled like the pockets of magic in the hazelwood thicket. She was perched comfortably on a large branch, just about to pluck one of the flowers, when she heard a voice from the forest floor below.

"I wouldn't pick that one if I were you. The Wild doesn't like it when outsiders come in and take its most precious blooms."

Her good mood dissipated as fast as the honey butter she'd made earlier. Finndryl. She clenched her jaw in annoyance and a little bit in fear. Did he follow her here? Would he tell Gryph?

She hated to admit it, but the thought of disappointing the graying tavern owner made her uneasy.

She lowered her hand and leaned back against the trunk of the tree. "What would happen if I picked it?" She glanced at him, expecting him to look smug, but was surprised to see that he stood below her with a hint of a smile on his face.

Clearly, it was a trick of the moonlight.

"Your hands will blister painfully until they eventually weep a nasty, glowing pus for six days and nights."

He would probably love it if that happened to her. That explained the smile, then.

She leaned away from the beautiful flower. "The forest must prize it very much, then. How do you know this?" Lore climbed down before landing lightly on her feet. The soft earth and thick moss of the forest floor softened her landing.

"I climbed up there myself when I was little. It was the longest six days of my life."

Lore grinned, reaching into her apron and pulling out a handful of the glowing flowers. "Funny, because I've been collecting these for three days now and nothing has happened to *my* hands."

Finndryl stumbled back, eyes widening. "Impossible. I wasn't even able to pluck the flower from the vine before my hand was on fire."

"Didn't you say the Wild doesn't like outsiders taking their precious blooms?" She placed the flowers back in her apron, careful not to bruise the delicate petals. She had several ideas for how to use them. She was full-on grinning now; getting one over him was a delicious feeling. "I guess that means I'm the chosen one."

He grimaced, but it did little to remove the shock from his face. "Who *are* you? Where do your kind come from?"

Lore shrugged. "No one knows. There are legends, of course, that claim my ancestors are from a world of our own. One ruled by humans because there is no magic and no fae at all. The stories say that one day, someone angered a frivolous god, or maybe a malevolent one, depending on who is telling the story. Either way, humans were lost to the darkness for a hundred years."

She removed her apron so as not to crush the flowers, plopped onto the ground, and pulled her knees up to her chest to hug them.

"Some say they were *not* lost for a hundred years and that it was only a moment of complete darkness. But the only thing we know for sure is, when my ancestors came to, they were in the heart of a forest. They had to fight monsters that shouldn't exist and fend for themselves with only what had been in the vicinity around them when the world went dark."

She pulled her arms in tighter. She hated this history of hers. "It wasn't long before those who ruled Alytheria found them and subjugated them. Without magic, humans never stood a chance."

Finndryl frowned. "It must be hard, not knowing your true history or where you come from."

"Yeah, it is. It's mostly frustrating, though. My people could be so great if we also had magic, you know?"

"But you *do* have magic. I suspect you used it just now to grab those flowers without harm coming to you." He stepped closer to her, dropped to the ground beside her, and grabbed one of her hands gently, like he would hurt her if he applied any pressure. He turned her palm up and brushed her glowing fingertips lightly with his own. "It must be magic."

"It's not really mine."

He glanced up from her hand, meeting her eyes with confusion. Her hand was still in his. He was sitting so close to her and not wearing a look of contempt for once.

The last time they had been this close, she had just been poisoned.

She had to remind herself to breathe. She'd climbed sea-soaked cliff faces. She'd fought armed guards and lived in the woods for days. She was brave.

Brave enough to weather his rejection, should it come to that. "Will you help me? I can't read it. The book, I mean. If I press a flower to it, words and diagrams appear, but I can only understand a fraction of it. I feel like my magic is being held hostage by my ignorance."

"I thought the book spoke to you."

"Not since we were in my room at Wyndlin Castle. I think it was the strongest there, perhaps powered by something in the castle. Or maybe it could only talk to me when making a bargain? I don't know." Lore pulled her hand free, frustrated.

Finndryl frowned again before nodding slowly. "Okay."

She smiled. "You'll help? Thank you!" She almost threw her arms around him before remembering that this was Finndryl. He would probably put a dagger through her chest before he would ever embrace her.

His brows pulled together. "I'm not helping you because I want to. It's because of how much you've done for my father. I haven't seen him this happy since I was a kid. You've given him a reason to enjoy life again—I would repay that."

CHAPTER 22

The next day, after the dinner rush had come and gone, Lore cleaned up, filled a basket with food for Flix for his kids, prepped for the next day's lunch, and waited for Finndryl to kick the last of the stragglers out and close the tavern.

She was just placing lit candles on one half of the large oak table that she usually reserved for preparing food. But this evening, she'd cleared the space, scrubbed it twice, and set out two steaming mugs of tea.

When Finndryl finally appeared, his tall frame filled up the entire doorway and he had to dip his head to miss hitting it on the frame. He surveyed the kitchen, jaw clenched as he took in the cascade of drying herbs that now hung from the rafters, the cabinets overflowing with spices, and finally, the two mugs on the table.

Lore wiped her apron, suddenly hyper aware of the sauce stain on the front just over her right breast. She shouldn't care what he thought of her outfit, and yet, she did. She should have changed.

Her own eyes flitted from his arms to his face and back down. He was holding an armful of scrolls.

"You're here. I wasn't sure if you had changed your mind or not."

"What gave you that impression?"

"Well, when I didn't see you this morning, I thought . . . I don't know what I thought." A nervous laugh escaped her. "That you had changed your mind, I guess."

"I woke up early. I wanted to go to the library before the tavern opened." He took the last step into the room.

"Please, sit. Let me help you with those—" She reached out, but he skirted around her.

"It's fine, I've got it. Is this surface clean?" He eyed the table, squinting at it with suspicion.

"Yes, I wiped it twice, just now. It should be dry—"

"Will you move the tea? I don't want to risk any spills."

"Of course." Lore grabbed the teacups and placed them near the hearth, trying not to grit her teeth. She had to remind herself that he was here to *help*, even if he seemed determined to rile her up.

With one more once-over of the table, Finndryl must have decided it looked clean enough because he placed the scrolls down, almost reverently. "Treat these with care. Technically, they're not supposed to leave the library. They belong to the Master Scholar, but I've known him since I was young." Finndryl pulled a chair out and sat, beginning to unwrap the cords securing the scrolls together. "I used to spend a lot of time at the library before we moved. He told me I could keep the scrolls as long as I needed, but eventually, I'll have to return them."

"I didn't realize Tal Boro had a library. This is a pretty small town, isn't it?" Lore sat as well, wishing she had something to do with her hands. She didn't dare touch the scrolls without Finndryl's permission, so she tucked her hands into her lap.

"You can hardly call it a library. My father almost has more books in his apartment than the library has in its entire collection. It's nothing like the Edgemoor Library in Rywandall—

where Isla and I went to university. Though, the Master Scholar I mentioned? Rickeul? He has quite a collection himself. They belong to him, but he keeps them with the other scrolls and books."

"Why don't you have a collection of your own?" Lore thought back to the books and journals in her room, the ones that were now, probably, still buried beneath the ceiling.

"I don't usually read books more than once."

"Why not?" Lore thought of all the books she'd read again and again. Some of them she could almost recite word for word. Rereading a favorite book was like coming home after a long time away.

"I don't need to. Once I read something, I don't forget it."

She opened her mouth to ask him another question, but he unrolled a blank scroll before she could. "Let's start with the old alphabet. It's quite similar to the Alytherian language spoken today. Most of the words are directly descended from Old Alytherian, in fact." He spread out a blank piece of parchment and began to write out the old alphabet from memory, without even glancing once at one of the tomes or scrolls.

Lore raised an eyebrow. "So, you *were* lying that day when I showed you the grimoire. I thought Isla's reaction to you not being able to read it was odd. It was like she didn't believe you."

Finndryl didn't have the decency to even pretend to be embarrassed at being caught in a lie. "Of course I knew how to read it. My main course of study at the university was alchemy, and almost every source of knowledge I was assigned to study was written in one extinct language or another. Sometimes a book was even written in three extinct languages."

"So, you just decided not to tell me."

He sat back in his chair, the hint of a smirk appearing on his face. "It wasn't so much a *decision*, Lore. It was more that I didn't know you, nor did I trust you."

"Fair enough." She couldn't fault him, not really. But did that mean he trusted her now? And why did that thought make her insides glow?

"I asked Rickeul if he'd ever heard of a grimoire like the one that you possess."

Lore looked at him sharply.

"Don't worry. I made it seem like I was researching ancient grimoires for my alchemical studies." He rolled his eyes before continuing. "He said he'd heard a legend about one from back when he was studying to be a scholar, but of course, he figured it was just a myth. There aren't any direct accounts on record. Only hearsay, poems, songs, or children's tales. But he did say that *if* such a grimoire existed—one that could be infused with so much magic it had the power to make decisions on its own and speak to someone—then I needn't bother looking for it."

"Why not?"

"Because any object that held enough magic to gain sentience would disintegrate."

Chills rose up Lore's spine. She glanced at her grimoire. There it lay, not disintegrated. In fact, from this angle, it looked like any old book—a fancy one with hand-stitched embroidery, colorful vines and flowers, silvery shimmery moons, and gold-foiled spine, sure.

But a book, nonetheless.

"I was thinking about that: about magic and how it works." Lore began to pick at a rough spot on the edge of the table. "When I was little, I didn't even know magic existed. We didn't have any, and because my parents kept me away from any fae who came into Duskmere, I had never seen it. It's not something we humans like to talk about, because when we do, the Alytherians punish us. It's become a sort of taboo conversation among my people. But once I discovered it—that there was this entire resource that millions of creatures all over the world had access to, but we didn't—I couldn't stop thinking about it."

She licked her lips, unable to meet Finndryl's gaze. Not wanting to see his response.

"I craved it," she continued. "I always thought, if I could harness magic, Duskmere would be so much better off. We wouldn't have to worry about earthshakes, drought, or other natural disasters. And then, when I became the first in living memory to leave Duskmere, I found that hardly anyone uses magic at all. It surprised me. That magic is not only a finite resource, but that not everyone can do every kind. Yet, when I go to the thicket of hazelwood trees in the Wilds, it's *filled* with magic. So why isn't anyone out there collecting it for their enchantments?"

Finndryl had gone preternaturally still. The kind of still that a human could never achieve.

Lore sat up, looking around. The hairs on the back of her neck stood on end. Could he hear something she couldn't? Was someone out there in the tavern? The kitchen had gotten so hot earlier she'd removed her scarf—if they came in, they'd immediately see she was human.

"What's wrong?" she asked.

"Are you telling me that you can *see* magic?" He leaned toward her, his eyes roving over her face.

"Can't everyone?"

"No. Nobody can. And only some of the most talented practitioners, those who've trained for decades, can even feel *Source*. It's known that those who have an affinity for earth magic, like Asher"—Finn's mouth twisted with dislike when he said Asher's name—"can usually obtain it in the woods, and it's best when drawn through the soil."

"*Source?*"

"It's what alchemists call that which fuels our enchantments. There are two types of magic. The kind that every being has—this kind is often related to one's species. The sirens in Olan can all influence the tide to an extent. They're born with the inherent ability. Some of the dark fae can actually communicate with the animals of their clans, and others can shift entirely into that species. And then there is what I think you are talking about; it's what alchemists call *Source*. It's much like the wind. When it is near us, those with the skills can feel it, but we can never see it. For most alchemists, it takes years of training to be able to call to *Source*, let alone harness and wield it successfully."

Lore's mouth had gone dry. She stood on shaky legs, clutching her grimoire, and strode across the kitchen, skirting the large cookstove in the center. The moon was almost full, and some of its silvery light shone through the ground level windows near the ceiling. Lore held the grimoire up, standing on tiptoes, and extended her arms as far as she could, until its pages were bathed in moonlight. "When I do this, what do you see?"

Finndryl's eyes were alight with curiosity. "I see the grimoire. It looks the same as it did over here on the table."

Lore tilted her head, eyes narrowing at the bright, illuminating light that was exploding from the grimoire and bathing her hands and wrists. "Do my hands look any different to you?"

Finndryl shook his head.

She dropped her arms and quickly crossed the space, sitting back at the table, a little breathless. "Are you jesting? Is this another lie?"

Finndryl rolled his eyes. "I only lied that one time. Though I suppose I'll regret it now if it means you're going to doubt my integrity." He leaned toward her, his voice lowering. "But more importantly, what do *you* see when you put the grimoire in the moonlight? What happened to your hands in your perspective?"

"The book glows. With magic. Or, *Source*, I suppose. It looks the same as the magic that collects in the thickets. But the grimoire has so much of it, and when it's under the light of the moon, it's so bright it's *blinding*. It bleeds onto my hands, almost like it needs somewhere to go, and since I'm holding it . . . well, it flows into me like a moonlit river."

"Can I try it? It's all right if you say no."

"I don't see why not."

Finndryl picked up the book with even more care than he'd shown the scrolls earlier. But when he held the book up to the moonlight, though the book shimmered, his hands remained the same, beautiful in their mahogany tones.

They did not glow. The magic did not seek him out as it did Lore.

"I don't feel any stronger, nor do I feel the *Source*, as you say the book has." Finndryl dropped down beside her, handing the grimoire over. "Well, I suppose that is just another way that the book is unique. It chose you, and so you have access to its *Source*."

So many thoughts were racing through Lore's head. She felt a little dizzy. She thought that with Finndryl's help, she could finally tease out the grimoire's secrets. But the more she learned about magic—or *Source*—it seemed as if she gained more questions.

She'd always been able to see the magic swirling around Duskmere, though it did not enter the town. It appeared something, or someone, kept magic outside of Duskmere. Were there others in Duskmere who could see the wisps as well? Or was it just her? She wished she'd asked, but her mama's voice came back to her, urging her away from the forest where the wisps lived, refusing to broach the taboo subject of magic. Lore had just never made the connection, and now it was too late. There wasn't another human around to ask.

"Do you think the Edgemoor Library would have any scrolls on the grimoire? Your scholar may have called them legends or myths, but in my experience, there is always truth hidden within a good story," she said.

"I'm sure there are, but I wouldn't be able to grant you access. Only those who attend the academy, esteemed alumni, or the very important or wealthy have access to the ancient archives. The grimoire is at least one thousand years old, correct?" He coughed, gaze skittering away. "I am also, sort of, banned from the library."

Disappointment bloomed in Lore's chest. Why couldn't anything just be easy for once?

At least there was something else to focus on. "You must tell me the story of how you got banned from a library." The only one she'd ever been to was cursed. But in books, libraries were the most magical of places, ones that celebrated knowledge and welcomed all.

He grinned, his sharp canines glinting in the candlelight, and rubbed the back of his muscular neck. "Let's just say that if the scholar had denied these scrolls that I brought with me today, I would have found my way in tonight and simply taken them. Only, I wouldn't have gotten caught this time."

"This time? What was so worth taking?"

"Younger me didn't care about being caught or whether a plan was reckless. The scrolls weren't even that important; I just wanted to see them, and they had denied me access. I was a student, but I was neither important enough nor wealthy enough, so the scholars at Edgemoor wouldn't give me access. If my sister was here, she would probably chime in about how I've always had a problem staying out of places I wasn't wanted." Finndryl's grin turned sheepish.

Lore smiled in return. "I think that might be true for both of us."

The two went to work and the next two weeks blurred together in a haze of lessons. Lore and Finndryl poured over tomes as thick as a candle and translated spell after spell. Despite their best efforts, some remained untranslatable, their words too inde-cipherable for even Finndryl's mastery of four languages.

Although Lore was exhausted from the day's work and Finndryl was often sticky and tired from the tavern, Lore learned to translate the ancient symbols and words. She learned to read and write them and even to recite them, carefully.

Sometimes, their fingers would brush when they dipped their quills into their shared inkpot and the shock would startle Lore. The brief contact birthed a quick heat that shot from the brush of their hands to her core, and the feel of his fingers against hers would linger long after they'd closed their books for the night.

It wasn't long before she yearned for the day to end, for the patrons to leave, and for Finndryl to step through the little door that led to the kitchen.

Lore was a fast learner. She'd always had a love for languages, and the first time she translated a full page of the grimoire on her own, a passage about a special bark that could combat the effects of certain poisons, she glanced up, startled.

Finn's eyes met hers and his nod and accompanying rare smile spoke volumes. The edges of his full lips pulling up sent a thrill through her. The sight of his black eyes watching her, pools of ink so dark they could tell a thousand stories, trapped her. The heat radiating from his broad chest, the sureness of his muscled shoulders pressed near her own, and the spicy scent of him stirred something in her.

Lore lay awake that night, feeling guilty and missing Asher. She wished she could tell him everything she'd learned. She yearned for him to return.

And yet, in the moments right before sleep, she would wonder. What was building between her and Finndryl?

Lore tried to bank those feelings, suppress them, but despite how often she chased the thought away, it kept finding its way back. A stubborn, inconvenient thing. She would give anything to have Grey with her right now. He always had advice for when her emotions were involved.

$$))) \bullet ((($$

Although Lore picked up the language quite quickly, it was weeks before she successfully harvested *Source*. Unless she was holding the grimoire, she couldn't hold on to it. She could coax moonlit wisps to her palms, feel the warm tendrils of their lights wiggle in her hands and begin to bleed into her, but they always slipped from her grasp.

It was frustrating, but not as frustrating as daybreak.

At night, Lore could soak in moonlit power, which filled her up and made her stronger and faster. She could even swear that food tasted better at night in those woods, but when the woods turned mauve with the coming dawn, the power within her would dissipate like grains of sand through her fingers. Dawn brought with it the acrid taste of longing.

Eventually, she and Finndryl exhausted the collection of both the Tal Boro library and its scholar, without a single mention of a book even remotely like the grimoire or a whisper of someone being able to see *Source*.

But it wasn't all frustration. The first spell Lore successfully cast was a spell for Asher and Isla. It took three nights of sitting among the clovers while surrounded by the hazelwood trees for them to get it right.

She was holding a wooden bowl filled with water from a stream between her hands, chanting the words from the book again and again for the third night in a row, when an image appeared on the water. It was them—the image was little more than a flash, as if she were seeing them in a dream, but it was undeniably Asher's antlers and Isla's locs.

"Finndryl, I see them!" Lore's voice rose through the quiet wood, startling Finndryl where he had been dozing against a tree, a book forgotten on his thigh.

He'd taken to keeping her company in the woods, even if he spent the whole time "resting his eyes."

But now, Finndryl jumped up, his book forgotten in the moss. He kneeled beside her, heat radiating from his muscled shoulder, and peered into the bowl. "What do you see? It looks just like water to me."

"They're safe. On the road. They've acquired horses somehow." She smiled at him.

Some of the tension that lived behind his eyes and crept into his shoulders dissipated. Despite his insistence that Isla was too stubborn for anyone to actually succeed in hurting her, it was clear he'd been worried. "I'm not surprised. Isla prefers to travel on horseback. She was always meant to have horses."

"I'm sure one day she will."

Finndryl raised his eyebrow. "Yeah, if she would ever settle down and get a decent paying job."

"She could always marry a rich lady and acquire them that way."

Finndryl's eyes crinkled, and his lips turned up at the corners. A thrill shot through her; she'd coaxed a rare smile from him. "I can't see one lady ever being enough for her."

"Even if that lady owned a hundred horses?" Lore bumped his shoulder. The water sloshed over the bowl and soaked into the fabric of her dress.

He placed a hand on his chin, pretending to consider it. "Well, maybe then, but this lady better be willing to accept my sister constantly running off to chase adventure."

Lore placed the bowl down, pushed her fingers into the soil, and drew more *Source* from the surrounding wood. "Duskmere next."

Finndryl stilled beside her, all jest leaving his tone. "Are you worried about what you will find?"

Lore picked up the bowl, her hands glowing—though only to her eyes. "Yes."

She closed her eyes, chanting the words, quietly thankful for Finndryl's firm shoulder pressed against hers. He seemed to lean into her, gifting her some of his strength.

When she opened her eyes, the water had turned murky, cloudy. She leaned closer, trying to see through the clouds. "There is something blocking Duskmere, I think. A veil. I can't see through it." She thrust the bowl down, unease coursing through her.

"What if you look for a certain person instead of the town itself?"

Lore bit her lip, picking the bowl up. Her hands shook with trepidation. She'd already known there was a spell surrounding Duskmere, so what was stopping them from also adding a shroud over the town?

How else would so few people know about humans?

Lore chanted the words again, thinking of Aunty Eshe. She pictured her broad, proud shoulders, which hadn't folded with age. The permanent laugh lines that seemed to grow more pronounced every year.

Aunty Eshe, where are you?

When she opened her eyes, she saw the same shroud blocking her vision.

"No, it's not working." Fear crept into Lore's voice.

"Okay, don't panic. Try someone else close to your heart. The more you care for them, the easier it will be. What's your friend's name? Grey? What about him?"

"He's in Duskmere too. I don't see how that would work." She could feel her chest tightening and her lungs beginning to ache for air.

"Just try."

She looked away from the cloudy water. Finndryl was watching her, assessing. Lore inhaled a shaky breath.

"All right, let me try."

Grey.

Grey.

She pictured her friend. His easy, crooked grin. His black hair that seemed to curl into his face in a way that drove all the girls—and many of the boys—back home wild. Not that he was interested in them. The easy way he would grab her hand and pull her into a hug any time she needed one.

Goddess, she missed him.

She focused on their friendship. She knew his face better than her own. His voice was as familiar to her as the sound of rain.

She chanted the words; they came easily to her now, spilling from her lips like a hymn as the moonlit power coursed through her. Her lungs stretched, allowing her to breathe easily. Her heart beat with a firm, steady, beat.

She opened her eyes and saw him.

Grey was no longer in Duskmere.

CHAPTER 23

D escribe to me what you saw one more time, love."
Gryph sat across from Lore at his dining room table
the next morning, nursing a cup of coffee.

Lore set aside her toast, untouched. Her stomach was in knots;
she couldn't even think about eating. "It's hard to tell. I can see
him. He's in a palace. It's beautiful. Every surface of the room
around him is ornamented. There are statues made from gold and
the ceilings are covered in paintings. Others gather around him,
dressed in finery, like they're the gods and goddesses themselves."

"And you can't get the bowl to show you where this palace is?"

Lore bit her lip, eyeing the bowl in question. During the day,
it was a normal wooden bowl filled with water.

"No. I can only see Grey and the ballroom he's in." Lore
closed her eyes, trying to focus on the details. "I saw a throne
on a dais with a female sitting on it. Her hair is piled high above
her head like a beehive. Beside her is a small orc with pale green
skin and tusks. They're beautiful. They're definitely celebrating
something." She couldn't stop shivering. "I'm worried about him.
He looks thin and tired. His eyes are glassy and unfocused. They
passed him around to dance like he's a . . . a puppet. And then he
dropped, exhausted, at the feet of the throne."

Finndryl and Gryph shared a glance.

"What is it? What do you know?"

"I think I know where he is. How he got there is beyond me, but . . . the female you saw on the throne, you said her hair resembled a beehive? Was it white, almost silver?" Finndryl asked.

Lore nodded. "Yes!"

"That would be our queen, my dear," Gryph spoke quietly. He was usually the loudest in the room, so his whisper was slightly shocking.

"Grey is with your queen?" Lore's mind tripped over itself.

Grey, her best friend who had been trapped in Duskmere just like her, was now, somehow, hundreds of miles away from home with the Queen of Rywandall.

Finndryl looked at Lore with a grimace. "She's more than four hundred years old. Queen Riella tends to seek out anything new or exciting, so it makes sense she would have 'collected' a human."

Lore's shivers increased, and her hands started shaking. "Nothing about this makes sense." Her voice pitched up an octave. "Do you think he's allowed to leave, or has he become her prisoner?"

"I'm sorry, love. She doesn't really let them go, not if she wants them," said Gryph.

Lore ground her teeth, anger seething out of every pore. "Grey is a person, not a pet to add to a fucked-up collection!"

Gryph and Finndryl exchanged a glance again, only adding to Lore's frustration.

"Don't do that. Don't keep things from me like I'm a child."

Finndryl's voice dropped low, cautious. "I would never keep anything from you. Forgive me, I'm trying to put this delicately. The queen has a host of alchemists in her court. It's said that once one eats her enchanted food, they *choose* to stay."

"What's so bad about eating enchanted food?" Lore looked at Finndryl with wide eyes, imploring him not to break her heart.

He returned her gaze, his eyes filled with regret. He reached a hand toward her before clenching his fist and withdrawing it. "All other food will taste like ash upon their tongue. All other drink will feel as if they're quenching their thirst with sand. Those who eat her food become consumed with want, and they will do anything for the chance to taste her wine and eat her cakes again."

"No. That wouldn't happen to Grey. He wouldn't eat it." Lore slammed her fist on the table as she shook her head. "Grey is the strongest person I know. He would fight it."

"Lore . . . how would he have known to?" Finndryl asked.

Lore felt like she was drowning. She didn't answer Finndryl, choosing instead to focus on the task ahead of her. "I have to get him back."

"Love, even if you managed to infiltrate the grounds, navigate the palace, and then somehow find Grey, *your friend would not wish to leave.* From how you described his eyes, he has surely tasted her food," Gryph said, sadness in his eyes.

Lore shook her head. "That isn't a good enough reason to leave him."

"What is one human girl going to do against a powerful fae queen?" Finndryl asked, his voice gentle but firm.

Lore stood up so fast, her chair crashed to the ground behind her. She ignored it, lifting her chin in defiance. "This human will do what I have always done: fight back. I will find a way."

She stormed down the rickety stairs and waded through icy mud to unlock the Exile. She needed to be alone. She needed to think. She pressed through the empty tavern, closed the kitchen door behind her, and began to pace.

Back home, there were some who couldn't handle the hardships of life in Duskmere. They grew a plant, a beautiful one with pink petals covered in a fine dust and the palest of green stems. When the plant matured, they plucked the petals, crushed them, and mixed them with water. When this mixture became putrid, stinking of rot and decay, they drank it.

It made them forget that they were starving, in debt, over-worked, and trapped, but it came with a price. The more they drank, the more they craved.

Dust water allowed them to forget their worries, but it also made them forget they had families, children, parents, and that they needed water and food. Those who became addicted died of dehydration with smiles on their faces.

Lore had seen it happen too many times. Desperate families came to her aunt, begging them for a cure, but Aunty Eshe *couldn't* help them. Only by looking inside themselves and finding strength could they break their habit.

There was no way Lore would leave Grey to a fate like that. Grey was family. He was the single most important person in her life and Lore would risk anything if it meant saving him. She stopped pacing, rifling through pages of notes, diagrams, and scrolls until she landed on a map of Rywandall.

That night, as the sun set and the shadows began to collect in the kitchen, Lore snuck out the back door and slipped silently into the forest.

CHAPTER 24

L ore was led through the palace gates with the sharp end of a sword pressed into her back.

Bitter, icy winter wind blasted her cheeks, and her curls blew wildly around her face, embracing their freedom where Lore could not. She stilled for a moment, boots skidding on a mosaic of multicolored tiles, looking toward the flickering lights cast by torches as they turned the pretty courtyard into one of nightmares.

She cast her eyes past a fountain, its water frozen in a gravity-defying filigree, before landing on the palace. Vines crept up the gleaming stone, in bloom even at night, and their flowers cast their cloying scent around every visitor. Servants milled about in matching uniforms, completing the day's tasks. They studiously ignored the prisoner being directed into the house; either this was commonplace, or they were well trained not to meddle.

The guards directed her through a side entrance, and she stepped into a colossal foyer. Marble statues lined the room, all fae in different levels of undress. The marble was carved with such skill that their clothing appeared to flow in a permanent breeze. Their faces were alive with emotion, alight with either pleasure or horror, depending on the scene chiseled by the artist.

The details of each statue made Lore's breath catch in her throat.

If circumstances were different, Lore imagined she could look upon each one for days and never have her fill of their beauty. Unfortunately, she barely had a moment to take in the room before she was pushed forward, through sparkling corridor after sparkling corridor, until she was spat out into a ballroom.

It wasn't the one she'd seen in her vision.

This one was smaller and more private, but no less grand. The party from the night before seemed to be dwindling; there was only a single violinist left in the corner. The rest of his quartet had joined the festivities. He played by himself, an eerie melody that sent chills down Lore's spine.

Many of the revelers who had been dancing in her vision were now sleeping in bundles around the room—on the stairs, against pillars, or even under the ornate buffet table still overflowing with food and drink.

Then, she saw her, sat upon the dais.

Queen Riella.

She wore a gown that was beautiful in its simplicity. The thin, ribbon-like sleeves slipped down her shoulders, seeming to celebrate the large swell of her breasts. The dress was short, hugging her knees. She wore high stockings that kissed her shapely calves, and her heels ended in points so sharp they could skewer someone easily. Her white hair was gathered high atop her head, artfully woven with glistening pearls and bright gemstones. Her red lips popped against deep ebony skin.

The queen was as beautiful as she was terrifying.

The guard pressed the sharp point of her sword into Lore's back, urging her toward the dais.

She couldn't make her feet move; that dais spelled death, terror, horror.

But she had to do this. For Grey.

Lore swallowed thickly as she shuffled her feet forward a millimeter at a time. She'd made a terrible mistake.

Except, no. She *hadn't*, because there Grey was, asleep below the queen. His head was on the lap of the queen's consort, who looked at Lore with a blank and apathetic expression, despite her sharp tusks. The queen's consort ran a hand through Grey's hair, the pale green of her skin contrasting starkly with his silken black waves.

"Who is this, Naevrys? They've missed the party." The queen sounded bored, almost drowsy.

"We caught her trying to infiltrate the palace in a shepherd's cart, Your Majesty," the guard, Naevrys, spoke behind Lore, her voice raspy. She twisted the sword viciously into Lore's back.

The queen laid her head on her hand, slouching into her throne. "You know what we do with thieves. Kill her and be done with it. Feed her to the pigs."

Naevrys hesitated. "She is a human, my queen. I thought you would want to see her before deciding."

The queen bolted up straight, suddenly awake. "Two humans in the same week? Bring her closer. I wish to see her better."

Lore didn't wish to go any closer, well aware that she smelled like animal shit, covered as she was in dirt and grime from the sheep-filled wagon she'd hidden in. Her hands were still tied behind her back, the ropes biting into her wrists, and her hair—now half tied back and half wild curls—displayed her human ears for all to see.

She suspected the guards would have killed her if her ears hadn't been so clearly human.

"Move."

Lore had no choice but to obey. She shuffled closer, keeping her eyes on the floor.

"At last, a human girl! I must admit, I've been curious since your kind appeared in the north. I was little when the news came of a creature who could walk and talk but wasn't from our world—you all are such poor things, cursed to live without magic. I remember asking my mother for one of you. The greedy Alytherian king denied my request, of course."

Lore stayed quiet. The queen had admitted that she'd once asked for a human, as if they were little more than pets. Lore needed to figure out the rules here.

The queen continued, eyeing her up and down again. Her gaze snagged on Lore's wild hair, and she wrinkled her nose at the smell wafting off her. "I have to admit, you aren't as pretty as the human boy I have."

Lore gritted her teeth, widening her eyes in surprise. She decided to pretend she hadn't recognized Grey the moment she'd seen him. He was still asleep, though she could hear his ragged breathing now that she was so close to him. He didn't sound well.

"More wine!" the queen ordered, startling one of the many servants lining the back wall. The one closest to the double doors at the back of the room—a smaller creature with skin like pebbles at the bottom of a riverbed—exited hurriedly, coattails flapping behind them. "Please sit while they fetch the wine. Are you hungry? Thirsty?"

Lore shook her head and looked around for a place to sit. Apparently, the queen meant for her to sit on the floor. She stepped forward eagerly, relief flooding her when the sword at her back fell away. She dropped to the marble floor, shivering as the coolness instantly started to leech through her clothing.

She finally got a good look at the guard who had discovered her. She was small for a fae, though her powerful, feathered wings made up for her height. She was brown like Lore, with shockingly blue eyes, full lips, and vibrant red hair that curled around her face, like a fiery version of Lore's own. The winged female scowled at her; chin raised as she pointedly put her hand on her unsheathed sword.

What was a dark fae warrior doing working for the rival queen? Lore thought tensions were high between the two kingdoms.

Lore didn't avert her gaze, instead raising her chin and stilling her features.

"Oh, Naevrys! Stop scaring the human and untie her bonds. She won't hurt me," ordered the queen.

Naevrys scowled, clearly not liking the command, but she quickly sliced the rope wrapped around Lore's wrists before stepping back a few paces. Lore watched as Naevrys sheathed her sword and stood straight, hands behind her back and wings folded in.

"Girl, do you speak?"

Fear forced Lore to raise her eyes to the queen again, flinching at the annoyed twist of her features. "Yes, Your Majesty. I apologize. I've never met a queen before, and in truth, I am stricken by your beauty."

The queen smiled with delight. "Oh, you are a doll, aren't you? Isn't she a doll, Bea?"

Her consort, Bea, paused in playing with Grey's hair and sniffed. "She stinks of sheep."

"That is because she was caught hiding with the sheep. Isn't that amusing?" She paused, her smile faltering. "Now, why would a human be sneaking in here?"

Sweat dripped down Lore's back. Grey should have heard her voice by now. Why wasn't he looking at her?

The small attendant returned with a decanter of wine and two mugs. He poured a thick red into each, then handed one to the queen, who waited as the attendant walked over to Lore. She didn't want to accept, but she suspected refusal would mean death. She grabbed the offered chalice of wine; it looked like blood but smelled sweet, like summer rain.

"Please, drink with me. You must be thirsty. We shall toast to our friendship and then we shall have a celebration in your honor." The queen drank deeply from the cup, tipping it back until she'd swallowed every last drop. When she pulled the chalice away, her red lips had deepened in color, now so purple they were almost black.

This was a terrible idea, but she held out hope. With shaking hands, Lore placed the chalice to her lips and drank.

The wine was decadent and thick. Sour. It made her jaw ache, but then it turned sweet like ripe strawberries. Then there was something Lore couldn't place, but it made her eyes prick with tears.

It wasn't a flavor. It was an emotion.

Home.

Just then, Grey lifted his head.

He didn't stir at the sound of her voice, but he must have smelled the wine.

Dark circles lined his eyes. His shoulders jutted through the silk fabric of his shirt, birdlike. He looked around the room, passing over Lore without a second thought. He reached for the queen's cup; his fingertips were blue.

"Is there more wine, Your Highness?"

"Not for you, my dear. You've had enough today. If you drink any more, it will make your tummy hurt."

Anger flashed across Grey's features and then just as quickly dissolved. His shoulders slumped, dejected. "It won't. My throat is parched." He eyed the attendant with the decanter in his hands. His expression darkened.

Lore had never seen that look on his face before. It looked foreign, wrong. She glanced between her friend and the attendant.

"Hush now. You know I hate when you beg." The queen's reply was sharp and vicious, her beautiful features marred with annoyance.

Grey lay back, paying Lore no mind. The attendant, she noticed, seemed relieved that he wouldn't have to fight anyone. He took the opportunity to bow and retreat, taking his place back against the wall.

Had Grey even noticed she was there? Hadn't he recognized her?

The queen's consort leaned down to whisper into Grey's ear. Whatever she said contented him for the moment, and he settled against her lap once more, closing his eyes.

"What is your name, girl?"

"Tella." It had been a long time since Lore's mother's name had passed through her lips. She wasn't quite sure why, but something in her gut told her to lie.

"Tella, follow Naevrys. She will have you bathed and changed while we liven up the celebration. Come back to me and I will give you more wine."

No. No more wine.

Although, more wine sounded nice. Lovely. It was so very sweet. Lore frowned. Why had she lied to the nice queen about her name? She was about to open her mouth to confess, suddenly needing the queen to know her real name, when someone clenched their fingers around her arm, jerking her painfully toward them before she could. "Let's go," the voice said.

"You're hurting me." Lore said. Or thought she said. But now, she couldn't feel the lady with the wing's fingers at all. Had she really hurt her?

No, she wouldn't have. She must have imagined it.

Three beautiful palace attendants in matching uniforms washed Lore. They sang to her and marveled at her ears, touching the rounded tips like they were marvelous. They thought it was so silly how flat her teeth were. Lore opened her mouth wide, delighted that it made them laugh.

When they were done with the bath, they brushed out her hair, adding oils and creams until her coils shined like the sea at night. It had been so very long since anyone had brushed Lore's hair. The thought made her sad, but that was silly—wasn't she getting ready to celebrate something?

When her tangles were gone, two of the attendants wove flowers through her curls while the other rubbed a soothing oil all over her body.

A fourth attendant walked into the room; arms loaded down with dresses. They draped Lore in a satin slip and secured a taffeta corset embroidered with mushrooms and vines around her middle. Someone pinned a velvet cape around her shoulders—it was the color of the inside of a ripe plum.

She eyed herself in a tall, ornate looking glass. The dress hugged every one of her curves. Lore twirled easily in delicate slippers, marveling at how the dress seemed to cascade like a waterfall. Her lips were stained red from the wine and seemed to shine in the dim light. She pressed her fingers to her lips, unable to take her eyes from her reflection.

"Will there be more wine at the party?" Lore's mouth was dry, her throat parched. Someone else had said their throat was parched earlier. *Who was it?*

"Oh yes, Tella. You can have all the wine you wish."

Lore frowned, breaking free from the beauty in the mirror and eyeing the attendants. Tella was her mother's name. Why were they calling her that? But then she remembered that soon there would be more wine, and she smiled instead.

"I think I look very beautiful," Lore said, breathless and beaming.

The attendants exclaimed in agreement and began to drag her from the room toward the celebration.

When she entered the ballroom, Lore was handed a cup of wine with delicate flowers floating on top. Gone were the sleeping folks strewn around the room—in their place, a revelry in mid-swing. There were musicians stationed in every corner. The music filled her up and made her body hum.

A male in a velveteen vest and slippers took her hand and led her to the dance floor. His hand gripped her waist and pulled her to him. She threw her head back and danced with him before being passed to a woman wearing nothing but chiffon and an orb filled with moths upon her head.

It was the queen. Lore's legs turned liquid under the queen's gaze, her attention a toxin of its own.

"You look lovely, Tella." The queen reached out, cupping Lore's cheek.

"Not as lovely as you," Lore breathed. Her breath mingled with the queen's own.

The queen laughed, euphoric. "Dance with me."

"I would be honored."

The designs on the walls seemed to twist and twirl along with Lore, and the vines along the ceiling grew and began to sag with ripe fruit. Lore reached up, plucking a purple one from a vine, and bit into the flesh, laughing as the juices exploded from her lips, rich with sugary sweetness. She held the fruit out to the queen, overcome with joy when the queen gripped her hand and pulled it to her, biting into the plump fruit.

The juices dribbled down her pointed chin. Lore was mesmerized by the sight. She reached a hand out and wiped the juice, which seemed to shimmer with *Source* itself. She brought the shining liquid to her own lips to taste.

The queen's eyes fluttered with desire, and Lore's core clenched in response.

The night was lost to dance. As Lore spun from eager hands to hands, the music flowed through her like a waterfall, until she lay down beneath a sparkling chandelier, breathless. Her cheeks were sore from laughing.

Her chest heaved with breath, just as her stomach gave a sudden twinge and pain blinded her for a moment. It was like a knife stabbing into her abdomen, twisting, yanking, and pulling.

But when she pressed her hands to her stomach, there was no knife. No wound. Just internal, cramping pain.

As the chandelier began to come into focus, the haze of the wine began to lift. Lore remembered the bark she'd peeled from a tree and chewed for hours as she followed the map and found her way to the palace. She'd swallowed it just before she climbed into the farmer's wagon, and nuzzled in with the sleeping sheep, the taste of bitter bark coating her tongue.

Finally, it had soaked up the properties in the wine, allowing her to remember.

Now, she just had to pretend to still be heady with wine as she sought out Grey.

$$)) \mathbf{)} \bullet \mathbf{(} (($$

She found him swaying to music by one of the many hearths in the ballroom. Despite the smoky heat from the flames, he shivered, his skin covered in goosebumps.

"Grey." The breathless cry of his name fluttered from her mouth, though he did not turn. She wanted to pull him into her arms, grip him tightly, and shake him until he looked at her, but she dared not. Nobody had seen her stumble over here with a decanter of wine clutched in her hands, as she pretended to drink from it. "Would you like more wine?" she asked him.

He turned to her then and smiled.

Her heart fluttered with joy as she pulled him into an embrace. She thought of the moment he'd found her after the earthshake. It was so different from now, as his arms did not lift or wrap around her.

She leaned back, looking into his face—at his wavy, black hair and the piece that always fell in front of his eyes. Dread marred her joy. The marks of his time here were clear on his face: his bloodshot eyes; dry, cracked lips speckled with ruby beads of blood; and the hollows in his cheeks more pronounced than when she'd seen him in the vision in her scrying bowl. His shoulders were bony where she pressed against them, sharp through the fabric of his tunic.

"Wine?" His voice was rough, gravelly.

She steeled herself, clenching her jaw. "Yes. I have wine for you, see?" She swirled the wine in the decanter for him to see. She felt gross and evil as she tempted him with the very thing that was killing him, but there wasn't time for another plan.

She hadn't truly believed that he wouldn't recognize her. She was having to scramble now.

Grey leaned into her, toward the wine, and she pulled him, tugging on his wrist, until he took one halting step, and then another. She led him from the room, wishing more than anything that she had her grimoire. The palace was filled with *Source*, but without her book, it would not come to her when she called it.

She dragged him from the palace, sticking to the shadows. Her breath hitched when they passed a guard or a couple pressed together, but despite the danger around every corner, Grey followed Lore's whispered promises of wine, soon.

They burst out of the palace and raced toward the protective wall. Icy wind kissed Lore's glistening skin, and the moon greeted her like an old friend.

She placed a stopper into the pitcher of wine and tossed it over the barrier. It was the only way to encourage Grey to climb. His limbs shook with exhaustion, but eventually he made it over, landing with a cry on the other side. Lore scrambled after him, fingers scraped raw from the stone wall.

She dropped to her hands and knees and searched the ivy-covered ground. Somewhere around here was a large stone, and beneath that, her grimoire. She just needed to find it.

"No, not yet!" she hissed.

Grey had just pulled the stopper from the wine and was tipping the decanter toward his mouth, his movements jerky and rushed. She pulled the decanter from him—or tried to. His grip was iron-like, and he yelled, the sound torn from his chest and carrying over the wall.

Lore heard an answering cry from the guards. They'd heard him.

Fear enveloped Lore. She was out of time. She let go of the wine and looked away as Grey drank from it greedily, a man in a desert who'd just found his oasis.

The shouts of the guards were getting closer. She just had to find the rock. She tore at the ground. Goddess, had she made a mistake? Was this not the correct wall?

She almost despaired, just as her hand scraped painfully against a rock and brushed against the spine of her grimoire. She thrust the rock away and pulled the book into her arms.

She held it with one bloody hand and thrust her other into the dirt, pulling the *Source* from all around her. The sound of the guards climbing over the garden wall rained from above her.

She had but seconds—the *Source* was strong here near the queen's palace, and she wondered if this was why she'd built her palace here. Was it that, with so much *Source* around, the queen and her alchemists had flocked here?

Alight with *Source*, her hand began to glow, and Lore spoke Old Alytherian. She'd memorized this spell, had been practicing it for weeks. Finally, the shadows all around her leaped up to cover her. She rose, stumbling to where Grey knelt with the decanter, and she grabbed his hand. The shadows expanded to cover him, too.

"Hey, where did they go? I just saw them!" There was a guard on top of the garden wall, preparing to leap down, and another just behind him. They looked around, their eyes passing over Lore and Grey.

She pressed her mouth to Grey's ear and whispered. "Stand up. I have more wine at home. Come with me."

Grey stumbled, drunk, as she pulled him, but they went together into the dark.

CHAPTER 25

Finndryl was waiting in the Exile's kitchen when Lore and Grey stumbled through the door just as dawn was beginning to lighten the sky.

"What were you thinking?" Finndryl seethed. His eyes were wild and they alighted across her body, taking in her silk and chiffon dress and her slippers, which were now muddy and torn. When he was done assessing her, he visibly relaxed at her lack of obvious injuries.

Then he looked at Grey, who stood, swaying on his feet, his lips stained from blood and wine. His eyes were vacant and lost. He was slumped against Lore, his body giving out from exhaustion and neglect.

Finndryl closed the space between them. Despite his bared teeth and clear anger, he didn't hesitate to relieve Lore of her friend's weight. The moment Finndryl had Grey in his grip, the slighter man leaned into him, instantly asleep. Finndryl set him down in a seat at the table.

"Were you followed?" Finndryl stepped over to Lore, where she still stood by the door. His body radiated heat and warmth. She wasn't sure if she could take another step.

"No." The word tumbled from her lips.

He stepped closer to her, and she realized he was visibly

shaking. With rage? Fear? Lore wished she could read him more easily. She wished she could reach out and thread her fingers through his. But even if guilt wasn't holding her back, his hands were clenched into fists at his side.

She met his eyes.

They darkened, fury seething within their depths. "I'll make sure you weren't followed."

"I wasn't."

"I wish I could believe you."

"I used a spell. We weren't followed."

"How am I supposed to trust you when you put yourself in danger so willingly?"

"You ask this like you've ever trusted me to begin with. Besides, I had it handled." A wave of nausea swelled through her, and she felt her forehead. Goddess, she was sweating.

"We can speak about this more when I return. Just don't leave m— Don't leave again." He led her to the table where he'd set Grey down. He pulled a chair out for her, and she collapsed into it, leaning against Grey.

"Lore."

"Yes?" Her eyelids fluttered open.

"Promise me you will be here when I return." His voice was soft, barely carrying over the soft snores of Grey's sleeping form. The sound of his words sent an ache through Lore, and she glanced to where he'd paused in the doorway.

His back was to her and his head was bowed.

"I will be here."

Without another word, Finndryl picked up his sword and slipped out the door.

Lore hadn't realized she'd fallen asleep, but she woke up to Finndryl's hand on her shoulder, nudging her awake. Water was dripping from his locs and his sleeves.

It must be raining.

That was good. Rain would have helped cover Lore's tracks, in case her spell failed. He was furious still: his jaw was clenched and his brow was furrowed, but Lore thought that, underneath the fury, he was relieved.

She thought that because she felt the same. Just being near him again righted a wrong. She wanted to stand up and toss her arms around him and thank him for being there for her again. But she resisted the impulse.

"You weren't followed. We must bring him up now and strap him down. I'm not sure what he'll do when he wakes up and realizes there won't be more of the queen's food or drink."

Lore nodded. "Let me get the door."

Finndryl carried Grey up the stairs easily. Although her childhood friend was almost as tall as the average fae male, he'd lost so much weight and muscle mass that he looked as if he weighed nothing.

"I shouldn't have left without telling you. It was impulsive. Dangerous. And wrong." Lore could hardly keep her eyes open, and her stomach was still cramping painfully, but she couldn't end the night without admitting this to Finndryl.

"It's nice to hear you admit it. Now get some rest. When you wake, I expect you to tell me how you managed to break your friend out of the palace and live to tell the tale."

It took a week for Grey to stop calling for the queen's wine, his voice hoarse from screaming in agony as withdrawal racked his body.

Lore alternated between forcing bark and water down his throat and praying it wasn't too late for him. But the grimoire had not steered her wrong. It just took a lot longer for the bark to pull the poison from his body. He would sleep until his body heaved violently, and he would throw it up, the bark now black with poison.

It took another three days for Grey to recognize her, but when he did, the whisper of "Lore" was quiet between his lips. His eyes were clear, alert. His face twisted in fear and confusion, and Lore clung to him, her tears soaking his borrowed linen shirt.

"Yes. It's me. I'm here."

"Why does my body feel like a carriage ran over me?"

Lore laughed, the sound thick with tears. "That's so funny because I said that same thing a few weeks ago."

Grey groaned. "I want to laugh, but it hurts. Everything hurts."

"I know. You've been through so much." Lore squeezed his arm. "For now, just know you're safe. I'm taking care of you. Let me grab you some broth."

Grey closed his eyes, nodding softly.

Lore ran downstairs and burst into the tavern. The place was empty save for Flix, asleep in a corner booth. Finndryl eyed her from where he stood behind the bar, slicing up ginger root.

Lore's steps didn't falter. She raced behind the bar and threw herself into his arms. "He's awake, Finn! He's awake, and he knows me! The detox worked."

Finndryl laughed, dropping the knife to return Lore's embrace. He picked her up and spun her around, her skirts rustling against the counter. She pressed her face into his neck, her smile wide, and breathed him in. The spicy scent of him was enhanced by the smell of fresh ginger clinging to him.

Finndryl slowed the spin, his laugh catching in his throat as if he realized—at the same time Lore did—that this was the closest they'd been since that night when he'd carried her back to his father's house.

He let go, and Lore landed gently on the floor, clearing her throat. "Anyway, I wanted to come here and heat up some broth for him. I think he'll finally be able to keep it down."

"Right. I'm happy for you." Finndryl smiled again, running his hand through his locs. "Why don't you put some of this fresh ginger in it? It will help to settle his stomach."

"Oh, yes! I should have thought of that myself."

"You have a lot on your mind. If I can think of ways to help, I will." Finndryl scooped up a few slices of ginger and placed them in Lore's palm. He folded her fingers around the ginger and squeezed them.

Lore's stomach tumbled at the feeling of his hand on hers. "Thank you."

Finndryl nodded, giving her hand one last light squeeze and then pulling away to busy himself at the bar. Lore had to stop herself from reaching back out, if only to feel his touch for a moment longer. Lore turned to walk to the kitchen. She paused just before skirting around the edge of the bar. "For everything. Thank you for everything. If you hadn't helped me with my grimoire, Grey would have been lost to me forever."

"It's nothing." Finndryl's voice was thick. He went back to slicing the ginger, turning his back to Lore.

She stepped into the kitchen; her fist clenched around the ginger.

Finndryl's scent danced in her senses.

CHAPTER 26

I didn't think I'd see you again."

Lore sat beside Grey on Isla's bed; they'd been sharing it while Grey recovered. Light from the moon shone through the window, kissing her hands with its light. She frowned, realizing her fingertips were stained black where they'd touched the grimoire.

How long had they been like this? She wiped them on her trousers, but the black pigment didn't come off. She was used to her hands being stained with colors; she'd worked in an apothecary since she was a child. Her hands were almost always multicolored from dyeing fabric or creating medicinal poultices. But this was different. It looked like her fingertips were just . . . black.

As black as the spaces between the stars on clear nights.

As if she'd been born with them this way.

Unease bubbled up in her stomach, but she pushed it down. She didn't want to worry Grey. This would have to be something she figured out later. Just another mystery to add to the ever-growing pile.

"I have so much to tell you."

"And I have a lot to tell you."

"Like why or how it is that you escaped from Duskmere?" Lore asked.

"*How* I escaped Duskmere? Well, I didn't have a choice. The fear. The sentries. I couldn't let them stop me from finding you. I knew I had to find you, and I knew that, when I did, you would have found magic. I've always known you would find a way." He squeezed her hand.

Lore grinned, excitement thrumming through her. "I did find a way." In hushed tones, she told him about finding the grimoire and the magic it allowed her to access.

When she finished, Grey sat across from her on the bed with his mouth hanging open.

"Say something!"

"Where do I start? How is it that you can communicate with a book? What did you give to it when you made that bargain? How can a human do magic? Can you teach me?" His voice rose an octave with each question.

Lore bit her lip, searching his eyes. "I don't have an answer to any of those questions. I honestly have no idea what I gave it other than taking it from the castle, but it doesn't matter. Without it, I would be in a dungeon or, more than likely, dead. I want to bring this gift home to our people. I want to carve out a real existence for us. No more of this half-life, no more being too afraid to explore this world. You know, when I saw the ocean for the first time, I couldn't believe that all this time we could have been fishing there. We could've been filling our children's bellies instead of watching them go hungry."

Her voice was beginning to rise as her anger ignited anew.

"We could've built ships and explored this world. Settled into a territory of our own and become a sovereign nation. With access to magic, maybe we can do what our ancestors never could—leave this vile place forever, you know?" She sat up, leaning closer

to him. "Any sacrifice that I make will be worth it if we can become our ancestors' wildest dreams."

Grey's eyes reflected her own determination back to her. He
understood. Her pain was his as well. Their history the same.
"Because of you we finally have a fighting chance. You having
magic changes everything." He pulled her into a hug and Lore
squeezed him back, taking a moment to sit in this safe, familiar
space with him.

"There was something I left out of the story, though," Lore
said, her voice tinged with mischief.

"Oh, gods, do I even want to know?" Grey said with a laugh.

"I might have, um—kissed someone." Lore's cheeks heated,
and her stomach tightened at the memory of Asher's lips.

Grey sat up, leaned his back against the headboard, and pulled
an embroidered pillow to his chest. "You're going to tell me all
about this, aren't you?" He waggled his brows. "How I've missed
your dramatic romantic endeavors! Better than any romance
novel." Lore inwardly grimaced. *If only.* Even though Grey wasn't
interested in a relationship himself, he'd always rooted for her
amorous attempts.

Grey's teasing reminded her of past lovers' fumbling kisses.
Of boys' clumsy fingers, and youthful territorial demands, as if
allowing them to touch her meant they now owned her.

"Yes, I am. In insufferable detail." Lore looked around at the
wallpapered walls and lingered on the closed door. Finndryl was
in his room just across the hall.

Could he hear them? She was sure he could.

"You weren't kidding about having a lot to tell me." Eyebrow
raised, he looked amused, but she could also see he was a little
freaked. If Lore had kissed someone after leaving Duskmere,
there was no way that person was human, and that in and of itself
meant things would be complicated.

Lore lowered her voice, and in hushed tones told him all about Asher. She waited with bated breath, afraid of what Grey would say. Would he tell her she'd been stupid for allowing a fae to squirrel his way into her heart? That kissing him would only make it harder when they ultimately returned to Duskmere? That she was a terrible person for allowing herself to be so distracted when Duskmere was in the state it was in? All of these thoughts that had swirled through Lore's mind would hurt a hundred times more if spoken out loud by him.

"You *would* fall for the enemy," Grey said through a grin.

Relieved, Lore playfully pushed him. "He's not the enemy. He's why I'm alive, to be honest. And when you meet him, you'll see why I just can't seem to stop myself from kissing him."

"I will, huh?"

"Yup. Now tell me, what news of home do you have?"

Grey's eyes glistened with unshed tears, and he spoke her name—or tried to, but his voice broke. He cleared his throat, trying again. "Lore, there is something I have to tell you, but I don't know how to say it. You asked me earlier why I left Duskmere. Before this morning, I wouldn't have been able to tell you. It's like Queen Riella's wine stopped the words. But they've finally come back this morning. I don't even want to tell you this because you've lost so much already but—" He reached out and grabbed her hands again, squeezing.

Lore pulled in a breath, steeling her stomach. She was used to bad news, but she was never ready. She could never be ready for it.

"Our people have been taken. So many of them. And Aunty Eshe . . . Aunty Eshe was hurt badly protecting Kyon and Milo. I don't know if she made it. Our elders tried protecting those they took, but the sentries were merciless. There was so much blood." Grey paused, letting this sink in. He continued. "We think they're being held at Wyndlin Castle. The fae wore the black and gold of Alytheria, and their sentries aided in the roundup. I was able to escape, so I came to find you, knowing you spent time there. I hoped you'd have enough knowledge of the castle to help us rescue them."

Lore's face crumpled, and hot tears burned her eyes. She bent in half, pushing her face into her hands. Agony like she'd never known burned through her entire body. It was one thing to lose a loved one—she'd lost the two most important people in her life by the time she was nine. But it was another thing to have everything she'd ever known taken away. And the uncertainty of where her people were—the thought of what horrors they must be going through—left her shattered.

She couldn't stomach it. How was she supposed to get through the *not* knowing?

Were they being hurt right now? Who was taking care of the other kids? Were they with Uncle Salim? Her heart broke again, thinking of the pain he must have felt when he saw his partner hurt. A soft sob escaped into her hands.

Eshe and Salim Okorofor had a love story out of a storybook. They'd been together since they were fifteen. Unable to have their own kids, they'd taken in every child who didn't have a home. They provided them with safety, food, clothes, and, more importantly, a family.

The dark fae had come in and taken everything from her. It was one thing to hurt her—but to hurt those she loved? She wouldn't stand for it.

Lore allowed herself one more moment to cry—allowed herself one more deep wave of grief to rack her body with sobs.

And then she stilled. Drying her face with her hands and pushing her damp hair away from her eyes, she looked at Grey, whose own eyes were bloodshot.

"We must leave tonight. How many were taken?"

Grey nodded, relief showing on his face. He'd come to find her because he'd known she would take action. She'd always been the leader in their duo, and he would follow her to the ends of the earth.

He *had* followed her to the ends of the earth. After all, here he was, sitting in front of her.

"Thirty, I think."

How were they going to get so many out of a spelled and fortified castle? They would need help. She thought for a moment of Finndryl and Gryph, but there was no way she could ask them to risk their lives. She was already the reason Isla was in danger.

Still, the thought of never seeing Finn again made her ill.

And Asher . . . who knew where he even was? She thought he would want to help, but she had no way of finding out where he was. Her locator spells had barely been able to let her know he was still alive. Grey and Lore were an entire kingdom away from him and Isla. And more importantly, could they make it there without being captured?

She would have to try.

She wanted Aunty Eshe to be safe and unhurt, and for her people to be settled somewhere new, far away from the dark fae and everyone who wanted nothing more than to see them harmed. She wanted every single person from Duskmere to be returned to their families unharmed. She wanted Grey to be there, safe, whole, and surrounded by his family.

She wanted the earthshake to have never happened and to sit next to Aunty Eshe at night, grinding flowers, discovering new pigments, and trying recipes for their scented oils.

She smiled, thinking about the time she'd mistaken *dekia* buds for *jassimine* flowers and her "perfume" had made the entire kitchen smell for a day. Aunty Eshe had laughed so hard, pinching her beautiful, wide nose and pretending to faint from the fumes.

Lore fell asleep with burning eyes and her grimoire in her arms. She dreamed of a future where she led her people to a new settlement, one by the ocean where they could build boats and travel the world, no longer unwanted prisoners on Alytherian soil, but a proud people with land all their own.

Lore woke with a start, sitting up and tucking the journal beneath the pillow.

Somebody was in the room with them.

CHAPTER 27

Lore reached out to shake Grey, but he wasn't there. He was standing by the window, talking to a shadowed figure with twin swords slung low on his hips.

Lore jumped out of the bed. Her feet tangled up in the sheets and she flipped off the end of the bed, landing on the floor on her back.

Asher ran over to her, kneeling beside her and laughing quietly. She would've died from embarrassment, but she was too busy laughing herself. Relief swept through her entire body like a balm.

How was he here?

"You are ridiculous, but I'm so happy to see you," Asher said through a quiet chuckle.

"Is it really you?"

"It's really me. I didn't expect to see your friend here, though." He looked at Grey with an eyebrow raised.

"Me neither . . ." Lore's voice trailed off as Asher leaned in toward her, cupping her cheeks. Long fingers curled in her hair, and he cut her off with a kiss. A low growl erupted from his chest, and she couldn't stop her own answering moan. His smell, his taste—everything about him was intoxicating.

She heard Grey leave the room, closing the door behind him softly. A true friend, that one.

Asher pulled her up until she was straddling him. His excitement at seeing her pressed between them, hard against her stomach. She wrapped her arms around his thick neck and slid her hands in his soft curls, wrapping her palms around his antlers as she ground into him.

Goddess, he tasted like blackberries. She pulled his pouty bottom lip into her mouth and nibbled it. Asher growled at that, tightening his arms on her back for a moment, deepening the kiss.

Through panting breaths, between kisses, he scolded her. "I heard what you did, leaving the safety of Gryph's house and sneaking into the palace."

Lore bit her lip. She was having trouble getting her thoughts in order. His eyes were dark with desire. She wanted to marvel at the heat in them, but she kept dipping down to look at that pouty lip. She wanted to bite it again. "I didn't have a choice," she murmured before leaning in to kiss him again.

Asher pulled back a moment, his eyes searching hers. "Did she hurt you?" Asher pulled her close again, threading his fingers through her curls, and pressed her cheek into his chest, growling. "I've heard what she does to those she collects. If she hurt you, tell me. You're mine to protect."

Lore's stomach tumbled at the word "mine" and she bit her lip in surprise— she'd never belonged to anyone before. She'd never wanted to be anyone's either, would not have tolerated it, but she loved the idea of being Asher's. She craved it. "I'm glad I have you on my side, Asher. I don't ever want to find out what it's like to be your enemy."

He threw his head back and laughed. "You don't have to worry about that, my little mouse."

She loved his laugh. She leaned in to kiss him again, thinking that maybe now was a good time to move to the bed.

Asher spoke before she could. "Isla and Finn are waiting for us downstairs. As much as I would love to continue our reunion, we have much to discuss."

Wait. "How *are* you and Isla here right now? Last I saw, you were on a mountain, leagues away."

He grinned. "You saw us? How? Ah, I see. Your powers have grown."

"In surprising ways."

"I can't wait to hear all about it."

"Are you two done?" Grey called through the door. "We don't have much time."

Lore leaned in and kissed Asher, wishing they had all the time in the world to taste each other, explore each other. Asher felt the same because he pulled her to him with his arm, crushing her to his chest, as if he couldn't get close enough to her. He kissed up her jaw, and sighed into her ear, and Lore thought it was the most beautiful sound, him breathless against her. She jerked her hips, unbidden, against his hard length that pressed against her, and he groaned at the sensation—Lore realized there was a more beautiful sound after all. Grey knocked again, and with a sigh, Lore slid off Asher's lap and pulled the door open. Hoping her cheeks weren't too flushed, she said, "Grey, remember? I told you about Asher. This is him." She waved her hand in his direction, as if he could have somehow missed the giant fae male in the room.

Grey raised an eyebrow, his eyes crinkling with amusement at the corners. "Mmhmm, we met while you were over there clutching your pillow like it was going to make an escape."

She was going to give him so much shit the next time they were alone. She rubbed the back of her neck. When had it gotten so hot in here? She glanced at Asher, giving him a shaky laugh. It was so bizarre seeing the two of them together.

Two worlds colliding.

Lore said quietly, "I have a lot to update you on. Grey brought grave news from Duskmere."

Asher frowned. "I think I know it. That's why we were on our way back. To tell you." He sighed. "I ran into a friend while we were in the mountains. He'd just traveled from Wyndlin and he—he was part of the troop that—" Asher looked ill, not wanting to finish his sentence. "He was in the troop that was in charge of rounding them up."

"Did he say why Wyndlin wanted them?" Grey was suddenly in Asher's face, no longer hanging by the door.

But Asher didn't back away. He took Grey's aggression in stride, no doubt realizing that no matter what, emotions were going to run high.

"No, I'm sorry. My friend wasn't briefed on that. Apparently, nobody low-ranking knows. The information has been kept between the officers and some of the royalty. They've tried to keep it hush-hush."

Grey looked ill.

Lore walked up to him, placing her hand in his. "We're going to save them, Grey. We're going to save them all."

$$)) \,\blacktriangleright\, (($$

The Exile was empty of patrons. Even Flix wasn't in his usual booth or perched at the bar. Gryph must have cleared the place out.

Lore locked the door behind her just before seeing a rush of sparkles. Lore pounced, pulling Isla into a tight hug. "I'm so happy to see you safe," Lore breathed into Isla, not letting her go just yet.

"You weren't really worried about me, were you?"

"I might've been." Lore pulled back from their embrace with a shrug.

"If everyone is done with the reunions, Isla just told me some disturbing news and I think we need to come up with a plan," Finndryl said from where he sat at a table beside Gryph.

Lore gave him a soft smile. She searched his eyes for any of the warmth that had been there just that morning when it had been only the two of them in this very room. She found none. Any kindness he'd shown her over the last two weeks had dissipated with Asher's return.

The dismissal stung.

She took her place beside Asher. Isla had filled Finndryl and Gryph in while Asher and Grey had been upstairs.

"So, you know that Grey and I must return to Wyndlin to rescue those who were taken. We'll leave in the morning." Lore looked at where Gryph sat between the twins, the giant with kind eyes. "I'm sorry to leave so suddenly. About the kitchens—"

"Don't worry about it, love. I've always known your stay here was temporary. I've already talked to Flix's oldest two kids. They are more than willing to cook for the Exile. Gods know they can use the work."

Lore nodded. *That's good.* Flix may have a sickness that meant he couldn't provide for his family, but Gryph did what he could to help. "Right. Well, we haven't much time to come up with a plan to somehow rescue—"

"You don't really think that we would let you do this alone?" Finndryl spoke up, his voice laced with ice.

"We could never—"

Finn cut her off. "Grey has barely regained his strength."

"But Isla only just returned—"

"I love helping my dad out with the Exile, but he's a big boy. He doesn't need his kids babysitting him all the time," Isla said, giving her father a light cuff on the shoulder.

"I didn't raise my kids to ignore those in need. Anything you need from here—food, supplies, anything—just take it."

Lore's eyes stung with tears. She'd hoped, but she couldn't have asked. "I don't know how or when I can repay you—"

"Little one, you've brought life back into this tavern. My business is booming. How could I repay you for that? The supplies are nothing at all. No, don't protest, I won't hear another word."

"All right. All right. I won't." Lore put her hands up before her, relenting.

Gryph was not one to be swayed once he set his mind to something.

"Look. I know the castle like the back of my hand. If I can have a piece of parchment and some charcoal, I can draw up a map," Asher said.

"I have a stash in the kitchen," Lore said, standing up.

"Good, love. Grab the supplies and let's get to work," Gryph said, his voice a rumble.

Lore hurried to where she and Finndryl kept their study supplies. She flicked through weeks of their work. Translations, alphabets, a doodle that Finndryl had sketched while Lore had been working on a particularly difficult passage. It was a simple sketch of their mugs where they had sat on the table, steam drifting up, swirling, artfully done. She remembered that evening, it seemed to take forever for their tea to cool enough for them to drink. Lore grabbed the paper and folded it up, slipping it into her pocket. If asked she couldn't say why she wanted to take this memory with her, just that she wasn't quite ready to let it go.

"The charcoal is up here, I moved it the other day," Finndryl remarked from behind her.

Lore jumped, spinning around. Had he seen her fold that drawing up and slip it into her pocket? "What?" she asked.

"I put the charcoal on the top shelf here. I figured you wouldn't be able to reach it."

"No, I can't reach up there." Lore's cheeks were burning. Finndryl hadn't seen her; if he had, he would be teasing her about it right now. Or maybe he wouldn't. Finndryl wasn't even looking at her.

"If you move, I can get it down for you."

"Of course. Why did you place it up there anyway?" she asked as she stepped to the side. Finndryl took her place in front of the shelf and reached with ease—his arms were incredibly long.

Finndryl shrugged. "I needed the table."

Lore frowned. That wasn't really an answer. "But you know I can't reach up there, and we use this charcoal nearly every—"

"You can't have thought we would continue our research with him back, did you?"

"Well, I don't see how—"

"Just drop it. Here." He shoved the charcoal at her, his eyes cold.

This wasn't right. Lore wanted to take him by the shoulders and shake him. "It doesn't have to be like this—"

"He's waiting."

Lore reached out, placing her hand on Finn's arm. "Wait, Finn, I—"

Finn jerked his arm away from her. "Just go."

Lore stepped backward in shock. He'd reacted like she'd stabbed his arm or something, and not just laid her hand upon it. She drew her lips into a thin line as she roughly scooped up the papers on the table, no longer caring if they got wrinkled. "Fine. Have it your way."

She returned to the table and handed Asher the papers and charcoal.

The group worked through the night, fine-tuning their strategy and preparing for the journey ahead. They knew it wouldn't be easy, but they were determined to rescue the people who needed their help.

As the sun rose, they were exhausted but satisfied. They had done as much as they could in the time allotted to prepare for the mission.

Gryph stood from the table and stretched. "Okay, let's get some rest while we can. You younglings have a long journey ahead of you."

The group dispersed. Asher and Lore stayed back to clean up the diagrams and maps. They stashed them next to the supplies Grey and Isla had packed for them.

"Asher, you've had a long journey. I can wash these cups if you want to head upstairs and get some rest. I'm too restless to sleep right now." Lore gathered the mugs and carried them to the kitchens.

"Let me get that." Asher ran in front of her and opened the door.

Lore slid past him, his body heat sending shivers up her arms. She dumped the cups into the sink. She was just about to fill the sink with water when she felt Asher step up behind her. He placed one hand on her hip.

His breath stirred the curls on top of her hair. "I just got back to you. Do you think I'm letting you out of my sight again?"

Lore's hands stilled just above the faucet. He had a point. She didn't want to let him out of her sight, either. She turned around to face him. Her skin flashed hot at their closeness and her chest constricted.

Asher was looking at her, his eyes dark with desire. Lore didn't ever have to wonder what he was thinking—he wore his emotions on his face. He wanted her and he let it be known. Things were easy with him, unlike with Finn. Warm then cold, one moment aloof and uncaring, and then risking his life for her the next. Every aspect of Lore's life was complicated. With Asher it was never confusing. She needed someone who would be open with her. She didn't want to question where she stood when it came to how someone felt about her.

"Good. I didn't want you to leave, anyway," she whispered. She wanted him closer. To *feel* the way he felt about her against her lips, her skin. She wanted to be sure about something, at last.

"You could've fooled me. I thought you were afraid to be alone with me or something." Asher lifted a finger up and brushed her flyaway curls behind her ear, taking a moment to caress the rounded tip.

Heat shot from that sensitive spot on her ear down to her core. Lore clenched her thighs together, but it didn't help ease the pulsing ache there.

"Mmm, do you like this? My ears are sensitive too, you know."

"I could—" Lore lost her train of thought. Asher had begun to swirl the tip of her ear between his fingers. And the hand on her hip tightened deliciously. "I could never be afraid of you."

A low growl of approval erupted in his chest. "You have never had a very good sense of self-preservation. Always running headfirst into danger. I sometimes wonder if you have a bit of adrenaline-seeking behavior, Mouse."

"I don't—"

Lore's protest died on her lips as his fangs glimmered in the purple light of dawn and he pressed his lips to her throat. He scraped down with his teeth until he reached the spot where her neck met her shoulder, then he bit down. Not enough to break the skin, but just enough for molten fire to shoot through Lore's veins. Nothing existed outside of the brand of his mouth on her.

"I'm so much stronger than you," he crooned. "You *should* be afraid of me. In fact, you should push me away right now." His words were spoken softly against her skin, the plea in them apparent. He was telling her to push him away, even if it was the last thing he wanted her to do.

Lore couldn't even if she'd wanted to. At some point, she'd brought her hands up and fisted them in his shirt, gripping him to her. "You couldn't hurt me."

"I could hurt you in more ways than you know. But I can't seem to stop tasting you," Asher murmured. "Simply delight-ful." He pulled her sleeve aside and began trailing kisses down her shoulder. He chuckled, although the sound ended in a groan. "Mouse, if you keep untucking my shirt, I'm going to do very bad things to you."

Lore began untucking it in earnest.

He pulled the thin skin of her throat into his mouth and bit. Hard. The sharp pain—mingling with pleasure—sent liquid heat straight to her core. Lore moaned, sliding her head back to give him more access. Asher reached up and gripped her throat, kissing and biting her harder.

"Asher." Lore breathed.

"Yes?" He was licking and nibbling at her collarbone now.

"Kiss me."

Asher froze for the barest of moments. Lore could tell he was warring with himself.

Ultimately, he lost.

Or won.

Lore wasn't sure, because every thought scattered from her brain as he picked her up and she wrapped her legs around him. He walked over to the table in three long strides and placed her on it. Her core pulsed to her heartbeat, and she ached at the feel of him between her thighs.

"If I kiss you, I won't be able to stop."

She pressed her legs around him as Asher searched her face for any sign that she didn't want this. Any sign that he should stop.

He found none.

And then he was kissing her, claiming her. His mouth was hot and insistent on hers. She opened for him, her tongue tangling with his, and she could taste the sweetness of him. The kiss was fierce and wild, like they were both starving for each other.

Asher's hands roamed over her body, cupping her breasts and sliding down her sides to grip her hips. She moaned into his mouth, her body arching up to meet his.

Closer. Closer. She needed to be closer. He'd been gone for so long—she needed to feel him. To see him. To know that he was really here.

Lore pulled Asher's shirt up over his head and marveled at the sight. It was all sharp angles and muscles, so different from her own body. She leaned forward and kissed a scar on his chest, marveling at the sweet and salty taste of him.

Goddess, his skin is smooth like butter.

But she didn't have long to explore because Asher was lifting her dress above her head. He cursed when he saw her full breasts for the first time.

"You're a work of art. Your maker must have spent forever perfecting you." His head dipped, and he pulled one of her breasts into his mouth, then bit down on her taut bud, swirling his tongue.

Lore cried out, pulling him to her.

His free hand trailed up her side, leaving goosebumps behind. He cupped her other breast, flicking the nipple between his agile fingers.

Her core was on fire. Goddess, this wasn't enough. She needed—she needed . . .

"More," she gasped out. "Asher, give me more."

Asher growled, pushing her back onto the table. Lore had chopped countless vegetables here. Translated a hundred texts.

She squirmed. She'd never thought that—

Oh, gods.

Asher was sliding her underwear down her legs and spreading her thighs. He dropped to his knees and licked his lips at the sight of her spread bare before him. There was no sign of the male who coaxed plants with gentle hands. He looked like a predator who would eat her alive.

He licked her slit before devouring her like she was an antidote and he was on the brink of death from poison. He licked and kissed, parting her to gain more access.

Lore closed her eyes as the ache that had been building up in her since his return grew. She felt like she was on fire. Every nerve ending was alive and tingling. She pushed up against him, wanting more. Needing more.

She moaned, wrapping her hands around his antlers and drawing him closer. She gasped when he drew her clit into his mouth and sucked. Her thighs began to shake, and Asher gripped each one in his hands, spreading her wider still while holding her in place as she writhed beneath him.

He teased her, raising her up higher and higher until the sweet pleasure of it all made her cry out in ecstasy.

Asher lapped up every last drop of her before kissing each one of her still shaking thighs. As tremors and aftershocks tingled through her body, Lore silently thanked the goddess Rahada, who surely must have sent Asher to her.

"Now that I've had a taste, I can't imagine ever giving this up," Asher growled.

She'd never experienced anything like this. She knew now that every fumbling boy back home hadn't had a clue what they were doing.

Asher stood, pulling her to him so once again he was placed before her. He kissed her softly. The taste of her pleasure on his lips was a decadent thing. Something to be savored. But she could feel the thick length of him pressing at his breeches, begging to spring free.

Lore reached out and felt him, wanting to do for him what he had for her.

But Asher stilled her with a hand on her wrist. "Lore, when I take you for the first time, it won't be with my friends within earshot of us. After we do what we have to in Wyndlin, I'll take you far away. Somewhere I can have you all to myself."

Lore wanted to protest.

"Don't pout. You need your rest. We leave in a few hours." He licked his lips, which did very little to calm her. "Come, I'll walk you upstairs and then I'll finish up these dishes."

CHAPTER 28

Lore, Asher, Grey, Isla, and Finndryl made an odd squad.
Finndryl was back to his old self: standoffish, glaring at
Asher, and not even looking at her. How had Lore forgotten how much she used to dislike him? And yet, she missed him,
despite him being only a few feet from her. It made her heart
ache, but she couldn't think of it now, because at the moment, she
could barely breathe.

They made their way north, though the path they took was
treacherous. Asher led the way through the uninhabited terrain
and, when Lore wasn't scaling cliff faces, or trying not to panic
as they walked through cave systems, Asher taught her how to
navigate by the stars. In return, she showed him some of the
new spells she'd been learning with Finndryl's help.

During a short break at a river where they refilled their water
skins and took a moment to breathe, Lore soaked her swollen feet
in the freezing water. As she ran her hands in the water, wishing
she had the power to control the flow, she saw Asher taking note
of her fingertips.

They were now completely blackened, and the insides of her
palms were stained, too. The black, ink-like stain had curled like

wispy smoke up the backs of her hands. She felt embarrassed for a moment—would he think they were ugly?

She quickly shook her hands dry and placed them in her pockets. "I think that every time I use a spell, more ink from the book stains my fingers," she started to explain.

He stopped her from saying more. "If the price for your power is ink-stained fingers, then I'll worship this ink. Power is beautiful and, Lore, you're the most beautiful creature I've ever laid eyes on," he whispered for her ears only. He gently pulled her hands from her pockets and kissed each fingertip in turn.

Her core warmed at each feather-light kiss.

Lore dropped her hands to her side. "My power only works at night, and dawn is coming."

)))●(((

They traveled for another two days, sleeping for brief stretches and switching lookouts.

Finally, after a luminous, dusky sky dawned on the fourth day, they made it to the Wyndlin Castle grounds just as vendors were setting up for market day.

Lore used a headscarf to cover her ears and Grey had tied her green ribbon across his forehead to cover his own.

They walked through the gates, purses heavy with coin Lore had glamoured from stones in the river, and acted like they were just a group of friends looking for a food stall.

Once they made it past the guards, the group split up. Lore had a plan and Asher knew the grounds.

Between the two of them, they would get in, no matter what.

CHAPTER 29

Lore cursed when her feet hit the marble floor of the library. She landed funny and her ankle smarted. She quickly moved to the side so Grey could drop in behind her.

They both sighed with relief when he tumbled through the open window and climbed down the shelf without vaporizing into dust or turning to stone.

They had discussed both very real possibilities—just because he was human didn't mean he could get through the wards. Lore didn't trust anything Chief Steward Vinelake had said, and she wanted Grey to know that.

But he was human, and he'd made it.

Lore and Grey went straight to one of the supply closets in the library, though Grey could hardly focus; he was so enamored with the library. Pride crept through the moth wings in Lore's stomach, settling in with all her nervous energy.

The place had really begun to look beautiful. She had put in work here, and it showed.

Lore smiled when she opened the closet, which was exactly how she had left it.

As she'd remembered, the library had not only been filled with books and scrolls—there were entire closets filled with extra supplies and relics, rusted and long forgotten. But she suspected some of the weapons she'd come across were spelled, because when she pulled one of the swords from the scabbard, it still gleamed like it had been polished that morning.

And when she gently pressed her thumb against the edge to test it, it sliced through her skin like a hot knife through butter.

"I can't believe there are really uniforms in here," Grey said, holding a guard's tunic to his chest. It was too big and faded with age, but it was the smallest size they could find.

"I know. They aren't current, but the symbol and color hasn't changed over the years, it seems. I think we can move through the castle without suspicion as long as we don't run into any guards."

They changed quickly, Lore tightening a sword belt along her hips. The short sword hung at her side, light as a feather. From its balance alone, she knew it must be worth a fortune. She had barely been able to lift Asher's military-issued swords. A piece of cloth from one of the tunics wrapped around the elaborate sword hilt obscured the fox head with ruby eyes carved into the handle. The sword would draw more attention than a faded uniform.

Grey attached a bow and arrows to his back. He'd been hunting for his family since he was a kid, and he was an incredible shot. He strapped another short sword to his own hips. His was of a similar design to Lore's but had an owl head on the end, surrounded by flowers instead of vines.

They grabbed three more uniforms and some more weapons, then climbed back up the shelf to the window.

The fox Lore used to feed was waiting on the roof at the top, and the morning sun glinted off its sienna-colored fur. It was waiting as if she'd never left.

"I don't have any treats for you today. I'm sorry."

The fox sat back on its haunches, tilting its head. It watched them with its otherworldly eyes, unmoving.

Lore kneeled next to Grey on the ledge and peered over to the ground. Almost everyone was at the market, but while they'd been in the library, two guards had moved to the smaller garden outside the library windows.

The guards were standing right at the base of the tree they needed to use to climb down. One guard pulled out a pipe and lit it with fire magic. Puffs of gray smoke billowed around him. Could there be a worse time for them to take a smoke break?

Lore and Grey had already taken a long time in the library, and they needed to meet the others in Asher's secret garden so they could suit up.

The fox chirped, swishing its tail around. Its large silver eyes were curious.

"I don't have any food for you, little one. We need to get down there, but I'm afraid this will be the last time I see you."

Lore tentatively reached out a hand; the fox was adorable, but it had incredibly sharp teeth and she wasn't stupid. When it eyed her approaching hand but didn't growl, she brushed its head.

The fox leaned into her, nuzzling her palm.

Grey gasped and Lore beamed. "It loves me!" she whispered.

She yelped when the fox suddenly moved, jumping off the ledge and onto a tree branch that stretched all the way across the grounds. It jumped down and landed on the fae guard with the pipe.

The pipe was knocked from his hand and tumbled to the manicured lawn, which promptly began smoking. The other guard swore, immediately standing to stomp on the embers.

The fox yipped, prancing around playfully before racing off across the grounds, looking like little more than an orange blur.

Lore swore under her breath. No animal should be able to run that fast, certainly not a small fox.

The owner of the pipe leaned down and picked it up from the ground, dusted it off, and slid it into a pocket in his uniform.

He mentioned something to his friend, scratching his head before they walked off toward the side entrance to the castle.

Break time was over.

Lore and Grey didn't waste a second. They scrambled across the tree branch and shimmied down the tree before racing to the entrance of the secret garden.

Asher was by her side the moment she pushed through the garden door. "I was just about to say fuck it and come looking for you," he said.

"I'm here! We had some trouble with some guards, but a fox helped us."

"What?" Finndryl asked.

Grey chuckled. "We can explain later. Let's go. The market is in full swing and if we want to get out of here with the crowd, then we've got to leave now."

The others put on the guard uniforms and weapons, though Finndryl didn't take any of the latter—he kept his grandfather's long sword strapped to his back, stating tersely that it was all he needed.

Lore had managed a cloaking spell on the sword; now, there was hardly a lump to be seen beneath his cloak.

It was time for the next part of their plan.

CHAPTER 30

Asher strode toward a statue in the corner of the garden. His long legs carried him there quickly. Lore followed hesitantly because the statue they were heading toward was shaped into a haunting visage.

The statue featured a female dark fae carved from marble. She sported tall, feathered wings that were spread wide. Twin black, curved ram antlers jutted out from her forehead and back toward her wings. Reptilian scales were etched into her muscular forearms and hooves protruded from beneath her dress. A spotted tail twirled behind her.

In juxtaposition to her other highly detailed features, her face was featureless. An ancient, rusted mirror stood in place of eyes, nose, and mouth, as if she were waiting for others to see their own reflection, no matter their heritage.

Lore couldn't shake the feeling that the statue was studying her and finding her wanting. She tore her gaze from it, brushing off chills. It was truly a work of art, but she wouldn't complain if she never had to see it again.

"Well, that's unnerving," Isla said from behind Lore. "What are we doing so close to the star of my future nightmares?"

Asher, who was kneeling in front of the statue, gave a muffled reply just before a grating sound broke out. He heaved his shoulder against the base of the statue until a square space opened, one leading to pitch-black darkness.

This was just like the secret door to the secret garden.

"My brother and I discovered this passage when we were little," he said, pushing the statue a little farther. "We were left on our own and spent hours playing hide-and-seek in the abandoned wing of the castle—the quarters that used to house the queens and royal children of Alytheria." He stood and rolled his shoulders. "Actually, the only reason we found this garden was because of this passageway, not the hidden gate out there." He motioned toward the gate they'd all walked through to get from the castle's gardens.

"You spent your childhood playing beneath this thing? That explains a lot, actually," said Finndryl from where he stood by Grey.

Asher grinned at Finn. "Just wait until you see the passageway."

Lore looked around at everyone. All her friends were here, risking their lives for people most of them had never met. "Thank you for coming with me."

They met her eyes in turn, knowing that, although they were all going to crawl into that dark space willingly, they might not all be coming out.

))) ● (((

The passage immediately opened onto a set of rusted stairs.

The farther down they went, the damper and mustier the air became. A glowrock balanced in Isla's outstretched hand lit the way. The walls on either side of the passageway were slick with moisture and a thick layer of moss grew in the wettest spots. Lore couldn't believe anything could grow here without light.

Soon, they were in a large cavern and walking on an old brick pathway. A roaring river rushed alongside the narrow path, and the sound of the thunderous water made Lore want to faint. She held her breath and walked with her hand pressed to the wall. Slick or not, she needed to feel something solid to support her.

"We only have another hundred feet or so before we come to another staircase that will lead us to the abandoned wing." Though Asher spoke in a quiet voice, his lilting words echoed back to them.

In all its multiplicity, the echo made it sound like there was an army of Ashers.

Lore *wished* they had an army.

She nearly jumped out of her skin every time they heard the slightest noise from farther down the tunnel.

Asher continued. "I heard a whisper a long time ago that the river beneath these grounds empties into the sea. We can lead your people here. If it doesn't lead to the sea, we'll see where it takes us and can come up with a plan from there."

Grey spoke up. "Right. The most important thing is getting them away from this place. We've already taken so long."

"I can't shake the feeling that we're walking toward our death with such a half-assed plan." Finn's voice was laced with annoyance.

"Well, if you can come up with a better one, please enlighten us, Finn," Isla snapped.

Lore slowed until she was walking in step with Finn. "You know, you don't have to do this. You can leave now and none of us will think any less of you."

"I *do* have to do this." His tone was curt and clipped. Even in the dark, Lore could see his hands were clenched in tight fists.

She frowned. "If it's because of Isla, I can talk to her. Maybe I can convince her not to come, either."

Finn and Isla were both risking their lives for her. She had no right to ask them to do this and, even though they had come willingly, she couldn't help but feel guilty.

"It's not because of Isla," Finn ground out. "As I've said before, she can take care of herself."

"Then what is it?"

Finndryl stopped walking, letting the others continue down the path ahead of them. Lore waited until he was ready. "You know, if you had asked me to come with you to rescue Grey, I would have."

"I—I'm sorry. I didn't realize."

"If you don't know that by now or why it is I'm here, then just drop it. It's probably for the best, anyway." His eyes flickered to Asher's retreating form. Lore opened her mouth to ask again, but he interjected before she could. "Leave it, Lore."

She would drop it for now. But only because Asher had turned around and was heading their way.

"We've reached the stairs," Asher said as he jogged up to them.

The stairs leading up to the abandoned quarters were identical to the ones beneath the dark fae statue. But this time, instead of a crawl space, a door waited at the top and they were able to walk out from behind a threadbare tapestry.

The room they entered was completely bare, aside from the tapestry behind them. The floor and boarded-up windows were covered in a fine layer of dust that kicked up when they walked and bloomed around them.

Lore stifled a sneeze.

They left the abandoned wing after passing countless other rooms, some with furniture covered by old sheets, others still filled with lavish decorations on display. Paintings, hand-painted end tables with delicate brush strokes, golden candlesticks, and even a tall instrument with fifty strings. All of them had been left behind and forgotten. Long ago, they had probably been cherished by an ancient royal.

It wasn't long before they began to see signs of life.

As they kept walking, the disrepair began to disappear. The floors were recently swept and the doorknobs and sconces gleamed, freshly polished by maids. The wallpaper was vivid and bright, not faded as it had been in the abandoned wing. They heard voices behind closed doors and passed servants carrying trays of food.

They were in the royal quarters; a place Lore hadn't seen before. Somewhere in these grounds, the King and Queen of Alytheria lived. They were ancient and childless, and when they finally succumbed to old age, they would leave no traditional heirs to the throne. The servants had talked during meals and expected mayhem from those distant relatives who would be in line to succeed. Alytheria's stability would be threatened for the first time in hundreds of years due to the monarchs' lack of a natural heir.

All of them exhaled a collective sigh of relief when they passed by guards standing at attention and exited the royal quarters. Apparently, the guards weren't looking too closely at anyone leaving the quarters, being more concerned with those entering them. They would have to make it back to the tunnel and the passage to the sea using a different route; hopefully they'd be able to wind through the crowd of people still there for market day.

When they reached the dungeons, they found that the entrance was only manned by two guards. Asher walked up to them, making some joke Lore could not overhear. Both guards snickered, glancing toward the dungeons. Asher took the opportunity to knock them out with two quick jabs.

Grey and Finndryl dragged the guards to a nearby storage closet, and the team descended the stairs to the dank dungeons, weapons at the ready.

Lore held her breath, the anticipation of seeing her people again thrumming through her.

At last, they reached the bottom of the stairs.

But her people weren't here. All Lore saw was a male, asleep on a mat in one of the cells. His membranous wings twitched in his sleep.

"I thought your source said they would be in the dungeons," Isla whispered, her voice strained with fear.

"He did," Asher replied, teeth gritted.

"It doesn't matter. They aren't here! Where else could they be? Think."

And then suddenly, Lore knew. She remembered once seeing a giant room in the servants' quarters, near where her own closet of a room had been. She'd seen the room for only a moment when a junior laundress had entered it, carrying bundles of sheets. The room was huge and filled with beds. At the time, she thought it was some type of infirmary room.

But it was big enough to house her people.

"I think I know where they are."

Stashing their weapons away, they raced back up the stairs to the hallway. The servants' quarters weren't far from the dungeons, but they would have to pass the servants' dining hall—the place where the guards ate as well.

Lore had a lot of hopes: hope that they wouldn't recognize and arrest Asher on sight. Hope that they wouldn't smell that Lore and Grey were humans or question why two light fae were roaming around the castle when things were so tense between the two territories.

All her hopes and dreams were riding on people not caring enough to take notice of them. The chance of that happening— of them being lucky enough to fly under the radar—made her want to laugh maniacally until tears streamed down her face.

But she stuffed that urge down and continued farther into the corridor, hoping.

They walked past the dining hall with purpose, and no one took note of them. They had two more turns before they arrived at the room she'd seen before. She was shocked when they arrived without being stopped. There wasn't a guard outside the door, but she didn't think too hard about it. She needed to know if her loved ones were in there, so she thrust the door open.

It was empty.

LORE OF THE WILDS

They all rushed into the room and Lore cursed, tears sting-
ing her eyes as she looked around at the vacant beds.

Only, they were no beds lined against the walls. There were
cribs. Each one had freshly laundered sheets, bordered by gleaming metal bars and shiny padlocks.

Chills rose up Lore's back and goosebumps erupted on her
arms. Why would anyone put padlocks on cribs?

Lore glanced outside a small window with iron bars screwed
into the stone of the castle wall. Lead filled her belly.

Asher spoke up. "There's one more place they could be, but
if they're there, then there is no way we can break them out.
It's heavily guarded by the Royal Guard. Those soldiers are the
best trained, strongest magic wielders, and almost all of them
winged. They're such an exclusive group. I don't even have any
connections."

"What do you mean 'winged'?" Grey asked.

"I mean that they've got wings. Most fae with wings are high
ranking and extremely loyal to the royal family. They're their
own kind of royalty among dark fae, so to speak. The families
are almost always wealthy and one hundred percent always in the
royal family's pockets. They're mostly assholes, to be honest."
Isla rolled her eyes. "They tend to look down on us 'grounders.'"

"Goddess. How are we going to find out if that's where they're
imprisoning our people?"

"We'll wait until nightfall. Then you can use your cloaking
spell and we can look through the windows."

$$)) \bullet (($$

The minutes ticked by like hours. Lore wanted to throw up with
every passing breath—her people's blood could be spilled any
moment, and she was stuck here, waiting for night to fall.

Finally, the moon rose and Lore felt her power build. It was a warm and comforting hum that whispered to her, reminding her that she was no longer the scared girl in the apothecary.

She had power now. She could do anything she put her mind to.

She and Asher left the others in the room with the cribs. They walked silently across the stone floor of the castle, cloaked and invisible to everyone they passed in the low-lit corridors. Asher led Lore down ocher-colored corridor after corridor until they exited through a small, nondescript door.

This part of the grounds was surrounded by high fences on all sides. It wasn't like the manicured gardens the castle displayed for visiting nobility, nor was it like the lively, open space where the market was held. This garden was wild and untamed, looking more like a small and dense wood.

They continued along a brick path until Asher turned sharply onto a trail leading through low brush and tall trees. If he hadn't shown her where to go, she would have missed it. They walked down the trail, still hidden by the cloaking spell.

Ahead was a tower. Lore craned her neck to see to the top of it.

Asher reached out to feel the stone, probably to test if they could climb it, but she grabbed his hand.

"Don't touch that. It's spelled," she whispered.

"You can tell?"

"Yes. I can't tell what the spells do, but there is a patchwork of them, woven together. I can see the shimmering of *Source*."

The tower itself was vibrating with it.

"Shit. Okay. I'd planned on crawling up there, but let me see if my magic will work."

"Let's get off the trail first, in case anyone comes down it."

They veered from the path, walking through bushes now. Asher, as always, made no noise. Lore could hide from sight, but there didn't seem to be anything she could do about the forest debris crunching beneath her feet. She picked her way carefully, stepping only where Asher stepped, but she was still louder than she wanted to be.

They circled the structure. It was wider than she'd thought. Multiple figures were in the air, keeping guard as they flew over the grounds.

"Okay, this should be far enough."

Asher leaned down and chose a young, curling vine and coaxed it toward the stone. In accordance with his gentle whisper, it grew strong and thick, hardening and stretching out. He directed the vine toward the stone wall, until the tip of the vine was within a few inches of the stone—it shied away from the tower. Its edges blackened and turned to ash.

Asher whispered faster, the crease in his brow deepening in concentration. But no matter what he did, the vine blackened and died where it touched the tapestry of enchantments on the tower.

He cursed and dropped his hands. Whatever spells were on the stone, his earth magic couldn't penetrate them.

"Let me try something," Lore said. She sat on the ground, crossing her legs and resting her wrists on her knees, and emptied her mind as much as she could while leaving a small thread of her magic to power the spell that was keeping them invisible.

She emptied her mind of the worries she felt for her loved ones and friends.

Her worry for the group she'd left behind in that room of cribs.

She even distanced herself from Asher, who was standing behind her, his hand on one of his swords, ready to protect her should anyone surprise them.

She cast her magic out around her.

With her eyes closed, she imagined that her magic was a web of fibers, one that looked like thousands of different colored strings. She unraveled them, then spread them out like a blanket. She first focused on the earth beneath her, then the plants all around her, followed by their stems and roots. Wild strawberries were growing here. And soon, in the spring, the flowers would bud and produce small, red fruit.

Spells began to filter through her mind, detailing all the things the sweet, tiny berries could be used for. She spared a moment of thought for the seeds and stems and leaves. If she harvested every piece of the plant, they could be used for a spell of desire. But she didn't need this knowledge. Desire didn't help her now.

She moved on, spreading the blanket farther out. There were so many types of ferns, each one with its own power living within its own tapestry of life. Each one could be harvested for different medicines, tinctures, and spells. Some could be used to heal, others to poison. Though her eyes were closed, she could see the grounds around her; whatever the moonlight touched, she could sense. The light was showing her a glowing map.

She could even see herself and Asher; they stood out on the grounds, looking different from the greenery around them.

She willed her moonlit sight to move farther out, toward the tower. With excitement that almost broke her concentration, she realized she could see it despite the spells around it. The tower was so tall, shouldn't she have been able to see it from the public gardens? Or was it cloaked from that vantage point like she was? She imagined herself like a floating spirit and she rose up, up, up, until she found a window. The moonlight was weak there though, so she moved away, toward the side of the tower facing the moon, and looked through that window.

There, the abducted women! They all huddled together on the cold stone floor, most of them asleep.

She moved farther up the tower, pushing her sight into a new door, managing to find the children. She spotted Milo snuggled up to Katu, sleeping with his thumb in his mouth.

None of this made sense. What did the dark fae want with humans? Didn't they already have everything they could ever want?

Then a cold feeling chilled Lore. They didn't have everything.

They didn't have many children. The royal family couldn't even conceive. And what had the merchants' child said? That the situation was so dire that they were stealing younglings. They must be kidnapping them to raise them.

Sweat broke out across her brow. It was harder to see now. The tower was getting hazier. No, no, no! She needed more power. She pushed herself harder, ignoring the splitting headache growing behind her eyes.

She raced farther up, probing farther into the tower. She found another room, one with more women. This room was much smaller than the last and it had six, no, seven women in it, all around her age. She recognized some of them.

This room was completely different from the first one. Tapestries covered the walls, and a fire flickered in the fireplace on the far wall of the room. Thick rugs lined the floor, and all the women had their own beds. It was a facade of warmth and safety, contradicted by the bars on the window. One woman, nearest the window, was strapped to the iron bed frame by her wrist, proving that this was anything but safe.

Lore wanted to scream.

Withdrawing her sight from the tower, she focused on herself down below. She felt so far away. A stab of terror struck her. She knew at once that this projection was dangerous. If she stayed away from her body for much longer or went any farther, there was a chance she would become disconnected from herself permanently.

She rushed back to herself and gasped in pain. Her nails had bitten into her palms. Her skull felt like it had split in two, so painful was her headache. Every bit of her was tingling all over and heat rushed through her cheeks. For a breath, she felt like her own body was foreign to her, but she steadied herself, willing herself to be calm.

Or as calm as she could be, given what she had just seen.

"Asher, they're using the human women to sire children." Her words came out slurred. She hadn't realized that casting herself out would cause so many problems. She had been reckless, but what choice did she have?

"What?" Asher's brown skin paled. He reached out a hand to pull her up. Her knees were weak, and she leaned on him for a moment, pressing her forehead against his shoulder.

"Yes. I'm pretty sure seven of them are with child already." Lore's teeth chattered when she spoke. Nausea rolled through her in waves. She was going to be sick.

"We need to get you out of here. All of us need to leave until we can regroup with the rest back in Duskmere. If we tell those who remain, maybe they can—no. We can't leave them here."

Tears of anger threatened to spill. Hot rage burned through her like nothing she'd ever known. She couldn't imagine the violation these women had faced in the last week. The children seemed safe, but for how long, and until what age?

"You are right. We can't leave them here. You have to break the wards, Lore."

"I can't break these wards. I'm not strong enough."

"You don't have a choice. What if this is the only chance that we get to save them?" Asher stepped toward her until the moonlight bathed him too, highlighting his antlers and shining on his sharp cheekbones. He slid his long fingers through her curls, gently cupping the back of her head, and pulled her to him. His eyes searched her own a moment before he closed them, pressing his forehead to hers. A deep rumbling sound came from his chest as he inhaled her scent. "Have I ever told you that you smell like the deepest part of the forest? Like frosted cranberries and verbena."

"No, you haven't."

"It's divine," he whispered before brushing the softest of kisses against her lips. He pulled her to him and his breath caught in a strangled growl as his tongue swept against her own. He was devouring her, tasting her, his lips insistent.

She opened to him fully, tasting blackberry and honey, relishing the feel of his hard chest against her own. She wound her fingers in his soft, thick curls, moaning into his mouth when he tightened his arms around her. The vines at her feet rose up from the ground, wrapping themselves gently around their legs, like he would tie her to him if he could, so he would never have to know what it was to be apart.

This kiss felt dangerous.

It felt too much like goodbye.

They both knew that going into that tower could be their end.

She broke away, panting. Asher's eyes were so pained she had to look away lest she lose her courage.

For a moment there, nothing had seemed worth putting what she felt for him at risk.

And then she remembered the woman in the tower, her wrist chained to the bed. She remembered Milo and Katu—Katu was only twelve and yet found himself surrounded by all those children who needed him.

She kneeled on the ground.

Asher crouched next to her. "Harness your power, Lore. You can do this. Break the wards."

She thrust her hands out, searching for any weakness in the threads of the spell.

Some things were worth taking a risk. Things like freeing those she loved and setting those responsible for their pain on fire.

CHAPTER 31

The entrance to the tower was on the other side of the forest path.

Two winged fae stood on either side of thick metal doors. Unlike the sleepy guards outside the royal wing of the castle, these stood at attention, alert in their gleaming golden armor.

Asher was right. The Royal Guard consisted of a different class of soldier.

The pair stood in front of the guards, hidden within the tower's shadow. The guards might have been bigger than them, with long staffs as weapons and bracketed by powerful, all-black feathered wings that could lift them high into the sky, but Lore and Asher had the element of surprise.

If Lore hadn't been cloaking them with her magic, Asher's knife would have gleamed as he thrust it out, slitting the throat of one and then the other in a single breath. Neither of the guards even knew what hit them as they clawed at their throats, trying and failing to keep their lifeblood from gushing through their fingers.

They might have been of the winged station, but they could die like any other.

Lore stood in front of the door with her hands splayed out inches from the wards on the doors. She could feel Asher's vines creeping forward, wrapping around the guards' golden boots and dragging them to the tree line, where they disappeared into the ground.

She couldn't find a hole in the network of wards here. She needed to think of this another way. She could feel the heat coming off the wards and, with her second sight, she could pass through them, but she couldn't figure out how to get her physical body through.

She and Asher were running out of time, but perhaps her earlier thought of setting people aflame hadn't been too far off.

Maybe fire was the answer.

She pulled her pack off her back and searched through it, eventually pulling out a small vial of glowing liquid. She held it up for a moment; it looked like she'd bottled moonlight.

Weeks ago, she'd ground up the flowers she'd plucked from the canopy in the wildwood, the ones that had made Finndryl's hands burn, bubble, and blister as a child. Back then, she'd thought that, maybe, she could use it as a weapon when she was in a tight spot.

But maybe, if she filled it with her intentions and entwined them with *Source*, it could become *more*.

"Step back," she told Asher, not wanting to splash him with the glowing liquid.

She twisted the stopper out of the vial and placed it on the ground before her. She closed her eyes, focusing on the contents, and began chanting under her breath, using bits and pieces of spells she'd learned in the circle of clovers alongside Finn.

She weaved them together: a spell for unlocking, another for unraveling, and a third for movement of an element. She rotated her hands, sweat dripping down her back, and put all her intentions into the spell.

She felt the liquid float up and out of the vial, spinning in midair.

Through Lore, it defied the laws of the world.

She twirled her hands and pushed them out, willing the liquid to do as she bid.

She chanted her new spell, imagining the liquid rushing toward the metal door and eating through the wards there, burning through them as if they were nothing. When it frayed the fabric of spells, she pushed it inward, toward the locks, until it ate through those, too.

"Lore, somebody is coming."

She opened her eyes at Asher's hushed whisper.

"Let's go. Stay behind me. Do not veer from my steps."

She'd made a rupture in the wards, just big enough for her and Asher to slip through. They didn't hesitate to enter.

$$)) \mathbf{) \bullet ((} ($$

Lore tripped up the winding stairs. It was too dim for her to see.

There weren't any guards in the tower, but they still had to be quick. Asher had seen others coming toward the tower right before they had slipped in. And the wards being tampered with might have alerted whoever had created them.

They burst through the first door Lore recognized. The women were huddled together, just as she'd seen. They startled away, many of them scrambling back from the door, terrified.

"It's okay. We aren't here to hurt you. We're rescuing you."

"Lore?"

One of the women stood and took a hesitant step forward. She was the eldest daughter of the Burgs—the family who owned the tavern. The young woman ran into her arms, and Lore embraced her. She smelled of old sweat and fear.

It had taken Lore so long to get here. Too long.

"Emalie! I'm sorry I made you wait."

Emalie stepped back, squaring her shoulders as she turned to the other women. "It's Lore from back home. We can trust her."

The other women stood now, and Lore realized that, through the dirt and grime, she recognized a lot of them. Not all by name, but their faces were familiar to her. They reminded her of home, but they weren't looking at her.

They were watching Asher, who stood by the door facing the hallway. His twin swords were brandished as he scouted for danger.

The women, understandably, didn't trust him. To them, he looked like the enemy.

"It's okay. He's on our side." To Asher she said, "Asher, sheathe your swords."

He was fast enough that, if anyone found them, he could pull them out in a heartbeat. If it got these women to trust them a little more, then it would be worth it.

"We have a way out of the castle. If you can hold on for a few more moments, we are going to grab the children and the—"

"I can hear the tower doors opening. They're here." Asher cut her off.

"Okay, change of plans. We need to— Finn?" Lore's voice broke and her heart stopped in her chest.

Finn stood in the hallway, dripping blood. It was on his face, his neck, and across his stolen black uniform.

Lore raced past Asher, immediately trying to find the wound. "Where are you hurt? Finn, where are you hurt? I can't—" Oh, goddess, she couldn't lose him. She *wouldn't*. Her mind was racing, hysteria threatening to bubble out of her. Her hands were red.

Goddess, there was so much blood.

Finn reached out, gripping her wrist and stopping her hands from checking for injuries. He tilted her chin up with his other hand so she was looking at him and only him. "It's not mine.

Stop fussing. The Royal Guard has been alerted. I killed three of them, but more are coming."

Lore almost fainted with relief. Finn's steady heart pounded against her wrist where he held it, pressed against his chest. His calm gaze settled her a little. He wasn't hurt.

Still, with the guard alerted, how was she going to get all the people from Duskmere out? "I'm glad you're okay, but maybe, next time, don't make such a mess?"

"A mess? I look lovely compared to them."

Lore's heart skipped a beat, and her stomach did a little flop at the tilt of his lips and hint of teeth. Only Finn would joke at a time like this. She couldn't believe he'd followed them.

Then again, yes, she could.

"We have to split up." She turned back to Emalie. "Can you lead the other women down? Grab the ones who are pregnant first. Go with Asher. He will take you to the woods. Hide there and I'll be down soon. I need to get the children."

Emalie led the others out.

"Lore!" Asher called her name from where he stood poised at the top of the steps. "If you don't follow us soon, I will leave them to come back and find you."

"I'll be down in just a moment, I promise. When you see the kids, take them to the tunnels. Don't wait for us. We'll meet you there."

She could tell he was unhappy with this plan, but he trusted her enough not to argue. He tore his gaze from her and looked at Finndryl, something new in his eyes, something Lore couldn't quite place. "Protect her," he said.

Finndryl placed his hand on Lore's shoulder. "I will."

"I know."

Lore would have to unpack this moment between Asher and Finn later. Shelving it, she turned and ran up the steps toward the children. Finn kept pace at her side.

Ahead was the door, just as she'd seen it in her projected dream state. Though it had been locked from the outside with a padlock, the lock was nowhere to be seen now.

A cold chill went up her back and she slowed her pace. She couldn't see any magical wards on this door; there was nothing that would hurt her if she touched the handle. Still, sudden feeling of unease or not, she didn't have a choice.

The door swung open on silent hinges, and she saw the children. Milo and Katu were no longer sleeping, but were now awake. She stepped toward them, already opening her arms to embrace them, when Katu shook his head, just slightly, and looked over her right shoulder.

She turned, just in time to see two winged soldiers advancing, their swords raised high.

Behind them, standing in the shadows, was the steward.

CHAPTER 32

D id you really think we were just going to let you take them? After we spent so long getting them here?" the steward asked, his voice dripping with malice.

His signature haughty tone made Lore want to gouge his eyes out with her thumbs. *Goddess, of course he's behind this.*

"I'm taking them all with me," she said.

"You're a sneaky little bug, aren't you? I couldn't seem to get my hands on you after you ran and took the one thing of worth in that godsforsaken library." He took a step toward her, his fancy slippers at odds with the filthy tower floor. "What I can't understand is how you knew the book was anything special. I was told it was spelled to appear blank."

He must not have known the book had called to her. That it had chosen her. How much did he know?

Lore rearranged her face to be emotionless. Better to leave him guessing.

"Tell your soldiers to stand down. You can't have any of us! We are not yours to take!"

The steward stepped forward between the two soldiers until he was in front of her and Finndryl.

"Oh, don't play the fool. I know you have the book. Syrelle

underestimated you—he didn't realize that the human he sent into the library would have her own motive. I told him. I said all humans were liars and thieves, little better than vermin who couldn't help themselves. They always want what they don't deserve." His eyes lit with fevered hate.

Lore's stomach churned. But it was best to keep him talking while she figured out a plan to get the children out. "We *never* deserved this." She cast her arm out around the filthy tower, the captured children.

The steward laughed. "You are right. You don't deserve the time or attention that cowardly excuse for a lord, Syrelle, gave you. Our race is on the brink of extinction, and he wanted to fix the problem by chasing after a *book*. One that we weren't sure even existed. But I had another plan. All I needed was the threat of war from the south. Do you know what another war would do to our numbers? The dark fae would be wiped out—and the king knows it. He gave up on his useless nephew's plans and finally invested in mine. We don't need the magic of a long-dead alchemist when your kind were there all along, just a carriage ride away."

Lore felt sick. The steward was walking toward her, his arms outstretched in pride. "The answer was simple, really. We will use the human women to carry the next generation—eventually we can breed out the stain in the blood. And in the meantime, we will raise the children to fill our barracks and secure our borders. You reach fighting age in no time at all, we will blink and the next batch of soldiers will be ready. Our precious youth need not go to war when we can train the human children and half-breeds to do it for us."

"You're mad if you think we will let you get away with this."

He smiled at her protest and barked at the soldiers behind him. "Cut the vermin down and bring her pack to me. I think I'll take the book for myself."

The soldiers approached.

"Wait for my signal, Katu," she whispered, eyes never straying from the soldier advancing toward her.

The sight of his gray wings punched horror through her entire body. If he was hoping to intimidate her with them, it was working.

She retreated a step, keeping the pointy end of her sword between them. She didn't have anywhere to go. Another step and she risked the children behind her.

"Don't you fucking dare." Finndryl moved in front of Lore. "If you want to keep your ability to fly, you'll disregard the steward's orders. Take another step toward her or any of the children and it will be your last." Finndryl's voice was a purr, but heavy with the promise of violence.

The female soldier threw her head back and laughed. "Like we're scared of you, *clanless.*"

Now Lore wanted to claw this female's eyes out for using that slur against Finn.

Finndryl tilted his head, homing in on the female. Lore couldn't see his face, but she imagined it was terrifying.

The winged soldiers advanced at the same time, swords arcing toward Lore. Finndryl brought his own sword up and blocked both of their weapons. The sound of the force of their blades rang through the chamber.

Lore took this opportunity to turn around and grab Katu by his shoulders. Thistle and Sage, it was good to be near them again. Over the clashing of metal, she yelled at the children, "Stay low, go out the door and down the stairs. *Run.*"

They bolted, Katu dragging Milo along even as the youngster's small arms reached out for Lore.

She tore her eyes from the boys and looked back to the fight just as Finn's sword cut through the female soldier's golden armor. A look of surprise crossed her face before agony took over and she dropped.

Finndryl wasted no time. He twisted, his feet dancing across the floor, and stepped over the soldier to deflect the second one's attack. But the first one wasn't down for long, and soon Finndryl was fighting them both again.

The steward's face turned purple with fury. "No matter. I'll do it myself. Come here, girl."

As the last of the children disappeared from view, Lore smiled. Had the steward really thought she would give up so easily?

She rushed toward him, sword raised, just as he thrust his hands out toward her. Fire erupted from his fingertips.

She ducked under the wall of flames, trying not to falter as searing heat rolled over her body. She rammed into his legs, knocking him off balance.

The steward fell hard. He may have been fae, but he was *ancient*.

Lore shifted her weight until she was kneeling above him. She gripped his braids and yanked his head up before she slammed his face into the ground. She thrust his head back and repeated the move. "Leave! Us! Alone!" she shouted, ramming his head into the stone with each word.

The steward went limp, and she dropped him.

He laughed and grinned, his sharp teeth red with blood.

Lore was so taken aback she hesitated for just a moment, and he took that opportunity to turn the tables, shoving a knee against her chest so hard she couldn't catch her breath.

He laughed as his blood dripped onto her face. He pressed harder, grinding his knee against her sternum until her vision began to waver. She clawed at his knee, her movements jerky and uncontrolled, as she tried to push him off. But she couldn't get any leverage from her position.

She was losing the fight and her vision began darkening in earnest.

The steward leaned in toward her. Lore scratched at him,

trying to dislodge his knee, but he twisted her hair and yanked her head painfully to the side to whisper in her ear. "In some ways, you should be *thanking* me. I have given the wasteful existence of your kind a purpose. I will swoop in like a plague and take more and more until I have used them all up. In fact, I think I *won't* kill you. I'll fill you with my spawn instead. How would you like to watch your own child hold the chains of your people?"

He lessened the pressure on her chest for just a moment, just long enough for her vision to clear and for her brain to catch up.

She reached to her belt, pulled the last glowing vial out, and broke it across his face.

The chief steward screamed as he launched himself backward against the wall, clawing at his face. But where his fingers met flesh, it peeled away like the skin of fruit left to rot in the sun. His body began to convulse as the poison ate into his face, his eyes, and his throat.

Even after his screams stopped, the tonic continued to eat at him until there was nothing left of his face or his fingers at all.

Was it over? *Please let it be over.*

Finn crouched beside her as she struggled to draw in a breath. He reached out, turning her face away from the smoking, stinking thing in the corner that had once been the steward. "Are you all right?"

"I will be once we leave this place forever."

"Then let us," Finndryl said as he hauled her up.

Lore glanced to where the two guards sat slumped on the ground, their blood spreading over the floor.

"How did you manage to take down two of the winged fae?"

"I've got my ways. A few tricks up my sleeve." Finndryl grinned. He had fresh blood splattered on his face and clothes. In his locs. Dripping from his sword. He risked his life for strangers. Lore thought he'd never looked so beautiful. "Besides, anyone who would participate in this fucked up experiment didn't deserve to live."

"You've got that right. The steward said the king himself signed off on this. I'm going to make everyone involved pay."

"Let's do it together."

"Deal."

CHAPTER 33

Lore followed Finndryl on unsteady legs down the stairs and onto the forest path.

When she saw the fox waiting for her, she wasn't overly surprised. The creature looked at her, its eyes so bright and intelligent. It was clear that Lore had missed, somehow, that this wasn't just an *ordinary* fox.

Its orange fur now glowed in the moonlight and its white tail sparkled like snow, glinting with *Source*.

Lore reached out her hand and the fox rose on its hind legs to nuzzle her palm before settling back down without a sound. Warmth spread from Lore's hand where it had brushed the silken fur and it spread to her chest. Something had just happened with the fox. Something she wasn't sure of, but she now felt connected to it. She could feel its heart beating beside her and feel the comforting presence that it—no, *she*—sent Lore's way.

A thrum through the invisible chord that connected them said, *"I am here. I am here. I am here."*

Lore spread her spell of invisibility out until it cloaked the fox as well as Finndryl.

Lore could still see the fox, just like she could still see herself, but the shimmer of *Source* let her know the spell was working. The trio walked silently, unseen, as winged and unwinged soldiers alike rushed through the castle, searching for them.

Soon, they would discover that the tower was empty, save for the dead guards and the steward's disfigured corpse.

$$))) \bullet ((($$

Lore and Finndryl eventually made it to the garden gate.

Lore heaved a sigh of relief as they slipped inside, closing it behind them. Soon, they would be reunited with Asher and the others. From there, they would make their way back to Dusk-mere and Lore would find a way to break the spell surrounding the town. Then, nothing would stop them from leaving and finding their own place in the world.

The humans would decide their own fate from here.

They walked through the overgrown garden, heading toward the faceless statue and the stairs that would lead them to safety. The fox yipped and wound itself around Lore's legs, not unlike a housecat.

"What is it, girl?" She knelt down to scratch behind its ears, then it glowed brightly and turned into a moon moth, its wings flapping silently.

Finndryl reached out a hand, surprise on his face. The moth landed on his knuckles and flapped its wings a few times before flying up to land on Lore's shoulder. The moth walked up her shoulder before settling beneath her hair.

"What—" Finndryl asked.

But Lore cut him off. "This fox was my buddy the entire time I was here working in the library. But that, well, that was new."

They walked farther into the garden, the moth's wings just

slightly tickling Lore's chin. It wasn't an unpleasant sensation; in fact, it was comforting in a way. The fox-turned-moth was a friend. Lore felt that in her bones.

Just as they arrived at the faceless statue, Asher stepped out from behind.

"Where are the humans? You left them?" Finndryl asked, his voice strained.

"Yes. Grey and Isla are leading them home. Finndryl, you should meet up with them in the tunnels below. I need to speak to Lore first."

"What's wrong?" Nightmarish thoughts ran through Lore's head. Perhaps one of the children had gotten hurt in the time she'd last seen them. Maybe they were lost. But no, Asher's face wasn't sad.

He looked calm, actually. "Finndryl," he repeated, "you go on ahead."

Finndryl didn't move from where he stood behind Lore. "I'm fine here with her. I'll stay with her until we've gotten her safely off the castle grounds, which is what we should be doing now, Asher. Anything you have to say to her can be said once we are in Duskmere."

Anger flashed in Asher's eyes. "You don't give up, do you, Finndryl? You think that she really wants you here with her? She can't stand you. Nobody can."

"Asher, stop it." What was he saying? Why was he being so cruel? Lore turned to look at Finndryl, preparing to reach out to him, thinking he might do something violent. "Asher, I'm sure you don't mean that. Finndryl is right. We need to go."

But Finndryl's head was cocked to the side as he surveyed Asher. "I knew it was only a matter of time until you showed your true colors. You've always had Isla and my father fooled, but you never deceived me."

"He needs to go, Lore. I need to talk to you. Don't you trust me?"

"I—yes. I trust you, Asher. Of course, I do. But I don't feel safe here."

"You're safe with me. I would never let anyone hurt you." Asher took a step toward Lore, and Lore had the oddest feeling that, in this moment, she needed to step backward and keep the space between them the same.

"Something isn't right. Lore, get behind me," Finndryl said. Even the moth hiding in Lore's hair was fluttering with agitation.

"Oh, come on now. You're going to believe this fuck-up over me? Lore, come here, now."

Lore couldn't believe this was happening. They had all been working together just fine. What changed within the past hour?

"Asher, I—"

Something in Asher changed. Suddenly, waves of power rolled off him. They permeated the garden, seeping into her pores and invading her body and mind. She'd felt this power before, but not from Asher.

She'd felt it from the noble fae male who had come into the shop.

That fae had had wings and short-cropped hair.

But, as if he were aware of her thoughts, Asher's face changed. His antlers morphed and seemed to disappear into his curly hair. His hair changed, turning from brown to the darkest black and shrinking to a short, cropped style. Wings sprouted from his back.

She knew him. She knew this face. The beautiful clothes. The feeling of such power.

"Syrelle?" The acidic taste of terror coated her tongue. "Where is Asher? What have you done with him?"

Finndryl growled from where he stood in front of her. It was a low, predatory sound. Lore didn't have to see him to know his face promised violence.

She spread her fingers out by her thigh. *Wait.* She hoped Finndryl saw her signal.

"I *am* Asher," the noble fae said. "I let your precious humans go, but I can't let you leave the grounds with the grimoire."

Lore's mind spun. She knew what he was saying, but his words sounded far away and muddled like he was underwater. Her heart pounded in her chest, and she couldn't catch her breath.

"You—what?" She couldn't make her mouth work properly.

"Do try to keep up, Mouse. You're a smart girl. Come with me and I'll even let Finndryl go."

Mouse.

Mouse.

How would an imposter know that was what Asher called her?

"Lore, run," Finndryl hissed as he drew his sword from its scabbard. He widened his stance, preparing to fight this Asher who was not Asher.

But Lore couldn't move. Her limbs weren't working. "Asher, stop. This isn't funny." Lore hated that tears were welling up in her eyes and clouding her vision. This couldn't be real. It was a trick of some kind.

"Call me Syrelle."

"Syrelle is the fae lord who tasked me with organizing the library."

The imposter smiled. Gone was Asher's easy grin. And in its place was something foul. A warped version of the smile Lore had come to love. "Yes. I wanted to thank you for finding my book for me. But I couldn't do that until now."

"*Your* book?"

"Well, it belonged to my grandfather. He's the one who put the spell on the library that barred anyone but his direct bloodline from entering and stumbling across one of the pinnacles of his life's work, the *Deeping Lune*. I've been searching for it since I was a boy. Looked in every corner of that damned library." His words took on a bitter edge. "*The Deeping Lune* should have come to me when I called it."

Syrelle took a step toward her.

"Don't come near her," Finndryl growled, venom coating his words.

"This is my grimoire. It belongs to me," Lore said, shaking her head.

Anger flashed in Syrelle's eyes before his amused mask appeared again. "It is a marvel that it has bonded with you, which is something I never expected to happen. But the book is *not* yours. My grandfather infused that book with his own rare form of magic."

Syrelle smiled, and Lore's stomach flipped at the sight of it, terror rising in her throat.

"I would know that magic anywhere. I could feel it the moment you stepped through the library doors with it, hiding it under your tunic. I can feel it, even now."

He stepped toward her again, placing his hand out, palm up.

"It's my birthright, but the grimoire would not share its secrets with me. I tried for years to find it and to unlock its mysteries. And then, I thought of something. If I could not make the book bow to me, then maybe my opposite can. A weak, magic-less human. And I was right—in a sense, although not about you being weak. Lore, don't you see? Now that you have awakened the magic and begun to master it, we can work together. Things don't have to change much. You can still practice magic and become stronger, so long as you do as I bid."

Lore wanted to faint. She wanted to forget the last few moments of her life. She wanted to scream in his face. She opened her mouth to do just that, but no sound came out.

Asher—Syrelle—had wanted her to find the book and awaken its power so that he could use it? Use her?

"No, that can't be. You know Finndryl and Isla. They know you. As *Asher*! They've known you for *years*," Lore said, her voice desperate. This couldn't be true. "What about you being conscripted into service? Or about your life as a grounder?" She waved toward his wings, which spread out behind him, a physical embodiment of all his lies.

"Yes. Since I was a child, I've had the ability to change my form. I often changed my appearance to that of a grounder. Only a few know that 'Asher,' the lowborn guard, is not real." The imposter frowned. "Sometimes being a noble can be tiresome." He took another step toward her, his gait filled with the same movement as Asher's smooth confidence. His steps made no sound when he walked. "I met Isla years ago on one such respite. Unlike her brother, I quite enjoy her company."

Finndryl made a sound behind her. Disbelief. Rage.

"What about the steward? Why would you just let the humans go? Why did you let us kill him?"

"What do I care about the humans? The steward was doing the dark bidding of the king and queen. They are obsessed with the idea that our race is dying out, but I know that with life comes *Source*, and with *Source* comes life. Once the book has been awakened and is settled back in our land, this blight will end."

Lore felt bile filling her throat. She was going to be sick.

She turned to run, but before she could, the world stopped. Some invisible force was holding her still. Everything, even her curls, stood stuck as if time itself had frozen. She couldn't move a muscle, not even to draw in breath.

She was suffocating, both because of a lack of air and under the weight of Asher's lies.

Terror shot through her. Was this how she died? Had she led Finn, too, to his death?

"Oh, no you don't. The book stays here. And you, Lore, stay

here. And, you know, I think I'll keep Finn, too. He might come in handy soon, to keep you in line."

Syrelle took the final steps across the garden until he was right in her face.

"The book has bonded with you. A human."

Distaste coated his words, and it was that, more than anything, that broke her. Asher, the sweet fae who had fought for her and bled for her, thought that she was unworthy because of her humanity.

"But, since you've bonded with *Deeping Lune*, that means you will hear the call of its sister book. You will lead me to it, Lore. We will be as we always have been. Together. A team." He reached for her and touched her fingers where they were stained black with ink.

Yesterday, he had performed the same action, and Lore had felt warmth and love.

Now she wanted to flinch away from him. To never let him touch her again.

But she couldn't move.

The edges of Lore's vision were turning black from the lack of air. Soundless, she tried to beg Syrelle to release her. To let her move. To let her breathe.

Behind her, she could hear Finndryl struggling to fight free from Syrelle's hold.

Asher should not have this power. Asher had the power of green, growing things, of life and earth. Asher could not do this.

But this was not Asher. This was Syrelle.

Just before she lost all consciousness, she heard Syrelle croon, "Sleep, for now. Tomorrow, we sail in search of *Auroradel*, the Book of Sunbeams."

TO BE CONTINUED

ACKNOWLEDGMENTS

Turns out writing a book is hard, and for most of this one, it felt impossible. But I actually managed to complete this one, and for that I will be eternally grateful to so many. I couldn't have done it alone.

To my mother, Robyn, who listened to my stories before I could even write them down—and who, some thirty-odd years later, is still listening to them. You've read every version of this book. Your encouragement and support of my craft has never wavered, and I can't thank you enough for that.

To Lamarr, the love of my life, my own personal happy ending, thank you for your constant ear, always being available to listen to complaints at three am. For constantly lifting me up when I feel like giving up, and for encouraging me in every facet of my life, I love you and I like you. Thank you for loving me.

To my Delilah, my delightful Delilah— everything I do, I do for you. You are my pride and joy, my inspiration, and my light.

To my agent, (YES, I have an agent!!!) Thao, I am half convinced I dreamed you up because you championed my book and made it possible for me to realize my wildest dreams. Without you, being a full time, published author would still just be a wish!

Tessa, my editor, I am floored by your support, you took my book into your skillful hands and it bloomed under your direction.

To the entire team at Harper Voyager, thank you for believing in my book, for seeing its potential, and for being the giver of dreams, I am awed by the team's hard work and dedication.

To Nicole for supporting my dreams and always making me laugh.

To the best critique partners Emma and Hayley— without your rallying, writing sprints, video chats, millions of voice notes, and invaluable advice, my book wouldn't exist.

To my first editor, who quickly became my friend—Jasmina, there is no one else I would rather sit with in silence while we both type for hours. And yes, I would love some tea!

To Jordan— the best cover artist I could've ever asked for. You managed to take my vague vision and turn it into the cover of my dreams.

To Jolee, for believing in Lore before even I did.

To the Books Are Magic girlies— Danielle, Emma, Hayley, Malene, Rebi, Kamila, Kat, Sol, Heather, Jenn, Becca, Sarah, and Kim, for reading my early (so early nobody should have even read it) versions of my book. For cheering me on and always being available to talk and to dream. For the book recs and the life advice.

To the community on Bookstagram— there isn't a better corner of the internet. Bookstagram is my happy place.

To my siblings, I love and miss you.

To my readers, you're my favorite.